# PROUD
# OUTCAST

W. Michael Farmer

# PROUD OUTCAST

**DAYS OF WAR, DAYS OF PEACE**

**CHATO'S CHIRICAHUA APACHE LEGACY**

**VOLUME TWO**

# W. MICHAEL FARMER

**WILL ROGERS MEDALLION-WINNING AUTHOR
OF *THE ODYSSEY OF GERONIMO***

HAT CREEK

# HAT CREEK

*an imprint of*
Roan & Weatherford Publishing Associates, LLC
Bentonville, Arkansas

**Library of Congress Cataloging-in-Publication Data**
Names: Farmer, W. Michael
Title: Proud Outcast/W. Michael Farmer |
Days of War, Days of Peace: Chato's Chiricahua Legacy #2
Description:First Edition. | Bentonville: Hat Creek, 2024.
Identifiers: LCCN: 2024943228 | ISBN: ISBN: 978-1-63373-874-4 (hardcover) |
ISBN: 978-1-63373-875-1 (trade paperback) | ISBN: 978-1-63373-876-8 (eBook)
Subjects: FICTION/Indigenous | FICTION/Historical | FICTION/Westerns |
LC record available at: https://lccn.loc.gov/2024943228

Hat Creek trade paperback edition January, 2025

Jacket Design & Interior Design by Casey W. Cowan
Jacket art by Herman W. Hansen (1854-1924)
*The Renegade, Apache Indian,* Watercolor on Paper
Editing by Amy Cowan

*For Corky, my best friend and wife,*
*the wind beneath my wings*

# ACKNOWLEDGMENTS

THERE HAVE BEEN many friends and professionals who have supported me in this work to whom I owe a special debt of gratitude for their help and many kindnesses.

Lynda Sánchez's encouragement and insights into Apache culture and their voices are a major point of reference in understanding the times and personalities covered in this work.

Audra Gerber provided excellent editorial support that contributed to this work's clarity.

Good friends, a rare and a true gift, Pat Fraley and Mike Alexander, supported me during numerous visits to New Mexico, allowing me time and a place from which to do research that otherwise would not have been possible.

The patience, encouragement, and support of my wife, Carolyn, through long days of research and writing made the work possible, and it is to her this novel is dedicated.

The histories listed in Additional Reading that I found particularly helpful were those by Angie Debo; Eve Ball, Nora Henn, and Lynda Sánchez; Alicia Delgadillo and Miriam A. Perrett; Lynda Sánchez; Sherry Robinson; Edwin Sweeney; and Robert Utley.

# TABLE of CONTENTS

# CHARACTERS

### APACHE

- **Alchesay:** *White Mountain Apache chief and scout whose bravery scouting for General Crook brought him the Medal of Honor.*
- **Bashdelehi:** *First wife of Mohtsos, mother of Begiscleyaihn (Helen), Chato's third wife.*
- **Benedict Jozhe:** *Lived with his wife in Guydelkon's village at Fort Sill. Future tribal chairman.*
- **Biyaneta:** *Wife of Perico, brother of Geronimo. She was taken in Geronimo's raid on Fort Apache in September 1885 to recover wives that Chato and his scouts had taken in camp raids in Mexico.*
- **Charley:** *A lead scout, one of ten who accompanied Chato to Washington, D.C. (also known as Askadodilges).*
- **Chato:** *Chief and feared war leader of Chiricahua Apache band (c.1854 – 1934). First Sergeant and lead scout for U.S. Army in 1885 after Geronimo left the reservation.*
  - **Chato's Family**
    - **Banatsi:** *Chato's widowed sister. Never remarried (c. 1857 – died at Mescalero, date unknown).*
    - **Gon-altsis:** *Chato's younger brother and scout known to the Mexicans as Patricio. He accompanied Chato to Washington, D.C. (c.1861 – died at Mount Vernon Barracks 1892).*

- **Begiscleyaihn (Helen):** *Third wife to Chato. Married at Fort Marion (c. 1872—died at Mescalero c.1944).*
  - **Maurice:** *Elder Son of Chato, mother was Helen, born Mount Vernon Barracks (1891—1915). Married Lena Kaydahzinne.*
    - **Esther:** *Daughter of Maurice (1911—1912).*
    - **Alexander:** *Son of Maurice (1913—?).*
  - **Blake:** *Son of Chato and Helen, born Fort Sill (1894-1908).*
  - **Cyril:** *Son of Chato and Helen, born Fort Sill (c. 1897—1898).*
- **Ishchos:** *Second wife to Chato (c. 1847 – died in Mexico, date unknown).*
  - **Maud:** *Elder daughter of Chato and Ishchos (c. 1873—1902).*
  - **Bediscloye:** *Son of Chato and Ishchos (c. 1876—died in Mexico).*
  - **Naboka:** *Daughter of Chato and Ishchos (c. 1879—died in Mexico).*
- **Nalthchedah:** *First wife to Chato; Divorced Chato, married Dexter Loco about 1896.*
  - **Horace:** *Son of Chato and Nalthchedah (c. 1879—1888).*

- **Chihuahua:** *sub-chief of Chokonen Apache, protégé of Cochise, primary leader of first group of Chiricahua shipped to Fort Marion in the spring of 1886.*
- **Cooney:** *Scout and long-time friend of Chato.*
- **Daklugie:** *"Nephew" (second cousin) of Geronimo. Daklugie's mother Ishton was Geronimo's cousin, but he called her his "sister" and claimed Juh was his brother-in-law. Apache cattle herd manager. Eight years of study at Carlisle Indian Industrial School. Married Ramona Chihuahua.*
- **Dadespuna:** *Also known as "Dexter." Son of Loco. Spent time at Carlisle School. Married Chato's divorced wife Nalthchedah.*
- **Dashdenzhoos:** *Mother of Lena Kaydahzinne who married Maurice*
- **Dutchy:** *Scout supporting Chato for Lieutenant Britton Davis in 1885.*
- **Eugene Chihuahua:** *Son of Chihuahua. Worked and learned to read and do sums with George Wratten. Excellent athlete. Became village leader after Chihuahua died.*
- **Eclahheh:** *Chokonen Apache. Second wife of Naiche who he shot in the leg during the March 1886 surrender to General Crook.*
- **Fun:** *"Brother of Geronimo" (second cousin), a Britton Davis scout who intended to kill Davis and Chato in 1885. His Apache name was Ilt'i' bil'ik halíí (which means "smoke comes out") because of his heroism and courageous fighting at Aliso Creek.*

- **Geronimo:** Di-yen *(Shaman) and war leader whose chief was Naiche (c. 1823—1909).*
  - **Geronimo's Family**
    - **Azul:** *A widow Geronimo married. His last wife. Apache name "Sunsetso" (Old Lady Yellow). After they married, they lived with Guydelkon husband and father of two sons of her niece who had died.*
    - **Chee-hash-kish:** *Wife to Geronimo, mother of Chappo and Dohn-say*
      - **Chappo:** *Son of Geronimo and Chee-hash-kish.*
      - **Dohn-say:** *Daughter of Geronimo and Chee-hash-kish. Married Mike Dahkeya, a Geronimo warrior.*
    - **She-gha:** *Wife to Geronimo.*
    - **Shtsha-she:** *Wife to Geronimo.*
    - **Zi-yeh:** *Wife to Geronimo.*
      - **Fenton:** *Son of Geronimo and Zi-yeh.*
      - **Eva:** *Daughter of Geronimo and Zi-yeh (Geronimo's last child).*
    - **Ih-tedda:** *Mescalero wife to Geronimo, taken in 1885, divorced in 1889.*
      - **Lenna:** *Daughter of Geronimo and Ih-tedda.*
      - **Robert:** *Son of Geronimo and Ih-tedda.*
- **Guydelkon:** *Important scout who accompanied Chato to Washington, D.C.*
- **Ha-oz-inne:** *Chokonen Apache and youngest wife of Naiche.*
- **Harold Dick:** *An old Chiricahua di-yen at Fort Sill who opposed the Jesus Road.*
- **Huera:** *Woman who escaped Mexican slavery and was married to Mangus. She was considered a master tizwin maker and helped talk Geronimo into escaping Fort Apache in 1885.*
- **James Kaywaykla:** *Adopted son of Kaytennae. Mother was Guyan. Attended Carlisle.*
- **Jason Betzinez:** *Nephew of and one time novitiate for Geronimo. Attended Carlisle.*
- **Kayitah:** *Scout with Chato in 1885 search for Geronimo in Mexico and a warrior wounded in Aliso Creek fight, and scout who helped talk the Naiche-Geronimo band into surrender.*
- **Kaytennae:** *Second in command to Nana and later leader of the Chihenne Apache. Accompanied Chato to Washington, D.C.*
- **Loco:** *Chief of the Chihenne Apache who preferred a path of peace.*
- **Lot Eyelash:** *Young warrior who rode with Geronimo in Mexico. Accused Geronimo of being a witch.*
- **Mangas:** *Chihenne Apache chief, son of Mangas Coloradas, named Carl Mangas by the army.*

- **Martine:** *Scout with Chato in 1885 search for Geronimo in Mexico and later with Kayitah helped convince Geronimo-Naiche band to surrender to General Miles.*
- **Mohtsos:** *Husband of Bashdelehi, father of Begiscleyaihn (Helen) Chato's third wife.*
- **Nahgoyyahkizen:** *(which means "kids romping and kicking") Young Chiricahua woman who married George Wratten and took the White Eye name Annie White. After two children she divorced Wratten and married Coonie.*
- **Nahzitzohn:** *Second wife of Mohtsos; stepmother of Begiscleyaihn (Helen, Chato's third wife).*
- **Naiche:** *Chief of Chokonen Apache, youngest son of Cochise, friend of Chato.*
- **Nana:** *Married to Geronimo's sister, Nah-dos-te, a war leader of the Chihenne Apache.*
- **Noche:** *Important scout with rank of Sergeant Major. Served as principle scout to Captain Emmet Crawford and accompanied Chato to Washington, D.C.*
- **Noch-ay-del-klinne:** *Cibecue Apache called the "Prophet." He created the Apache Ghost dance and claimed he could call back the great dead chiefs from the dead when all the White Eyes were gone. The Prophet was killed while being taken into custody by Colonel Carr in 1881.*
- **Perico:** *"Brother of Geronimo" (second cousin), Second Sergeant behind First Sergeant Chato in Britton Davis's scout command who intended to help Fun kill Davis and Chato.*
- **Ramona Chihuahua:** *Daughter of Chief Chihuahua. Attended Carlisle School. Married Daklugie.*
- **Tim Kaydahzinne:** *Father of Lena Kaydahzinne.*
- **Toclanny:** *Chihenne Apache scout. Longest serving scout (twenty-five years) in the Army. Served in Company I as an infantry soldier and soldier at Mount Vernon Barracks.*
- **Victorio:** *Great war chief and leader of the Chihenne Apache.*

## FICTIONAL

- **Yellow Boy:** *Mescalero Apache. Retired tribal policeman. Legendary shot with Henry rifle.*

## SPECIALIZED NAMES

- **Blue Mountains:** *The name the Apache used for the Sierra Madre.*
- **Coyote:** *Clever but sometimes foolish character in Apache teaching stories.*

- **Owl-man Giant:** *Monster in Apache mythology.*
- **People:** *Capitalized when referring to a collective group as a whole, like the Apache.*
- **Power:** *Power is capitalized when referring to supernatural power.*

## ANGLOS

- **Captain Emmett Crawford:** *San Carlos Indian Agent and with Captain Wirt Davis a chief of operations officer in Mexico for General Crook in 1885 charged with bringing in Geronimo's band.*
- **Captain Wirt Davis:** *With Emmett Crawford was a chief operations officer in Mexico for General Crook in 1885 and charged with bringing in Geronimo's band.*
- **Lieutenant Joseph H. Dorst:** *Accompanied Chato and others to Washington, D.C. and served as General Miles's liaison for the trip.*
- **Colonel Eugene Asa Carr:** *Commander at Fort Apache who arrested the prophet, Noch-ay-del-kinne, in 1881.*
- **General George Crook:** *Established the Apache Scouts. Directed the war against Chiricahua from 1882 until 1886.*
- **General Nelson Appleton Miles:** *Replaced General Crook and made surrender terms to the Chiricahua that were never kept.*
- **George Wratten:** *Trusted Anglo friend and interpreter for the Apache, who was with them at Fort Pickens, Mount Vernon Barracks, ran sutler store at Fort Sill.*
- **John Clum:** *San Carlos Agent 1874-1877.*
- **Joseph C. Tiffany:** *Agent at San Carlos 1880 – 1882.*
- **Lieutenant James Lockett:** *Commander of Chiricahua camps after Lieutenant Gatewood left.*
- **Lieutenant Marion P. Maus:** *Second in command to Captain Crawford, who after Crawford's murder by Mexican paramilitary Rarámuri negotiated Geronimo's March 1886 meeting with General Crook.*
- **Lyman Hart:** *San Carlos Agent 1877-1879. Freed Geronimo and his war leaders from the guardhouse upon arrival at San Carlos in 1877.*

# APACHE WORDS
## AND PHRASES

- *Ch'ik'eh doleel:* all right; let it be so
- *Di-yen:* medicine woman or man
- *Doo dat'éé da:* it's okay; it doesn't matter
- *Enjuh:* good
- *Googé:* whip-poor-will
- *Haheh:* a young girl's puberty ceremony
- *Hoddentin:* sacred pollen
- *Isdzán:* woman
- *Ish-kay-neh:* boy
- *Ish-tia-neh:* woman
- *Iyah:* mesquite bean pods
- *Nadah:* Baked Agave
- *Nakai-yes:* Mexicans
- *Nakai-yi:* Mexican
- *Nant'an:* leader
- *Nant'an Lpah:* Gray leader, the Apache name for General George Crook.
- *Nish'ii':* I see you
- *Pesh:* iron
- *Pesh-klitso:* yellow iron (gold)
- *Pesh-lickoyee:* nickel-plated or silver (literally "white iron")
- *Pindah-lickoyee:* White-eyed enemies
- *Shiyé:* Son

- *Tobaho:* Tobacco
- *Tsach:* cradleboard
- *Tulepai:* (Lit. Gray water) Corn beer, also known as *tizwin*
- *Ussen:* The Apache god of creation and life

### Reckoning of Time & Seasons
- *Harvest:* used in the context of time, means a year
- *Handwidth (against the sky):* about an hour
- *Season of Little Eagles:* early spring
- *Season of Many Leaves:* late spring, early summer
- *Season of Large Leaves:* midsummer
- *Season of Large Fruit:* late summer, early fall
- *Season of Earth is Reddish Brown:* late fall
- *Season of Ghost Face:* lifeless winter
- *Sun:* used in the context of time, means a day

### Spanish
- *Ándale pues:* Go on now
- *Ataqué:* attack
- *Arroyo:* a small steep-sided waterway with a flat floor and usually dry except during heavy rain
- *Bosque:* brush and trees lining a waterway
- *Capitán:* Captain
- *Casa:* house
- *Hacendado:* wealthy landowner
- *Llano: open grassy plain,* dry prairie
- *Playa:* the flat sandy, salty, or mud-caked flat floor of a desert basin usually covered by shallow water during or after prolonged heavy rain
- *Retirarse:* retreat
- *Rebozo:* shawl
- *Río Grande:* Great River
- *Segundo:* second in command
- *Teniente:* lieutenant

# CHIRICAHUA APACHE BANDS

• *Bedonkohe:* Located in eastern central Arizona and western central New Mexico. Originally Geronimo's band as a young man. Eventually merged with Mimbreños and other bands.

• *Chokonen:* Located in southern Arizona. Band of Cochise and later his son Naiche.

• *Chihenne:* Also known as Warm Springs, Mimbres, or Mimbreños, Located in the Mimbreño Mountains of New Mexico. Band of Victorio, Loco, Nana, and Kaytennae.

• *Nednhi:* Located primarily in the mountains of Sonora and Chihuahua in northern Mexico. Band led by Juh.

# INTRODUCTION

THIS IS THE second of two novels about the Apache chief and warrior Pedes-klinje, or as the Mexicans called him, Chato (meaning "Flat Nose"). The first book, *Desperate Warrior,* covered the years from 1877 to 1886, when Chato often rode with Geronimo as his *segundo* (second in command) in numerous raids and battles, especially in Mexico, after they escaped San Carlos Reservation in September 1881. During the years in Mexico, Chato lost a wife and two children to Mexican slavery after they were captured during a Rarámuri Indian attack led by Mexican military on the great Nednhi Chief Juh's winter camp in January 1883.

Losing his family was a defining event in Chato's life. He was desperate to get his family back and out of Mexican slavery. Five months after his family was taken, General Crook offered to get them back through high-level negotiations between the Chihuahuan state in Mexico and his big chiefs in Washington. Realizing this was his last, best hope of getting his family back, Chato vowed allegiance to the Army and to General Crook.

Chato understood that for General Crook's offer to work in retrieving his family, Geronimo had to stay peaceful on the reservation and not escape to raid in Mexico, Arizona, and New Mexico. He told Geronimo that if he left the reservation, he would destroy Crook's ability to get their families out of slavery, and he, Chato, would find and drag him back to the San Carlos guardhouse in chains. The White Eyes would imprison him there or on the little land in the western big water, Alcatraz, for years. Geronimo called Chato a traitor and a liar, and when he broke out of Fort Apache Reservation tried to have him killed. They remained enemies until Geronimo's dying day twenty-four years later.

The lives of Chato and Geronimo show striking similarities. Some historians have called Chato "Geronimo's doppelgänger." Although Geronimo was about thirty years older than Chato, they both claimed supernatural powers, rode together on many raids, were on the same reservations at the same time, lost wives and children to Mexican slavery, and were deadly rifle shots. Both men became Christians and then left the church to become again believers in the Apache creator god, *Ussen.* Geronimo was the acknowledged leader of the Chiricahua faction that wanted war to settle differences with the White Eyes. Chato was a major leader of the peace faction that believed peace with the White Eyes was necessary for Chiricahua survival.

The Naiche-Geronimo band of thirty-eight men, women, and children surrendered to General Nelson A. Miles in September 1886. Contrary to a surrender term, the women and children were shipped to Fort Marion in Florida, but the men were sent to Fort Pickens. All were held as prisoners of war. In one of the most shameful episodes in American history, the Army also made its loyal Chiricahua scouts, including Chato, and the peaceful Chiricahua who had stayed on the reservation after Geronimo escaped, prisoners of war at Fort Marion. Thus, all Chiricahua became prisoners of war for the next twenty-seven years. After the Chiricahua were shipped to Fort Sill as their future reservation, the similarities in the lives of the two men continued. Chato and Geronimo oversaw villages at Fort Sill during their captivity. Both men lost children to White Eye diseases. Both died in a hospital after catching pneumonia from drinking whiskey and lying soaked in cold water overnight. Chato's story does not drift far from Geronimo's.

After the Chiricahua were freed as prisoners of war, Chato, who never got his wife and children out of Mexican slavery, moved with his third wife and most of the Chiricahua to the Mescalero Reservation in south central New Mexico. Chato arrived at Mescalero in 1913. He died a bitter old man in 1934, still isolated from many of his People.

Chato's story of captivity and release to freedom is told here in Book 2, *Proud Outcast,* which covers the years from 1886 to 1934. During this time, Chato survived betrayal by the Army as a prisoner of war and endured, with his head held high, being treated as an outcast by some of his own People after they were freed.

As *Desperate Warrior* said, Chato's story is taken from history, but its truth is told through fiction as imaginatively seen through the eyes of Chato, whom Lieutenant Britton Davis, his former commander, described in 1929 as "the finest man, red or white, I ever knew."

# PROLOGUE

## APACHE SUMMIT, MESCALARO, NEW MEXICO
### 1930

TWO OLD MEN sipping from cups of scalding-hot coffee sat in rocking chairs by a potbellied stove in the main room of a small house. An old woman, her white hair streaked with gray, her fingers nimble and swift while manipulating thin reeds in a basket she was making, sat in a corner near the stove, paying little or no attention to either of the men as they watched, through a big, dust–covered window, the bright sunlight falling on the eastern mountains.

Blowing across the top of his cup to cool the black, steaming liquid, Yellow Boy said, "Chato, you've given me much to think about with the stories of your life as a warrior and a lead scout tracking the renegades who left Fort Apache. I understand why you told Geronimo you'd come after him and drag him back in chains to the guardhouse if he broke out and ruined any chance you had with *Nant'an Lpah* for getting your wife and children back. After you warned him that a breakout would prevent negotiations for your family, he must have understood that it would have the same effect on his family. I don't understand what he was thinking, but he didn't seem to care about getting his own family out of *Nakai-yi* slavery. In my opinion, that makes him a traitor to his People."

The wind rushing through the tops of the tall pines sounded like a distant river in full flow as Yellow Boy took a swallow of coffee and then scratched his chin.

"If my memory is correct, you told me that after four moons trying to catch Geronimo in the land of the *Nakai-yes,* you and other scouts needed rest and returned to Fort Apache to work your farms. That would have been by the last moon of the Season of Earth Is Reddish Brown. You weren't even chasing renegades. You and the reservation Chiricahua hadn't been in the land of the *Nakai-yes* for about three moons when Geronimo first talked of surrender with *Nant'an Lpah* in the Season of Little Eagles. Then, two suns later, after agreeing to surrender, Geronimo and Naiche broke the agreement and hid in the Azul Mountains in Sonora a few suns before they began raiding and *Nant'an Lpah* was sent to another place. That must have been when the White Eye big chiefs decided to make all the Chiricahua prisoners of war. I don't understand why they betrayed the peaceful Chiricahua, and I've heard you say the same thing many times. Maybe if you tell all you remember happening to you after Geronimo broke his surrender agreement, we can understand why the White Eye big chiefs did this thing only witches would do."

Chato stared at the hot stove and listened to the coffeepot bubble. Yellow Boy glanced at Helen sitting over on the other side of the room. She still worked on her basket, but he could tell she was listening to what was being said, especially by Chato.

Chato nodded and took another sip of his coffee. "Hmmph. Yellow Boy has a clear eye. I think a long time but never understand why the White Eye chiefs made the scouts or the peaceful Chiricahua prisoners of war. Geronimo must have laughed long and loud when he learned we were prisoners too. I tell you the rest of the story. Maybe you hear something I missed and we learn why the White Eyes do this hard thing to us. Maybe you need to come for more visits with the man nobody likes if you want to hear it all. I'll be glad to see you again, *amigo.*"

Yellow Boy smiled. "Speak, and I will listen."

# PROUD
# OUTCAST

# ARIZONA, NEW MEXICO AND MEXICO

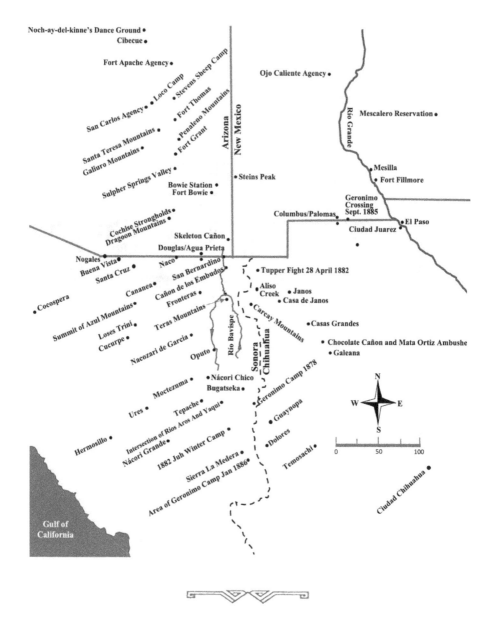

*Approximate locations in the history of Chato and the Chiricahua Apache beginning at Ojo Caliente Reservation, New Mexico, in 1877 and ending in the summer of 1886, when Chato and his delegation left Fort Apache for Washington. Modern locations are provided for common reference.*

# ONE

## KAYTENNAE RETURNS

A MOON AFTER I learned of the death of *Capitán* Crawford and that Geronimo and Naiche had told *Teniente* Maus they would meet with *Nant'an Lpah* in two moons, Gon-altsis, my brother and Dutchy, both Army scouts, came to my cabin to sit and smoke with me. They said *Teniente* Maus feared the renegades might attack Fort Apache to get back the families *Nant'an Lpah* had captured in the land of the *Nakai-yes*. Their first sergeants had picked them to go to Fort Apache, find out what we knew, and report back. They came to me and Alchesay, White Mountain chief and scout, to learn what we knew or had seen. Alchesay told them no one among the White Mountains had seen or heard anything that said the renegades were headed for Fort Apache. After we smoked, I told them the same thing. If we had seen or heard anything to suggest they were nearby, *Teniente* Lockett and I would have been after them.

They told us about the fights in the Blue Mountains (Sierra Madre) to run Geronimo out of his camps and the fight with the Rarámuri when *Capitán* Crawford was killed. They told me Binday—son of She-neah, the great medicine man who was killed when we wiped out Juan Mata Ortiz—had put a bullet in the heart of Mauricio Corredor, who led the Rarámuri. Dutchy said he killed the man who shot Crawford. I was happy to hear this. I thought, *If peace comes, other warriors and I won't be slipping off to Mexico to settle accounts with Corredor and the Rarámuri.*

Gon-altsis and Dutchy ate their evening meal with us. My women remembered Dutchy well and of course Gon-altsis from our first days on Turkey Creek and were glad to see them. They told us how good the sheep and horses on the farm looked now in the Ghost Face and that they believed we would have a good year in the growing season. They stayed the night with us and left the next morning.

I had asked them during our meal the night before if they truly believed the renegades would surrender. They nodded their heads. "Yes, Geronimo and Nai-che, they surrender, and then the others will too. *Nant'an Lpah* thinks bringing Alchesay, Naiche's mother, and the woman they took who later escaped will help convince them to surrender."

I said, "Hmmph. *Nant'an Lpah* is great chief with much light behind his eyes. I think they probably surrender."

AFTER GON-ALTSIS AND Dutchy left, I kept my eyes and ears open to any-thing that might tell me about the talks *Nant'an Lpah* and the renegades would hold near the border, but where they would be held, no one was certain. A moon later, word came that Geronimo and Naiche with their band had ap-peared at *Teniente* Maus's camp on the *Río* San Bernardino, claimed they were ready to talk, and thought a good place was near where the *Río* Bavispe makes its big turn south. *Teniente* Maus told them they were much safer from attack by *Nakai-yi* soldiers if they moved the council meeting closer to the border. They talked among themselves and decided the best place to meet *Nant'an Lpah* was Canyon de los Embudos. *Teniente* Maus sent word by talking wire and asked that the *nant'an* come quickly and said that the renegades were ready to talk. The *nant'an* took his time. He didn't want the Chiricahua to think he was eager to take them in. He didn't leave Fort Bowie for several days while he gathered the people and supplies that he wanted to go with him to help convince the renegades to surrender.

I was at the Fort Apache trading post to get seeds for the garden and fields my women were planting and stood outside by the hitching post, talking to *Teniente* Lockett about the big meeting with the renegades in the Canyon de los Embudos. Then he told me something I had not anticipated.

"I expect *Nant'an Lpah* will be leaving tomorrow. The train Kaytennae's on came in late yesterday afternoon."

I frowned. "Kaytennae is in chains on the little land surrounded by big water to the west. He won't be free for another harvest or two."

*Teniente* Lockett nodded. "You're right. That's the way it was, except he wasn't in chains there more than a moon. The story I hear is that *Nant'an Lpah* had him freed for him to attend the meeting talks. This'll show the renegades that they'll get their freedom back if they become prisoners and that they can learn white ways that'll help them when they're free. Kaytennae learned to speak English and to read and make tracks on paper while he was at Alcatraz."

Kaytennae and I had had our differences. He believed I told *Teniente* Davis lies about what he was doing to get him in trouble. I told *Teniente* Davis only the truth.

"Where Kaytennae go after big council?"

"Why, he'll come back here to be with his family. He's still Nana's *segundo*, ain't he?"

"*Sí*, still *segundo*. Has family here at Fort Apache."

I hope Kaytennae isn't holding a vow of revenge against me. I'd hate to kill him in front of his People.

THE NEXT EVENTS at the Canyon de los Embudos surrender meeting happened fast. They were like lightning arrows from Thunder's Bow, but we at Fort Apache learned about them suns later. The renegades, including Chihuahua, Ulzana, Nana, Geronimo, and Naiche, but not Mangas and his little band, who were not with the others, surrendered. The night of the surrender, those with Geronimo and Naiche got drunk, and a White Eye whiskey seller, who Geronimo trusted, told him that the White Eyes planned to hang him and others as soon as they crossed the border. At the last camp they made, before they crossed the border, Geronimo and Naiche and about forty of their followers took a couple of horses and mules and left the camp deep in the night for the mountains in western Sonora. *Teniente* Maus was low on supplies, but his scouts still followed them until the renegades scattered in all directions on foot.

The White Eye big chiefs far to the east blamed *Nant'an Lpah* for letting Geronimo and Naiche get away. They sent him away to serve as a *nant'an* someplace with the prairie tribes east of the Río Pecos. A new *nant'an*, Miles, came. He did things differently than *Nant'an Lpah*. He sent many more Blue Coats to patrol the border and to chase Geronimo in the land of the *Nakai-yes*, and he used no Apache scouts for fighting, only a few for tracking.

About fifty who did not break away with Geronimo and their leader, Chihuahua, were sent on to Fort Bowie, where—with about twenty-three women and children, other prisoners *Nant'an Lpah* had collected—they camped and in a few days were all taken to Bowie Station, put on an iron wagon, and disappeared down the iron road, into the rising sun.

ALCHESAY AND KAYTENNAE accompanied *Teniente* Maus and his scouts back to Fort Apache.

A few days later, I sat drinking coffee by Nalthchedah's outside fire after my morning prayers. I thought, *I wish I had killed Geronimo when I had the chance. Now he has driven* Nant'an Lpah *away, and my chances of the big chiefs in the east getting* Ishchos *and the children out of* Nakai-yi *slavery are gone forever. The big chiefs will no longer demand them, and Geronimo raiding in Sonora will cause many bad feelings between the Americans and the* Nakai-yes. *There won't be any desire to help free our People on either side.*

I was staring at my cup when a shadow crossed my hand, and I looked up. It was from Kaytennae. I was reaching for the knife in my belt when he held up his hand. "I come only for talk."

I stood and faced him. "There's coffee hot on the fire."

He shook his head.

I said, "Speak. I listen."

"Chato, I come to speak with you so, if one of us makes a mistake in understanding the battles to come, we will know not to blame the other."

I frowned and cocked my head to one side. "Speak clearly, Kaytennae."

"I wore my chains for a moon on the little land surrounded by the big water the White Eyes call 'Alcatraz.' Then they took the chains off and let me walk about the land and even let me go across the water with others to see the big town. At this place, I thought about you often and how, when I came back, I would gut you for telling lies about me to *Teniente* Davis."

I shook my head. "I spoke no lies to *Teniente* Davis about you or anyone else. I told him only what I had heard or seen with my own eyes and ears. His spies—I was not one—told him about you being drunk and nearly ambushing him. I was not even a scout then."

Kaytennae nodded. "Yes, I believe this. I have thought about it for a long time. Still, I think everything you told *Teniente* Davis, you told him to make me look bad. To pass the time on the little land in the big water, I learned the White Eye tongue. I speak and understand the White Eye tongue good. I learned to read their tracks on paper. Now anytime you speak to the White Eyes about what you see or tell us what you hear from the White Eyes, I will be there to see that you tell it straight, tell it true, and if you do not, I will."

I said, "I always speak true. You want to listen to me tell others what I know or think? If I don't speak true, then you speak what you think is true. Let the listener decide who speaks the truth."

He crossed his arms and stared at me for a moment. "*Ch'ik'eh doleel* (it will be so). I watch and listen to everything you say. Tell it true. If you do not, I will. Be warned, there are those—Geronimo, Ulzana, Chihuahua, and others—who believe you betrayed us by leading Crawford to their camps in Mexico or were a spy for *Teniente* Davis. Geronimo hates nothing more than disloyalty. You killed Ulzana's young son when you raided Chihuahua's camp. They want revenge for what you've done. They want your life. Watch your back. It won't be me who kills you. Maybe you live a long time. Maybe they get you quick. They are Apache. They don't forget." Then he turned and walked away.

# TWO

## THE DELEGATION TO WASHINGTON

THREE MOONS AFTER the renegades surrendered and the Geronimo-Naiche band broke away from the main group to continue raiding and making war in western Sonora, life was calm at Fort Apache as those of us who were left there and at Turkey Creek tended to our animals and crops. The new *nant'an*, Miles, didn't use scouts like *Nant'an Lpah* had, except a few for trackers, and brought many more soldiers to chase and fight Geronimo than *Nant'an Lpah* ever had. The soldiers were everywhere at San Carlos and Fort Apache. It seemed there were now more at San Carlos than when Noch-ay-del-kinne, the prophet who said he could call back the great dead chiefs, had been killed. At that time, there were so many soldiers on every trail they made the People believe the White Eyes planned to do something to them, and so we ran for the land of the *Nakai-yes*. Now we knew better and had no thought of returning to that hard land across the border. *Nant'an* Miles had no luck in his chase for Geronimo. As our crops and livestock herds on our Fort Apache farms grew fat, the Blue Coat soldiers hadn't captured or killed anyone in the Geronimo-Naiche band. We laughed at this among ourselves but said nothing to our agent or the Blue Coats.

One day, a Blue Coat rider rode up to the place where I and Horace were unloading and stacking hay from my wagon. I saw him coming but couldn't imagine why he came as I stopped forking hay out of my wagon and watched him come. He walked his horse up to the wagon, where I stood in its bed, which put us at nearly the same eye level. He touched his forehead with the edge of his hand like the Blue Coats do as a sign of respect. I nodded.

He said in the *Nakai-yi* tongue, "*Señor* Chato?"

I nodded.

"*Señor* Chato, *Nant'an* Miles wishes to have a council with the Chiricahua leaders next sun at the time of shortest shadows and asks that you be at the chief house. He says to tell you there is important business to discuss."

"Hmmph. Tell *Nant'an* Miles I come."

IT WAS COOL in the chief house, and windows provided most of the light for *Nant'an* Miles's council. He sat behind a big shiny table between a white chief from the east, whom I had not seen before, and Tom Jeffords. I was happy to see the old friend of Cochise, who now seemed to serve as a counselor and interpreter for the *nant'an*. Next to Jeffords was a man who made black water tracks on paper to help the *nant'an* remember what was said. I never understood why the White Eyes did this. Weren't their memories as good as ours? I thought, *Maybe they speak too many words to remember. Nant'an* Miles, unlike *Nant'an Lpah*, wore his best clothes, with rows of buttons wrapped in ribbon and pieces of shaped metal that hung from ribbons on the left side of his coat, close to his shoulder. He was a tall man, broad in his shoulders, with a big bush of curled hair that grew under his nose that no Apache would tolerate under his own nose.

Those who came to the meeting sat in a semicircle around his table, our rifles across our knees. Kaytennae made it a point to sit next to me, smiling as he sat down. I made it a point to ignore him. I saw the wrinkles in the *nant'an*'s forehead as he scowled, looking at our rifles across our knees. He turned to Jeffords and spoke close to his ear. Jeffords shook his head and said something back. The *nant'an* nodded, looked back at us but no longer scowled, and stood. He spoke through Jeffords, a few words at a time.

Jeffords first introduced the *nant'an*, asked that we hear his council, and said time would be given to ask questions. Then the *nant'an* spoke to us through Jeffords.

"Strong leaders of the Chiricahua, I bring you greetings from the Great Father who lives by the big water in the east. He is glad that you have kept your word to live here in peace even as Geronimo and others have stirred up the White Eyes, *Nakai-yes*, and other Apache against you. Other Apache and White Eyes don't seem to like you. The Great Father thinks, for your own protection, you should be moved far from here to a new reservation where you will not be attacked or your property stolen from you. The Indians at Fort Apache are getting drunk on *tizwin* all the time and killing each other. Deep in the dark night, the stillness is broken by rifles and revolvers fired by your own People in savage orgies. All these problems must be spoken to in council with the Great Father.

"I want you to choose a group of ten from among you to visit the Great Father and his big chiefs and tell them how you feel about leaving Fort Apache. He will think on your concerns before deciding what to do, whether you go or stay. On the way, riding on the iron wagon, we will stop and let you all look over the land at two sites and decide if either site would make a home for you, where you can support yourselves if the Great Father decides you must get out of the way of the angry White Eyes and *Nakai-yes* who won't listen to reason and want to spill your blood in revenge. We want to do everything we can to help you. Now is that time. Help us help you. Come back to this place in three suns at the time of no shadows and tell us who you have chosen to speak with the Great Father and to see the places of future reservations you might choose."

I turned to Kaytennae, who had been frowning as he listened to the *nant'an's* words, and asked, "What does this mean, this 'help us help you?'"

Kaytennae wore a crooked smile and shook his head. "It means we are taking your land and it's Geronimo's fault."

I didn't like the words of this *nant'an*. I had put much work into my farm. I didn't want to go to another reservation and start over. My sheep herd was growing. My ponies were fat. I had some hay already stacked for winter. I had a plow and kept it in good shape, and I had a wagon and team with harness that could pull the wagon or the plow. The corn and barley we had planted were growing well and would make a good harvest. My children were learning how to farm, something I did not know when I was their age. I was making money hauling things in my wagon for people who didn't have one. Why must we move? I was a first sergeant of scouts—that must count for something with the White Eyes. I had risked my life leading scouts for *Capitán* Crawford in the land of the *Nakai-yes*. The scouts had risked their lives too. Surely we could all stay where we lived well and in peace with the White Eyes and other Apache. The only darkness in my days was the thought that Ishchos and the children were still in *Nakai-yi* slavery, and my advocate for them to the big chiefs in the east had gone away. A thought came like a light in the night, *Perhaps I can go on this trip and speak with the big chiefs, maybe even the Great Father, and get them to speak to the* Nakai-yes *again about my family. Yes, I'll go. I can do that.*

Before we met again with *Nant'an* Miles, the men met in council and decided who would go east to speak with the Great Father and big chiefs and look at the new reservation lands. I was chosen to speak for the group. I had met with

*Nant'an Lpah,* who was a great chief, and he was always glad to hear my words on how to go after Geronimo. Others chosen included Loco and Kaytennae, who glanced at me, smiled, and said that since he was Nana's *segundo,* he must go to ensure he heard exactly what the big chiefs said. Loco insisted his two wives and a granddaughter go. Noche, Charley, Gon-altsis, and Guydelkon, who had been among *Teniente* Davis's most important and trusted scouts, agreed to go. We planned to ask three interpreters we trusted to go with us. These included Sam Bowman, Concepción, and Mickey Free.

WE MET AGAIN with *Nant'an* Miles, who spoke to us through Jeffords. He asked who we had chosen to represent us and to see the new reservation sites. Since I was our spokesman, I stood and told him who we wanted to go east and that we were ready. He nodded and waved for *Capitán* Dorst, sitting nearby, to come stand with him. Dorst was tall and lean and had yellow hair he pulled to one side. I had worked with him a little when I led *Capitán* Crawford's scouts. He was a reliable Blue Coat officer. I liked him.

The *nant'an* said, "I see you chose good representatives. Captain Dorst here with me will oversee your welfare when you travel. He will see that you eat well, board the right trains, sleep in the right places, speak with the big chiefs and the Great Father, and return home safely. Sam Bowman, Concepción, and Mickey Free will go with you to serve as interpreters. Captain Bourke, who you know was General Crook's assistant, is now working in the city of the Great Father, where you are going. He will help Captain Dorst support you when you get to the city of the Great Father. I hope the big chiefs will let you stay at Fort Apache or at least give you one of the two good land reservation sites you'll see on the way east. You'll leave Bowie Station in nine suns. Captain Dorst will make arrangements for wagons to pick you up and take you to Bowie Station, where you'll board the train east."

There was something about the way the *nant'an* looked at us as he spoke that made me think he also had plans he wasn't telling us, and it worried me. But there was nothing I could do except stay watchful. He ended the council. "Good luck, gentlemen. I'll be here with the Fort Apache commander, Lieutenant Colonel Wade, if we need to meet again."

I returned to my farm and, with my women and children, sweated much in labor for the next six suns to ensure all was ready for my leaving. I thought

I would be gone about a moon and wanted to be sure all the harness for the wagon horses was in good shape. We gathered and stacked all the hay we could and made sure that our fences and tools were in good repair and that our knives were sharp and ready to use.

Every evening as the day grew dim, the sun cast dark-orange, red, and purple colors across the horizon clouds, and the little smoke column from Nalthchedah's cooking fire in front of our cabin rose straight up in a smooth column until, high above us, it bent and flowed parallel to the ground and pointing east. Nalthchedah served her best meals, and we ate like starving people. Maud, Horace, and Banatsi were full of questions about the trip east. They wanted to know every detail, but I knew so little about what *Capitán* Dorst planned that I couldn't answer most of their questions. Nalthchedah was strangely silent, her questions few. She was eager in the blankets. *Ussen* had not yet given her another child, and she seemed desperate to have one growing in her before I left.

The night before I left for the place of the Great Father and big chiefs, I lay awake listening to the frogs on the river, the peepers in the trees, and Coyote calling his brothers. I wondered where all this movement was truly leading. I had no dreams to tell me, and I felt like a blind man wandering on top of a mesa knowing I was staggering around too close to its cliffs. One wrong step and there would be no more wandering, no more life as we knew it.

I HAD NEVER ridden an iron wagon and was amazed at how fast it went. Watching the brush and land fly by when we were into the flat country, I thought, *This must be the way hawks and eagles see the country as they fly close to the earth.* It seemed to me that the iron wagon pulling us must have a caged demon inside somehow harnessed to turn its wheels on the iron road. It blew steam and smoke and roared and whistled. It had to be fed with wood or black rocks and watered often. Where did the White Eyes get such a demon, and how did they control it? I had no idea. Often when we stopped for wood or black rocks and water, *Capitán* Dorst used the talking wire to advise the *nant'an* of our progress. Near the time of no shadows of the second day, *Capitán* Dorst told us the *nant'an* had learned that the sites the Great Chiefs wanted us to see for our reservation weren't ready yet and that we would have to see them another time. My blind man staggered nearer the cliffs. I feared it was a warning of days of darkness coming.

# THREE

## THE MEDAL

OUR LITTLE BAND saw many unbelievable things from the windows of our iron wagon. There were houses much bigger and finer than any *hacendado's hacienda* or those *Nakai-yi* big chief's, many iron wagons and iron roads, great chimneys filled with smoke sticking high out of great *casas*, unending villages with many *casas* large and small and much land being farmed, a great river none of us could swim across, and people without number everywhere we went. None of this surprised Kaytennae. He had seen many things like this in the *gran* village near the land of Alcatraz but, like the rest of us, had not slept in a great house with many rooms, a place to eat, and a place to drink whiskey. *Capitán* Dorst took us to such a place after we stepped from our iron wagon into the *gran* village of the Great Father. Dorst called it the "Beveridge Hotel." I did not like this place of many smells, scattered trash, dirty rooms, many people, long gloomy cave-like tunnels *Capitán* Dorst called "halls" with sleeping rooms every few paces on both sides, the noise from the wide wagon roads that crossed and ran by its sides, or the sly looks form those who worked there.

THE MORNING SUNLIGHT was bright, but the air felt heavy and looked hazy as *Capitán* Dorst led Kaytennae, Charley, the three interpreters, and me, with Loco, the women, and the scouts following behind along a wide path of large, smooth square stones that ran beside a wide wagon road. It was filled with buggies pulled by high-stepping horses driven by men in black suits sitting on a high seat, while others sat in the back of the buggy, smoking *cigarros* or reading big pieces of paper covered with the tracks the White Eyes made for words they called "newspapers." It seemed that someone or all the riders in every buggy passing us turned their heads and stared at our group following a Blue Coat *Capitán* toward the *gran casas* where the Great Chiefs made choices that had affected our lives for the past twenty harvests. I hoped their choice for us this time was a good one.

Today we were to speak to the Great Father, and later in the coming suns, the Great Chiefs Secretary of War William C. Endicott, in charge of all the soldiers, and Secretary of the Interior Lucius Q. C. Lamar, in charge of the White Eyes who were reservation agents. We Apache knew Endicott's men often argued with Lamar's men who oversaw us.

Soon, we saw a great white house with two rows of windows. At its front, near the middle of the house, was a big door shaded by a small roof supported by tall, smooth stones the size of big tree trunks. Not far from the wagon road leading past the door, a big stone bowl surrounded by green grass caught a column of water flying out of the ground. We turned down the path by the big wagon road leading toward the doors. *Capitán* Dorst turned but kept walking and waved an arm in its direction. He smiled at me. "We're going to the White House first. The Great Father lives and works there and wants to meet you and thank you for your service as first sergeant of scouts and leader of this delegation."

We walked under the roof over the door and went inside. My jaw dropped. I had never seen such rooms. The rooms had tall ceilings, and reaching to the ceilings were tall stones, smaller but like the ones that supported the roof, over the door. The floors were smooth and shiny, inset with symbolic patterns, and great paintings hung on the walls, covered with paper having many different patterns. *Capitán* Dorst led us to a man sitting behind a table with a book of paper in the middle and stacks of papers on either side. The man, tall and lean with a small bush of hair under his nose and sad drooping eyes, wore the usual long gray coat many white eyes in the *gran* village wore with a narrow piece of cloth tied around his shirt collar.

*Capitán* Dorst stepped up to the table. "Captain Dorst, U.S. Army, with the Chiricahua Apache delegation from Fort Apache to see President Cleveland."

The man behind the table pulled his round sun tracker the White Eyes called "watch" out of his vest pocket on the end of a gold chain, snapped it open, and looked at it. Then he ran his finger down the paper with tracks where the book was opened, stopped near the top of the page, looked up at *Capitán* Dorst, and smiled. "Yes, sir. The president is expecting you, and you're right on time."

He took papers, a writing stick, and a box covered with fine blue cloth and said, "Follow me, please." We followed him down a rug-covered hall floor to a door where he knocked, heard, "Come," opened the door, and led us into a big room with a desk at one end and enough chairs in front of the desk to seat us all.

A big, fat man lumbered out of his chair and around the desk with his hand out while the man from behind the table said, "Mister President, this is Captain Dorst with the Fort Apache delegation you wanted to meet. I'll just put this on your desk."

He nodded and then stuck out his hand to *Capitán* Dorst, gave it several gentle pumps, and said, "Grover Cleveland."

*Capitán* Dorst smiled and said, "My pleasure, sir. Captain Joseph Dorst, U.S. Army." Then he turned to me and said, "This is Chief Chato, who leads the delegation of Chiricahua Apache from Fort Apache to speak with Secretaries Endicott and Lamar."

I gave the Great Father's hand two good pumps as he smiled and nodded at me and then moved on down the line, with *Capitán* Dorst introducing Kaytennae, Loco, the scouts and interpreters, and finally the women.

Sitting just behind and to the right of the president's desk were two men, who stood when we came in the room. After the president shook our hands, he turned to the two men, both dressed in dark suits. One was older, his hair gray, and the other with a long face that had more hair on it than the other man's, and he wore big round glasses in front of his eyes. The Great Father motioned to them and said, "Ladies and gentlemen, I want you to meet the men who oversee you. The first gentleman, with all the gray hair, is Secretary of War Endicott, and the second is Secretary of the Interior Lamar, whose son I'm sure you know is your agent at Fort Apache."

Endicott and Lamar smiled and stepped up and shook *Capitán* Dorst's hand before he in turn went down the line, introducing each of us again for another handshake. After having my hand gripped and shaken three times, I thought, *White Eyes have very strange ceremonies and customs.*

The Great Father, standing in front of his desk, said, "Everyone, take a seat. I'm happy to see the delegation of peaceful Chiricahua Apache from Fort Apache. I know you have business to discuss with these two gentlemen seated behind me, which I understand you'll discuss in council with them later this week." He raised his brows and turned to look at the big chiefs, the secretaries, who both nodded. "I also understand that Chief Chato is your spokesman. Is there anything you wish to convey to me personally, Chief? I'm here to listen."

My heart was pounding. At last, I would speak to the Great Father for the People. I knew most of what we had to say would be said to the big chiefs. I said, "Great Father, know and understand we can make war no more against the Americans. We have no desire at all to make war. We ask only to work for our living as every man must. We are happy on our land at Fort Apache. That is all I have to say until I speak with your Great Chiefs." I sat down.

The Great Father nodded. "The words you say, Chief Chato, are good to hear. I assure you that so long as your People keep faith with the government, your interests shall be looked after. Now, sir, if you will stand here with me, I have something for you."

I moved over to stand beside the Great Father. Big Chief Lamar handed the Great Father the blue box that the man in the hall had left on his desk. He opened the box. Inside was a shiny silver medal. It was about three fingers wide and three quarters of a hand long and had a long cloth streamer attached to it. He took it out of the box and said, "Chief Chato, we want to recognize the great service you have done for us in helping our soldiers bring the renegade Apache in. We owe you a debt of gratitude and hope you will accept this small token of our appreciation."

I saw Kaytennae make a little frown when I made the all-is-well sign. The Great Father glanced toward *Capitán* Dorst, who barely nodded before the Great Father pinned it above the left breast pocket of my vest. It was a heavy medal with the image of a Great Father and tracks under him on one side. *Capitán* Dorst later told us what all the tracks said on both sides. The tracks under the image of the Great Father said, "Chester A. Arthur." On the other side was a carved picture of a settler standing with a Plains Indian. The settler was pointing toward the open, inviting door of his cabin. There were a few tracks above the cabin, which said, "Peace," and many more small ones along the bottom, which said, "From Secretary Lamar to Chatto."

I felt very happy and proud. This medal showed us the Great Father would let us keep our land if we worked hard at Fort Apache. It was a great day to be alive.

The Great Father shook my hand again and said, "Congratulations. Thank you, Chief." The two big chiefs, Endicott and Lamar, smiling, shook my hand again and said the same thing. Then they spoke to *Capitán* Dorst, and we left them while they spoke with the Great Father.

Outside, the sun was bright, the air wet and hazy, the heat worse than anything I'd felt in the desert, and our bodies leaked water as if pouring from some pot inside us. I thought the land would be desert except that water in places roared out of the ground in tall columns until it fell back and was caught in great bowls. There was so much water everywhere that grass grew green even in the dry Season of Large Leaves.

*Capitán* Dorst said we would walk back to the hotel and eat a midday meal. After we ate, he said he planned to hire a big buggy and have it drive around town to show us monuments and other big-chief buildings. He told me that, next sun, we would visit something he called the "Smithsonian Museum," a place where special things of long ago, and even near times, were kept for all to see, and that there was a man who made pictures who wanted to take ours for our historic visit.

That sun, riding in a big buggy with *Capitán* Dorst, we saw many great buildings, their roofs supported with the great stone pillars like the ones at the Great Father's house. One of the monuments was a thin, tall building of cut stone that reached high into the sky and was pointed on top. I didn't understand how such a building could be built, and upon seeing it, I knew the White Eyes must have more power than we could imagine.

Before we returned to the hotel, we drove by a great burial ground. Each place where a soldier was buried was marked on white stone with the tracks for the soldier's name and his standing as a soldier. The stones were laid out in many rows and columns and stretched across green fields crisscrossed with graveled walks. I thought, *Truly, a garden of stone.*

# FOUR

## ENDICOTT SIGNS A PAPER

THE NEXT SUN we spent at Smithsonian Museum. We had our pictures taken there, and we were filled with wonder at all the things the White Eyes had done over the span of many harvests. Our amazement at all the buildings and monuments we had seen the afternoon before grew and grew as we saw many fine things in the museum, some very, very old, made and used many harvests ago.

The next morning, we walked the same smooth stone path to talk with the big chiefs that we had used to go to the Great Father's white house. The big chiefs had their rooms in great separate buildings side by side, a little behind and west of the Great Father's house. Their buildings had three rows of windows and, above them, a fourth row that individually stuck out from the roof.

*Capitán* Dorst led us into the big chief house of Endicott. It was like walking into a cave, dark and gloomy, but lighted by oil lamps hung together in groups from the ceiling. We walked into a short hall through a big, heavy door, and in a few steps, we came to the middle of a big hall that ran the length of the building. Directly across this hall from where we entered were two sets of steps that I guessed led to rooms above us and must use the second row of windows. The long hall was filled with echoes of men talking and laughing and the slap of their shoes on the smooth shiny floor. *Capitán* Dorst led us down the big hall, past a few doors and big colorful paintings of men in Blue Coats fighting men in gray coats or red coats or Indians of all kinds. He stopped at a door with big tracks that looked like the ones the White Eyes made with black water on paper, but these were painted on a board stuck on the wall beside the door.

*Capitán* Dorst opened the door and led us inside where he spoke to a man sitting behind something that looked like a big table, with many boxes supported in frames under it that let the boxes be pulled out and easily shoved back into the frame. Dorst explained to the man that we had an appointment to meet with Secretary of War Endicott at this time. The man at the table reminded me of Naiche, tall and thin, with thick, black hair shining with oil and smoothly combed back from his face. A big growth of hair was combed under his nose to look like a set of horns, and while it was warm, almost hot, in the room, he wore a coat and tie around his high-collar shirt like the Great Father's man wore. Little trickles of water ran down the sides of his face, and he often used a white cloth to dab and wipe it away. He smiled and nodded and motioned for us to sit in chairs around the room while he went into to tell the Great Chief we waited for him. The man at the desk, *Capitán* Dorst called him "secretary," knocked on a door at the end of the room and then went in. I heard the secretary mumble something, and then a deep voice said, "Oh! Good! Right on time. Give me another five minutes with Secretary Lamar and his men, and then show them in."

Secretary closed the door behind him and, smiling at *Capitán* Dorst, said, "Secretary Endicott will be with you in five minutes."

Dorst nodded and leaned back in his chair, sitting up straight with his fingers laced together over his belly. I looked at the others with me. Their faces were blank masks showing neither fear nor gladness. They looked like they were ready to face torture. My heart beat a little faster than normal as I thought of how this man might have enough power to get my family out of Mexican slavery and keep us on our farms at Fort Apache as I had told the Great Father. He could make us move to a new place and start over again. I made a prayer to *Ussen*, asking that I be given Power to say good words when the Great Chief and I spoke.

THE DOOR OPENED from the great hall into the room where we sat. A Blue Coat walked in, nodded to the Great Chief's secretary, and, with a big grin, took the hand of *Capitán* Dorst, who, laughing, stood for a shake. I realized the Blue Coat was *Capitán* Bourke, once a *segundo* for *Nant'an Lpah*. We all liked and knew him. He had light behind his eyes, and he understood and studied our lifeways. He went around the room, shaking hands and speaking to each one of us.

I was the last to shake his hand and said as I gave his hand two strong pumps, "*Capitán* Bourke, I'm glad to see you. Do you work here in this *gran casa*?"

Bourke grinned under the big bush of hair under his nose and shook his head.

"I'm happy to see you here, Chato. Maybe you and the people with you can talk some sense into Secretary Endicott. No, I work a few streets away, trying to learn about the lifeways of your People and others to help guide the White Eye understanding of them. We want them treated fairly to prevent any more war between us. I came over here at the request of General Crook and Secretary Endicott."

I nodded, happy to hear what *Capitán* Bourke said to me. He would help us tell Endicott how we felt. The secretary stood at his desk, looked at a watch he pulled from his vest pocket, went to the door, knocked, disappeared inside, and came back out to motion us into the room where Big Chief Secretary Endicott sat.

Capitáns Dorst and Bourke led us into a room with big windows streaming in sunlight that slanted across a great table in the center of the room. A group of oil lanterns, also for light, hung from the ceiling. On one end of the room was a big, brown shiny desk, its top carefully arranged with many papers covered with tracks and the little tools the White Eyes used when they worked with tracks on the paper. The great table, arranged so the chief could sit in front of his desk and command one of the narrow ends of the table, was surrounded by twelve chairs. Chairs were around the walls, and two men sat in these. Big Chief Secretary Endicott stood up from the desk, and his secretary introduced us as we came in and motioned us to chairs. Capitáns Dorst and Bourke sat with the interpreters, and I sat between them. Kaytennae and Charley sat to the right of Bourke. Loco and his women and the scouts sat in the chairs along the wall to listen to what was said, but not to speak.

His secretary sat to Endicott's right and pulled a little black water spear from his pocket, uncovered its point, and prepared to make tracks of what was said in the meeting. During the meeting, Endicott's eyes stayed on each one speaking. It was warm in the room. He, too, kept his coat on, but his face showed no water like his secretary. He welcomed us and said, while motioning toward the two men who sat in chairs by the wall and smiled and nodded, that we had already met these men at the Great Father's house, Secretary of the Interior Lamar and his secretary, who was also making tracks on paper resting on a board in his lap.

Endicott turned to *Capitán* Dorst and, as Sam Bowman translated English into Spanish, and Concepción translated Spanish into Apache, said, "Captain Dorst, General Miles asked that I meet with your delegation from Fort Apache who have come to make their case for staying there, and I'm happy to listen."

*Capitán* Dorst said, "Sir, General Miles asked that these men come and make their case to you for them staying on their farms at Fort Apache. For the past three years, they have lived at Fort Apache, peacefully working their farms.

When Geronimo left the reservation, they didn't go with him. All you see here, and most of the men who didn't leave the reservation, served the Army as scouts and helped General Crook lead Geronimo to surrender. One of the Army's best scouts, Chato, is here to speak for them. He did exceptional work in tracking and finding the escapees and bringing them back to the reservation." Endicott smiled and nodded his approval toward me.

*Capitán* Dorst continued. "Apache is a hard language to learn, and it's rare to find an interpreter who can interpret what is being said in Apache directly into English. We have three interpreters to ensure that you correctly hear what the Apache say. Concepción will translate from Apache to Spanish. Sam Bowman and Mickey Free will translate from Spanish to English. If there is any confusion about what is said, Captain Bourke will help interpret the meaning of his words. Endicott nodded and said, according to Sam Bowman and Concepción, "Speak, and I will listen."

I made it a point of looking at Endicott's eyes so, as a White Eye, he understood I spoke straight. "I come to this place looking for good words, good advice, words as if God is speaking. I come also for a paper with tracks that records what we say so I can remember the words that you tell me here."

Endicott nodded and glanced toward his secretary, who was fast writing what was said and who also nodded he understood what I wanted. Lamar crossed his arms and cocked his head to one side, listening closely to what I said.

"I come to ask for our country, to ask for land where I live now—that is why I have traveled so far. At Fort Apache, what I plant grows up very well, the water there is very good, and I want to stay there."

Endicott interlaced his fingers, rested his elbows on the table, and leaned forward as if to hear better. He seemed to be listening to my words.

"The favor I want to ask of you is to ask for my land as if I was asking a favor from God. I hope you won't forget my words. It is to me as if God said that he and you had come together to talk. I think now God is listening."

Occasionally, Endicott and Lamar frowned at the translation as if they didn't understand what was said. *Capitán* Bourke then spoke, explaining what I meant, they nodded they understood, and then I continued.

"You may have some children. Everybody loves his son, loves him dearly, holds him in his arms and to his heart. I have a wife and two children in Chihuahua, this *Capitán* Bourke knows. I have seen their pictures, and so has *Capitán* Bourke, where they are held in captivity. There are other captives in the land of the *Nakai-yes* belonging to those who are not in our group who have also remained on the reservation. Another favor I want to ask of you as if I was asking a favor from God is for you to request the *Nakai-yes* return their Apache slaves to you, that these children may be delivered to my hands so I can take them to my heart again and have them with me at Fort Apache. I have feelings just like white people, and for that reason, I want to have my People once more with me. I cannot make big houses like this but can only take small sticks and make a house—even if my hands ache, I want to live this way."

*Capitán* Bourke explained my meaning after Endicott and Lamar shook their heads, and those making tracks on paper looked puzzled. "In speaking of his house, he means that no matter how poor a man is, his home, when it is the best he can offer, is the place for his wife and children to be. When he says he has seen their pictures, he speaks of the photographs that were sent by the Mexican authorities to General Crook to induce Chato to believe his wife and children were better off where they were in Chihuahua than they were on the reservation."

Endicott sat back in his chair, nodded he understood, and smoothed the bush of hair under his nose. Lamar crossed his legs and slumped back in his chair, stroking the long hair on his face that rested on his chest.

I said, "Before we came here, I had my picture taken at the place called Smithsonian Museum. I want to have some of them sent to the man in Chihuahua who has my family. I want my name, Chato, put on the picture so my wife will know it is me who sends them and longs for her."

Bourke said, "The best way to accomplish this is to send them to General Crook for forwarding. He's been in correspondence with persons in Chihuahua and knows exactly where Chato's family is."

Endicott looked first at Lamar, then *Capitán* Bourke, and finally me. He said, "We will get you some copies of your picture and ask Captain Bourke to send them to General Crook to forward to the right people in Chihuahua. I hope it does some good to hasten the return of your wife and children."

"Do any of the other delegates have anything to add to what Mister Chato has said?"

Kaytennae cut his eyes toward me and then shook his head, as did Charley.

"No? Then I yield the floor to Secretary Lamar."

Lamar pulled a chair to the table and sat beside Endicott. He said, "Chief Chato, you have said you and your People want to stay at Fort Apache. Are there things you need in the way of farming tools?"

I saw this as a good opportunity to get things we could all use. I said, "More wagons and machines to cut and gather hay would be very helpful to everyone. More lumber to make shelters for our livestock and hay will help much."

"Very good, sir. If you return to your farms in Arizona, I'll see that you get those things. Go home. Work hard, behave yourselves, and we all will be happy. On your way home, you can go by way of the Carlisle School, where I know several in your group have children they will be happy to see. Go and visit them. Take your time and have a good long visit. It may be a long while before they return with all the training that will help your People increase and prosper."

I knew Great Chief Lamar was right, and, glancing over my shoulder, I saw the happy faces of Loco, Noche, and two or three others who longed to see their children. The Great Chiefs were treating us well.

Endicott leaned over and spoke in a whispered voice to his secretary who had been making tracks on paper as we spoke. Secretary nodded, still making tracks on paper, as Endicott whispered his instructions. When Endicott finished, the secretary smiled, picked up his papers and writing board, and went into the next office.

Endicott said, "My secretary will prepare you a paper for my signature that you can carry with you. Mister Lamar and I thank you for coming and explaining your position to us. We will do the best we can for you. You can wait here while my secretary finishes writing it, and I will sign it."

Great Chiefs Lamar and Endicott shook hands as the White Eyes always do and walked out with Lamar, saying, "Good luck with your farming, gentlemen."

Great Chief Endicott returned with the paper I had requested, sat down at his desk, and made his name tracks on it. He handed it to me, and I gave it to *Capitán* Dorst to read aloud so we all knew and understood what it said.

*Chato, chief of the Chiricahua Apache, has been on a visit to Washington to see the president. He has made known his intention to refrain from war and to work for a living. President Cleveland has assured him that, so long as he shall keep faith with the government, his interest shall be looked after. In a more prolonged interview with Chato, I have endeavored to impress upon his mind that his future prosperity depended upon his following the path of peace and civilization.*

*{Signed}*
*William C. Endicott*
*Secretary of War*

We smiled with relief, believing we would be allowed to stay at Fort Apache.

# FIVE

## THE IRON ROAD TO DARKNESS

LOCO HADN'T SAID much on our trip. He just shepherded his wives and granddaughter and spoke to the Great Father and Great Chiefs, even then not saying much. I knew he was taking in all the sights, sounds, and smells of our trip, stunned as the rest us, except maybe Kaytennae, with how fast the iron wagons moved, the great strength of the demon iron wagons, the towns filled with *casas* and great buildings that reached into the sky, farms filled with crops and livestock, the awful stench and smoke in some places, and White Eyes without number.

I asked Kaytennae how the White Eyes did all this. He stared at me for a time, his crooked smile frozen in place, and then shrugged.

"I think maybe many White Eyes have light behind their eyes and learn how to do and make all kinds of things. Then they keep the memory of how they do something by making tracks on paper so all who can read the tracks understand what they need to do for making the same thing. Many times, those who read the tracks make better things, and they build machines to make things over and over to the same pattern. They don't use slaves to do this. It's why they have so many guns and bullets. Machines make them."

I had understood how White Eye tracks on paper had power. Didn't we have tracks on paper with power from the Great Chief Endicott? But I didn't realize that the track's power could be passed to all who could read the tracks. Truly, this was something of great power.

We rode an iron wagon to a village near the place called "school," took an easy horse-drawn wagon ride, and came to the place of school in the village of Carlisle. There, Loco and his women found his son, Dadespuna, the one the

White Eyes named Dexter. Loco had not seen Dadespuna for over two harvests and was astonished at the looks of the young man he called son. The boy could easily have passed for a dark White Eye. Like all the boys, his hair was cut and shaped to look just like that of a White Eye, and he wore a White Eye suit and a narrow strip of cloth called "tie" with a big knot around the collar of a white shirt. I remembered Dadespuna well from the days in the Sierra Madre before *Nant'an Lpah* came with the scouts. Now, I would never have recognized him if we had passed on the road.

Loco stared.

Dadespuna said, "Father? Don't you know me?"

"My son, I would know you anywhere, but I would not recognize you. You have grown tall, a fine man. You speak the White Eye tongue, and your hair is worn like that of a White Eye. Are you learning White Eye secrets and how to make tracks on paper others can read?"

"This I do, Father. There is much to know. I will never learn it all, but enough, I think, to help my family and the People."

Loco's smile made the scars around his bad eye stand out like mountain ridges on the *llano* as he said, *"Enjuh* (Good or all right)! *Enjuh!"*

"Father, come, sit with me and tell of your adventures to see the Great Father and his chiefs and your life at Fort Apache." Dexter moved chairs to a circle near the room's corner and motioned his family to them.

Kaytennae saw a young man from his family, Lorenzo Bonito, and they talked a long while. The boy was younger than Dexter and wore a uniform, but he looked just as much White Eye as Dexter and knew the White Eye tongue.

Noche and Charley also met with their young people, with expressions of wonder at how they had changed and looked so different in White Eye clothes. I had no one at school with whom I could visit, but I remembered many from the early days of their youth and hoped that my children would one day learn White Eye secrets at this place.

*CAPITÁN* DORST INTRODUCED us to *Capitán* Richard Henry Pratt, who had started the school and was its chief. He found the children and young men and women at the school for us to visit and then took time to show us the buildings where many children learned White Eye secrets and let us watch their training and all they went through in learning a White Eye skill. We spent nine suns at school. It seemed to me that *Capitán* Dorst wanted to keep us there, but we were too old to learn at school. Every day, *Capitán* Dorst spoke to his Great Chief in the Great Father's town on the talking wire.

The more I watched school, the less I liked it. The children could never speak the tongue or practice the family customs of their fathers. Everything they did, from going to their blankets at night to how they ate their food, was controlled by signals, bells ringing, or whistles. The boys stayed fit by running or wrestling or playing games with balls. It wasn't nearly as hard as what we usually did every day, but it was enough. The girls were taught to cook and sew and keep their places clean. I liked the teachers showing the children how to read and make tracks on paper. This is what they should do. If all these other things I didn't like helped them learn White Eye secrets, then let them be. They were much easier than what we required them to do in our camps.

During the eighth sun at school, *Capitán* Dorst told us we would climb on the iron wagon and return to Fort Apache the next sun. I was happy to hear that. There was much work to do on my farm now that Great Father and Great Chiefs Endicott and Lamar said we would stay where we were and not go to another reservation.

As the sun fell into the hills, we mounted the iron wagon that would take us to Fort Bowie, where we would take wagons to Fort Apache. There were no other people in our iron wagon. We had room to sleep on the seats as the iron wagon made the same thumpity-thump noise like a pot drum at a dance and swayed gently side to side as the iron-wagon demon roared and pulled us into the night. I watched the stars as we traveled and could see we were headed southwest, the only stops being to water the iron wagon demon or to get more wood or black rocks to feed it.

Early in the night, after riding for three days on the iron wagon, we stopped again for water and wood or black rocks. *Capitán* Dorst left the train to use the talking wire again as he often did when we stopped. When he remounted the iron wagon, it pulled slowly away and made a long swooping curve toward the north. It didn't bother me. The iron wagon often went the wrong direction for a while before swinging back in the right direction but deep in the night, I looked at the stars out my window. We still traveled north. My guts cramped and left a bad taste in my mouth like I had eaten bad meat. I had a bad feeling like my Power was warning me of something bad.

Not long after the gray light of dawn, we passed through a big village with many livestock corrals filled with cattle and passed places where cattle were being driven into iron wagons. I asked *Capitán* Dorst about this place later. He said the place was named Kansas City. It was a big gathering point for shipping cattle driven from as far away as Texas or Oklahoma. I could only shake my head in wonder. The White Eyes always did things in a big way.

Early that morning, I dozed back to sleep. I awoke as the iron wagon slowed to a stop. There was banging and clanging in the glowing sunlight above the edge of the rolling prairie swells, and then all was quiet. I looked out the window down the side of our iron wagon and saw the demon wagon that had been pulling us going away. I saw the men uneasily looking out their windows and then at each other. West up a bank and across the tracks, I could see a few buildings scattered along wagon roads. On the other side of our wagon was a wide river running north to south and then more prairie.

Kaytennae saw me looking out the windows and again, with his lower lip stuck out, looked at me and slowly shook his head. The sour feeling grew in the pit of my stomach. Three wagons pulled by horses came down a road and stopped at our iron wagon.

*Capitán* Dorst stood. "The Great Father asks that we wait here a few days while he considers the best thing for your reservation. Take your things and climb on the wagons outside and we'll go to a place where you can eat and sleep."

I said, "But Great Chief Endicott gave us a paper that said we could stay at Fort Apache. Why can't we go there now?"

*Capitán* Dorst nodded and motioned us through the door. "I know. I'll explain everything when I learn what the Great Father has decided to do. Come with me." His voice sounded more like a command than one asking us to follow. We followed him off the iron wagon and climbed into the wagons waiting for us by the iron road. It was a beautiful golden-light morning with night water still shining like jewels on the grass and prairie larks calling.

THE WAGONS CARRIED us to a big house with two rows of windows. It was large enough for us to have rooms with Loco and his women in one room, the three interpreters in a room, Kaytennae and me in a room, the scouts in a room, and *Capitán* Dorst in a room with a writing desk. Three or four soldiers stayed in rooms below us. There was a long, wide table surrounded by chairs for food in a big room and a Blue Coat who cooked. We were comfortable but uneasy. Was the Great Father changing his mind about us?

We ate a little later that day. I asked *Capitán* Dorst where we were. He answered, "Fort Leavenworth, Kansas." He said that he would show us around if we were here more than a sun or two and that we should not worry but let the Great Father decide what was best for us.

We stayed at the house for nearly a moon. After we had been there a few suns and still no word came from the Great Father, *Capitán* Dorst took us in wagons to the great town with many cattle corrals a little south of where we slept and ate. He showed us Fort Leavenworth and a big place with high stone walls and many watchtowers where the Blue Coats kept soldiers who disobeyed orders and White Eyes who disobeyed the Great Father's commands. *Capitán* Dorst called it "prison" in the White Eye tongue. The suns, like leaves lying on a slow-moving stream with no beginning and no end, drifted by.

I wondered if *Capitán* Dorst planned to keep us in his prison like White Eyes who disobeyed the Great Father's commands. We had done nothing wrong. We were still scouts paid by the Army. Then the day came when *Capitán* Dorst said word had come from *Nant'an* Miles on what the Great Father had decided and asked that we come to sit around the big table where food was served while he told us what had been decided. Sitting beside him was a Blue Coat who had a paper nearly filled with tracks and a jar of black water and a little spear for making tracks on the sheet under where the tracks already were.

*Capitán* Dorst said, "My friends, the Great Father has spoken. The White Eyes who settled in the places they call 'Arizona' and 'New Mexico,' where you raided and made war many times, where you killed many and took much livestock, are demanding the Great Father take you away. Their chiefs want you in ceremonies they call 'trials' before they make you dance in air, hanging by your necks from the ends of ropes, for all your murders, burnings, and livestock thefts—all those things you did before you agreed to return to San Carlos and Fort Apache reservations."

He waved his hand toward the paper filled with tracks.

"*Nant'an* Miles on this paper with tracks says this agreement will be done if you accept what it says, and the Great Father's chiefs agree. If this happens, you will become 'treaty Indians' living on a great reservation of six hundred square miles, where you will be reunited with those who surrendered to General Crook and were sent to Fort Marion in Florida and possibly with the bands of Geronimo and Mangas. Each family will receive six hundred dollars' worth of farm equipment and livestock. Fifteen of your chiefs and leaders will be paid twenty to fifty dollars a month besides being given good houses and other valuables. If you do not accept these terms, you will be treated as prisoners of war."

I held up the paper Great Chief Endicott had signed and given to us. I said, "This paper says we can return and stay at Fort Apache. Why is this paper no longer any good?"

*Capitán* Dorst nodded. "Yes, Secretary Endicott gave you that paper, but it says only that you visited him and the Great Father in Washington and that you will be treated well if you return to Fort Apache. Those are not treaty terms. You did not sign it that you agreed to what was said. Since you were given that paper, many White Eye settlers have begged the Great Father to make you dance on air for your past murders and theft. The Great Father wants to get you safely away from those who want to hang you. Now, who will be the first to touch the pen and have his name written on this paper?"

I looked around at the faces sitting at the table. Kaytennae, who sat next to me with arms crossed and eyes narrowed, was not smiling. He looked at me with disgust filling his face and his lips curling in anger. Loco sat frowning, and Noche and the other scouts sat staring at *Capitán* Dorst like men who had bet heavily on the wrong horse in a big race. I felt like a fool and was outraged, more at myself than any other, for thinking the silver medal and Endicott's paper showed we could go back to Fort Apache. Maybe this was a good agreement, maybe no good, but it was the only one we had. I didn't want to dance on air at the end of a short rope. I locked my jaws so my anger wouldn't let loose the bad words I wanted to say, and I made my face an unchanging mask. I was spokesman for this group. I stood and walked to the Blue Coat holding the little spear that made tracks on the paper and touched it.

*Capitán* Dorst smiled and nodded and said to the Blue Coat holding the little spear, "Chato."

Kaytennae, Loco, and the others all came forward to touch the black water spear. Then *Capitán* Dorst made his mark that he had seen us touch the pen. After all names had been signed, he took the paper, rolled it up, and put it in a leather carrying tube. "We're good with General Miles now. We leave in a few suns."

EIGHT DAYS LATER, *Capitán* Dorst told us that we would travel the next sun. Early in the dusk of the following sun, wagons picked us up and carried us to the iron wagon we had left a moon before. The demon iron wagon waiting to pull our iron wagon sat puffing and blowing water smoke as the light slowly disappeared into darkness falling over the rolling prairie and the fort buildings.

We climbed into the old fire smell on the iron wagon and took the same seats we had when we arrived. Doors were closed, windows opened to let in cool night air, and the demon iron wagon pulling us made a loud groan, as it always does before it moves, and then began to creep forward with much creaking and clanking. We picked up speed, moving south toward the great village with the many livestock corrals and then east across a wide river. None of us had any idea where we were going except to this big reservation *Nant'an* Miles had said covered six hundred square miles, where we would join our People from Fort Apache.

We stopped only to get wood or black rocks for the demon iron wagon and to give it water. At a few of these places, *Capitán* Dorst bought us food and let us walk around a little to help our legs stay strong. It felt good to have the windows open and the air blowing in to keep the heat down. I liked watching the towns and farms and woodlands fly by and to see how they changed as we moved south and crossed great rivers and passed through forests of many tall trees.

Near the end of the third day, we passed into unending forests filled with trees that I had never seen before. Water covered land where towering trees grew with gray hair-like grass growing off their limbs and their roots holding them in the water like giant fingers. Great lizards two or three times the height of a man in length with a mouth full of big knife-like teeth worse than those of a great bear rested on banks and little bumps of sand rising out of the water, some holding their mouths open and taking in the sun's heat.

Looking south out the window in the gathering gloom, I saw lights in a big nearby town. We rolled to a place in the town where the demon iron wagons stopped to let their riders off. I was surprised to see several Apache men, scouts in their Army coats, along with Blue Coats with rifles, waiting for our iron wagon. Among them was the powerful warrior and chief I knew well, Chihuahua. He was dressed in a *capitán's* uniform with the crotch cut out of the pants so he could easily wear his breechcloth inside them. My heart sank. We were at no six-hundred-square-mile reservation. We were where the Blue Coats kept their prisoners of war, Fort Marion.

# SIX

## FORT MARION

WE GATHERED OUR things and made our way out of the iron wagon to a place where *Capitán* Dorst stood motioning for us to gather around him. We all looked at Chihuahua and the scouts as we left the iron wagon, and he nodded, acknowledging each of us, even me. I knew that he and his brother, Ulzana, wanted to kill me for the death of Ulzana's son, but we all knew this was not the time or place for a fight. I knew Fort Marion would be a very dangerous place for me. Accidents and death by sickness happened every day.

*Capitán* Dorst said, "Fort Marion is a mile or two down the street. The Great Father has decided you must stay there until the details of your reservation are decided. I'm glad to have served with you, and I expect and hope that you'll soon be on your reservation." He motioned toward Chihuahua and the others with him. "These gentlemen will show you the way to Fort Marion and help you find your quarters there. Now, I return to serve *Nant'an Lpah. Adios.*"

We watched him climb back on the iron wagon and wave a white cloth in long up-and-down sweeps. The demon-wagon driver fed the demon more wood and pulled a series of levers, and the iron wagons began moving down the track, disappearing in the darkness, like a snake going in a hole, leaving us abandoned to the scouts and soldiers.

I felt the paper crackle in my pocket holding Great Chief Endicott's signed paper that said we could stay at Fort Apache. I knew then that I would never see Ishchos and our children again. I clenched my jaws shut, wanting to scream in rage and cry in sorrow. I had done everything I knew to do to get my family out of the land of *Nakai-yes* and to keep the People on their farms at Fort Apache. I failed on both counts because I trusted the White Eyes to speak straight.

Chihuahua said, "Seeing my People makes my eyes feel good but my heart sad that we are far from our deserts and mountains. This is a place of many storms and much rain. Thunder and Wind come often with lightning arrows. There are many little insects that will bite you. It is better to wear a shirt with long sleeves and be hot than be attacked by them. Remember, it is only for two harvests before we can return. Come. Follow me, and together we will do the best we can until we leave this edge of the great water."

I wondered, Where is this great water? I saw many long and wide places filled with black water where trees grew and what looked like the edge of a great moldy-smelling river filled with black mud as we passed through the trees to our stopping place. Maybe that's what Chihuahua meant by "the great water." There were "hmmphs" and nods of acknowledgment from all the men, including me, as Chihuahua led us out of the stopping place for iron wagons and down the road, past big houses and trading posts. The horizon to the west looked covered with trees. Toward the northeast, across what we thought was a great river, we saw the bright glow of a full moon rising from below a smooth horizon.

In less than half a hand against the horizon, we stood in front of high stone walls with arrowhead-shaped corners and lookout towers. There was a big ditch filled with bad-smelling water and green slime that ran around the bottom of the walls. We passed through a guarded gate and crossed the water around the walls on a wooden bridge attached to chains that I learned later could be used to pull the bridge up if the place were attacked so the attackers had to cross the ditch filled with water just to get to the gate in the high walls. We entered the hole through the walls through a double-door gate guarded also by Blue Coats. The walls were maybe fifteen or sixteen long paces thick, and on top of them, we saw the tops of many white tents. Past the last door inside was a grass-covered compound maybe a hundred paces on a side. The inside walls had windows on two levels. The White Eyes called the rooms holding the windows "casemates." Each room had an upper window and a door at ground level. From some of the casemates, smoke drifted out the door. I thought, *Probably from cooking fires. There were blankets over the windows on the second level. If those are separate rooms, then people might sleep there.* I quickly learned that the best sleeping quarters were in the tents on top of the walls. The rooms inside the walls leaked, and it rained and stormed here often. The People were allowed to cook in the leaking casemates when it rained but had to share fires.

When we entered the compound, Chihuahua stopped and faced us. To our right were steps on two of the inside walls that together led to the tops of the walls. He motioned toward them. "Those steps lead to sleeping tents. There are many tents set up now on top of the walls. Choose any one you want not being used, but it cannot be moved. You can cook in corner places on top of the walls or, when it rains, in a few places down here where you see smoke. When you want to cook, take a little wood in the bottom room, next to your left side here, for your fire. There's very little wood for us all. Don't burn more than you need for yourself. There are three wells no more than two-men-high deep and filled with fresh water you can pull up with a bucket, one of two left in your tent. Nearby the well over in a corner there, the one with buckets around it, is a room for men to bathe and a room for women and children to bathe, but for only one adult at a time. Do your personal business in a bucket at your tent and, each morning, dump it in the trough with flowing water in a room next to the bathing places.

"Every morning, when the sun is two hands above the horizon, I hand out rations to each family. Our ration should be as much as a soldier gets, but a big chief has decided that soon he will give us less and that we can fish in the big water to feed ourselves if we are still hungry. The big chief does not understand—*Ussen* does not want us to eat fish, and we will not disobey *Ussen*. Soon you see how we do things. We must all work together to survive. Your tents are up those stairs. Get some rest."

I climbed the steps with the others in our delegation, feeling angry and betrayed. A conical tent with waist high vertical walls next to the eastern corner wall, where a good breeze blew, was empty, and I took it. I could tell from all the empty tents on the wall top that many more people were to be brought here. I had no doubt who they must be. The White Eyes didn't hesitate to betray anyone who helped them. Soon we would see our People from Fort Apache.

THE SUN WAS just below the horizon, and the pesh-gray light outside my tent was enough to see to walk about. I made my morning prayer to *Ussen* and made water in the bucket left for us. Looking east over the edge of the fort wall, I thought I was seeing a wide river, but looking directly toward where the sun rose, I could see a wide break in the far bank and water as far as I could see. There is the great water.

In two suns, we learned all we needed to know about the fort and its rooms and how best to live there. Chihuahua and his scouts helped with everything from keeping the place swept clean to keeping water moving from the well to the baths, organizing who took baths when and maintaining proper sanitation. During the day, the gate guard on the other side of the little bridge let us come and go as we wanted if the women or children told him they were leaving or if the men had a scout accompany them, and we all promised to return before the sun went away. In town, our People sold things they made and, with the money, bought the rest of the food they needed and wanted.

There was nothing for the men to do unless they could get the materials to make toy bows and arrows for White Eyes to buy or for the women to do their bead work on cloth, some to even weave baskets from the reeds growing along the water ditch around the walls. Some were even selling their personal things to get enough to eat.

The first sun after we arrived, I looked at every space I could in the walls, visited with those I knew from the days before Geronimo led the breakout, and watched how Chihuahua and the men kept order and maintained cleanliness. The casemates reminded me of leaking caves. If you slept in one, you were sure to get wet but must sleep that way because that was your place. The commander of the place made sure the rations and firewood were kept dry, but that was about all he could do with what he had.

On the second sun after we arrived, Gon-altsis and I walked into town with some scouts. There were puffy white clouds starting to fill the sky, and it was cool with a steady breeze off the water. I wondered if this was the way storms grew here in Florida, but the warm sun was fast getting hot.

Gon-altsis said, "Chato, everyone calls you Chato, a name the Mexicans, fearing your raids, gave you so all knew who they were talking about after a raid. I'm not near the warrior you are—still, this is Spanish-tongue country. The Spanish built that old fort where the White Eyes keep us. I think I will start using the name the Mexicans gave me—'Patricio.' I like that name, Patricio. What do you think?"

I shrugged. "Your name, your choice. I like Patricio, too."

He grinned. "Then Patricio it is."

THE STORES WERE on a street shaded by big trees and big houses scattered among them. People stared at us as we walked by, but nothing was said. The storekeepers were friendly, and most spoke the Spanish tongue. I saw women buy orange and yellow fruits and sell their baskets and beadwork for money. They had dealt with the storekeepers long enough that they felt comfortable haggling with them over price. The storekeepers were happy to haggle with the women, and I soon realized that the haggling and keeping the Chiricahua in their store brought in many more customers who were anxious to see the Apache women and men asking for a better price without killing the storekeeper. The Chiricahua men also liked to see the women haggle. More customers then bought their toy bows and arrows and wood carvings. The People spent their hard-won money before they left the store and bought everything from food to cloth to pots and pans to *tobaho* and papers. I bought a coffeepot, coffee, and *tobaho* and papers with money I had brought with me. I had not smoked to the four directions since I left Fort Apache.

THAT EVENING, THE scouts, who had been part of the band who had gone east to visit the Great Father and his chiefs, cooked together in a wall corner near my tent. They had taken tents along the south wall where I camped. I had not eaten a midday meal and hadn't felt hunger until the sun was falling into the wet forests far beyond the great water. I ate nearly all Chihuahua had given me that morning, the same ration a soldier was given, and was satisfied. I made a pot of coffee and drank a cup with my fellow scouts as we watched the night settle over us like a warm blanket and brighten the lights of the town around us. We smoked to the four directions, and I looked around the men sitting near the fire, watching the last bit of cigarette turn to ash in our little fire.

I said, "The Great Father and his Great Chiefs have betrayed us. Why they wanted us to ride east to meet them, then north to see our children, then southwest back toward home, only to stop for a moon at a fort on the prairie before hauling us back to the southeast to stay in the same fort as the Apache who surrendered, I do not know. We worked hard with the Army to round up the People who left Fort Apache with Geronimo and in the land of the *Nakai-yes* risked our lives, suffered in the heat and cold, and left our families to look after our farms. This is the reward we get. I am very bitter about this." I spat a bit of *tobaho* off my lower lip as the others nodded agreement. "I wish there was a way to make the White Eyes pay for this betrayal, but I don't see how. Now we can't even go in the forests without them watching us to gather materials that could be used to strike them. The Great Father and his chiefs hold all the cards and deal the ones they want. They think we are helpless. I know this is not so. We must be patient, change with the events where we have no control, and work together to get out of here. Don't do anything that will get us in trouble with the White Eyes until we are ready to make things right. I don't care how powerful they are—we can find a way." I looked at every face and saw that they all understood what was needed. *"Ch'ik'eh doleel.* Go to your blankets and sleep well, my brothers."

I cleaned up around the fire, went to the wall, and leaned on it to watch the big river flowing by the fort, coming in from the great water. There was little wind, but the river made slapping water noises as it passed the fort, and far in the distance, out over the great water, were low clouds that flashed light, but I saw no lightning arrows, nor heard Thunder.

"Coyote waits, Chato."

Only years of warfare and discipline kept me from jerking in surprise as I turned to face Chihuahua. The knife I had hidden and brought east to defend myself was in the bedroll in my tent. His arms were folded over his chest. Still, I watched his hands for attack.

He smiled, showing white teeth in the darkness, and spoke in a low voice that only I would hear. "I don't come for trouble. Let us smoke to the four directions and talk." He pulled out his *tobaho* pouch and a paper as I nodded.

We sat down, side by side, and leaned against the wall in the dark. We could hear our children playing in the fort compound and White Eye children outside on the street below. The moon was rising but was still only a golden glow on the horizon. I realized how noisy the water and the insects were and wondered why Chihuahua of all people had chosen to speak with me.

We finished the cigarette, and he ground it under the heel of his boot. We were quiet for a time, and then I said, "Speak. I will listen."

Chihuahua looked across his right shoulder at me and said, "Either you pulled the trigger or you were responsible for who killed my nephew, Ulzana's son. Ulzana led a raid around Fort Apache. Found you and your wife working in a field and was enjoying the thought of how best to kill you when someone, somehow, warned you, and you and your wife got away. Now you are here, Ulzana is here, and I am here. By tribal law, my family has a right to avenge the killing of our son and nephew. But I stood in the shadows, listening, when you told your brother scouts that we must be patient and change with events to get out of here. These are my thoughts also, Chato. You may be a killer of boys, but you are a wise man and, for your People, a good chief."

"Yes, I killed that boy. He was shooting at us and could have killed one of us. He didn't have enough training to know how deadly and foolish it was to stand in the open and fire at his attackers. Whoever made him sentinel was a fool, and it got the boy killed. Both you and Ulzana are great, deadly warriors. I don't fear you. Come for me when you want. I'll kill you both. Are you saying now that you two will wait for your blood revenge until the White Eyes free us? If that is so, I say, *Ch'ik'eh doleel.* Let us work shoulder to shoulder until we are free, and then we can settle your case for revenge as men, not as snarling dogs tied to posts."

Chihuahua slapped at little insects gathering on his arm and waved his hand to drive more away. Far away, west, on the big river running by the fort, a great horn sounded, its noise crawling away in the heat of the night.

He said, "Yes, that is what I say. *Nant'an Lpah* said two years here and then we return. My brother and I will not seek your blood until we return. Do you agree?"

"There is nothing for me to agree to. I have no quarrel with you until you try to strike. Then there will be blood."

"As I said, you are wise, Chato. Now I ask that you help us." He motioned to the tents crowded together on top of the wall. "Soon I believe these tents will be filled with our People. I don't know why, but it's the only reason I know for putting them up. If our People are sent here, this place will be much too small. They'll be living on top of each other, and with nothing to do, the men will get in trouble and the women in their own peculiar kind of trouble. We must control them. We need strong chiefs to lead them and to work with the Blue Coat commander. We need you to help keep us out of trouble. When Geronimo and his People are brought here, the chance of trouble will grow, but we'll just have to keep a tight fist against it. Do you agree?"

I nodded. "Geronimo is the reason Ishchos and my children will live out their lives in Mexican slavery. Yes, I will help you, and I'll work even harder when he comes."

I saw Chihuahua's teeth flash again in the low light. *"Enjuh,* Chato. Now we are brothers. One sun, we will settle our quarrel as men. Coyote waits."

I smiled. "Yes, Coyote waits."

# SEVEN

## THE PEOPLE COME

THE DAY AFTER our talk, Chihuahua led Sam Bowman to translate and me to talk with the fort commander, *Teniente* Colonel Loomis Langdon. He had a big bush of hair under his nose and a patch of hair growing from his lower lip to his chin like goats the *Nakai-yi* herders had. His hair was gray, his eyes honest, and he spoke to us like we were men and not children. I liked him and so did Chihuahua. He was already aware of who I was and from where our delegation had traveled. I made a point of wearing my silver medal to ensure he understood I had spoken with the Great Father. I was not just any scout sergeant.

Chihuahua said, "Colonel Langdon, another chief, Chato, and a few others with him have come. Chato is ready to help make the People as comfortable as possible."

Langdon said, "Good. I need all the help I can get. I know who Chato is by reputation, and I think he will be of great help to us."

He told us what we had already guessed.

"All the Chiricahua who were living at Fort Apache will arrive in two or three days. There are nearly four hundred of them, including maybe seventy men. We must fit them all into Fort Marion. There must be strict sanitation rules or the fort will get disgusting and dirty in a hurry, and many diseases will come. There must be even food distribution among the families. The men must not fight for any reason. If they do, they will spend many days in my calaboose."

Chihuahua and I glanced at each other, both half smiling, and nodded that we understood.

"I told my commander that Fort Marion is much too small for all who are coming here. I recommended that they be sent to Carlisle, near Captain Pratt's school, where at least the children could go to school, get their education, and still live with their parents."

I had visited the school at Carlisle a moon earlier and knew he was right and nodded I agreed with him.

"Unfortunately, my big chief ignored my recommendation and ordered me to make ready to hold the Chiricahua here at Fort Marion."

We talked a long time about what to do and how to do it, and the more we talked, the more I liked Langdon. Near the end of our talk, a soldier brought a talking-wire message for Langdon. He read it and sighed before telling us to expect the People late the next evening at the place they called "station," where my delegation and I were met. He asked us to take every man we trusted to shepherd the People to the fort and get them bedded down after they arrived. He planned to have the rules for living in the fort explained to all the first thing the next morning, before the rations were handed out. He said a big load of rations was coming in that afternoon, and he wanted us and the other men to help with stacking and protecting them in the storage rooms next to the compound.

We were standing to leave when he said, "Another bit of news you may not have heard is that Geronimo and Naiche have surrendered with eighteen men and twenty-two women and children. They were put on a train headed in this direction about the same time as the People from Fort Apache, but their train was stopped in San Antonio. They wait there until the president can decide what to do with them."

Chihuahua and I looked at each other and frowned. Chihuahua said, "What means this 'until the president can decide what to do with them?'"

Langdon shook his head and made a face as if disgusted. "If Geronimo surrendered, then our military law says he and his People are officially prisoners of war and the responsibility of the Army. If they were captured, then the president can treat them like the outlaws they are and turn them over to territorial authorities for trial. These are territories where they murdered and pillaged. No doubt the territorial authorities would hang them. General Miles claims to have captured them, but others say no, the Geronimo-Naiche band surrendered. If they surrendered, then they and their People come here. And we'll have to find more room."

Shaking our heads in disbelief, Chihuahua and I left Langdon. I knew Geronimo was never captured. The only way he could have been taken alive was him surrendering. I knew Geronimo's Power would protect him even as bullets were flying. I didn't believe he would be hanged, which meant that they would be sent here.

As we left Langdon's workplace, I saw Ulzana, arms crossed, leaning against a wall on the far side of the compound, watching our doorway. At first, he made no move when he saw me. Chihuahua gave the slightest shake of his head, and Ulzana walked away.

With Chihuahua, Ulzana, Kaytennae, and Geronimo and two or three of his best warriors coming with him, who all wanted to kill me, in one place, I knew I would be in great danger. My knife could protect me against any one of them, but against five or six in an ambush they might set for me, I had no chance, and the odds were good they would get away with killing me. Let them come. I don't fear to die like a man. I'll take some of them with me to the Happy Land.

I WATCHED THE People climb down from the iron wagons at the station. If all the Chiricahua at Fort Apache had been sent to Florida, then my family should be with them. I hoped, because I wasn't there, that Nalthchedah, Banatsi, and the children might have escaped the roundup. My hopes flew away like crows around eagles as I looked down the line of twelve or thirteen iron wagons with people climbing down their steps and saw them, hefting their bundles and stepping down from an iron wagon far down the line. I hurried through the crowd, trying not to lose sight of my family. I was angry that they had been forced to come to this place, but I was very happy to see them.

"Nalthchedah! Nalthchedah!" I called as I weaved my way through the crowd. I saw her face light up with a smile as she turned in my direction and, pointing toward me, said something to the children and Banatsi. At last, I wiggled through the crowd and joined them. I wanted to hold them all, but that was bad manners. Affection was something to show in the privacy of our tent. They were all saying, with big smiles as they spread their arms, chanting, *"Chato! Chato! Chato!"* I touched each one as I greeted them, and then, like water pouring from a kettle, the crowd began to spread down the wide road toward the fort. Maud chattered in a low voice as we walked down the street. She told me about their trip and how tiring it had been since they changed iron wagons with seats that wouldn't let them lie down to sleep two suns ago in the great village of Saint Louis.

Many Blue Coats, on the outer edges of the crowd, watched the People streaming down the road to the fort, being shuffled along, saying nothing. Tree peepers and insects filled the night with their music, and the half-full moon cast its cool white light on the trees lining our way, making deep, black shadows that would make it easy to slip away even with Blue Coats watching, but no one even tried. We crossed the little bridge into the fort, and Blue Coats motioned for them as Sam Bowman, Concepción, and Mickey Free yelled for them to stand in the compound for their orders. I moved my family over next to the steps leading to the tops of the walls where the tents stood. When the last of the People passed through the doors leading to the compound, a White Eye soldier in a white coat stood on the little platform where the steps, halfway up the wall, made a left turn along the adjoining wall for another run of steps leading to the top. With Concepción interpreting, he said, "Go up the steps from where I stand to the top of the walls. There, you will see many tents that are empty. Choose a tent. That tent is where you will live here at Fort Marion. You can have any tent not already taken, but the tents must stay where they are put up. Buckets for your personal use are in the tents. They need to be emptied every morning in the trough with water flowing, near the rooms where there is bathing. There is another bucket, which holds water for drinking and cooking water. Rations are passed out in the morning. We will meet again the next sun to discuss all the fort's commander's rules. Behave and problems can be worked out. If you don't behave, there will be much time spent in the calaboose. Now find a tent and rest. Mister Chato and his family will lead you up the steps."

I held up my arm with my hand waving a white flag in the moonlight so they could see me lead my family up the steps to the tent I had taken. In the tent, the women and children gave me hugs and said how glad they were to see me, took a drink from the water bucket, and, after spreading their blankets, lay down for much-needed rest.

I left the tent to help Chihuahua and others straighten out disputes over tents and to answer questions about bathing and sanitation and how and where rations were distributed and where to get firewood. When I finally returned to my tent, all my family were sleeping, drawing in deep restful breaths. I lay down by Nalthchedah and felt her arm fall lightly across my chest. I heard her whisper, "My husband lies in our blankets. I thank *Ussen*. Tomorrow our new life begins. It will be hard, I know, but we are alive and together. It is *Ussen's* gift to us."

# EIGHT

# BEGISCLEYAIHN

OUR DAYS, LIKE drying mud, soon hardened into a common routine. Get up, get wood, start a small fire in a corner across from the tent, get rations, carry water from a well, cook, eat, clean up, and wait for the next meal. About the time our People came from Fort Apache, a big chief in the Army decided we needed fewer rations than a soldier and had them cut back—and then, in the middle of Ghost Face three or four moons later, cut them again. The People from Fort Apache soon learned from Chihuahua's People to make things they could trade in the town for food and other things they needed or wanted.

The White Eyes in town always watched us, curious in a friendly way, as we walked down the little walkways in front of their trading posts and looked at and bought things there. They didn't seem angry the way the White Eyes were in the land from where we came. The women worked hard to make beaded cloth and other trinkets the White Eyes would buy, and some men, me among them, made toy bows and arrows that also made us money. Although our rations were short, enough was bought and shared that none went hungry.

The bathing places were in constant use, the men drawing water to help a line of people waiting to take their turn to bathe. One of three wells was used only for bathing water, the other two for drinking and cooking.

The younger children were allowed to run and play on the grounds outside the fort walls, while the older children helped their mothers, but there was little for them to do. Langdon told a council of the chiefs and leaders that he was recommending that the children be sent to Carlisle School unless the older girls were already married. The big chiefs in the place where the Great Father lived had to agree to this, but he didn't know when that might happen. He told us that he had placed *Teniente* Mills in charge of deciding who would go, and he would begin selecting them in three suns. There wasn't a happy face leaving the council. I was sad at the thought of Maud and Horace going away so quickly after I had just started living with them again. I knew that Nalthchedah would be very unhappy at losing Horace and even Maud, although she was not her child.

That night at evening meal, I told my family what we had been told. Horace and Maud shook their heads, no, they didn't want to go. Nalthchedah looked at me in fury and said through clenched teeth, "Chato, you must stop this."

I said, "Woman, I have no power to do that. Horace will probably have to go. Maybe we can find someone for Maud and claim she's married. I will try."

The fury in Nalthchedah's voice rose again. "Foolish man! She can't marry. She hasn't had her *Haheh* (womanhood ceremony) yet."

I felt my own fury, but at Nalthchedah. I wished I had a stick. I would make her understand I would do all I could but that I was in control of our family and that she must mind her tongue around me. She saw the anger in my eyes and realized she had crossed a line, looked away, and said nothing more.

I STOOD STARING out across the water the next day. It was cloudy, and I could see rain pouring out of clouds advancing toward us like it walked on big, stubby giant's legs. The sound of steps approaching from behind made me close my fingers around my sheathed knife just under my vest, on the left side. I kept perfectly still and tensed, ready to fall and roll to my left while slashing up with my knife. But the sound of steps stopped three or four paces away and were replaced by a woman's soft voice.

"Chato, I would smoke and talk alone with you about a serious matter."

"Who speaks?'

"Bashdelehi, woman of Mohtsos. He left me when he went to Mexico with Geronimo and took another woman."

I grimaced with relief. "Bashdelehi. I know you. You and Nahzitzohn have raised your family well by yourselves. Let us go outside the gate and sit on the wall facing the great water."

Bashdelehi said, "Hmmph. That is a good place to talk. We go."

I spoke enough of the White Eye tongue to tell the Blue Coat guarding access to the bridge that Bashdelehi and I wanted to sit and talk a while on the great wall keeping out the big water. He nodded and said, "Stay where I can see you."

I found a place where we could be seen sitting between two trees on the edge of the great wall, our feet dangling over the edge by the big water.

After making a cigarette, I lighted it, smoked to the four directions, and then passed it to Bashdelehi. I had bought the *tobaho* two suns before the Fort Apache People came. It had a good strong smell, and I enjoyed smoking it with Bashdelehi. According to custom, we first talked a little while about this place and how little there was for us to do and how hard the trip from Fort Apache had been. I found myself nodding often to what she said because I knew what she said was all true.

There was a long silence between us after she spoke of the trip hardships. We listened to the water washing up on the thin line of sand below our feet and saw the stumps of rain pouring out of the clouds walking slowly toward us. The children had seen the rain coming and ran inside. The great white seabirds always wheeling above the fort and the water nearby were clustered together on the grass, expecting the storm.

Bashdelehi, nervous, ran her tongue over her lips and said, "Now let us speak of important things."

I nodded and said, "Speak. I listen."

She looked down at the water below our feet as though she was ashamed of what she was about to say. "Soon the White Eyes will take our children, and we will never see them again. I lost much eye water in our blankets last night when Loco told us this after the council last sun. I have a fine daughter, Begiscleyaihn, who will be made to go to the place the White Eyes call 'Carlisle' and the school there. She is a good girl, sweet tempered, hardworking, knows cooking as well as me, and had her *Haheh* two summers ago in the Season of Little Leaves before Mohtsos followed Geronimo into Mexico, leaving me, Nahzitzohn, and the children. I heard he had another woman down there. Since then, I have refused six offers for Begiscleyaihn. She wanted none of those boys or young men, nor would I have wanted her to accept one. How can she know she marries a man who can provide for her if he has not been accepted as warrior? How can a young man prove he is ready as a warrior if he cannot raid as a novitiate to prove his worth with men who are truly warriors?"

I nodded and, looking out to the big water, saw the flashes of light in the clouds from unseen lightning arrows and wondered where Bashdelehi was going with this conversation. Every word she said was true. I had thought often of how our young men could be recognized as adults, as warriors, without becoming novitiates.

"Chato, we live in hard, confusing, uncertain times. Never have the White Eyes had such power over us. We seem so helpless, and they lie to us much and often. We can't even keep our children near us and teach them if the White Eyes send them away to this school place. I want the best for my daughter. I know you lost a good wife in Ishchos and two of your children into Mexican slavery. Now you have only Nalthchedah, her child, Horace, the child of Ishchos, Maud, and your sister. Nalthchedah has not carried any more children in her belly since we left for Mexico with Geronimo five harvests ago. When will you have children with her again? Maybe *Ussen* gives her no more. You are a man respected by all, hated by a few. You need more sons for your memory. You need another wife. Take Begiscleyaihn as your second wife. She will not always be number-two wife, this I promise you. And I say the only thing for a bride gift I want is for her to be near me and not a long ride away on an iron wagon to the place called school in the land of Carlisle."

I stared at her profile next to me and wondered if my ears had heard such a thing. Begiscleyaihn was only a year or two older than my daughter Maud. It was not common but not unusual for older Apache men to marry young women. Many thoughts ricocheted about in my mind.

Nalthchedah had not been happy with me since my children no longer grew in her belly, and I was beginning to believe she didn't always speak straight with me. Maybe I did need another wife, one who could give me more children. But one who was nearly twenty harvests younger than me and her mother asking me to take her?

I rubbed my forehead, trying to think, as waves lapped against the seawall where we sat.

Bashdelehi said, "I ask you as a man, to help us, Chato. Don't let this child be taken from me."

I sighed. "I will speak with Begiscleyaihn first, at this place at this time next sun. Bring her with you. I will give you my answer in four days."

The relief I saw in Bashdelehi's eyes said much as she answered, "You are a good man, Chato." She stood and walked back toward the little bridge. I sat a long time, watching the rain approach from over the big water and then walked away.

# NINE

## BEGISCLEYAIHN SPEAKS

NALTHCHEDAH AND I sat with our backs to the chest-high wall that ran around the top of the fort walls. Smoke from the fading coals of her cooking fire kept away the no-see-ems, those tiny insects that came in great swarms to bite us in any uncovered places, leaving each bite covered with a red dot of blood. Banatsi visited with friends ten or twelve tents over, and the children were playing with others in the central compound in the center of the fort. I pulled my *tobaho* and papers from my vest pocket, made a cigarette, and said, "Woman, we talk?"

She knew, if I was making a cigarette, it must be serious business and, nodding, said, "We talk." I lighted the cigarette from a wood splinter in the fire coals, puffed to the four directions, and gave it to her. She smoked easily and returned it to me. I took a couple more puffs and tossed the remains in the fire. She watched my every move—I knew she was trying to guess what I would say—and, after the cigarette disappeared in smoke, said, "Speak. I will listen."

I puffed my cheeks and blew, hoping to blow away the whirlwind of anger I knew my words might provoke.

"I talked today with Mohtsos's first wife, Bashdelehi. You know he left her and his second wife, Nahzitzohn, and three children when he left for Mexico with Geronimo and took another woman. At Fort Apache, Bashdelehi and Nahzitzohn and their children worked hard and made it through Ghost Face warm and without hunger." I nose pointed in the general direction of the family tent. "They are settled over there, their tent on the far side of the fort walls from us."

Nalthchedah looked and nodded, a frown of curiosity growing on her face. "Yes, I know their tent. I know the family. They all work hard. Why did you speak with Bashdelehi?"

"Loco and his leaders told their People what they learned in council with Colonel Langdon two suns ago. The Blue Coat chief told *Teniente* Mills to decide which children should go to the place named school at the village called Carlisle. Only married girls and those who are sick will not go to school. This probably means Horace and Maud will have to go to school."

Nalthchedah's frown turned into a scowl. "Yes, I've already decided they probably would have to go. You said they needed to learn White Eye secrets and how to read and make tracks on paper, even speak the White Eye tongue. What has this to do with Mohtsos's family?"

"Bashdelehi has a daughter, Begiscleyaihn, who is fifteen harvests. Her *Haheh* was two harvests ago. She is certain that the child will be picked to go to the school at Carlisle and is afraid she will never see her again. Many who *Nant'an Lpah* sent there when we first returned to San Carolos have already gone to the Happy Place. I saw their markers in the school burying place when the Great Father sent us there."

"So what does this child have to do with you?"

"Bashdelehi begged me to marry her daughter to ensure she'll be kept here and not be sent away to school."

Nalthchedah, her eyes furious, glowing like coals of fire, raised her voice. "That's the most nonsense I've heard in many moons. Our men already have more women and children than they can take care of now. You told her to forget you marrying her daughter... didn't you?"

"I told her I would think about it."

"Chato, don't be a fool. That child is only two years older than Maud. Even if she had already had her *Haheh*, you wouldn't let her marry."

I felt anger squeezing my guts, and I spoke in a low, lethal voice she had heard before. "I said I would think about it, and I meant what I said. You watch how you speak around me, or I'll beat you for disrespecting me."

Her voice lowered and sounded civil again. "I don't mean to disrespect you. You are a great chief. But I say this, if you marry that girl, she will not live in our tent. You will have to provide for our family and hers. Can you do that?"

I stared at her for a few breaths and then said, "I can do whatever I think is right. If you want to leave me because I take another wife, then leave. I have said all I will say."

I SAT WAITING at the same place on the seawall where I had spoken with Bashdelehi the sun before. The sky was cloudless, a polished blue, holding a fiery sun. The mirror-like big water took the sky's color and mixed it with its own blue shade to form the color of blue stones (turquoise) found far away in the land of our fathers. Great white-and-gray birds, some with black heads, sailed in long looping spirals, making squeaky-sounding croaks as they looked for anything to eat, or landed to float nearby in the still water, where they bobbed and dived for fish in the shallows. Those birds ate anything. They were disgusting, like vultures of the big water.

I heard the soft swish of skirts behind me and turned to see Bashdelehi followed by a young woman with skin darker than mine, her raven's-wing-black hair in a long single braid lying over the shoulder of a calico-print shirt that looked new. She wasn't thin, but she wasn't fat either, and she looked strong, her wrists big and her fingers long. She was attractive and desirable but not what many would consider beautiful, the kind of woman any man could want.

Bashdelehi smiled and said with deference, "Chief Chato, this is my daughter we spoke of. As you asked, she comes to talk with you. As her duenna, I sit on the wall at a respectful distance so you may speak in private."

I said, *"Doo dat'éé da* (it's okay). Begiscleyaihn, come sit to my left so your mother always sees you, and we will speak of many things."

Bashdelehi squeezed her daughter's shoulder and walked far enough down the seawall to where the sound of the waves lapping against it would drown out anything Begiscleyaihn and I might say, expecting privacy. With natural modesty, Begiscleyaihn sat down about an arm's length from me, but I motioned her closer, and we sat shoulder to shoulder. I knew she must feel like a horse someone considered buying. I didn't want her to feel that way. She must feel free to speak her mind. First, I tried to learn what she wanted to know and do. Maybe her mother was forcing her to stay.

"You know why we talk?"

She nodded her head but continued to look down in deference to me.

"Lift your head to see me, that we may both know the other speaks straight. I know your mother does not want you to go to the place called school in the faraway village of Carlisle. Do you want to stay here or go to school? Speak. I will listen."

She turned and looked at me, no fear in her eyes. "I want to stay near my mother. I care nothing for learning White Eye secrets. I'm skilled at making baskets the White Eyes and the People pay us much for. I want to help my family stay alive during the hard times the White Eyes now put us through and because my father went off to Mexico with Geronimo. That was not right. The People you spoke to who scouted for the Blue Coats after you returned say you said so yourself."

I nodded. All she said was true.

"My mother has refused six bridal-gift offers for me and rejected them all because I didn't want any one of the men offering them, and she didn't like them either. Four offers came from men too young, unproven in battle or in making a living in the White Eye world. Two offers came from old ones who needed help even to stand. I doubted they were still able to give me children. Apache women must give the People children. I won't waste my body giving an old man his pleasures when he can't make a child grow in me. I would rather have no children and lose my life force for having children than be a slave for an old man."

I smiled and nodded. "You're a wise woman. I'm happy to hear your words. Tell me more of your thoughts."

"This is an awful place to camp. There are too many of us in this little place. I can hear those in the next tent when they try to make a baby or argue. I admit I learn much about marriage this way. It's not like what I thought it would be when I was a child."

"And hearing this, do you still want a husband?"

"Yes, I want a husband who I know will be gentle with me and patient, not like the man in the next tent. I tell Mother this, and she only smiles."

"Tell me more about what you dislike about this camp."

"We must wait a long time to bathe. I don't like being dirty. I want to bathe every day. Using a bucket for personal business is dirty and miserable. Is this the way the White Eyes live? If it is, they are dirty people. I would never take a White Eye husband. There is little wood to use for cooking. There is little food. The air feels thick and heavy, like we are always underwater, and the sun feels like hot iron against my skin. No-see-ems are everywhere and bite us every day. But I will not leave here unless my family goes with me.

"I have spoken with Chihuahua's People who came here first. Many get sick in this place and die from the worms the White Eyes call 'tuberculosis.' Or they have the same shaking sickness that came when we camped by the Gila. We must move away from here or all die. It is no different than Blue Coats killing us in battle.

"Soon a Blue Coat will say I must go to school. I don't want to go, even if it means I must marry. I won't go. My mother says you are the best of grown men who might take another wife, and I should consider being one of your wives even if I am number two. I know you are a great chief able to take care of two or three wives. I like that. But I want to know the man *Ussen* knows, not the one described by his enemies. I want to know the man who would be father of my children. Speak. I will listen."

# TEN

## HELEN

I LIKED THIS girl. She had sense and understanding far beyond her years. She knew how to work hard, and she had a clear eye for the conditions in which we lived. I stared out over the big water and asked in my thoughts, *Ussen* guide me in all this.

I said, "Before *Nant'an Lpah* came to the Blue Mountains and led us back to San Carlos, many times I rode with Geronimo. On raids and at war, I was his *segundo*. I had little use for those who were slow to fight and kill the *Nakai-yes* and White Eyes who came to take over our country, and I made my feelings known in council. This made me enemies. After I became a Blue Coat scout at Fort Apache, some called me a spy and a traitor, but I am none of these. In the days before I was a scout, I killed many *Nakai-yes* and White Eyes. I do not regret this. It is what warriors do.

"In the Ghost Face before *Nant'an Lpah* came, the Rarámuri looking for Apache scalps to make money paid by the *Nakai-yes*, came, led as *Nakai-yi* soldiers, and attacked Juh's camp where my first wife, Ishchos, and I camped with our three children—Bediscloye, a girl of seven harvests, Naboka, a boy of four harvests, and Maud, a girl of ten harvests. The Rarámuri took Ishchos, Bediscloye, and Naboka for *Nakai-yi* slaves. Maud got away from them during the attack and is still with me. She is two harvests younger than you. Geronimo also lost his wife Chee-hash-kish, taken during a *Nakai-yi* attack on us at Casas Grandes, and another wife and child were taken by the Rarámuri. Naiche also lost family members in that Rarámuri attack.

"Geronimo, leading warriors who had lost family, and I went to eastern Chihuahua looking for *Nakai-yi* hostages we could take and trade back for our family members in slavery. But, before we could take any important *Nakai-yes* and make trades, *Nant'an Lpah* came and led us back to San Carlos. I know you remember that long walk back."

Never taking her eyes from me, she nodded yes.

"When *Nant'an Lpah* came, I knew he must have power far beyond anything we had. He led Apache scouts, our own People, against us, found our camps in the Blue Mountains, and crossed the border with Apache without *Nakai-yi* soldiers opposing him. I decided I must follow his Power. Even more important, he promised us to free our People who were slaves in the land of *Nakai-yes*, and to me in private, he said that he would do all he could to get my first wife and children out of *Nakai-yi* slavery, through his big chiefs bargaining with their big chiefs. I vowed that if he did this, I would help him all I could in doing whatever he needed. This I did. Geronimo's People hate me for helping the Blue Coats. Loco's People know I do the right thing for all the People. I would do anything I could to free Ishchos, our children, and others even if it meant helping the *nant'an* find those who left Fort Apache. I made the mark on their paper that said I would do this.

"Geronimo and men like your father, who left Fort Apache nearly two harvests ago and then broke their word of surrender to *Nant'an Lpah* in the Season of Little Leaves, made sure I will never get Ishchos and the children back again. No one any longer speaks for us to the White Eye big chiefs about them convincing the *Nakai-yi* big chiefs to give us our People back. There is no one now like *Nant'an Lpah* to help us. I told Geronimo before he left Fort Apache that if he did this, I would find him in the Blue Mountains for the Blue Coats and drag him back in chains to the guardhouse at San Carlos, where he has vowed never to return."

I beat my fist against my chest. "There is a great sadness here for the loss of that part of my family. Time and events forbid me from seeing them ever again, but Ishchos will always be my first wife."

I went on to tell her of what happened when I spoke with the Great Father and how disappointing that had become. His big chiefs had lied to us. I made the mistake of trusting the White Eyes, but not all White Eyes were liars. Then I told her of my current marriage as a warm breeze blew in from the big water and waves slapped against the wall where we sat.

"The wife I have now is Nalthchedah. She is my second wife. We have a son of eight harvests, Horace, but *Ussen* gives us no more children. She lived with me and Ishchos but wouldn't go with me to Mexico when I left with Geronimo after the prophet was killed. I divorced her before I left San Carlos so she could find someone else when the rest of us ran into Mexico. When I came back without Ishchos, Nalthchedah had not remarried. It was a good thing for us to join our lives again. She works hard and is a good mother. She wants more children, and we have tried to start a baby many times for five harvests, but *Ussen* lets no child grow in her belly."

I paused my story, interlacing my fingers, and pulled up a knee to lean against as I decided how much I should tell this child. A flash of understanding filled my mind. Everything, I should tell this child everything. I was considering her to be my wife, and she must understand what she was committing too at such a young age. The breeze died, and the sound of waves slapping the wall where we sat grew weaker.

"I told Nalthchedah that I had talked with your mother and would consider taking you as a wife to keep you here and out of school. This made her angry. She says another wife will not live in her tent, that I must keep another wife in a separate lodge. I think it is a good thing to keep peace in my family. I don't think we will remain married many more moons. She says I act a fool considering you for a wife. I've told her if she does not respect me, I'll beat her. I don't believe she can hold her tongue, but in truth, I won't beat her. We'll just go our separate ways."

I paused and rubbed my chin, thinking, Yes, that is the way it will be with Nalthchedah and me, and looking out over the big water at the big white birds circling high, looking for food, and flying low over the water to feed on fish near the surface.

"I have spoken. Are there other things you want to know?"

She frowned and said, "Your wives give you no children for five harvests. Do you want more children?"

"Yes. More children are a good thing. They are *Ussen's* blessings. The Chiricahua always need more children. You are attractive. Men already show they want you by asking for you and offering bridal gifts. Your strong spirit and fine shape would stir any man. But I think you are still too young to have children, not that you couldn't, but that your body needs to grow and mature more so working in the camp and carrying a growing baby in your belly is not too much on you. I will not join you often in your blankets until you are ready for children. Maybe wait three more harvests—then you should have as many babies as *Ussen* would give us."

She smiled. "Babies are much hard work. When there are enough, I will tell my husband."

"I have told your mother that if you want me, I will decide within three days from now if I ask for you. If you do not want to go to school and want me as a husband, you need to decide before *Teniente* Mills starts selecting children to go. Think on it four days yourself. If we want each other, then I will give your mother a bridal gift even though she came to me. *Ussen* says it is the right thing to do."

She smiled. "Chato is wise. Yes, I will decide in four days." She stood and waved to her mother that she was ready to leave. They walked away, leaving me with my thoughts.

Few words passed between Nalthchedah and me for the next three days. She knew I had many thoughts about Begiscleyaihn while I worked with Chihuahua. A sun passed after I spoke with Begiscleyaihn. Still, *Ussen* had not spoken. I took a light blanket and lay down by the smoldering coals of Nalthchedah's cooking fire and stayed out of the tent with Nalthchedah, Banatsi, and the children. The camp was growing quiet. A man shouted at his wife. A baby cried. Above the walls of the fort, the smoke and light from the coals of many little fires hung like morning mists on a river, and the stars cast their light from the darkness above us to peek into the smoke cloud over us. Peepers and insects in the trees across the road that led into the town made much noise. My eyes closed.

Someone called to me, "Chato. Chato. Come. Help us." I knew the voice. It was Ishchos. She was framed in a small window covered with bars on the ground floor of a great *hacienda*. I darted between tall, spreading creosote bushes, thorny mesquites, and tall stalks from mescal as I ran toward the window in the darkest night I had ever known. The night's only light was a low flickering glow from a candle near the little window. I reached the window and whispered, "Ishchos, I am here." The window light grew brighter as she moved the candle closer to the window. I could barely see her face. My heart pounded with joy. At last, I had found her. I grabbed the window bars and jerked with all my might on them, but they wouldn't move.

She pushed her hand out through the window bars. "Touch me, husband. I have not seen or felt your hands in many moons." Watching in all directions, I stretched my arm out to reach her hand and felt its warmth and power, and I heard her sigh. "It is true. You still live. The *Nakai-yes* tell the children and me that the Blue Coats killed you. I wouldn't believe it. Now you are here."

"Yes, I'm here. There are waters in my eyes. Waters of rage and frustration. I've tried everything I know. Geronimo and I were looking for *Nakai-yi* captives to trade for you, but *Nant'an Lpah* came and took us back to San Carlos. *Nant'an Lpah* promised to help me get you back. I asked the Great Father of the White Eyes to get you out of this place. Nothing I've tried has freed you and the children."

"It is *Ussen's* will that we stay here, husband, and live without you. We are not mistreated, but we are not free. You must live your life the best you can where you are. You have much yet to do. Take another woman. Have more children. *Ussen* has told Nalthchedah she will have no more babies. She hides this knowledge from you. I'll be happy when *Ussen* gives you more children. Make the Chiricahua great once more. Give them all the children you can."

"Woman, I can't leave you and the children."

"You can leave, and you must. Go, before the *Nakai-yes* try to kill you. Always remember that I, too, am your wife, but I am here. I lift my hands to *Ussen* for you. Go, husband. Make a new family, but never forget the rest of your family."

Shouts came from out in the desert. *Nakai-yi* soldiers, some with great torches held high and others with long knives on the ends of their rifles, ran toward me. I had to run to escape them. Her last words to me were, "Run and live, husband." The light from the torches was so bright I had to squint to see past them and where to run in the darkness.

My eyes snapped open. Light from the rising sun filled my face. My heart racing, I sat up and looked around. Tents and beginning fires near them were everywhere. The People were beginning to stir. I puffed my cheeks and sighed with relief. My dream had been a vision. *Ussen* had spoken.

AS I PROMISED, I met with and told Bashdelehi four suns after our talk on the seawall that *Ussen* had spoken to me and that I would take her daughter, if she wanted me, as my third wife. Ishchos would ever be my first wife.

The next sun, I met Begiscleyaihn at the same place while Bashdelehi again stood farther down the seawall to give us some privacy. She took my hands, looked up at me, and, smiling, said, "I will be proud to be third wife for Chato. My mother wants us married as soon as possible so the Blue Coats won't send me away to school at the place called Carlisle. After we marry, I want you in my blankets. Come as often as you need and think is wise. I will never refuse you unless it is my moon time. If Nalthchedah wants no other wife with her and there is no room for a new tent here, then my mothers say you can sleep in their tent, and they and the children will sleep near the fire or they can stretch a separation canvas between us in the tent. I am strong enough and know enough to do a wife's work even if we are not in the blankets. I want to do that. Come to me when you are ready for me. I wait with much feeling for you. You are a great chief. I am proud to be one of your women."

I made the all-is-well sign and smiled my happiness that she had accepted me. "I'm proud and happy you choose to be my wife. I will go to those who make tracks on paper and record it is so. I'll visit your tent before this sun is gone to tell you and your mother all is done that can be done and to bring her a bridal gift."

WHEN I TOLD the clerk who makes tracks on paper about my marrying Be-giscleyaihn, he looked through his papers and smiled when he found her name. "You just got under the wire on that one, Chato. Lieutenant Mills has her on his list to see and probably choose for school tomorrow. He had already given her the name Helen because he couldn't pronounce her Apache name."

I crossed my arms and nodded. "Hmmph. There will be others marrying to stay away from school. This I know. Tell *Teniente* Mills that Begis—Helen is married to Chato, and I want her here with me."

# ELEVEN

## LAST DAYS AT FORT MARION

I GAVE BASHDELEHI a bridal gift of a small sack of gold coins from the few I had left. I thought it would be enough to buy her family rations and a few nice things from trading posts in the town. It wasn't much for a young woman like Helen, but Bashdelehi happily accepted it and asked that I come for a meal Helen would make for me the night of the next sun. Our joining ceremony was little more than me appearing for the meal, and I promised Helen that one day, when times were better, she would have a proper ceremony to celebrate our joining.

Helen's meal was good, made from things she had traded for one of her baskets. I wore the silver medal the Great Father had given me to make her proud of being the woman of a man who had spoken to the Great Father. After eating, Helen and I were the only ones in the tent. Her mother and stepmother, Nahzitzohn; her full brother of twelve harvests, Bailtso; a full brother of two harvests, Mohtsos; and her half-brother, Ahtay, stayed outside near their little fire. Helen's green beans, corn, white potatoes, and pieces of meat, fried in a pan with a brown sauce she said the White Eyes called "gravy," were all very good, and she had pieces of sweet fruit, peaches and apples, which I had not tasted since raids against Navajos and *haciendas* along the Río Grande.

Helen and I hardly knew each other except for what we'd shared of our lives while talking on the seawall. We drank coffee and shared stories about our families and lives and how we felt about those we called our friends. It was the best we could do to make up for months of courting that would have let us come to know and understand the other's best and worst selves.

We finished our coffee, and she disappeared from the tent, where her mothers outside made giggling comments to her too low for me understand as I leaned back on my elbows on her blanket in the deepening gloom of the tent. Soon she returned and tied the tent flaps closed. I could barely see her outline in the darkness as she unbuttoned her shirt and undid the belt around her skirt, slid out of her clothes, and then folded them neatly in a pile on her side of the blanket. I smelled the sweet yucca-blossom fragrance of her body and saw the shadowed curve of her figure against the outside light on the tent wall.

She lay down facing me with one hand and forearm supporting her head while she used her other hand to stroke my shirtsleeve. She said, "I am young and have never known a man. I desire you, husband. Make me your woman."

So young, yet she stirred passion in me that I had not known since I had first taken Ishchos as my wife. I sat up and began pulling off my moccasins and pants and then my vest, tie, and shirt. I lay back down beside her and took her in my arms. I kissed her and felt her breath quicken. She hesitated and wasn't sure what to do next. I stroked her bare back and spoke loving words to her as I pulled her to me. I was very gentle with her in our first communion, letting her decide how far to carry it as we whispered our devotion to each other.

Our first taste of our passion passed like fast water rushing over rocks in a mountain stream and then coming to rest in a deep, quiet pool. We lay back to sleep, her head in the crook of my arm as she said, "Husband, you've made me glad I'm a woman. I know there is much for me to learn for our pleasures and for us to make a baby. I want to make one now, my body wants you again, but I know I'm not yet ready. I'm eager for the moon when we will try many times to make a baby."

I smiled and hugged her. "That time comes soon enough, woman. I'll stay here with you as often as I can. Now, let *Ussen* fill you with good dreams."

She whispered, "Yes, he already does."

THE DAYS PASSED slowly at Fort Marion. The Great Father decided that Geronimo and Naiche's men had surrendered. They weren't captured, which made them prisoners of war. He directed that they be separated from their women and children. They were kept far away from the rest of us in Pensacola, at Fort Pickens on an island in Pensacola Bay. Pensacola was a long day's train ride from Fort Marion where we had to make room for twenty-two more women and children. Some shared tents with others, and a very few squeezed into two or three new tents all crowded together, but it was still better than sleeping in the leaking rooms in the walls of the fort. I didn't think we had room for anyone else, but a few more came after Mangas surrendered, and we crowded them in, too.

The big White Eye chiefs working for the Great Father must have decided they could make room for the new People by shipping our children off to school at the place called Carlisle. We didn't want this, and it was made worse because the big White Eye chiefs never gave warning what they planned to do or how. It was like trying to deal with some evil spirit that kept striking you or making your life miserable and you couldn't fight back.

*Teniente* Mills first sent forty-four children to school in Carlisle. I dreaded him sending Maud to school, never being able to see her again, but I told him she was the last one left to me in my family with Ishchos, whom General Crook was trying to return to us. Mills decided Maud needed to stay with me until her mother returned, and I was never more grateful to a White Eye than to him for this favor. He told me one evening as we sat smoking that choosing the children who had to go to Carlisle was the hardest thing he had ever done. Their parents were in tears as the iron wagon carrying the children left the place called the station, headed for Carlisle, and he saw the children hiding their faces in their hands or in their clothes as though their tears were shameful. He made some boys go to school even though they had married. I thought that was a good thing. They needed to learn White Eye secrets to support a family. They would never be warriors who could take what they wanted when they wanted it.

In the first group that went to the school at Carlisle, *Teniente* Mills planned to send twenty boys and fifteen girls, who left about a moon after I took Helen. Four more of the children the White Eye *di-yen* (medicine woman or man) had said were not well enough to go with the first group as well as those who had missed the first group and others—including Geronimo's nephew, Daklugie, youngest son of Juh, who had come in with Mangas's group, and Chihuahua's daughter, whom the White Eyes had named Ramona—were sent a moon later.

Chihuahua had begged Mills to leave him one child for him and his wife, and Mills agreed the boy later called Eugene could stay. My son Horace, Bashdelehi's son Bailtso, and Kaytennae's adopted son Kaywaykla were not sent to school until five moons later, just before we were all sent to Mount Vernon Barracks a long day and a half's train ride west past Pensacola. In all, about one hundred children were sent to school at Carlisle. Nearly half of them died from worms, the disease the White Eyes called "tuberculosis." Most of those who lived came back to their parents, who survived seven years at Mount Vernon Barracks and eighteen years at Fort Sill.

FOR THE YOUNGER children and those who did not go to school far away at Carlisle, the Catholic Church had a *hacienda* where they were taught by *di-yens* who were never-married women and who practiced the same ceremonies together. The *hacienda* was named the Convent of Saint Joseph. The women were called "sisters" and all dressed the same. Before the children were sent away to school, the sisters came to the fort and taught the children on the grass in the center of the fort. But some days it rained, and there was no teaching. After most of the children were sent to school, the big chiefs decided that those who were left, either too young or too sick, could go to the sisters' *hacienda* for their school. Every day, they would be taught twice the time they had on the grass at Fort Marion. They also had more school days at the *hacienda* because they had their teaching done inside, out of the rain. Until the *hacienda* was made ready for the children to come, the sisters still came to the fort but used one of the dark, leaking rooms in the fort walls to teach. Two young sisters came to teach the children, and all the People grew to like them very much. Mother Alypius and Sister Jane Francis were their names. They taught the children to speak in the White Eye tongue, to read and make tracks on paper, to draw pictures, and to sing. They also brought hats, shoes, books, paper, and pencils for the children.

The men, most of whom had little or nothing to do except keep the fort clean, began to watch the sisters teach the children. They became so interested in what the sisters taught that they began doing the drawing lessons with crayons and paper the sisters gave them and singing religious and patriotic songs with the children.

After the sisters began teaching the children at their *hacienda*, they also taught them how to behave in the land of the White Eyes. I thought this was a very good thing. The People thought the sisters were much to be respected and were kind, good women. Helen and I never forgot them.

SICKNESS AND DEATH made their lodges at Fort Marion. Among the nearly four hundred People from Fort Apache, seventy-six were sick, and sixty of those had shaking sickness like we had when we camped along the Gila at San Carlos. Within three moons, twenty-four (one man, seven women, and sixteen children) had gone to the Happy Place. So many were getting sick that the big White Eye chiefs agreed that a man named Herbert Welsh and *Capitán* Bourke could come, see how we lived, and report back to them with a clear eye.

*Capitán* Bourke saw everything Welsh did at Fort Marion and served as his interpreter when he talked to us. Welsh came to Fort Marion around the end of Ghost Face, after he had seen our children and how they survived at school in Carlisle. He thought they were well cared for, but many were dying and none of their *di-yens* understood why. When he arrived at Fort Marion, he talked with Colonel Langdon, who had recommended that we be held at school, where there was much more room and children could go to school without leaving the house of their parents. He visited the fort and saw how crowded we were. He was very angry at how close the places the Blue Coats called "latrines" were to where we took our drinking water.

Welsh talked to me for a long time. I dressed in clothes as good as those of any White Eye. He even said so. I told him how the Blue Coats treated the scouts who had helped force Geronimo to surrender. There were fourteen of us, and the Army still employed us while we were prisoners. We got no pay for our last days of work, and the fruit of all the labor on our Fort Apache farms had been taken from us. He clenched his teeth, mumbled words under his breath, shook his head, and made many tracks on paper. I told him my story and showed him my great silver medal the Great Father had given me. I said, "Why did they give me this fine silver medal to wear in prison?" Welsh snorted and shook his head. He didn't know either. He told me he would make many tracks on paper and try to make the big White Eye chief see that they must take us to a place with much more room.

Within a moon after Welsh left, we learned that the big chiefs were sending us to a new place with much more room for us than Fort Marion. It was called Mount Vernon Barracks and stood in the pine woods north of a place named Mobile Bay, west of Pensacola and Fort Pickens.

# TWELVE

## THE ROAD TO MOUNT VERNON BARRACKS

IN THE SEASON of Little Leaves, late in the moon the White Eyes called "April," Colonel Ayers, the new commander of Fort Marion, told the chiefs and leaders for the People to pack their things, that we were being moved to a place where there was much more room and life would be better. Two days later, we walked back to the station and were put on iron wagons in the middle of the night. All the women and children in the families of the Naiche-Geronimo band held at Fort Pickens were put in the same iron wagon, which was last in the line of those heading west.

Late in the afternoon of the following sun, the iron wagons carrying us stopped. The wagon carrying the families of the Geronimo-Naiche band was unhitched and left by itself near a *hacienda* at the beginning of a plank road that led out into the big water. A big white boat puffed smoke out a tall stack like an iron wagon and waited out in the big water, tied to the end of the plank road. We watched through our open windows as the Geronimo-Naiche People stepped down from their wagon and Blue Coats studied tracks on paper. They were guided by the Blue Coats into the *hacienda* and soon appeared on the plank road, guided and guarded by Blue Coats as they walked toward the boat puffing smoke at the end of the road. The many reflections caught from the setting sun by waves on the big water looked like gleaming jewels scattered on a dark blanket. In the distance, I saw the low profile of a small land rising above the water. It met the water with wide white sand. Trees waved in the breeze, and behind them, a short straight line of stone walls rose above their tops.

I thought, *That must be Fort Pickens. The women and children at last go to their men with Naiche and Geronimo. Maybe there is hope for all our families.* I turned to my women and children around me and told them what I thought. Nalthchedah looked away and out the window at trees and buildings on the other side of the aisle from where we sat. She was still angry with me for marrying Helen and blamed me for our son Horace being sent off to school in Carlisle three days before we left Fort Marion. I understood her anger about my marriage to Helen, but I couldn't stop Horace from being sent to school. Helen, Maud, and Banatsi were eager to see what I had seen, and they stared toward the women and children walking out to the puffing boat at the end of the plank road. The iron wagons suddenly jerked forward as the demon iron wagon moved toward the setting sun. Some of the women in our wagon wailed and moaned, believing they would never see their friends and relatives again.

The iron wagons traveled all night. The rocking back and forth and slow rumble of the iron wagons on the iron road made it hard to sleep. My mind wandered far across memories of good times with Ishchos and our children. I remembered the day Juh and Geronimo had led warriors to catch and burn Juan Mata Ortiz, days as first sergeant with *Teniente* Davis at Fort Apache, and days farming at Fort Apache. My closed eyes filled with the images of the great White Eye villages, especially the one of the Great Father and great White Eye chiefs who now controlled our lives but knew nothing about us and didn't seem to care how badly we suffered until Welsh came. The iron wagons stopped four or five times during the night to get water and wood for the demon pulling us.

Dawn's light crept filtered through the forest of great trees growing out of the water on both sides of the iron road. As the day brightened, we passed through a place of many iron roads and White Eye *casas*, and after making a stop, we changed our direction from due west to north as the sun floated above the tops of the great trees and mists off the water surrounding the trees. Great shafts of sunlight speared through the thin clouds of mist and trees, casting spots of brilliant light on the black water. Great white birds with long legs flew through the trees or waded in the black water, looking for fish that they grabbed with their long, orange-colored beaks. They crunched the fish and then gobbled them longways into position to slide down their long throats. I had seen little of this world and wondered how the big White Eye chiefs planned for us to survive at Mount Vernon.

THE IRON WAGONS stopped two or three hands above the horizon after dawn had passed. I saw no buildings, only trees on both sides of the iron road that continued in front of us, up a gentle slope. I thought I could see black water through the trees behind us on the east side. Looking out through the windows on the west side of our iron wagon, I saw a wagon road curving up a gentle hill and disappearing into the trees. A Blue Coat sergeant who had helped us often at Fort Marion opened the door to our wagon and, with the help of Concepción, said to us, "Your new place to stay is just up the road you see going up through the trees. This is Mount Vernon Barracks land. The soldiers will show you the way. The commander will tell you the rules and his expectations for you at his command post where the soldiers take you. Good luck."

We took what we had off the train and followed the soldiers up the hill. You could tell which families had sick women from the men carrying things their women normally carried. There were more of our People here than I'd first thought, and I was glad to be away from Fort Marion, where sickness was everywhere. I thanked *Ussen* that my women were healthy and strong enough to carry our belongings.

Near the top of the hill, the road forked. We were led down the left fork toward an open gate guarded by Blue Coats. We walked through the gate, and the Blue Coats soon had us sit as families on the ground in front of a *hacienda* that Concepción said was the Blue Coat chief's place of command.

We waited. It was getting hotter in this place, and the air felt heavy, wet, and hard to breathe. The commander came out of his *hacienda* and made a talk. I remember he said many fine things and told us the Blue Coats would always have a *di-yen* here to help us with our sicknesses. He motioned toward tall trees close to great brick walls, where tents like those we had used at Fort Marion had been put up in the dark shade of the trees. He said they were our tents for families, to make our camp there and, if we needed more, to ask and they would be issued. All the wood we needed for fires was loaded on some big wagons near camp. We could use that wood while we cut more, and he said we would be called to come collect our rations before the sun was gone. Water for drinking and cooking came from a well near our tents. He said we were free to move about as we wanted, the only rules being that we couldn't leave the village before sunup and we had to be back by sundown. Looking up toward a sky turning gray, he said we would be wise to choose our tents first and then make our living arrangements because it usually rained in the afternoons.

We had much more room than we'd had at Fort Marion, and the women and children were able to put what little they had in the tents, big Blue Coat tents that could shelter four men, some even more, with families camped near their leader's tent. Helen chose our tent near her mothers'. Nalthchedah, Maud, and Banatsi had a tent on the other side. They were far enough apart that each place had some measure of privacy, unlike the village on top of the walls at Fort Marion. Maud helped Helen with her tent, so each of my tents had two women making a place for a cooking fire and unpacking their things, making the work go fast. Maud and Helen went to the wood wagons where we camped and gathered small fallen limbs to help start a fire after returning with their arms carrying freshly split firewood. They made a lean-to with a sheet of canvas we had kept from Fort Marion, to use as a shelter from the rain when they cooked and to keep the firewood dry. They were quick to make a smoky fire to drive away the clouds of no-see-ems leaving drops of blood everywhere they bit. They were worse than anything we had suffered at Fort Marion. They also used sharp sticks to make trenches to channel the rainwater away from the tents and keep the insides dry.

Just before it rained, the Blue Coats called the women to come for their week's rations. The food rations were short, as they had been at Fort Marion. If we hadn't added to our rations at Fort Marion, with food bought using money from selling our crafts or the blankets the Blue Coats gave us, we would have stayed hungry. We sold and traded our goods to stores or to people coming to see us like caged animals, wanting something to show their friends they had visited with "wild Apache." I was very glad we had saved enough money from the things we sold in town at Fort Marion so that we could buy more food from farmers or stores. But I wondered where and to whom we could sell our things to keep buying food.

Thunder rolled, and the rain came. Water pattered on the branches over us and then, growing in intensity, fell on us in a rush. Many of the women and children had to stand in the rain while they waited for their turn to take rations. The rainwater washed through our camp, leaving sticky mud on paths we had made while finding camping sites and setting up tents. We knew we would have to make ditches to drain the water when it came or soon sleep on the wet ground in water-soaked blankets. We knew it rained often in this land of water everywhere, and we would have to make the ditches quickly. My women had made good trenches around our tents, and the ground inside stayed dry, but I could tell, if it had been a big hard rain, we might have been soaked.

# THIRTEEN

## MOUNT VERNON BARRACKS

THE DARKNESS UNDER the trees where we camped made it hard to tell when dawn came. Something light green, almost a blue stone color, started to grow on everything—moccasins, clothes, baskets, unused food... *everything*. Every day, the women had to scrape it away.

Although we had far more room at this place than at Fort Marion, the everyday rains, mold growing on everything, the hot and wet air we had to breathe, the clouds of no-see-ems, and camping under the trees in deep-shaded and shadowed darkness made life miserable for us. If we wanted to see the sun, we had to climb to the top of a tree and spread its branches.

The People still suffered much sickness. They coughed, wheezed, and spat blood in the thick, wet air. Their eyes turned red and developed sores on their eyelids. Some were covered by little red spots for a while, others became weak because their bodies didn't keep food long enough to use it, and still others had shaking-sickness spells where they shook and said they were cold even as the sweat poured from their bodies.

By the Ghost Face, we had buried ten women, nine children, and two men. Nearly all the men and women had died from the shaking sickness. No Apache or White Eye *di-yen* knew how to cure the shaking sickness. When we lived at San Carlos, we could get away from becoming sick with it by moving away from the river and up into the mountains, where the air was cooler and dryer. Here, there was no place to go.

I began to believe the big chiefs were crueler than we had ever been when we made war and killed many men, women, and children quickly with our weapons. These chiefs wanted to wipe us out by keeping us in this place of sickness and shadow, mud and great swarms of no-see-ems, and by starving us after we no longer had any money to buy food.

After a few minor chores at the beginning of the day, there was nothing to do. A few men still made toy bows and arrows to sell to White Eyes who came to stare at us, and the women made their fine baskets, for which the White Eye women made their men pay a good price. When we first came, the men wandered over the area and into Mount Vernon to find and visit stores with their wives. We wanted, needed, to learn the lay of the land. We weren't as closely guarded as we had been at Fort Marion. The Blue Coats knew miles of knee-deep black water nearby were filled with the giant, armor covered lizards the White Eyes called "alligators" that had huge mouths filled with great dagger-like teeth and big, ugly, poisonous snakes waiting to bring painful death. Nana, who had Power over rattlesnakes, said he had no Power over the big, ugly snakes or the giant lizards. Tall trees reaching high in the sky to block out the sun surrounded us and grew everywhere in the black water. Escape, too risky and dangerous, was the furthermost thought in our minds. Women and children could not possibly get across those stretches of black water, and no man would leave without his family.

To pass the time, men played monte and other card games but had little to bet. The women had their games too, including monte, but their chores kept them from playing as much as the men. One day crawled to the next this way for six moons. The men grew increasingly restless and spoke openly of somehow escaping. I counseled against doing this, saying they would never return alive in trying to get across wide stretches of black water. They gave me knowing smiles and slowly shook their heads, aware that, once, I had worked for the Blue Coats and was probably a spy again as they turned their backs on me.

AROUND THE TIME of the sixth moon after we came to Mount Vernon Barracks, the White Eye big chiefs, without a word of warning, doubled our rations and a Blue Coat *di-yen* came to our village after we began to complain to the first sergeant that our tents were leaking and coming apart. We couldn't sleep, and our clothes stayed wet, making more People sick. He looked at every tent and agreed something had to be done. We held a council with the Blue Coat chief. It was decided that he would have us build log cabins and do away with the tents. Each cabin would have two rooms separated by a breezeway, covered with a common roof we would need in the summer. Each room would be four paces on a side and the breezeway four paces wide. Our council was near the time of Ghost Face. Since the suns were often cold, he wanted every able-bodied man to work on the cabins. There were only thirty of us in the camp. The rest were sick or too old and feeble to work.

The able-bodied men were divided into two groups of fifteen. The first group worked half a sun, and then the second group worked the rest of the sun, and both groups worked every sun. At last, we had productive work to do and didn't waste our days or money on playing monte. The work was very hard at first. We had never done work like this. We had to learn to pace ourselves to have enough energy for the time we were supposed to work. We were fortunate that we had many tall and straight pine trees, their wood easy to work with sharp axes and saws, and that there was plenty of good clay to fill the cracks between the logs as the house was built. Each cabin had dirt floors, and we slept on the ground or on boards. There was a circular firepit to cook over, and we were given an iron, cone-shaped wood-burning stove for heat. The Blue Coat first sergeant called it a Sibley stove. When the cold winds shook the trees around us, I and my women were glad to have its heat.

In less than two moons, we had built sixty-two cabins and had enough logs for maybe twelve or thirteen more cabins. The two-room cabin was ideal for me. I put Nalthchedah and Banatsi on one side and Helen and Maud on the other. I told them to take turns cooking for the entire family, and I spread my blanket with the women who cooked.

Nalthchedah continued to carry her anger at me for marrying Helen and rolled away from me in the blankets even though we slept close together for warmth. After Horace was sent to the school at Carlisle, she understood better why Bashdelehi was desperate to keep Helen near her. Nalthchedah was distant with Helen, but they were civil and respectful of each other. She no longer blamed Helen for becoming my third wife but now blamed me. She no longer wanted children with me.

I didn't argue for more with her.

Helen continued to grow into a mature woman, almost ready to have children. Her desire for me increased, but I told her we should wait until we knew what the White Eye chiefs planned for us and when. Even with the cabins to keep the rain off us, but still cold in the Ghost Face and hot in the Season of Big Leaves, we needed better living conditions, and I needed to be able to provide for my family like I had before I left Fort Apache.

WHILE WE WERE cutting trees for the cabin logs and had even built a few in the moon the White Eyes called "December," two women who knew Herbert Welsh came to talk to us to learn if we wanted a school at Mount Vernon so our children could learn to live and make their way among the White Eyes. They saw the cabins we had already built and, after talking with us, thought the cabins and what we wanted—productive work to support our families, land to grow our own food and animals, and our children able to deal with the White Eyes—showed we had the energy to farm on our own. Of course we did! It's what we wanted in the first place, but the big chiefs wouldn't let us go back to Fort Apache. If the White Eyes now on our land in the west wanted to attack us if we went back, then we were willing to farm in the east but not here at Mount Vernon. This is what we told the women when we were in council with them.

Nana listened to this talk of staying in the east. Then he talked a long time and with great truth about how we should be sent back to our homes in the west. The council was held in the Blue Coat commander's place. After Nana's words were interpreted for the women, one of them walked over to a big round ball on the commander's table and motioned to it. She said to Nana through Concepción and to us all, "This ball shows us all the land and water the sun sees every day and night. The land is covered with people, so you can no longer roam as you please. You and the white men must learn to work together like brothers."

Nana stared at her, slowly shook his head, and then, burying his head in his hands, sighed. "I'm too old to learn that."

The women told us that they would tell their people we ought to have a school here for our children and that they should send teachers here to Mount Vernon for our children. We chiefs all said, *"Ch'ik'eh doleel."* We asked that they come quickly. But it was nearly a harvest before the teachers came.

IN THE SEASON of Little Eagles, everyone had a cabin in the low place close to the gate. The White Eye *di-yen* said the Blue Coats should burn all the tents since they were rotting and falling apart and could be a source of disease. We had a big fire one night, and then we lived no more in tents at Mount Vernon.

I began to wonder if the White Eyes would ever let Geronimo and Naiche and their People join us. If they came, then I would always have to be vigilant.

Geronimo hated disloyalty and had called me a traitor. I knew he would again try to kill me, probably joining forces with Chihuahua, Ulzana, and Kaytennae. I didn't fear these men. I had friends, too, and I knew *Ussen* would keep me safe.

In the Season of Little Leaves, the air warmed and grew heavy again. Flowers were everywhere, and the flowers on creeping vines the White Eyes called "honeysuckle" gave a sweet scent to the air. It was raining much, yet we had plenty of food to eat, and there were few who were sick. We had rested for a moon after getting all the cabins built and living arrangements made. It was a good time to be thankful to *Ussen*.

During the new moon the White Eyes called "May," the chiefs and leaders had a council with the commander. He told us that we had done well building our cabins and that we needed to continue to cut more trees for firewood and to build more cabins.

We looked at each other and frowned. Why did we need to build more cabins? Chihuahua spoke for us. *"Jefe,* why do we need to build more cabins?"

The commander smiled and said, "Your People are increasing. In half a moon, Geronimo, Naiche, and their People come."

# FOURTEEN

## GERONIMO COMES

CHIHUAHUA CALLED A council of all the men after we learned that the Naiche-Geronimo band would join us soon at Mount Vernon Barracks. The big White Eye chiefs had decided to put all the Chiricahua in one place. I learned later that this was one of the terms of surrender that Geronimo wanted. Chihuahua had called this council because there were many in the camp, me among them, who blamed Geronimo for many Chiricahua becoming prisoners of war when they didn't deserve exile in the east.

We gathered around a smoky fire to drive away the no-see-ems. Chihuahua stood with his arms crossed in the hazy firelight and looked around at all of us, a questioning frown wrinkled on his brow. Thousands of blinking lights from insects flying and crawling through the brush and trees surrounded us while croaking frogs, tree peepers, and insects added their songs to the night, and overhead, no clouds stopped the light from myriad stars in a smooth, black sky.

Chihuahua said, "I think you all know that soon the Naiche-Geronimo band comes to join us. The White Eye big chiefs finally put all the Chiricahua together in a place we don't want, with some brothers we don't want, who blame us for being here in the first place.

"I want us to speak our minds and then agree not to cause trouble when they arrive. If there is trouble, the comandante will throw those who start it in the calaboose, and maybe those who don't deserve to go. Once, I wanted to kill Geronimo, but he got away from me, and after I learned why he lied to me—he thought he was speaking the truth—I cooled down and decided to ride with him. I don't know why he broke his word to *Nant'an Lpah* after we surrendered at Canyon de los Embudos. He went his way. I went mine. It was his choice to make. We are not *amigos*, nor are we *enemigos*. How will you choose to treat him? You must think on this. This is all I have to say. I ask Chief Loco to tell us how he thinks about the return of Naiche and Geronimo."

Loco moved to the center of the firelight. The firelight glittering in his good eye and on his scarred face made twisting shadows, giving him an odd ghost-like look. "In the Season of Little Leaves six harvests ago, Geronimo led more than seventy warriors from Juh's camp in Mexico to my People's camp near the Río Gila at San Carlos. Three times, he had sent warriors asking us to come to Mexico. Three times, I said no. I had given my word to the White Eyes to stay at San Carlos, and I would keep it. When the warriors came, they forced me and my People to leave San Carlos. At first, I wouldn't go, but Chato, who was Geronimo's *segundo*, cocked his rifle and pushed it against my chest and said he would kill me if I didn't lead the People away. I believed Chato. At Geronimo's direction, I led the People east and then south to the land of the *Nakai-yes*."

Loco paused, crossed his arms and stared at the stars seeming to collect his thoughts. "We lost one or two running for the border. After we crossed the border, we rested three suns. Two suns later, nearly half the People had been captured or killed by the Blue Coats and *Nakai-yes*. Geronimo and some of his warriors fought hard for us, but they brought us to that killing ground.

"A harvest later, after *Nant'an Lpah* brought us back to San Carlos, Fort Apache life was good for a while until we all decided to break *Nant'an Lpah's* laws against making *tizwin* and keeping our wives straight. It was none of his business what we drank or how we treated our wives, and we said so. That was when Geronimo decided to leave and took Chihuahua and Naiche with him after he lied about killing Chato and *Teniente* Davis. My People stayed at Fort Apache and minded our business until the White Eyes decided we must be prisoners along with Geronimo. After all, they must have thought we were all Chiricahua and supported Geronimo. You and I both know this is not so, but the White Eyes are more blind than my bad eye.

"The White Eye cannot understand how the Chiricahua can have blood feuds across the whole band. Why not? The White Eyes have blood feuds across their country every sun. I tell you there are many reasons for me and every Chihenne to have a blood feud with Geronimo. I tell you I will not take my revenge against Geronimo. Every Chiricahua, good or bad, who can survive must live or we will disappear forever from the land. The White Eyes are more numerous than the leaves in the trees, more numerous than sand by the big water. The White Eyes could kill their other half in a feud and still be more numerous than the leaves in the trees. I say we forget our reasons for revenge against Geronimo or anyone with him. We do not need to be his *amigo* or his *enemigo*. We need all Chiricahua to survive so we survive and grow strong once more. That is all I have to say."

The chiefs and leaders around me were nodding. Chihuahua moved into the light again and said, "Who will speak next?" No one moved. He pointed in my direction. "Chato, my brother and I have business to settle with you, but for reasons I've said here and what Loco has said, we wait until we are no longer prisoners and the Chiricahua are strong once more. Chato has been on both sides of Geronimo. I ask him to tell us what he thinks we should do."

Chihuahua stepped back, and I walked to the speaker's place by the fire. I saw the men lean a little forward and cock and slightly twist their heads to one side to listen.

"When I was first sergeant for *Teniente* Davis, *Nant'an Lpah* was working with the big White Eye chiefs to get the *Nakai-yi* big chiefs to agree to let our women and children in slavery come back to us. He told me that, to get the People free, the Chiricahua had to behave so the big White Eye chiefs wouldn't stop talking with the *Nakai-yi* chiefs. I was, and still am, desperate to get my first wife, Ishchos, and two children back and did everything I could for *Nant'an Lpah* to see us behaving. I knew how Geronimo thought, and I knew he wanted to leave Fort Apache. He feared the guardhouse and wanted to stay far away from anyone who would put him there. I privately told him not to leave the reservation. I said if he did, he would destroy the chances of our getting our women and children back. I made him understand that if he left, I would help the Blue Coats find him or I would bring him back myself and do everything I could to send him to the little land in the big water that once held Kaytennae. Geronimo called me a traitor. I am no traitor. I saved many Chiricahua and White Eye lives in the work I did with Capitáns Crawford and Davis and other scouts who sit here with us. After I returned to my farm, I told the other scouts to treat the escaped Chiricahua as *enemigos*. The scouts also did much to make those who left the reservation decide to surrender—even Geronimo, until he changed his mind.

"Now Geronimo and Naiche's band return to us. We have all submitted to the White Eyes. Chihuahua and Loco speak true. The one thing we must do is survive. Those who come are not *enemigos* or *amigos*. They are Chiricahua who must help make us strong by living. Maybe one sun, when we are all free, there will be a time of revenge, but it must not be now. I have said all I will say."

I saw heads nodding as I finished. Chihuahua asked if there were any others who wanted to speak, but none did. He ended the council by saying, "I think you have heard wise words this night. Follow them."

The People moved off toward their cabins. They had much to consider.

THE PEOPLE WAITED, and most made up their minds that the Geronimo-Naiche band People were Chiricahua, neither *amigo* nor *enemigo*. Three suns passed. The morning of the fourth sun, children playing near the gate saw a line of people. Blue Coats were leading them up the hill toward the gate. Running to the village cabins, the children told everyone, "Chiricahua come! Chiricahua come!" Those who had been working outside or lounging around or playing monte moved into the cabins. Not one Chiricahua could be seen in the village.

I watched with crossed arms, sitting in the darkness of a cabin room door, as the people trudged through the gate and were led, as we had been, to the comandante's place where he would tell them the rules and where their places were in our village they saw below. As I counted, there were forty-six men, women, and children. There were vacant cabins for some, but a few more would have to be built. Those without a cabin would stay in tents until the cabins were done.

The People sat down to wait. They looked down the hill toward the village. I knew they must wonder what had happened to us. Were we all away working in the woods or fields? Had the Blue Coats shut us up somewhere? We stared at them from the darkness of our cabins and thought, What we should do with these People who returned to us. The air was still, wet, and growing warmer. Somewhere up in the tree branches, jays squawked. In the deep shadows of the tall trees, insects made their music. We all were held prisoner of the moment. No one moved, barely daring to breathe.

Geronimo stood and walked a little beyond where the others sat and looked over the village cabins and around the soldier *haciendas* before staring out over the treetops in the valley to the east. A young woman walked out of her cabin, her head held high and her chin up. I saw streams of water rolling down her cheeks as she passed by my doorway. Her name was Dohn-say. She was beautiful, the wife of Mike Dahkeya and the daughter of Geronimo and Chee-hash-kish lost to *Nakai-yi* slavery like Ishchos.

She went up the steps from the village, toward the People waiting for the comandante. People turned to watch her. I knew Geronimo saw her coming—his sharp old eyes rarely missed anything around him—but he continued to stare out across the trees in the valley east of us. When Dohn-say reached the path leading to the group, she ran toward Geronimo. He never moved a muscle. She threw her arms around his neck and buried her face in his shirt. He continued to stare at the treetops, seeming not to acknowledge her, but that was just good Apache manners. I knew how glad he must have been to see her and saw him hug her with one arm while he patted her back, saying something private between them. I saw her nod her head.

She went over to speak with Geronimo's two wives—a young woman with a baby, a Mescalero woman named Ih-tedda, whom Geronimo had taken to replace the wives that *Nant'an Lpah* had hidden from him at Fort Bowie, and an older woman, Zi-yeh, who had a boy with her, Fenton, eight or nine years old. I didn't see She-gha with the other two and wondered if she had gone to the Happy Place. I remembered that when she was at Fort Marion, she was often sick.

People began to drift out of their cabins. Those who had relatives or friends in the Naiche-Geronimo band moved up the hill to the group, speaking words of welcome and making signs of all-is-well. I saw my friend Naiche, sitting with his wives, stand as Chihuahua approached, both making the all-is-good hand wave and speaking with long-lost smiles on their faces, remembering days past. The scenes of welcome and greeting spread through the waiting group.

Helen, anxious to tell her father she had married a chief, and I went up the hill to find and visit with Mohtsos, but neither of the women he'd left behind at Fort Apache when he rode south with Geronimo and taken another woman, had anything to do with him. They hadn't gotten off the iron wagon at Pensacola to join him at Fort Pickens. I believed they were done with him and would take new men who were less careless with them.

Mohtsos saw us coming and stood to welcome Helen with a happy face. He said, "Ho! Daughter, *Nish'ii'* (I see you)." Even though it is considered bad manners to show affection in public, he hugged her anyway.

Helen said, "Father, at last you return, and we are together again. My heart sings a happy song." I stood back a little from them, but she turned and, with a big smile, took my hand and pulled me close to them. "Father, I have married since you left. I'm sure you know my husband, the great chief, Chato."

Mohtsos's face fell, his eyes narrowed, and his jaw raised as he slowly nodded. "I know Chato. Once a warrior of great Power, then first sergeant of scouts at Fort Apache. He chased us north of the border and in Chihuahua and Sonora. He and the other scouts destroyed many of our camps, taking our supplies and animals, and making our lives hard. Now he is my son-in-law. Geronimo says he is a traitor. *Ussen* turns his face from me for my daughter to claim such a man." He crossed his arms and turned his back to us.

Helen's eyes were close to spilling water. I gently took her by the arm and pulled her away. "Come, wife."

# FIFTEEN

## NANT'AN LPAH COMES

WE FINISHED THE cabins for the People from Fort Marion in a moon. Nearly all the anger and resentment against Naiche and Geronimo and warriors in their band, we buried in our souls to raise some other time when we were free or finally forgot. We all suffered together. More died that harvest and were buried in secret places in the dark shadows of the tall trees. Young and old, men and women, the People died. Many babies were born, more than normal, but we were dying off faster than babies were being born.

Nalthchedah studied the men who returned with Geronimo and Naiche but found none to her liking. She no longer came to me in the blankets, and I didn't tell her to come. Little was said between us. I knew, when she found a man she wanted and could maneuver into taking her, she would divorce me and leave. That would, I thought, make us both happy. Helen continued to grow into a fine-looking and talented woman. I was glad I had saved her from school and that she wasn't wasted as a wife for some young fool.

Naiche and I had been good friends for a long time before he rode south with Geronimo. Before the prophet had been killed and we all escaped to the Blue Mountains in the land of the *Nakai-yes*, we lived in misery near each other at San Carlos. My village had been next to his, and we smoked and talked often about how to make things better for the People and about the good days when his father led the People. He didn't hold it against me, as many did, for being first sergeant of scouts for *Teniente* Davis and helping Capitáns Crawford and Wirt Davis chase him and the other renegade Apache. He would never have left Fort Apache if Geronimo hadn't told him *Teniente* Davis and I had been killed. Once more, we talked and smoked often.

George Wratten, the young interpreter who had stayed with the People at Fort Pickens, also came to Mount Vernon. He spoke Apache better than any White Eye I had ever known, better even than Sam Bowman and Concepción, who had both returned to Fort Apache and their families. Nearly all of us liked and enjoyed George Wratten, but for reasons I never learned, Geronimo had little to do with him. The comandante made George Wratten our work supervisor, and at last, we had work to do, from raking leaves and grass around the Blue Coat *haciendas* to cutting brush for clearing the poor land for planting gardens in the next year and trees for firewood, which we always needed. This work was better than spending all day playing monte but did nothing to help the men provide for their families.

Two White Eye women came to teach the children six moons after the Geronimo-Naiche band arrived. They were sent and their wages paid by the same group who had sent the two women nearly a harvest earlier who had come to learn what we needed. The thing we needed most was to return to our homelands, which was beyond their power to provide. The second thing we needed was a school, so our children could learn White Eye secrets while they lived with us instead of attending the big school far away at the place named Carlisle. This they provided.

The comandante gave the teachers a big room for their school that would hold all the children and their chairs and still leave room for the women to have worktables with places underneath for their supplies and chalk writing boards to hang on the wall. The People were happy the teachers came. When Geronimo learned why and how the teachers came, he was so happy he appointed himself schoolmaster and sat through classes with the children, holding a long stick and threatening to use it on them if they misbehaved.

ALTHOUGH WE HAD work to do with the coming of George Wratten to supervise us, the days had a kind of gray-sky sameness. Except in the times of Ghost Face and Little Eagles, it rained nearly every day, mold still grew on everything, no-see-ems came in great biting clouds, and people with hacking coughs and spitting blood died. The good times were from our children being taught White Eye secrets of speaking the White Eye tongue, writing, and reading tracks made on paper or their chalkboards. Parents often tried to watch their children's classes and learn with them. I encouraged Helen to go every day, and she was fast to learn the White Eye tongue and making and reading tracks on paper. When we were together in the evenings, she taught me what she had learned. I thought, *The things these women teach our children are very good to know.*

A HARVEST PASSED. One sunny morning early in Ghost Face, I sat drinking coffee by the iron stove we used for heat. As if lightning had struck out of a cloudless sky, we heard a young boy running through the village yelling, "*Nant'an Lpah* comes! *Nant'an Lpah* comes!" Along with me, several others ran out of their cabins. Looking up the hill, I saw a gray beard and a face I would always remember, talking with Chihuahua and Kaytennae and three or four Blue Coat officers with him as they moved down the path toward our village. A crowd of excited people ran up the hill to see *Nant'an Lpah* again.

He shook hands with two or three in front of me, laughing and sharing little memories of long-ago days with them. When I reached him, I stuck out my hand and said in the White Eye tongue, "*Nant'an Lpah*, you remember me?"

He laughed as he grabbed my hand, "Remember you? How could I forget you, Chato? You did some outstanding soldiering in helping bring in the renegades."

I reached my other hand to hold him with affection behind his neck, when I realized it wouldn't be good manners to do that with a great chief like him and quickly let it fall to my side.

We led him over to see our school. He walked in the door and was introduced to the teacher in charge, a young woman named Sophie Shepard. Geronimo was sitting off to the side with the stick he used to make the children behave, but *Nant'an Lpah* didn't seem to notice him. The teacher showed how well the students were learning by writing words with few tracks on the board for them to read and speak. I could tell they had done this often and memorized a good answer because they were shy and didn't even look at the chalkboard when the teacher made tracks on it.

*Nant'an Lpah* watched them and nodded. He said, "Thank you for the fine work you do with these children, and I know their mothers and fathers must be very proud of what they've learned."

She smiled and said to the children, "School is ended for the day. I know your parents want to visit with General Crook."

We went outside, and he pointed to a grove of trees where we might sit in the shade. "Let's go down to that grove of trees and talk." As we walked under the trees, he picked up a stick and walked on.

GEORGE WRATTEN SAT next to *Nant'an Lpah*. The comandante for Mount Vernon sat on the other side, and Tenientes Foster—who worked with Wratten—and Kennon—who traveled with the *nant'an*—sat next to their chiefs. Chiefs and leaders gathered in a half circle, sitting around the Blue Coat chiefs. We were taking our places when Geronimo came up to speak to *Nant'an Lpah*.

The *nant'an* saw him and made a hand motion waving him back and said to George Wratten, "I don't want to hear anything from Geronimo. He's such a liar that I can't believe a word he says." Geronimo scowled, stepped back, sat down, and crossed his arms, waiting to listen. He often said bad things about *Nant'an Lpah* after that.

*Nant'an Lpah* had been whittling on the stick he had picked up as we gathered around him. He spoke to us as old friends. "I come to Mount Vernon at the request of the big chief for war, Mister Redfield Proctor, who has learned that this place is not good for you and too many of you are dying far too soon. I want to hear from all of you who came here in their separate ways and learn what you are enduring and what you need. These things I will put in my report to the big chief for war. I have seen a piece of land in the mountains of North Carolina the Cherokees would be willing to sell to the government for you and a piece in Virginia where you might farm that is near a school where you wouldn't lose your children to Carlisle School. My opinion, which I will write to the big chief for war about these lands, is that they are too small to support you. You need to be moved to Oklahoma, where there is much land to farm and grass-covered land to raise cattle. I'm here to ask questions and learn."

I was happy to hear this. Maybe someone near the Great Father would hear our cries and help us.

# SIXTEEN

## NANT'AN LPAH'S COUNCIL

*NANT'AN LPAH* LOOKED at Naiche. "You are a chief we all know and respect. You gave me your word that you had surrendered, and yet two days later, you broke off and ran with Geronimo. What made you do this?"

Naiche shrugged and looked off into the trees. "When we left there, so far as I was concerned, I didn't know anything. I didn't know how to work. I didn't know how to dig up roots, or break ground or break rock, and I thought I wouldn't like it. I was afraid I wouldn't like to work. All of us thought that way."

The *nant'an* frowned and said, "How did you come to leave that night?"

"I was afraid I was going to be carried off somewhere I didn't like, someplace I didn't know. I thought all who were taken away would die. I've learned different since then. I've worked much after that time. Nobody said anything to me that night. I worked it out in my mind.

The *nant'an*'s knife sent a long, curled shaving off his whittling stick.

"Didn't the Apache talk about it among yourselves?"

Naiche lifted one side of his face in a smile. "We talked to each other about it. We were drunk."

"Why did you get drunk?"

Naiche shrugged again. "Because there was a lot of whiskey there, and we wanted a drink, and we took it. The others didn't want to go out. I don't know why the others didn't know of it. I thought they all did."

*Nant'an Lpah* nodded and, while making another cut in his stick, said, "You had promised not to kill more people, but you killed everyone you came across. Why?"

Naiche crossed his arms, puffed his cheeks, and blew. "Because we were afraid. It was war. We knew anyone who saw us would kill us. We did the same thing. We had to if we wanted to live."

*Nant'an Lpah* nodded he understood. "How did you come to surrender? Were you afraid of the troops?"

Naiche shook his head. "We wanted to see our People."

"Did the troops force you to surrender?"

"We weren't forced to do it. We talked under a flag of truce. We all said we had enough of run, fight, run and wanted to surrender."

*Nant'an Lpah* stuck out his lower lip and nodded. He had known the answer before it was given. "How many of you had been killed?"

"One woman had been killed by the *Nakai-yes*, but none of the warriors were killed by anyone."

Naiche told me later while we were drinking coffee by a fire that he had told the same things to *Nant'an* Stanley when they were held at Fort Sam Houston in San Antonio, and the *nant'an's* man with the little spear, black water, and paper made tracks representing what he said.

*Nant'an Lpah* said, "How long did the white flag of truce last when you made the last surrender?"

Since he had been at their surrender with *Teniente* Gatewood, George Wratten spoke up. "When Lieutenant Gatewood and I left Fort Bowie, we were under a white flag. On the trail in Sonora, Kayitah and Martine saw where Naiche-Geronimo camped on top of a flat mountain and carrying a white flag on a yucca stick, ran up to the trail to ask the warriors to listen to Gatewood, who brought terms of surrender from General Miles. They were lucky. Geronimo knew they were scouts. He hates scouts. When they approached, Geronimo told the warriors to kill them. But they had relatives among the warriors who threatened to kill anyone who harmed the scouts. Geronimo said to let them come.

"Kayitah spent a long time talking to them, and they agreed to meet with Gatewood the next day. They trusted Gatewood and talked with him all day. Then we left and that night camped with Captain Lawton's troop nearby. The next morning, the warriors came in and laid their weapons down. They had chosen peace. We rode up to Skeleton Canyon in escort to prevent Mexicans and soldiers from attacking them, and we discussed terms with General Miles there before Miles and Geronimo made a surrender arrangement."

*Nant'an Lpah* nodded his head often as he listened to George Wratten's story. I had heard bits and pieces of it from a few people but not the story from beginning to end.

*Nant'an Lpah* said, "Could the surrender have been made without the scouts?" George Wratten looked him in the eye and shook his head. "I don't think so." "What were the conditions of surrender?"

"The conditions were that they should give up their arms and surrender, that they would not be harmed but would be taken to their People in Florida."

The *nant'an* asked Naiche about numbers who had surrendered, the number who came in to Fort Bowie with *Capitán* Lawton, and the total number of his band who had kept so many Blue Coats chasing them for five moons. The numbers Naiche gave him were the same ones he had told me when we talked about that time.

*Nant'an Lpah* looked around at the faces staring at him. "Tell me what has happened to you since the surrender." He nose-pointed toward me. "Chato, first sergeant of scouts at Fort Apache, what happened to you? What do you hope will happen to you and your People?"

I told him about being asked to lead a group to see the big chiefs and the Great Father and how we spent time at the school at Carlisle, stayed a moon and a half at Fort Leavenworth, and then woke up one morning at Fort Marion. I told about the letter *Nant'an* Miles sent to us while we waited at Leavenworth that said White Eye settlers would make war on us if we stayed at Fort Apache and that he had a big new reservation for us that covered six hundred square miles, where the chiefs and leaders would be paid twenty to fifty dollars a moon to live there. We all thought that we needed to stay away from White Eyes wanting to kill us, and the money to pay us was good, so all the men agreed and touched the pen when *Capitán* Dorst wrote our letter saying we agreed and signed our names. When we got to Fort Marion, I didn't believe it was six hundred square miles.

*Nant'an Lpah* said, "How many Chiricahua were enlisted as scouts by *Nant'an* Miles when you chased Naiche and Geronimo?"

I said, "Twenty-five. Nineteen of those were men who had farms. The others were young men or boys."

I was wearing the heavy silver medal the Great Father had given me. I unfastened it from my vest and held it out for *Nant'an Lpah* and the rest to see. "Why did they give me that to wear in the guardhouse? I thought something good would come to me when they gave me this, but I have been under confinement ever since.

"I left everything I had on my farm and crops in the field to make a long trip to speak to the big chiefs and the Great Father so that we might keep our farms at Fort Apache. I was working on my farm and had one field planted in wheat and another in barley. I had a wagon and made good money hauling hay, supplies, and other things. I didn't leave the farm because I wanted to. I had sheep, about thirty head, that were becoming greater in number all the time. I had to leave them. I made money shearing them and selling the wool. I had horses and mules that were worth a lot of money.

"The big chiefs made us come here and leave it all behind. They say they pay us for all we left. They take all and sell. Give us five dollars a moon from what they sell. My horses and mules were worth a hundred and fifty to two hundred dollars. They sold all the horses for ten dollars and the mules for twenty-nine dollars. They sold the sheep for two dollars a head—that's about right. I worked hard for my family. The big chiefs took what I worked hard for and gave nearly nothing back.

"You, *Nant'an Lpah*, told us about farms. I got a plow and took good care of everything. Now all I owned, all the labor I put into it, gone. Gone! I can't even hunt to feed my family. My wives and me no longer live where they can bake mescal or look for other good things to eat. We went hungry four moons here and all the time we were at Fort Marion. Then big chiefs tell Blue Coats to give us more food. Our living comes only from what the big chiefs give us. This is not right."

Chihuahua said, "Many of those sent to Florida with me had horses and mules, too."

Kaytennae said, "I haven't been paid for my wagon either."

*Nant'an Lpah* crossed his arms and shook his head at my words. "The way you and the other scouts have been treated is shameful, Chato. My words to the Great Father will say so. Let me hear from other scouts." He looked over the heads of those around him and smiled. "Noche! You were a sergeant major at Fort Apache and led us on many trails after the renegades. What happened to you?"

Noche sighed and looked at the ground where he squatted. "*Nant'an* Miles asked my advice often. I even said he ought to send Kayitah and Martine out with *Teniente* Gatewood to find Naiche and Geronimo. But after they surrendered, we were rounded up, put on a train, and sent to Fort Marion. I had a good farm I had to sell—with horses, and I've been paid for them, but they never paid me for ninety cords of wood."

Toclanny and Coonie told the *nant'an* how the Chiricahua and Chihenne had been taken from Fort Apache after being told they all needed to come early for their rations but then were surrounded, put in wagons, and taken to a train, and they told how disgusting and miserable it was riding to Fort Marion.

Kaytennae spoke of how he had helped the *nant'an* talk to the Naiche-Geronimo band at Canyon de los Embudos just before their supposed surrender.

"I talked your talk to them and your mind to them. They listened and knew you spoke straight. I never did anything wrong and never went on the warpath since I saw you. I tried to think as you told me to and was very thankful to you and was very glad to see you again this morning. All of us were, even to the little children." He lifted his hands palms up and frowned.

"I work hard all the time with my hands, but not for my family. I help build roads, dig up roots, build houses, and do all other kinds of work. Leaves fall off the trees and I help sweep them up. I was working this morning when you came here. I don't know why I work here all the time for nothing. I have children and relatives, lots of them, and I would like to work for them before I'm too old to work. I'd like to have a farm long enough to see the crops get ripe."

*Nant'an Lpah* said, "Yes, I understand all you say, Kaytennae. I'm doing everything I can to get you that farm."

Kaytennae smiled. "The *nant'an* is a good friend."

Chihuahua nodded and said, "I would like a farm, too, and will go right to work so that my children can have plenty to eat. I have a daughter and two other near relatives far away in the school at Carlisle. I want to see them again soon. Won't you make it so I can see them very soon?" Looking up into the trees around him, he said. "Here, there are trees everywhere. I would like to go where I can see."

Others told the *nant'an* much the same thing. We all wanted to leave this place.

As the sun began casting long shadows, our council ended. As *Nant'an Lpah* rose to leave for his train, he said, "I promise you, your words will fill the Great Father's ears, and I will work hard to help you get to a better land and better times. *Adios.*"

Yes, as Kaytennae had said, it was good to have *Nant'an Lpah* for our friend.

# SEVENTEEN

## TENIENTE WOTHERSPOON COMES

THREE MOONS AFTER *Nant'an Lpah* had a council with us, a dark cloud of sorrow filled our village. We learned that he had ridden the ghost pony. *Ussen* had taken him. Geronimo, never blaming himself for anything, believed *Ussen* took him as payback for all the grief he said *Nant'an Lpah* had caused the Chiricahua. A White Eye *di-yen* told Major Kellogg, the Mount Vernon Barracks commander, that the *nant'an's* heart had stopped. I, like most of the others in the village, regretted that *Nant'an Lpah* had been taken. I believed he spoke straight with us and did the best he could for us. I prayed that *Ussen* would speed *Nant'an Lpah's* ghost pony on its way and welcome him as a great chief to the Happy Place.

A moon later, we learned that before *Nant'an Lpah* had ridden the ghost pony, he had sent to the Great Father black water tracks on his talks with us and his search for a better place for us to live. After reading *Nant'an Lpah's* black water tracks, the Great Father began talks with the council of big chiefs. He also made another Blue Coat chief our commander. Major Kellogg, as chief of the Mount Vernon Barracks, had little or no time for us as our commander and had done little to help us. The chiefs and leaders understood that a new commander, chief only for us, could help us more than Major Kellogg.

*Teniente* Wotherspoon, our new commander, came to Mount Vernon with his family in the moon the White Eyes called "June." He was tall and straight and had a long straight bush of hair growing under his nose, eyes that missed nothing, and the voice of command. He walked through our village, looking at the cabins and talking to the men and their women, asking them what they needed or wanted. He seemed to do what other commanders had not. He listened to us.

He looked through our food supplies and worked out trades to buy foods the White Eye *di-yens* said we needed to eat when sickness came. He talked to the White Eye *di-yen* helping us and built a place where the sick who needed blanket rest and checking often were brought. He made a kitchen and feeding place, which soldiers called a "mess hall," into a place with White Eye beds covered with clean white cloth and a place for the *di-yen* and his helpers to work. The *teniente* called it his Apache hospital.

As Major Sinclair had done when we first came to Mount Vernon, Major Kellogg had also put us in groups for work. Some cut firewood, others cleared land for gardens, old men and women planted and kept the gardens, and others kept the leaves and dead grass raked up and carried away. *Teniente* Wotherspoon continued using the work groups but swapped them around in what they did. He also started paying the work-group leaders ten dollars per moon of service and encouraged all of us to work for money by agreeing to let us work for White Eyes who paid us for cutting wood or working on their farms. By the middle of the Ghost Face, he had let four of our warriors and their families live and work on a farm a three-hands-on-the-horizon easy run (about fifteen miles) from our village.

At the beginning of the Ghost Face, *Teniente* Wotherspoon called the men to a council one evening in the big room where the white lady teachers taught the children. He sat in a chair by their worktables while we sat or squatted on the floor around him. George Wratten interpreted for us. I sat with the leaders up front, close to him. We smoked to the four directions, and Geronimo prayed that *Ussen* guide us in our talks.

*Teniente* Wotherspoon said, "The first thing I did after I arrived here was to visit your village. I spoke with each of you and your wives. I saw the log cabins you built and live in. I saw the mold and dirt everywhere that made it very hard for your wives to keep your lodges clean. I saw how water collected in your village every time it rained and how the no-see-ems attacked you. I heard of and saw your sicknesses. I learned your village is not a good place to live.

"I want to build you a new village on the big sand ridge a long rifle shot from the post gates. You know the place. We can see its top every day when it's not raining. Water won't collect there like it does in your village. This means mold shouldn't be nearly as bad or the paths as muddy as it is now in the village. Your new village will have good new houses, not cabins, to keep you and your families dry when it rains and warm in cold weather. I've spoken with my chiefs. They are willing to buy materials for your houses and to pay for two carpenters to begin building them. They will also teach you how to build good houses for yourselves. If you agree, we can begin building new village houses before the end of Ghost Face. What say you?"

Wind swept through the tops of the trees, making the sounds of big water waves and clattering sticks as limbs whipped against each other, seeming to demand an answer. There was silence as the men looked at each other, wondering what the White Eyes wanted them to do for the new village. I thought, *This is a very good thing. The houses will be more comfortable than the cabins we have now, and we won't be wet all the time. Maybe sickness will go away. I'd like to know how to build a house. Maybe Helen and I can now enjoy the pleasures of beginning our first child that she asks me about many times.*

*Maybe....*

Geronimo stood and, crossing his arms, said, "New lodges are good. Less mold and dirt and sickness is good. Having dry paths is good. I ask, where is the reservation Miles promised us? Why can't we have that?"

It was the same question Geronimo asked in every Blue Coat council, and the Blue Coat in charge nearly always answered that he didn't know and that the big chiefs were trying to find good reservation land. We all studied *Teniente*'s serious face and eyes and saw that he spoke straight. He argued a while with Geronimo over getting us a new reservation before he said, "I ask again, shall I ask for new houses to be built for you in a village on the big sand ridge?"

Questions began to flow from the others. They asked, where would the lumber come from, and who would build the houses, and when would the work begin? Wotherspoon answered all their questions, and if he didn't know the answer, he said so and would try to find out. All agreed that a new village on the sand ridge was a good thing.

After Wratten told the *teniente* that we all wanted a new village, he grinned and made the all-is-good sign by waving his forearm parallel to the floor and saying one of the few words in our tongue he knew, *"Enjuh."*

I WALKED BACK to the village with Naiche. Neither of us had anything to say during *Teniente*'s council. Behind us, we could hear Geronimo telling his brothers and other followers how *Nant'an* Miles had lied to us about having our own reservation and how something ought to be done about it. Same old Geronimo, always trying to cause trouble. The trouble with Geronimo is, he's usually right until he loses his mind thinking he'll be thrown in the guardhouse and makes a bad judgment call.

There was no sound except for the wind through the trees, the shuffle of our moccasins on the path, and the mumble of talk behind us. The darkness covered us like a cold blanket with only stars showing between drifting clouds. Naiche said, "You said nothing tonight. Do you think we ought to build a village up on that ridge?"

I said, "Yes. This new village sounds like a good thing. You know that once the carpenters show us how to build a house, we'll wind up doing most of the work. I don't care. At least it's something to do besides raking leaves or cutting firewood." I smiled. "My worry is that as soon as Helen learns of this, she'll want our first child in her belly. I'll have to work all day and stay up all night."

Naiche laughed. "Every man should have such problems."

I laughed too but said no more. The thought of at last enjoying the pleasures of beginning a child with my young wife stirred me and pulled back the blanket over memories of the times Ishchos and I had enjoyed each other while making our children. I didn't understand how such pleasure could lead to the sorrow I had when they were taken and when I couldn't get them back. I remembered the words an old *di-yen* had told me harvests long past. *Ussen* knows how to make life sweet and bitter at the same time. Drink all the portion he gives you.

We walked into the village and went to our cabins. It was my night to sleep on Helen's side of the cabin. I pulled the blanket back from her door. It was warm and comfortable in the little room. Cedar wood crackled in her fire. It gave the room a nice, sharp smell. She sat by her fire, working on a basket she hoped to sell to one of the stores in Mount Vernon or the iron-wagon stop at the bottom of the hill. People often rode an iron wagon from the town they called "Mobile" to see the wild imprisoned Apache. With Geronimo organizing the People's selling, she thought she might get a better price for her work than in the little village. None of my other women were with her. She had asked Maud to sleep on the side with Nalthchedah and Banatsi so she could have some private time with me.

As she saw me come under the door blanket, a smile lighted up her face, and she was immediately up and wrapping her arms around me for a hug. I marveled that this fine young woman was mine. She said, "My husband comes. This night, we are alone. Will you have coffee?"

Releasing her, I hunched my shoulders. "The night air is cold. Hot coffee feels good in my belly."

She poured her coffee in a blue speckled cup and handed it to me. She said, "I want to talk with you while we have our alone time. Tell me of your council."

I took the hot steaming cup to my lips and sipped through the steam rising before my eyes. I told Helen about what the council had learned and what had been decided. A smile filled her face as I told her the details and ended by saying, "By the next Ghost Face, we should be in a fine new house and not this mold-covered, dirt-floor cabin."

"*Ussen* blesses us, husband. My spirit has wings."

"I think you speak true, wife. We've waited three harvests for your body to ripen and become that of a grown woman ready to give us children. You're a beautiful grown woman. You work hard, and your kind beauty stirs me often with desire for you and your pleasures while we wait for you to become a strong grown woman. Now we expect a better, safer place to live without sickness and attacks by clouds of no-see-ems. I think we are ready for our first child. Do you share my mind?"

Her arms flew up, and she almost yelled but then kept her voice low as she laughed and said, "Hi yeh! *Ussen* is good to us. When you returned from council, I planned to beg you that we begin our family, that we share our pleasures and begin our first child."

I laughed with her. It was the happiest time we had shared since she became my woman. I had made her my woman once but treated her like a woman who had just had a child and planned to wait for three or four harvests before we shared our pleasures to make another. Just watching her every day had often stirred my desire for her, but I had waited. Now the time was upon us, and I was glad I had waited.

She set her basket work aside and stood in the light of the little twisting flames in her cooking firepit, painting her beauty in dark shadows and making her eyes glitter as she smiled down at me. She had to pull only two strings on her shift, and it fell at her feet before I could blink. She reached down and, taking my hand, pulled me up to her body's warmth and smell of crushed flowers as her nimble fingers opened the buttons of my shirt, and my desire for her grew strong and powerful. She whispered, "Come to my blankets, husband. My body yearns to have you. There is much for us to do."

# EIGHTEEN

## CHANGES COME

IRON WAGONS BROUGHT lumber to Mount Vernon within a moon after the council agreed to a new village on the big sand ridge. Rain or shine, we drove our wagons down to the iron-wagon stopping place at the bottom of the hill to unload the pungent, spicy-smelling lumber for our houses. With mule teams straining to pull the heavy wagonloads to the top of the ridge, we labored hard to off-load the lumber and stacked it by size in piles across the ridge where our houses were to stand. We had to be careful to stack the pieces with space between the boards so that air circulated and water didn't collect in the layers.

We were able to haul two wagonloads a sun. It was hard work, but I was glad to feel my body strain as I lifted the heavy wood timbers rather than let my arms and legs grow soft from sweeping leaves and twigs from around the commander's *casa* or chopping brush with a woman's axe. I was weary and dirty when I went home in the setting sun, but I always felt better after I bathed in water my women poured in a washing tub for me and then ate their fine meals. After eating, we often talked together for a while, drinking the last of the coffee. Nalthchedah was curious about what the new houses would look like and how they could be that different from the cabins in which we already lived. I could only shrug and tell them I didn't know. I hadn't seen a house built yet.

Every night, Helen and I took one of the cabin rooms for ourselves. Although I was weary and sleepy from my labor and my belly full of the night's meal, Helen kept learning new ways to pleasure us in the smoky darkness that made me want her more than the night before. She might be a young woman, but she had somehow learned the ways of older women with men. She was determined to have my child in her belly sooner rather than later, and I wanted her to have one.

IN THE SEASON of Little Eagles, two White Eyes who knew how to build houses, *Teniente* Wotherspoon called them "carpenters," came to Mount Vernon to build the first houses in the new ridge village. The *teniente* soon held a council for us to meet the carpenters and gave us White Eye names the carpenters could remember and pronounce. Since I was first to ask about learning how to build a house, he told the carpenters to call me "Alfred" even though the carpenters, strong, tough men who laughed often and enjoyed their work, had no trouble calling me Chato. The *teniente* also gave each of us a few carpenter tools. Some got squares, levels, folding measuring sticks, war clubs he called hammers, and wide-bladed saws with many fine teeth to make smooth, narrow cuts unlike the saws with big, coarse teeth we used for cutting logs when we made our log cabins. Others received only hammers and saws. To carry the tools, our wives made us bags out of old tent canvas *teniente* gave them.

We helped the carpenters build the first house. They showed us how to lay out the house shape with stake and string, use rocks for the foundation pillars, and measure and cut the floor timbers for the outline frame and cross timbers they called "joists" with our saws; where to hammer the right-sized nails to hold the outline frame and joists together; the right way to lay a floor; and how to frame the walls and roof. We often had sawing contests to see who could make the fastest cut. The carpenters watched and coached us on how to make a good straight cut with the least effort as if, in a frenzy, we were jerking the saws back and forth. Kaytennae often challenged me to sawing contests, and bets were made on who would win. Geronimo watched and cheered for all who challenged me. His bets were always against me and not for the skill of my opponent. Sometimes he won, sometimes he lost, and sometimes the contests ended without a winner for one reason or another. I more than held my own with Kaytennae, although I was about ten harvests older than him.

We finished and painted the outside of the first house, finished it inside, and even made a table and chairs and a bedframe for it and put in a new cook stove the *teniente* bought for each house. Those carpenters taught us all a lot. I could see how limited my understanding had been of building a good house even after building log cabins at Fort Apache and at Mount Vernon. After finishing the first house, the carpenters let teams of us start several houses at the same time while they watched and told us what to do to avoid mistakes or how to fix things when we made a mistake.

One sun after we had begun the second round of houses, I walked back to our cabins with the others who worked and learned how to build houses. It was the same sun-after-sun custom we'd followed when building the first house on the big sand ridge. As I neared my cabin, something didn't seem right. The women weren't there, but my washtub had warm water and, as usual, the canvas was across the breezeway openings to give us privacy when we bathed. I undressed and, standing in the tub, washed away the grime and stink on my body after my sun's labor. Several of the men had commented, and I laughed and agreed with them, that now that we did White Eye work, we stank like White Eyes. "Maybe," they said, "the White Eyes won't know we're Chiricahua anymore and will let us go."

But my mind said, *That'll be the day.*

I dressed, went in the cooking room in the cabin, and poured coffee heating on the fire with a bubbling pot of stew that had a good smell of beef, onions, and potatoes. I sat in the breezeway and watched the sun falling into the trees to send us the darkness of the night. In the dimming light, I saw Helen leading my women down the path to our cabin. They were singing the old welcoming song for men successfully returning from raiding or battle. The women came to the breezeway where I sat, stood in front of me, and sang another round of the welcoming song and then stopped. I didn't understand at all what was happening. Helen laughed at the frown of confusion on my face, took my hand, and said, "Come inside, husband. Your evening meal is ready. We have something to tell you."

I went to the cooking room with them and ate a fine evening meal. Nothing was said while we ate together and I waited to hear their news, the women knowingly glancing at each other and smiling. After we finished eating, they cleaned up around the cooking fire and washed the iron soldier plates from which we'd eaten the stew. As I sat with arms crossed, watching them and waiting to hear their news, Helen stood in front of the family's women and said, "This sun, my sisters and I visited my mothers' cabin. My birth mother performed a ceremony for me that has been in her family since the grandfathers. The ceremony tells for certain what I expected myself. Husband, I carry our first child. *Ussen* has blessed us with new life coming."

A smile filled my face, and all that sun's weariness left my body. Even Nalthchedah was smiling. It was a blessed day for living. I stood and hugged Helen and then the rest of my women. Truly, I thought, *Ussen* blesses us. There is joy even in the White Eye prisoner camps for the Chiricahua.

SOON AFTER WE learned to build houses, *Teniente* Wotherspoon called a council of the men working on the houses. After we smoked, he spoke to us through George Wratten. "The big chief in the city of the Great Father thinks the Chiricahua would make fine Blue Coat soldiers. He first wants to start Company I of the Twelfth Infantry, which will be manned only by Apache soldiers. He wants you to have the same pay, to train and work just like White Eye soldiers, and to be given Blue Coat uniforms, guns, bullets, and other necessary supplies—and live together in a big house you will build called a 'barracks.' Some of you will continue building houses on the big ridge, while others will build the barracks. You will be able to enjoy weekends with your families. If there are not enough here to make a complete company, then we will take volunteer soldiers from San Carlos, maybe even some of the older boys at Carlisle, to join with you who volunteer here. I will be your first commander. You'll learn to read White Eye tracks on paper and to speak the tongue of the White Eyes, to count with their numbers, how to march and respond to drill commands. You'll learn to"—here, he smiled and we all laughed—"follow trails White Eye style, fight your enemy man-to-man, accurately shoot your weapons, and attack on command.

"In about a moon, if you decide you want to serve as a soldier, you will be asked to touch the pen for your name signing to a paper that says you agree to be in the Army for three years, you will follow all commands from those of higher rank, and you swear allegiance to the United States. Are there questions?"

We all sat staring at *Teniente* Wotherspoon in disbelief. How could we be prisoners and at the same time be members of the Blue Coat Army that held us captive?

Geronimo spoke. "If we are given our reservation away from this place, will the soldiers still have to be soldiers for their entire three years and serve where their comandante says?"

The *teniente* said, "Yes, they will still be soldiers assigned here unless the commander sends them elsewhere."

Kaytennae said, "We will each have our own rifles and pistols and bullets?"

"Yes. You'll be responsible for keeping them cleaned and oiled. But just as for all soldiers, they'll be kept locked in the barracks until the commander tells you to take them as part of an assignment."

Perico asked, "Will we be able to see our wives whenever we want?"

"No. You can visit your families only after your commander gives you a pass that says when you can go and for how long you can stay."

Our questions went on for a time but then stopped. We needed time to think about becoming Blue Coats. *Teniente* closed the council by telling us to decide what we wanted to do and to tell him in a few days. With our count, he knew how many outsiders from San Carlos or grown children from Carlisle he needed to bring to Mount Vernon to make a full company of soldiers.

BY THE TIME I returned to my women, I had decided that I would touch the pen and become a Blue Coat. The thought of having a rifle in my hands again and being paid money, as much as a Blue Coat soldier made, meaning my family could have nice things, was overpowering. My only worry was Helen thinking I was abandoning her and our child to become a Blue Coat.

That night as we sat together, I told her about the council and my thinking. Her eyes widened in the flickering firelight. "You want to become a Blue Coat? Before the Ghost Face comes, our child will come to us. You will not be here for his birth unless your chief says you can come."

"I do this because I want to feel a rifle in my hands once more. I want to feel like a warrior again. I do this because I can make money like a White Eye soldier. I'll have enough to give you and our baby good things and keep the other women comfortable."

She leaned forward, staring at the flames, her arms wrapped around her knees. At last, she puffed her cheeks and blew. "In the days of raids and battle, chiefs and warriors might be gone for two or three moons and go far. Who knew what enemies they might face or even if they returned alive? Their women had their babies and began the child's first suns without their men being nearby. It is the way of our People. You may not be with me, but you won't be far when our baby comes. You should be a Blue Coat if that's what you want. I will not complain. I want what my husband thinks is best."

I drew her to me and hugged her, *I'm a lucky man. This is a fine woman.*

# NINETEEN

## BLUE COAT

A FEW SUNS before touching the pen to join the Blue Coats, Naiche and I were in the same group building a house on the ridge where the new village grew. We had been working hard all that morning, putting up a couple of walls, and now decided to take a little rest and sat down in the shaded tall grass near the back of the house.

Leaning back on his elbows, Naiche glanced at me. "Chato, you become a Blue Coat? Ha-o-zinne tells me your woman has your first child in her belly. You join Blue Coats? You might not be here when the baby comes. What you do then?"

I picked the stem of a piece of grass to chew on and nodded. "Yes, Helen carries our first child, but I join the Blue Coats. Maybe so I won't be close when the child comes, but I come as soon as I can. You join Blue Coats?"

He shrugged. "Probably not. I have two wives and in-laws, Ha-o-zinne's People, and a tribe of children less than twelve harvests to look after. Why did you decide to join the Blue Coats when Helen might have your baby and you might not be here?"

"Hmmph. Helen and me, we talk about this. She says Apache women had babies all the time when their men were off on long raids or in wars. She has her mothers and my other women to help her. Men don't help women having babies unless no women there. She says I should join the Blue Coats if I want. I want. I want to feel like a man again, one who has weapons and can fight, even if it means I am a warrior for the Blue Coats. I want to feel the wood and steel of a rifle or revolver in my hands. I want to learn White Eye secrets in reading tracks on paper and speak better the White Eye tongue. You see how much we learn from the White Eyes building these houses. Yes, I'll touch the pen to join Blue Coats."

Naiche made a little frown and nodded. "Chato speaks wise words. He has a good woman."

IN THE MOON the White Eyes called "May," forty-six Chiricahua from the Mount Vernon Apache Village and eighteen Tonto, eleven San Carlos, and one Coyotero from San Carlos Reservation touched the pen to sign the paper that said they were Blue Coats. Company I of the Twelfth Infantry was born. My good friend Naiche and I were among of them, but Geronimo and twenty-eight men, most too old to join the Blue Coats and teenage boys old enough to use weapons, were not.

The same day Naiche and I talked, *Teniente* Wotherspoon and George Wratten went to the children's school. They asked to speak with Geronimo, and the teacher lady, Miss Shepard, told him the class would be fine if he left for a while. He put aside his children's discipline stick and went with the *teniente* and Wratten to sit in the shade under some trees not far from the school room. My sister Banatsi was with a group of women nearby, sewing on clothes in the bright sunlight, where it was easy to see the fine thread and needles work their magic to hold the cloth together. The women later claimed they heard every word that passed between *Teniente* and Geronimo. Banatsi told us about what she'd heard after our evening meal, and I had no reason to doubt her words.

She said, "*Teniente*, Geronimo, and George Wratten came from the school and found a shady place near where the women worked."

I knew *Teniente* must have wanted this conversation kept private, but he ignored the women who were working nearby as if they didn't exist. He had good eyes with much light behind them, but sometimes he didn't use either his eyes or his light.

Banatsi continued, "*Teniente* said, 'Geronimo, I have important work for you. If you take this work, you won't have time to join the Blue Coats because you'll be a village leader.'

"Geronimo frowned and raised an eyebrow in question. He expected to become a Blue Coat soldier. 'What you mean 'important work,' *Teniente*?'

"'I want you to be the judge, or as the White Eyes might say, the 'justice of the peace,' in your village. A judge is someone who hears both sides of an argument, decides what the truth is, and, if rules are broken, decides who will be punished and how.'

"Geronimo said, 'Hmmph. I never see a judge work before. I wouldn't know how to act.'

"'There is a White Eye justice of the peace holding court in Mount Vernon tomorrow. I'll ask George Wratten to take you down there so you can watch what's going on, and he'll tell you what's being said. Will you be a judge?'

"Geronimo studied the *teniente* and George Wratten for a moment and said, 'Next sun, I go watch judge with George Wratten. If I think I can do, I be judge.'"

I shook my head when Banatsi finished her story. Naiche and I laughed. We believed *Teniente* didn't want Geronimo, whom the White Eyes considered too old to be a soldier but in better physical condition than nearly any of the Whites Eye soldiers, stirring things up as a Blue Coat. Geronimo must have liked what he saw at the justice-of-the-peace court because he didn't touch the pen on the day the Chiricahua chose to become Blue Coats. *Teniente* Wotherspoon was a smart man to find Geronimo an important job that stopped him from becoming a Blue Coat troublemaker.

THE FIRST THING the Blue Coat sergeants began teaching us in our training was how to take care of our weapons and other things given to soldiers. They made sure we understood there was only one way to take care of our equipment, and that was their way. A man the sergeants called "barber" came. He cut our hair to make it look like that of White Eye soldiers, our ears showing and what hair was left combed away from our faces. On our first day, we set up big four-man tents inside the brick wall that surrounded the soldier buildings, and we were shown where to bathe and eat our meals together and places to do our personal business, which they called "latrines" like we'd found at Fort Marion.

During the days that followed, we all spent time learning how to dress like the sergeants wanted, march Blue Coat style, and respond to commands for changing the march direction as a group or for holding our rifles differently on command. The Blue Coat sergeants called these times "drills." I knew some of these commands after serving *Teniente* Davis as a first sergeant of scouts at Fort Apache, but there were many others I didn't know and was glad to learn them.

The first moon as soldiers, we drilled every day in our uniforms and began learning how to read tracks on paper before we changed into work clothes and broke into groups for building our barracks and continuing to work on the new village houses. *Teniente* received approval to build our barracks outside the brick wall close to where our houses were. He said that if the barracks and our houses were close together, then it was reasonable to let some of us live in the houses with our wives while others spent time in the barracks. When Helen heard this, her belly had started to show a bump. My living at our house with her made all my women very happy.

In two moons, we had drilled enough that we could join the White Eye Blue Coats stationed at Mount Vernon in drills that involved more than one company of soldiers. *Teniente* Wotherspoon told his sergeants he liked what he saw, and he wanted to promote some of the better soldiers to a higher rank so we would have our own commanders. All the chiefs were suggested for promotion to corporal, but Mangas and I refused. We knew what it was like to be responsible for men and didn't want the burden. Naiche served for a while as a corporal and decided being a Blue Coat *comandante* was not for him either and became a private again. Fun was promoted to corporal, and Toclanny, who had always been close to the Blue Coats as a scout, was promoted to sergeant.

When I said to Naiche, "Why didn't you want to be corporal?" he answered, "Once, I was a chief. I made my own judgments about what the warriors should do. When I told them to go to a place, it was because I had decided it was the best thing to do. If I made a mistake, it was on me. As a Blue Coat commander, I just relay orders from a higher chief to the men for whom I'm responsible. Sometimes the command is right, sometimes wrong. When I see it's a bad choice to follow a command, I'm responsible even though it wasn't what I would have done. I don't like commanding this way and won't do it."

I nodded I understood and said, *"Doo dat'éé da."*

IN THE SEASON of Large Fruit, our houses on the sand ridge were finished inside and out and had a cooking stove with a bed and table and chairs ready for use. We used wagons to carry our things to the houses that had been assigned to us. My women often walked over to the ridge to watch us building the houses and the barracks. They knew what to expect from the house when we started living in it and had talked often about how they wanted to decorate their house inside. When we moved, I drove the wagon, but the women wanted to walk.

We didn't have much, and the women soon had the wagon unloaded. Nalthchedah, Banatsi, and Maud lived on one side of the house. Helen and I lived on the other side. With floors and furniture and a cooking stove, we were far more comfortable than we had been down in the low place with dirt-floor log cabins and swarms of no-see-ems. The women decorated the house walls with baskets, blankets, and even bows and arrows I had made to sell to tourists.

Since Helen was carrying our first child, *Teniente* Wotherspoon had no reluctance in allowing me to live in our new house if I reported to the proper sergeant, place, and time for duty. We had grown used to hearing the Blue Coat horns sounding to tell soldiers when to do just about everything. After becoming a Blue Coat, we had to learn the meaning of the different calls, and since our houses were close to the barracks, it was easy to hear the horns from our houses for when to leave for duty and drills.

A MOON AFTER we moved, I was sitting on the steps of our house, listening to the night noises of tree peepers, insects, and loud bullfrogs on the little creek below us. Helen was visiting with her sisters on the other side of the house. I heard the creak of saddle leather and an occasional jingle of riding gear coming toward me. I stared into the darkness, wondering who it was and why someone would be riding a horse in the dark here among our houses. The fingernail moon gave just enough light to see the rider coming toward me. I felt for the knife in my boot, left my hand just above the boot shaft, and waited. The horse and rider came within a couple of paces of where I sat and stopped. I recognized *Teniente* Wotherspoon in the cool darkness.

He grinned and nodded as I stood and saluted as I had been trained to do for any officer. He saluted back and said, "At ease, Private Chato, this is an informal visit, one I prefer you say nothing about. Is there someplace we can talk privately?"

I pointed my nose toward a big pine tree in dark shadows about twenty paces away. "Yes, sir. No one see us talking there."

He nodded and dismounted to lead his horse as he followed me into the shadows. We sat side by side and leaned our backs against the tree's ruffled bark. He made a cigarette, and we smoked.

After crushing the last bit of burning *tobaho* with his boot heel, he said, "Chato, I have a problem I want you and a few others to help me solve. Are you interested?"

"Speak, *Teniente*. I listen."

"As you know, I've made Geronimo the justice of the peace for your village here. Most of the cases he's heard have to do with drinking whiskey. After you Apache drink a little whiskey, you seem to lose your minds fighting, arguing, destroying store property, passing out to lie snoring in the middle of the street, and wasting your money when you buy it. Where does this whiskey come from?"

I shrugged my shoulders and started to speak, but he held up his hand and said, "I know. It comes from two places. White Eye store and saloon keepers sell it to anyone who has the money. I have a local lawman named Baker who's on the case, and I expect he will make arrests soon. If we can put one of those fools in the calaboose for a few years, whiskey sales from stores will stop in a hurry. The other sources of whiskey are the bootleggers who have stills hidden on their farms. Believe me, it's bad water and can make you go blind and crazy even if you drink only a little."

I nodded. I knew everything the *teniente* said was true. I personally knew where three of the whiskey-making places were in the woods and swamps just outside the post boundary. And I had known men who disappeared into the swamps after drinking it.

*Teniente* Wotherspoon crossed his arms and didn't take his eyes off me. "I believe that if we can get rid of the whiskey makers around us, there'll be far fewer drunk Apache. That's where you come in. I want to put together a group of four or five of your warriors in the Army, find the places where the whiskey is made, and destroy the whiskey and the still that makes it. I know you don't drink, or if you do, it's not much. For the warriors, I was thinking Naiche, To-clanny, Martine, Noche, and you would be a good group. I'd try to send you out one night a week to find a still and destroy it with dynamite. If somebody shoots at you, you can shoot back. What's being done is highly illegal, so no one will be interested in bringing in the law to catch who did it. I'll give you all the explosives you'll need to blow those places to hell and gone. Toclanny will be a sergeant soon. I'll ask him to lead the raids. What do you think? Will you be one of whiskey raiders, Chato?"

I thought about it for a few breaths. It would be very good to go on a raid again with my brothers while being paid to do it.

"*Sí, Teniente.* I be whiskey raider."

# TWENTY

## WHISKEY RAIDS

THE MOON, BIG and yellow, just above the northeastern horizon, cast its cold light through the twisted black outlines and shadows of oaks and tall pines. The air was still and growing cold. We lay in the shadows on the moist, pliant ground among bushes and little thumb-diameter saplings surrounding a high place in the swampy woods. Following *Teniente*'s orders, Toclanny had led us running and wading across four miles of the woods until we reached this high place, where we took cover and waited for the sun to disappear.

There were five of us, *Teniente* Wotherspoon, Toclanny, Naiche, Noche, and me. We were scouting for a whiskey still *Teniente* Wotherspoon believed supplied whiskey directly to two or three store owners in Mount Vernon who sold or traded bottles of it to our People. He had seen a sharecropper wagon with a big load of sugar headed out of Mount Vernon earlier that day and had asked us to track through the woods to the place where he thought the sugar was being used to make whiskey. He told Toclanny that if we had the opportunity to destroy the still, we'd for sure do it, but we first had to ensure that's what it was.

Just when the moon began casting a bright glow in the dark night sky as it climbed toward the horizon's edge, we heard the creak and clink of harness, the occasional squeak of a wheel on a dry wagon axle, and men talking and laughing in low muffled voices. We could see the dim outline of men as their wagon pulled to the center of the high place and stopped as they began jumping off the wagon's load of sacks.

I counted four men. Two disappeared in the darkness on the other side of the wagon, and one unhitched the mules to tie them on a tree, where they nibbled at brush but were soon munching grain out of feedbags. The fourth man began unloading the sacks and stacking them on the other side of the wagon. Soon came sounds of an axe and the puff of a man splitting wood for kindling. A fire was lighted in a firepit ready to gobble up split wood.

As the fire grew larger and brighter, we could see an old White Eye sitting on a log near the fire, puffing on a bent stem pipe. He wore what the local farmers wore, canvas pants held up with straps across the shoulders they called "overalls." A straw hat that looked torn or cut in a couple of places on the brim covered his head, and a shotgun was lying across his knees. Even with the hat shadowing most of his face, I could tell he had white hair, a long drooping bush of gray hair under his nose, and splotches of short gray hair growing on his cheeks. I thought, *If you were in the Army, your sergeant would make you shave every day.*

The other men with him wore overalls and chewed-up straw hats too, but their skin tones ranged from dark brown to shadow black, and while they did all the work, they seemed to enjoy it. As the fire grew larger and spread its circle of light, I could see off to one side barrels around a mechanical contraption on top of a big pot. One of the men built a fire under the pot. A long pipe making many circles ran out of the pot's top, over to a big clear jug. Other barrels nearby seemed to hold other liquids or mixes of grain and liquid that made a kind of strong smell. The brush on the high place made it hard to see the barrels and mechanical stuff until you almost stumbled over it.

After the fires were lit and a mix of stuff in the barrels was poured in the mechanical contraption along with a couple of bags of sugar in the other barrels, the men gathered around the fire to warm themselves and talk about crops and farming.

One of the dark men said, "Mista Jordan, what you planning to plant for yo' crops come spring?"

The old White Eye spat in the fire. "I ain't rightly figured it out yet, Mose. It shore as hell ain't gonna be no cotton. Can't make no whiskey and not much money with cotton. S'pec it'll be corn or barley. Got any idees about what you want to plant?"

Mose grinned. His bright-white teeth seemed to glow in the dark as the moon rose higher. "Well, suh, I thinks it oughta be corn. It makes some mighty strong 'shine that them injins over to the barracks got a powaful hankering fer. Mista Richardson over at the sto' said the Army tryin' mighty hard to stop folks from selling their good whiskey to them 'paches. If'n we can't make whiskey with our corn no mo', then we'n always sell it on at the market and keep it in cribs for stock and shelled for home use like we usually do."

I could see what looked like steam starting to blow out the end of the long curly tube and a steady trickle of clear liquid, which I thought was water, begin to empty into the jug under the end of the tube. The moon, only half full, was rising higher. There was enough light on the scene to show a real whiskey-making operation with nearby barrels, buckets, and several big clear jugs standing ready for use.

The old White Eye shook his head and knocked the ashes out of his pipe. "Ol' Richardson ain't gotta brain in his head. For the money he's a making off this 'shine, he'n afford to take a risk or two. We shore as hell ain't workin' our tails out here in the swamps fer nothin'. We'n sell to other fools or sell it our own selves. I know how to do it. We gonna make our money, boys, one way or the other."

The men standing around the old White Eye nodded, saying, "Yas, suh, yas, suh. That right, Mista Jordon."

The old White Eye said, "Reckon that settles it, Mose. We'll plant corn come next season. I'll order the seed in the next day or two. I got some left in the crib we'n use for seed. You got any?"

Mose shook his head. "No, suh. I barely got enough to feed my animals and family through the winter."

"Well if you need any, let me know. I can always put it up against yore share next crop."

Mose grinned. "Thas mighty generous, Mista Jordon, but I think we be awl right for now."

Jordon grinned, showing ugly, yellow, stained teeth, and said, "That's good, Mose. Okay, boys, let's get a little whiskey bottled outta our last barrel and—"

A voice out of the darkness made all the men jerk with surprise and Jordon throw up his shotgun as *Teniente* Wotherspoon said, "No need to do that, Mister Jordon. It would be very good for your health if you dropped that old twelve-gauge. This still is about to be put out of business. We represent the United States Army."

There were four loud, unmistakable metallic snaps as we all cocked our rifles. Mr. Jordon laid his shotgun down against the log and raised his hands. "No need to git carried away here. We's just making a little to sip at home this winter, that's all."

Toclanny walked into the circle of light, his rifle cocked and aimed at Mr.

Jordon. The men with dark faces were trembling and looked like they were ready to run.

From the shadows, *Teniente* said, "This isn't an arrest, Jordon. You all just need to take it easy. I don't suspect you'll want to say anything to anybody about what happens here. My boys are going to wipe out your operation. No more whiskey making and selling it to the Apache for all the money they earn. I catch you making it again, I'll put you all in the calaboose for a long time. You boys understand?"

They all nodded while the old White Eye frowned a mean scowl.

*Teniente* said, "You boys hook up your team. Take Mister Jordon with you and get out of here. Jordon, you can get that old scatter gun at the post gate if you still want it. Now get out of here."

Mose said, "Yas, suh, we's a going, and we ain't makin' no mo' whiskey. No, suh, we sho ain't, is we, Mista Jordon?"

"Aw, shut up, Mose. Let's just git on home. I'll be coming fer my shotgun and maybe yore hide, Mista."

*Teniente* nodded and grinned as the men ran to bring the mules to the wagon. It was the fastest harnessing job I'd ever seen. Mose soon had the mules smartly trotting down the trail ruts through the woods the way they had come.

We had all been trained in the use of dynamite and had enough in our little packs along with simple fuses to turn everything in that whiskey still into smoke and little pieces of wood and metal falling out of the sky. We placed it like the *teniente* wanted, made long slow-burning fuses, and left running back along the same path we had come. It wasn't long before there was a bright flash of orange light and then a boom like angry thunder. The trees and bushes around us shook and then were still, and we heard what sounded like the patter of rain on the water where we waded, but it was the pieces of the whiskey still that was no more.

THE MOON WAS falling into the western horizon when we returned to our new village houses. I hadn't felt so good in a long time. Raiding and making war was what a man was meant to do. Even if I had to take Blue Coat pay and training to do it, it was worth it.

I eased open the house door, left my equipment on the eating table, and used a bowl and pitcher of water to wash up just like a White Eye. I feared I'd wake Helen. She was due to birth our child anytime, and her belly was stretched into a big ball that made it very uncomfortable for her to sleep. I pulled off my boots and shirt and went to our bed to lie down beside her.

Helen wasn't in the bed. I looked on the other side of the house and none of the other women were there either. I knew that her time must have come and that they had probably taken her to the White Eye *di-yen* at his place where sick people were given medicine. We had talked about her having the baby here in our house but decided the White Eye *di-yen* had much power. If she needed his medicine, then he would be there quickly to help her along with the women from our families.

I dressed in fresh clothes and ran down the tree-shadowed trail to the main gate and hospital. The sky was turning gray, and stars on the horizon were fading. Dawn was coming. As I ran, I prayed to *Ussen* that my fine young woman would be safe bringing our child into this world.

Lantern lights shone in a back room near the place the *di-yen* worked. When I reached the building, I walked fast through the door for the lighted room. A young man who helped the *di-yen* appeared in front of me as if by magic. He held up his hands for me to stop. He said, "Are you sick? Can I help you?"

"I Chato. Look for wife. Maybe she has baby."

The young man grinned. "Congratulations, Mister Chato. You have a strong new son. She's fine and right yonder in that room with the baby and your other ladies."

"*Gracias, amigo.*"

I brushed past him, my heart pounding in the hope the words he spoke were true.

The door to the room had a golden glow, and I stuck my head through the doorway to see my women and the *di-yen* as they spoke to Helen, her hair wet with sweat and past strain showing on her face. She held a white blanket–covered bundle to her breast. She saw me in the doorway and, smiling, said, "Husband, you come. You have a new son. He is a strong one and healthy."

The women and *di-yen* turned to see me, and all looked very happy. The *di-yen* said, "Congratulations, Mister Chato, your wife and son are fine."

I bowed my head. "Truly, *Ussen* blesses us."

# TWENTY-ONE

## THE DEATH OF FUN

THERE WERE GOOD suns that harvest in the season of Earth Is Reddish Brown. Helen with the baby in her arms walked through splashes of golden sunlight, and the other women in both families came back to the house singing a happy song like they sang for returning warriors in the long-ago days.

Helen, after resting in our bed, was up making an evening meal and then nursing the baby. He was a fine-looking child, and we were very proud of him. We gave him a White Eye name, Maurice, which we both liked. The name seemed to roll off our tongues and make a sound like wind passing through high grass on the edge of swampy ponds of water. Helen's mother, Bashdelehi, always smiling around her new grandchild, had already made a *tsach* (cradle-board) for him using special woods and yucca sticks George Wratten had given us. His Apache friends at Fort Apache and San Carlos had sent them to him for his child's *tsach*, with enough extra for maybe two or three others.

Wratten had married a young Chiricahua woman named Nahgoyyahkizen (which means "kids romping and kicking"), who was an orphan and niece of my friends Lot Eyelash and Binday. The White Eye school teachers had let her sit in on the men's classes to learn to speak the White Eye tongue and to read and make tracks on paper. Many in the village thought it was scandalous that a young woman associated with a group of men, but they never commented openly. Wratten did some interpreting for the teachers during the class and saw that the girl was quick, with light behind her eyes, and that the teachers were very impressed with how fast she learned their lessons. Wratten must have been impressed with her too, and she with him. They soon married. She took the White Eye name Annie White. Wratten was quick to give her their first child. She and Helen expected their babies at about the same time. Their first child, a good-looking baby girl they named Amy White, came early in the moon the White Eyes called "October." Our son was born a moon later.

*Teniente* Wotherspoon continued teaching us and training us in Blue Coat customs and ways of fighting and playing ball games like baseball and football. We learned much, but we also taught the White Eye Blue Coat sergeants a thing or two when we trained using pretend wars and skirmishes. In the time of the Ghost Face, *Teniente* Wotherspoon took his whiskey raiders and destroyed two more whiskey stills with dynamite. One place had so many barrels *Teniente* thought it must make half of the whiskey sold in the country around Mount Vernon.

PROBABLY THE BEST Chiricahua soldier among us was young *llt'i' bil'ik halii* (which means "smoke comes out"), who had become a Chiricahua hero while fighting the Mexicans at Aliso Creek. The White Eyes had named him Fun because they couldn't get their tongues around his Apache name. *Teniente* Wotherspoon was so impressed with the light behind Fun's eyes, his leaving whiskey alone, and how well and fast he developed as a Blue Coat that he promoted him to corporal.

Fun had a good wife, an older woman, and a couple of children with her, but he was smitten by a beautiful young woman and decided he had to have a second wife to help give his family more children. She was even more a girl than Helen had been when I married her and still had to learn her manners around her husband rather than treat him as a brother. One day, she spoke disrespectfully to Fun. He told me later that it was only the latest in several times it had happened and that he had already beaten her once. *Teniente* learned what had happened and told him not to let it happen again. But again, Fun lost his patience with her, grabbed a fancy walking stick carved for tourists Geronimo had given him, and gave her a good beating. She had some ugly bruises on her face and arms from that beating, but nothing was broken. *Teniente* Wotherspoon learned about it, had the White Eye *di-yen* look her over, and was very angry after the *di-yen* told him what he'd found.

*Teniente* had Fun in his office for over a hand above the horizon—or as the White Eyes say, "an hour"—and warned him that if it ever happened again, he would be kicked out of the Blue Coats and spend some time in the calaboose. Fun and his young wife got along well for about two moons after that until George Wratten, who supervised the men who hadn't joined the Army, noticed how depressed and sullen Fun had become. He learned Fun believed that his wife was having "undue intimacy" with two men. Wratten talked with them in his office and learned the problem. He told *Teniente* Wotherspoon, who investigated and found no evidence anywhere or from anyone that Fun's wife had been unfaithful to him. Wratten talked to them again and showed Fun *Teniente* Wotherspoon's investigation results, which Fun accepted, but he soon believed again his wife was unfaithful. Wratten asked Geronimo to council with them. Geronimo talked with them for two hours that evening. Again, they seemed to reconcile.

The Blue Coat big chief let companies of soldiers demonstrate their fitness by marching a hundred miles as a ten-day training exercise. *Teniente* Wotherspoon was very proud of his command, Company I, and asked the big chief to let us demonstrate our fitness with a hundred-mile march. We expected that we could march a hundred miles in a day and night if we had to, but *Teniente* asked for ten days and was given permission to make the march with Company I. He planned to march us to Mobile, camp, give us a day or two of leave to spend our pay and see the sights, demonstrate our drill capability to the people of Mobile, and then march back to Mount Vernon using a different route.

In preparation for the hundred-mile march, we took several long one-day marches that covered as much as forty miles and found the long marches nothing compared to what we often did when we were running wild and free. As the days counted down to our march to Mobile, we cleaned and oiled our equipment, and it was inspected by the sergeants at least twice. Our tents, rations, cooking supplies, and tools we might need in training exercises along the way would be carried in a wagon, pulled by a four-mule team, and driven by a White Eye soldier assigned to the Mount Vernon quartermaster.

Helen was a good mother and had all the help from both families' women she could possibly want or need. When we had our evening meal together, she kept the baby in its carrier while we ate and talked about the day. A favorite subject of gossip among the women, and one Helen often mentioned at our evening meal, was Fun, his wife, and the seeming tension between them. Fun had not beaten her since an angry *Teniente* Wotherspoon had warned him not to do that again if he didn't want a court martial and time in the calaboose. She had walked a narrow line doing everything she knew to do to avoid even looking at other men for any reason. At the same time, she had her pride and walked erect with her chin up and kept their house spotless. Still, Fun was not happy with her.

I asked Helen, during one of our evening talks, what she would do if I acted like Fun with her. She didn't hesitate to answer. "I'd pack my things, take my child, and go to my mothers' house. I would not be your woman anymore."

I crossed my arms and smiled. "Helen is a wise woman."

She laughed. "I've made a few good choices in my life. One of them was to be your woman."

THREE DAYS BEFORE we were to begin the march to Mobile and back, Fun's mind fell into a deep black hole. It happened the next sun after Geronimo had counseled Fun and his wife. That sun, Fun acted normal. We all watched one instructor show us how to make sure water didn't make us sick. Fun supervised men at target practice and, as corporal of the guard, took his turn at guard duty at the village gate. He sat in the company guardhouse doorway watching his house while he cleaned his rifle. Then he continued the rest of the day staring at his house.

The sun fell behind the western hills. As darkness grew and stars began to show, Fun picked up his rifle, loaded it, and walked to his house. He found his wife sitting on the floor and, without a word, shot her. Its noise crashed like a thunder arrow through the village houses. An old woman nearby ran inside and, yelling and screaming, attempted to jerk the rifle out of his hands. He shoved her away, telling her that if she didn't leave quickly, he'd kill her too. He put the end of the rifle barrel to his head and fired. The shot blew his hat off but barely grazed his head, not even enough to stun him. With the old woman screaming at him and begging him to stop, he calmly reloaded, put the barrel behind his ear and fired again, blowing half his head away.

A few men ran to the door, saw the scene inside the house, and started demanding revenge. When I saw what was happening, I ran from house to house, telling those inside to hide anything that might be used for a weapon and to stay inside. The men demanding revenge, from whom I had no idea, soon cooled their anger without access to weapons. Officers with soldiers ran fast to the house and talked to anyone who had seen anything. By the time officers finished asking their questions and making tracks on paper, the only sounds in the village were the wails of women related to Fun.

Fun's wife suffered a little wound not amounting to much. The White Eye *di-yen* bandaged her up and kept her in his "hospital" a few suns before sending her home to her parents. All thoughts of revenge against her had disappeared.

Geronimo had let it be known that he had spoken with Fun and his wife the night before Fun tried to murder her and then killed himself. From his talks in counseling them, he was convinced their problem was in Fun's mind and not from any intimacies she might have had with other men.

Wratten had been wise to ask Geronimo to counsel with Fun and his wife. After the People learned his opinion, they held nothing against Fun's wife, and she lived peacefully among us.

# TWENTY-TWO

## THE HUNDRED-MILE MARCH TO MOBILE

TWO DAYS AFTER Fun was buried, I told my women I would see them when the soldiers returned from their march to Mobile and back. The sun was two hands above the horizon and cast shafts of brilliant white light through the tops of trees. Jays and mockingbirds were squawking, insects and frogs were tuning up for their morning songs, and crows were cawing as they left their trees and headed to brush along open water in the swamps to the east.

Three White Eye officers, three White Eye sergeants, four Apache corporals, two Apache buglers, and sixty-five Apache privates (four privates were sick in the hospital) marched out of our village at Mount Vernon in two columns, followed by the supply wagon. We each carried blankets, a canteen, a haversack, a field belt, an entrenching tool, and a rifle, which was loaded with blank cartridges. In my column, I marched behind Naiche and Toclanny, and Kaytennae and Noche were behind me.

We followed the iron-wagon tracks toward Mobile. The wagon stayed on the wagon road while we marched in a zigzag path from the road across the iron-wagon iron road, into the woods and swamps, and back to the wagon road. Three hands before the sunset, we stopped to camp near a place called Gunnison Creek, where the water was fresh and smelled clean, the grass tall and thick. One of the sergeants bought a goat from a farmer, and we had fresh roasted meat with our usual field rations of hardtack, dried beef, potatoes, and coffee.

THE BUGLERS, SAM Haozous and James Nicholas, blew their horns two hands before sunup, telling us to eat and get ready to march through the wisps of fog floating off the creek. We were on the march crossing Gunnison Creek by the time the sun lay on the horizon. We again zigzagged across the iron road three times and passed through swamps, walking single file on logs we cut and laid end to end. The columns often changed the rear guard to practice protecting the rear as the column marched. It was good training for us to learn how to cross swamps while men guarded our rear. I learned much on this march.

When the sun was halfway to the time of no shadows, *Teniente* turned toward Mobile and met the wagon with our supplies on what I heard a sergeant call the "Sawdust Road." We were marching at a good pace and feeling the strength flowing again in our legs. Soon we were passing little houses, almost like the log-cabin shacks we had once had to build and live in, sitting close to the edge of the road. Women and children, white and black, quiet and staring, sat in their house breezeways and watched us march by. Soon there were fine, great white *haciendas* fronted by big porches with roofs supported by tall, fluted columns and green yards with many varieties of flower beds, the grass all the same height, each porch filled with chairs for ladies dressed in their finest and using their little soldier glasses on a stick to study us as we marched by. The road grew wider and harder and was covered with a kind of caliche that let wagons roll at good speed past big brick buildings with wide, tall windows showing things the store offered. Wide streets crossed the one we were on. We saw more big buildings—some were stores, and others had huge, wide doors open like big barns and were used to hold materials wagons brought or carried away. *Teniente* wanted to show us off, and we wanted to show off our marching skills. Sergeants shouted commands for what they called the "manual of arms," which dictated how we held or shouldered our rifles and wheeled and turned as if one man marched to resume our first formation.

Crowds gathering to watch us gave us a sense of pride that made us march tall and straight with our chests out. I thought, *We're not prisoners anymore. We're part of the Americans, part of their warriors.* I felt good. We marched for three miles from the center of the big brick buildings to a place the Americans called "Frascati Park" near the big water. The *teniente* planned for us to camp there under the great moss-covered trees and short green grass. When the tent and supply wagon arrived, we were quick to set up our tents and then ready to eat. Some in the crowds had followed us there along with a few wagons and watched us work. A few of the men went to the beach to collect driftwood for fires, and soon our midday meal was being made.

We set up a big tent for the *teniente* as his place of command. He and his officers had invited many important White Eyes, men and women, to a mid-sun fiesta and to see his soldiers in action. That afternoon, after we'd eaten the meal and the paymaster had given us our month's wages, we were given passes so we could leave camp and see the sights around Mobile. We had to be back by eleven and were given strict orders not to buy or drink any whiskey even if it was offered to us free. We were warned that we could be put in the calaboose for a long time if we were caught drinking or getting drunk. *Teniente* Wotherspoon and his officers begged his mid-sun fiesta *amigos* not to sell or give us any whiskey. His guests promised not to give us any alcoholic drink and to tell people they knew to keep alcohol away from us.

Before going into town, we washed up and put on our dress uniforms that had been packed safely in the wagon. I went to town with Naiche, Kaytennae, and Toclanny. We walked down wide streets in cool shade provided by massive trees in great green grass yards like we had seen before when we had marched down Sawdust Road, into town from the other direction. A warm breeze drifted off the big water and kept the afternoon comfortable and pleasant.

Once in town, we saw many things in the store windows. I looked at jewelry for my women and a leather-covered baseball for Maurice for when he started to walk and play with other children. There were so many stores that I decided to look in the windows of as many as possible and then, next sun, buy the pieces I liked best. I bought some *tobaho* and cigarette papers for myself, and the men with me did the same. Naiche decided to buy his gifts the next sun also, but Toclanny and Kaytennae bought their gifts as soon as they found them.

We walked down many streets and looked in many windows. As the sun was setting, we had hunger and decided to eat in a place called "Bayside Diner." It served big plates of food, including beef, potatoes, vegetables, baked bread, many varieties of fish (which we wouldn't eat), and sweet cakes and pies. I was glad the Blue Coats had taught us how to use a knife and fork to eat our food, at least we didn't appear unlearned about White Eye ways of eating to others at nearby tables. I still preferred to eat with my knife and fingers but was comfortable using a knife and fork. The beef we ate was overcooked for my taste but still very tasty. I liked the potatoes that had been mashed up and covered with something that was a mixture of beef grease and flour—I remembered Helen had told me the White Eyes called "gravy." When the other people there realized we were Apache soldiers, they stopped eating and watched us eat for a while. After they decided we wouldn't kill anyone and were eating normally like everyone else, they lost interest in us and returned to eating their meals.

We finished eating and told the one who had brought our food we were ready to pay. He disappeared into the kitchen. Soon a big fat man wearing a white cloth tied over his clothes and splattered with stains from food being prepared came waddling out of the kitchen door and headed for our table. He looked over our plates, saw there wasn't the first scrap of food on them, and grinned.

He said, "You boys with the Apache soldiers in town?"

Naiche nodded and said, "We Apache soldiers."

The fat man said, "Happy to meet you, boys. My name's Charlie Beam. I own this here eatery. My cook took off and left me high and dry, so I'm having to cook until I can find another. How's your meal?"

Naiche said, "We eat all on plate. Good. Ready to give you money for it. Then we go."

Charlie Beam grinned. "I tell you what, boys, since you are on our side now and you mind your manners, keep your money. I'm giving you your first big meal in Mobile."

Naiche frowned. "No money for food you cook?"

Charlie Beam shook his head. "No money. I pay the bill."

Naiche nodded and said, "I know White Eye custom is to say, 'Thank You,' for gift. We say thank you. Maybe we help you sometime."

Charlie Beam grinned and nodded. "Maybe so. If you behave yourselves, you have friends in Mobile. Well, boys, I've got to get back to the kitchen. See you around."

We all stood and mumbled, *"Gracias,"* as he disappeared through the kitchen doorway.

Back walking down the street, we found a stream of people going into a building and giving a man at the door money or a little piece of paper to get in. The sign above the door said, "Primrose and Rose Minstrels." Before we left camp, a sergeant had explained that places like this were called a "show" and that we should understand none of it was real, just fun to watch. We had never seen a "show" and decided to learn what the sergeant was talking about. It cost us each a dollar to get in the door, and we found seats in the back row where we could see it. The show was strange. The men who did the show were White Eyes who had blackened their faces, wore fancy suits, and talked like black people we saw on the streets. They sang songs and told stories the White Eyes called "jokes" that were supposed to make those who heard them laugh. I don't think we knew the language well enough to understand the story. We learned to clap to show our appreciation when a song or story was finished. Some songs and stories weren't so good. I didn't think they deserved clapping, but everyone else did, so we did too. White Eyes are people with strange customs.

After the show, we found our way back to camp and checked in with the corporal of the guard. It had been a long sun, but we had learned a lot and had a good time.

The next day, we had our morning meal and were inspected by an officer before we were given our day passes. Naiche and I walked up the quiet streets and past places with tall towers with bells next to their roofs where the White Eyes went to speak to their *Ussen*. Then we found a bench near the stores where we wanted to buy presents for our families and sat there enjoying the shade and cool breeze off the big water while we waited for the doors to open. It was so peaceful that we had nearly drifted off to sleep when the store owner opened for business.

We went to the store and bought what we wanted for our families. It took about half of a month's pay, but I didn't care. The best feeling after a raid was bringing things back for your family and the People. I was sure the best feeling of the long march would be giving presents to our families when we returned. We carried the gifts back to camp and then spent the rest of the day on the sand at the edge of the big water. As the sun disappeared, Naiche and I agreed that this had been a good day. The next day would be a day of show-off drills, and then we would leave the next morning.

The show-off drills were a big success. So many came to the late-afternoon drill that they crowded onto our drill space and kept us from doing some drills the *teniente* had planned. Even so, he was happy to see so many people interested and impressed by our drill skills.

The next morning, Sam Haozous and James Nicholas were on their bugles again, two hands before sunrise, and we were marching out of Mobile as the sun's edge appeared on the horizon. It was good to be moving again and feeling the strength in our legs as we moved along, real warriors even if we wore the clothes of the Blue Coats. *Teniente* Wotherspoon took the wrong road to the place where he wanted to camp in a place called "Oak Grove," but we found the way and made it to camp by the time the sun was halfway down to the western horizon. I heard one of the White Eye sergeants say, as he shook his head, that it was 3:00 p.m., when we had marched twenty-one miles and weren't even tired. In the harvests before *Nant'an Lpah*, it was nothing for us to cover four times that distance in a sun.

We were on the move again at sunrise and became lost again, but one of the sergeants got a local farmer to show us the way to the road, where we camped at a place named Citronelle about an hour sooner than we had the day before. Naiche told me that he heard a sergeant say we had marched twenty-three miles and the commander of Mount Vernon had come to see how we were doing. The next sun, it was raining too hard to make it worthwhile to march, so we rested in our tents.

The next sun, the rain had passed. We marched about two hands above the horizon before coming to a place named Cedar Creek and in the middle of the morning made camp on a ridge above the creek. The *teniente* told us to build a "corduroy road bridge" across the creek, which wasn't very wide, but it was about neck deep and flowing fast. We trained at Mount Vernon to build such bridges, and in a hand past the time of no shadows, it was done. Including the approaches to the bridge, it was about twenty-five paces long. We tested how much it would support by marching over it followed by the supply wagon. It held firm and steady. We were proud of our work. *Teniente* Wotherspoon's grin stayed on his face a long time that day.

The next day, in less than three hands, we marched to Mount Vernon, where the proud *teniente* saluted us and said we had done a fine march any commander would be proud of. He dismissed us and gave us all leave for the rest of the day and the next.

OUR WOMEN SAW us coming and welcomed us singing as though we were warriors returning from war or a raid in the long-ago days. I was happy to see my women, and they were happy to have the necklaces and other bits of jewelry I brought them from the stores in Mobile. I showed Helen the ball I bought Maurice and told her to put it away and give it to him when he wouldn't chew it up while his teeth grew. She thought that was a wise idea.

My women made a special meal for the middle of the day and listened while I told them stories of the hundred-mile march to Mobile, which every man who had marched was proud of, but none more so than *Teniente* Wotherspoon. The ten-sun march to Mobile had taken eight suns, with one sun camped in place for rain, a sun and a half's leave in Mobile, a sun showing off in drills at Mobile, and a half sun building a corduroy bridge over Cedar Creek. *Teniente* Wotherspoon told his sergeants there was no other company in the Army he would rather march with.

# TWENTY-THREE

## CAPTAIN MAUS AND
## TENIENTE SCOTT COME

TWO HARVESTS OF good times and bad passed after our hundred-mile march with good behavior in Mobile. Our training continued even though the San Carlos Apache who had only signed on for a harvest left after their harvest of commitment. Even the five San Carlos soldiers who had taken Chiricahua women for wives left them to return to San Carlos because the women were still prisoners of war and weren't allowed to leave with them. *Teniente* Wotherspoon gave us passes to go to Mobile by riding the iron wagon early after sunrise and returning the same sun as it disappeared in the west. All the soldiers wanted to visit Mobile, some to take their families, others to look for a bottle of whiskey. I was one of the soldiers who took their families to look in the big stores and buy things we needed. After reaching Mobile, it was fun to watch the women stare at the things in the store windows as the soldiers had during our weekend passes after camping at Frascati Park. I laughed when I heard the women say they wondered why anyone would want or need the stuff they saw in the store windows.

As part of our training, we learned to use little machines called watches. Watches showed by numbers where the sun was in the arc of the sky, each increasing number being about an additional hand width above the horizon. The iron wagons going to Mobile were supposed to be at the Mount Vernon place at a number on the watch and then return from Mobile on another number. The comings and goings of the iron wagons were usually nearer to the next number on the watch, and we had to wait for the iron wagon if we wanted to ride.

Maurice grew fast and was soon crawling and then walking in our house, but Helen was a good mother and stayed patient with him as she worked on her baskets and kept our side of the house clean.

One night as we finished our evening meal, she looked at me with a sly eye and said, "Maurice grows fast, husband. By the time he is weaned, I should be carrying his brother. Our blankets call us. Will you come to me tonight?"

Her playful words stirred me, and I grinned and nodded. "I have waited more than two harvests to hear these words you give me. I hunger to hold you in the blankets as a man holds his wife."

Helen giggled. "Soon, husband. Soon."

MAUD WENT TO school every day. She was becoming a beautiful young woman and had learned to speak the White Eye tongue and to make tracks that captured what was said. I was very proud of her. Nalthchedah didn't have much to say to me, but she did her share of the women's work. I never attempted to go to Nalthchedah's blankets after I took Helen as my woman. My sister Banatsi and I sometimes talked together over coffee. She told me Nalthchedah would leave as soon as she could find a man who wanted her and that she had a couple of innocent flirtations with three or four soldiers from San Carlos who had joined our company. I thought, *She's lucky she didn't marry one who then left her at Mount Vernon when he returned to San Carlos because I wouldn't take her back.*

*Teniente* still used his whiskey raiders to find stills, but we didn't blow them up. After we found one and learned who used it, *Teniente* had them arrested and put on trial for selling unlicensed whiskey to Indians. Finding good whiskey after a few of the whiskey makers went on trial became harder and harder. I didn't care. I had stopped drinking whiskey, except for an occasional nip, but was never again drunk after losing Ishchos and two of our children to *Nakai-yi* slavery.

Three moons after our march to Mobile, *Teniente* Wotherspoon was made *capitán*. Six moons later, although he was still our commander, *Capitán* Wotherspoon was sent to serve General One Arm Howard. We were not happy to see Wotherspoon leave us. He was a good commander and our friend. Tenientes Charles C. Ballou and Allyn Capron were put in charge of us while *Capitán* Wotherspoon was supporting General Howard.

During these harvests, many died, including Seeltoe, who, like Fun, believed his wife Belle was committing adultery with another soldier, Nah-to-ah-Ghun. Seeltoe saw Belle and Nah-to-ah-Ghun enjoying themselves together and shot and killed both before killing himself. Then Dutchy and Ditoen, drunk, were killed one night in a fight with White Eye Blue Coat soldiers. At Mount Vernon many others died from diseases they caught that neither the White Eye *di-yen* nor our *di-yens*, even Geronimo, could cure.

Too many were dying. Our leaders worried that disease would soon take us all. As we were to learn, the Army big chiefs were worried about this, too, as well as the newspaper stories telling about how badly we were treated. They decided that if we wanted to leave Mount Vernon, then they would move us farther west, past the great river. To learn what we wanted, they sent *Teniente* Maus, who was now a *capitán* serving under General Miles, and *Teniente* Hugh Scott, who came from Fort Sill, to have a council with us. I knew *Capitán* Maus from when we both served *Capitán* Crawford, chasing Geronimo in the land of the *Nakai-yes*.

THE DAY BEFORE Maus and Scott arrived, we held a leaders' council and chose Geronimo to speak for us all. A sun rarely passed that he wasn't giving any Blue Coat who would listen an argument demanding that we be given the reservation Miles had promised us. Even though the old man and I were virtually enemies, I thought he was the right choice as our speaker.

We gathered in a big room in the commander's *hacienda* the next day. *Capitán* Maus and *Teniente* Scott met us and acknowledged each of us as *Teniente* Capron led us through the door. We sat in chairs around their table loaded with supplies for making tracks on paper. *Teniente* Scott made many tracks on paper to record what we said, and this was given to the big chiefs as a record of our meeting. Wratten sat near the officers and interpreted what each side said for the other.

*Capitán* Maus started the council by saying they were glad we held a council for them, that their big chiefs had sent them to listen to us and learn if we wanted "to go to some other locality."

The room became perfectly quiet, so quiet the old men's raspy breathing was louder than distant children at play. We all looked at Geronimo, who, with a cough to clear his throat, seemed to shake his lethargy and stood up in front of his chair with crossed arms. He looked at all of us and then at Maus and Scott and spoke in his raspy old-man voice.

"I am very glad to hear you talk—I have been waiting for a long time to hear somebody talk that way. I want to go where we can get a farm, cattle, and cool water. I have done my best to help the authorities—to keep peace and good order, to keep my house clean. God hears both of us, and what he hears must be the truth. We are very thankful to you—these poor people who have nothing, and nothing to look forward to. What you say makes my head and whole body feel cool—we are all that way. We want to see things growing around our houses, corn and flowers. We all want it—we want you to talk for us to General Miles in the same way you have talked to us.

"Young men, old men, women, and children all want to get away from here. It is too hot and wet. Too many of us die here. I remember what I told General Miles—I told him that I wanted to be a good man as long as I live, and I have done it so far. I stood up on my feet and held up my hand to God to witness what I said was true. I feel good about what you say, and it will make all the Indians feel good. Every one of us has got children at school, and we will behave ourselves on account of these children. We want them to learn. I do not consider that I am an Indian anymore. I am a white man, and we'd like to go around and see different places. I consider all white men my brothers, and all white women are now my sisters—that is what I want to say."

*Capitán* Maus nodded and looked around the room at all of us before saying, "I understand it to be your opinion that all of you want to go somewhere else."

Geronimo held up his hands and shrugged his shoulders. "We all want to go, everybody." Then he sat down.

Naiche stood and said, "We live just like white people. We have houses and stoves just like them, and we want to have a farm just like other white people. We have been here a long time and have not seen any of us yet have a farm."

Chihuahua said, "God made the earth for everybody, and I want a piece of it. I want to have things growing. I want the wind to blow on me just as it blows on everyone else. I want the sun to shine on me and the moon as on everybody else."

Nana wheezed, "Although I'm too old to work, I want to see all the young men have a farm. I could go around and talk to them and get something to eat."

I wore my big silver medal the Great Father gave me. I stood so all could see it. "If I could say anything that would hurry up the farms, I wish it would. You can find some of the old people yet—the grandfathers and grandmothers—but most of them are dead. That is why I do not like it here. I want to hurry—I want to tell you to tell General Miles to get us away from here in a hurry."

Kaytennae, who sat next to me, spoke up. "I had lots of friends—cousins, brothers, and relatives—when you last saw me, but since coming to this country, they have all died. I have children here and am all the time afraid that they will get sick and die."

Loco rumbled, "It's just like a road with cliffs on both sides—they fall off on both sides. Nobody killed them. Sickness did it."

Chihuahua stood up this time and, crossing his arms, leaned toward the officers. "I went to Carlisle to see my children, and it made my heart feel good to see them in the white man's road—but I want to have all our children together where I can see them. I want my children wherever I go." He tapped himself on his chest. "*Capitán* Maus, I want you to look at me and see that I am not like what I was when you last saw me before escorting me and my People back to Fort Bowie."

Mangas, in his quiet, whispery voice, told of his life in hiding and his attempt to get by to Ojo Caliente before he decided he had to surrender and said, after he got to Fort Pickens, "I have been, up to this time, a good man and have never stepped off the good path."

*Teniente* Capron nodded and held up his hand palm out to stop Mangas in mid speech. "Just a moment, Mangas." He turned to Scott and said, "This man has the best record of any man in Company I Twelfth Infantry." Then he waved for Mangas to continue.

"As for where we live here, in this little bit of reservation—there are lots of trees here, yes. They give shade, but when you put your foot on the ground, it burns you."

Someone else said Mount Vernon was no bigger than a thumbnail and the trees were so thick one had to climb to the top of a tall pine to see the sun rise.

When he heard this, *Teniente* Scott said, "I can promise you that you'll be sent to a place where you can not only see the sun rise, but you'll be able to see the mountains."

We all said, as if by one voice, *"Ch'ik'eh doleel."*

*Capitán* Maus and *Teniente* Scott promised we would learn soon what their big chiefs had decided to do with us.

# TWENTY-FOUR

## THE ROAD TO FORT SILL

IN LESS THAN half a moon after the council with *Capitán* Maus and *Teniente* Scott, *Teniente* Capron held another council with the leaders. He spoke, and Wratten interpreted, although most of us understood what he said from our Blue Coat training.

He smiled and said, "I have good news. The big chiefs have decided that you'll move to Fort Sill in about a moon."

We looked at each other and nodded. At last, the Blue Coats had listened to us.

*Teniente* continued. "There is much to do before we leave. You need to take the windows and doors off your houses, your table and chairs and beds and all your big personal things, and load them on freight cars that will be sent on a different train. You'll have to build new houses at Fort Sill. Use your doors and windows on them, and the inside things you want to keep will be yours. If you are in the Army, you will be sent to Fort Sill with your families. The big chiefs expect that the Army will leave Fort Sill in a few harvests, and it will become your reservation. Lieutenant Scott will be your commander and the chief of all the Chiricahua and Chihenne sent there. I'll be his assistant."

I thought, *At last we'll be closer to places of our birth in Arizona, and maybe the big chiefs truly give us this place as our reservation or send us home from there. Maybe Geronimo won't turn this change bad by trying to escape. I think if he does, I kill him. I kill them all who cause trouble for the rest of us.*

The *teniente* spoke of all the other things we had to do to leave and who would be responsible for those jobs. When he finished, he asked if there were any questions. We had none.

My women were working away from the house when the council was over.

I decided to wait until the evening meal to tell them about our leaving Mount Vernon and went to marching drill. Our company didn't look as powerful as it had been when *Teniente* Wotherspoon was commander. We were down to about fifty men after those from San Carlos decided they didn't want to reenlist and returned to their families on the reservation.

THERE WAS NO need for me to tell my women the news. Mangas told his wife we were moving, and the news spread among the women like lightning arrows between the clouds. At the evening meal, they were full of questions, but I couldn't answer most of them.

Helen's belly was swelling with our next child. She was worried she might give birth on our way to Fort Sill. What would we do then? I told her she was too young to remember, but our women in the long-ago days sometimes had their babies while we were on the run. The older women who were *di-yens* for births would know what to do.

Maud told her not to worry about Maurice, that she would take care of him while Helen took care of herself. I was proud of Maud. She sounded more like a grown woman every day and was a great help to us.

Nalthchedah and Banatsi wanted to know what personal things they could carry. I said I would find a box about the size of what the White Eyes called a "trunk" that would be big enough to hold all our treasures. The women looked at each other and smiled. They knew a trunk was not big enough for the six of us, but I knew they would work it out.

THE PACE FOR preparing to leave increased day by day. I had enough money to buy a good trunk and went to a store in Mobile and bought one. It had more room in it than one might guess from looking at the outside. After the women looked inside, they thought it would be enough space for them to get all our things in it.

While the women packed the trunk, I began taking the window sashes and doors off our house. The men who drove the wagons to pick them up made writing tracks with a carpenter marker on the window-sash frames and on the door edges to identify who they belonged to. We had to cover the holes left by the windows and doors with canvas just like we used to do to *wickiups* in the long-ago days. After the doors and window sashes were taken to an iron wagon, the wagons came back for our table and chairs, bed, stove, and box of personal belongings to load on an iron wagon.

Helen told me that she had heard Geronimo was keeping his trunk to carry with his family on the iron wagon. Gossip in the village said his Power had warned him to keep his family's things with them. The same night Helen told me about Geronimo's trunk, I had a dream where a stack of trunks like ours was burning in a great fire. I woke up in a sweat, the dream vivid in my mind as if it were more real than a vision. I decided *Ussen* was telling me to carry our trunk with us on the iron wagon like Geronimo was carrying his.

As the day approached for us to leave for Fort Sill, we lived more and more like we did in the long-ago days, sleeping outside and cooking over an open fire. Those days brought back many memories. There were hard times, when we had to run, fight, run, and hide. There were good times when we returned from raids with many presents, killed and avenged enemies, burning the worst ones like Juan Mata Ortiz. Most of all, we had our freedom. We could go where and when we wanted and take what we needed. Now we had to do what the Blue Coats said, even to the point of becoming a Blue Coat. We weren't free, but we weren't slaves either. Our sun-to-sun lives were much easier. Even so, I still valued the freedom taken from us over the easier life given to us.

WE HAD WALKED up the hill from the iron wagon stopping place when the Blue Coats first brought us here. Now we walked back down the hill to wait for the iron wagons to take us away. In Mobile, we mounted iron wagons that went first to New Orleans, then to Houston and Fort Worth, and finally to Rush Springs in Oklahoma. At every stop in the big towns, crowds gathered to see the Apache prisoners who were heading west. They wanted to see us all, even to the point of some walking through our iron wagons to see us like we were pieces of carved stone. It was Geronimo they most wanted to see, and they paid money for items he sold, like buttons off his shirt or a hat he wore. After we left the station, he sewed more buttons on his shirt or pulled another hat out of his trunk to wear to the next station.

In those days, Rush Springs was as close as the iron road came to Fort Sill. We arrived when the gray light of dawn was growing brighter, the sun increasing its golden glow behind the horizon. High clouds were catching lightly tinted reds and purples as the sky turned a light blue. It was like seeing a big blue stone behind thin cloth. The land, gently rolling prairie, and trees all along the creeks and rivers had changed little since we had left Fort Worth. I could tell already that our new homes would be on land that would produce much without the extra-hard work we had to put into what we planted at Mount Vernon without gaining much produce for our labor.

Our family trunk made it all the way to Rush Springs. Naiche helped me get it stashed on board when we changed trains in New Orleans and Fort Worth. We were fortunate. No one stopped us from loading our trunk in our iron wagon, perhaps because Geronimo had one too. We learned that the iron wagons carrying our window sashes and doors, our household goods, and boxes of personal effects had been taken to New Orleans and had somehow caught fire and burned while they sat waiting for us. Most of the People who had not brought their treasures with them on their iron wagon had nothing left. We would all have to start over at Fort Sill.

I was worried about Helen giving birth to our second child while we were on the way and made sure I knew which iron wagons the *di-yens* who helped with births rode in. But Helen moved to get on board the iron wagons like the big ball she carried in her belly wasn't there and never showed any sign of a birth pain.

The Army had sent cook wagons to feed us while we rested that day from the long ride on the iron road. We spread our blankets in the shade of trees near to shedding their leaves by a creek and enjoyed the cool dry air sweeping over us. Children played, but most of the adults napped.

As the sun left us in darkness among the grassy rolling hills, Coyote called to his brothers, and they answered. I saw water run from the eyes old women who heard them. They said in their cracked voices, "At least it sounds like we're back home."

As we were eating our morning meal, a long line of wagons appeared on the road. *Teniente* Scott was coming to meet us with many Comanche and Kiowa in their wagons to welcome us with hand signals we didn't understand and give us a ride. It had been many years since any of us had seen or used sign language. Unfortunately, neither side could speak the other's language. Even those called Kiowa Apache sounded unintelligible. We called them "Half Apache" because we could only understand about half of what they said. *Teniente* Scott realized former Comanche and Kiowa Carlisle students who spoke the language of their parents could talk to our former Carlisle students in the White Eye tongue and then, in turn, speak the tongue of their parents. Thus, speaking through two Carlisle students, the Comanche and Kiowa welcomed us to the Oklahoma country and fast became the friends and new neighbors who lived nearby.

The Comanche- and Kiowa-driven wagons had come to help carry our personal supplies and assist people like Helen or old ones who would move slowly to Fort Sill. Since it was only thirty miles, it would be an easy walk for the rest of us. I looked forward to it.

The road carried us across the rolling hills of the prairie, including three or four creeks, and we stopped that many times to take a little rest and take care of personal business before continuing. The sky was a brilliant blue, and the warm air was filled with the calls of birds. I saw Geronimo intently studying the land and had no doubts he was considering how he might escape. If he tried to escape, I hoped the *teniente* would ask me to help track him down. He had caused all of us much suffering that had to end.

NEAR THE END of the day, our column passed through a big gateway with a sign over it that read "Fort Sill." In the distance, we could see the tops of buildings and a low-lying dust cloud hiding most of them. At last, we could see our destination, and our feet hurried us forward.

The soldiers at Fort Sill had big pots of stew and freshly made bread for us to eat and had prepared tents for us to shelter in for two or three days until we had our places set up where *Teniente* Scott directed along Medicine Bluff Creek. It was too late in the season to begin building houses, which would have to wait until the Season of Little Eagles. *Teniente* Scott, after learning that a fire on the iron wagon hauling all our window sashes and door frames had left us with nothing for our houses, hired a master carpenter to start making them.

# TWENTY-FIVE

## A NEW BEGINNING

THE MEN OPERATED as a military unit clearing brush for a wagon trail along Medicine Bluff Creek. We built large *wickiups* that could survive the Ghost Face from saplings we had trimmed and saved. *Teniente* Scott gave us canvas to cover them and all the rope we needed to make them tight to the frames, with an adjustable hole at the top, over the fire, to let out smoke and keep cold air from blowing in. The creek was low, and that made it easy to get the stones we needed for *wickiup* fireplaces. We hauled wagonloads of firewood from the fort's supply and stacked it where women could get it when needed. Every day we hauled a couple of wagonloads to keep the *wickiup* fires burning. Most families lost their cooking pots and other necessities in the New Orleans iron-wagon fires, but *Teniente* Scott provided the women the cooking pots they needed. The *wickiups* were close to the creek, which enabled us to dig several good shallow wells, giving the women easy access to clean water.

We had our first night in the village a few suns after we arrived. It was a strange way to live. It felt like we were going backward in time, from living in houses to our old way of life in *wickiups*. After going back to the *wickiups* for a while, I never heard anyone say they wanted to return to the way we had lived before we became prisoners.

A few suns after we arrived, a few of the leaders were loaned horses or mules to ride so they could follow and understand the perimeter and how large an area Fort Sill covered. Its area was greater than we had imagined, easily large enough to support the cattle herd that we all wanted. *Teniente* Scott told us that the big council of chiefs in the Great Father's city had provided money to buy each family a few head that we could keep in one big herd.

A few days after we arrived, following the evening meal, *Teniente* Scott had a council with all the parents who had children over five or six harvests old. The *teniente's* wanting to speak with parents of children older than a certain age told me that this council would be about school. I went to the council because Maud had not yet had her *Haheh*, but I didn't think she should be going off to school anywhere. The lady teachers at Mount Vernon had offered to come with us, but neither the Army nor those who supported them wanted to continue paying them for teaching the children at anyplace except Mount Vernon. Now the People's children were without White Eye teachers to show them the way to learning more.

A big fire had been built where the council met. When *Teniente* Scott stepped into the firelight with George Wratten just behind him, the low rumble of voices stopped, and all eyes were on them. *Teniente* Scott thanked the People for coming and told why the Shepard sisters, who had done much good with the children while teaching at Mount Vernon, hadn't come to Fort Sill.

He then said, "There's a boarding school the plains tribes' children attend thirty-five miles from here at Anadarko. It has been agreed that the Chiricahua children can attend school there."

He stood a little closer to the fire so all could see his face. "Four days from now, wagons will take your children to Anadarko. I expect them to be clean and neatly dressed and carrying the extra clothes they need to stay at the school. I know this is hard for you parents not to see your children as they grow, but it's the best thing we can do now. If you want to visit your children at Anadarko, I'll be happy to give you a pass so you can go. Are there any questions?"

There was complete silence in the crowd, the only sounds coming from the crackle of the wood in the fire. When there were no questions, the *teniente* looked at Chihuahua and said, "Do you have anything to say, Chihuahua?"

Chihuahua, holding his bowler hat over his chest with both hands, stepped forward and said, "*Teniente*, of course we don't want the children to leave us for a school, but we have been prisoners long enough to know that an officer's orders are carried out. The children will be ready."

*Teniente* Scott smiled and nodded. *"Enjuh."*

A FEW DAYS after we settled into our *wickiups*, I awoke one morning to find all my women gone. I saw a damp spot where Helen had been sleeping and knew she and her sisters must be at the birthing *wickiup*, where they and *di-yens* would be busy helping her deliver our child. I built up the fire and was thinking of what I could eat this day when Maud ducked into the *wickiup* carrying Maurice in her arms and smiling. She sat the little one down, and he threw up his arms and ran toward me, laughing with delight. As I swooped him up in my arms, Maud said, "This sun is good, Father. A strong new son has come to you. Your wife was blessed with a safe and easy delivery. She knows you need to eat and go to your job at the sawmill. She asked me to come and cook you a morning meal."

"You're a great help to your father, Maud. My heart is glad you're my daughter. I'll make coffee and eat some warmed fry bread Helen made last night. It's enough that you take care of Maurice until Helen can manage the new baby and him at the same time."

She made the all-is-well sign. "This I do. Now, play with your son, and I'll fix you something to eat."

AS I WALKED to the sawmill, I stopped at the birthing *wickiup* and spoke to an old woman, a *di-yen* who had birthed most of the children in the band, who now sat warming herself near a fire. I asked to see Helen. She gave me a grin that still had a few teeth and pointed toward the entrance blanket. I pulled the blanket back and stepped into the flickering shadows made by the fire near the far end. It was warm and comfortable in the *wickiup*. Several pots sat on the fire, one with water bubbling enough to leave steam in the air. As my eyes adjusted to the light, I saw Helen reclining on blankets, the baby asleep, its head resting between her breasts. When she saw me, she put the edge of her hand to her lips to signal silence and then curled them, motioning for me to join them.

I knelt by her as she whispered, "Husband, you have a strong new son. He came in the middle of the night. I saw no need to wake you. All is well?"

I gave *Ussen* thanks for this woman who was giving me such fine children and nodded as I whispered, "All is well. Did you suffer much?"

"No. It wasn't a hard birth. The birthing pains didn't last long, and the *di-yen* made a hot drink for me that keeps the pain away after birth. I'll return to our *wickiup* before you finish your day's work."

"There's no hurry for you to do this. Come when you're ready, and keep yourself warm and comfortable. I'm very proud of this child."

She nodded as the baby kicked once and began chewing on its fist. "I think we come before the sun goes."

I swelled with pride at having Helen as my wife, nodded, and left the *wick-iup* to a chorus of squawking blackbirds that had landed in the trees around us. They soon fluttered away, their numbers so great they sounded like high water sweeping over big rocks, as young boys with slings dropped a few out of the trees to the yells of delight of their brothers and friends.

WITHIN A FEW days after our arrival, *Teniente* Scott had us working long days after getting our *wickiups* framed and covered. He managed to get fifty mules transferred to us, which were owned by the Army and intended to be sold when Camp Supply closed. He and Wratten laid out on a map where villages would be on the north side of Medicine Bluff Creek and the nearby fields where crops could be grown. Wratten proposed, and *Teniente* Scott saw the wisdom in having twelve villages, with related people in each village and near each other, all with similar interests. Wratten also suggested who the Army should use as village chiefs and made a list. It was the village chief's responsibility to see the homes were kept clean and harmony maintained in the village.

Before village chiefs were named, Wratten and *Teniente* Scott went to each candidate to ask if they would serve as a village chief. I was surprised to find them at my *wickiup* door one rest-day afternoon, asking if they might meet in private with me to discuss work they wanted me to do. I welcomed them into my *wickiup* as my women left for a walk.

We had a cup of coffee and then rolled a cigarette and smoked to the four directions. Wratten had a long round tube with him that was used to carry maps. He opened the tube, pulled out and unrolled his map, and laid it out on the ground with small rocks to hold down the corners. He said the map showed where the villages of the houses we were going to build would be located and where the land would be used for growing crops for each village.

*Teniente* Scott said he wanted me to be a village chief on the western end of the villages on Medicine Bluff Creek. Naiche's village would be east and next to mine. Loco and Chiricahua Tom's villages were next to ours to the north, and north of them would be Toclanny's, Mangas's, and Kaytennae's villages. Geronimo's village would be the farthermost east on the east side of Cache Creek between Kayitah's and Perico's villages. Perico's village was closest to the fort.

*Teniente* Scott explained that, as a village chief, I would be paid like an Army scout, and it was my responsibility to see that the shaded area next to our village on their map were village family's cultivated fields. Each family was to get ten acres. They needed to plant five acres in Kaffir corn (a kind of sorghum that could be used for cattle feed in the winter but didn't burn up in the dry summer sun and prairie winds), three acres in cotton, and two acres in vegetables of their choice. *Teniente* Scott said the first order of business at these village sites was to plow the land with tools and mules he had found for us and plant winter cover crops for animal feed in the spring before the Ghost Face made the land unworkable.

I agreed to become a village chief. *Teniente* Scott said he was happy that I would lead my People and that when all the village chiefs were named, he planned to have a meeting with the leaders and village chiefs to explain why the People would want to stay in their villages and not go wandering off. I had been wondering myself how he planned to keep Geronimo from running for Arizona and starting a new war while we were still suffering the penalties from his last one.

AFTER THE VILLAGE chiefs were named, *Teniente* Scott held his meeting around a great fire with the village chiefs and leaders. Most of the rest of the People sat in the cold darkness to listen to what he had to say.

*Teniente* Scott said, "Your People have made a good start here at Fort Sill. We are all proud of your progress. There are no fences on the Fort Sill reservation borders, and if you were thinking about leaving on your own, it looks easy to get away. I want to tell you tonight what will happen if you decide to run."

I smiled when I saw Geronimo sit a little straighter, cross his arms, and lean in to better hear the *teniente*.

"It's seven hundred miles from Fort Sill to the Mescalero Reservation in New Mexico, and from there I'm sure you could find your way to your old camps in Arizona or Mexico. I've talked to a Mescalero who lives with the Comanche. He has shown me all the trails and waterholes along the way to Mescalero. I've had two maps drawn of those trails and water holes between Fort Sill and Mescalero. I've given one of them to General Miles, and I'm keeping the other. I also have a pack outfit in the mule barn, and it's loaded with twenty days' rations ready to go at any time. The Comanche, who know the plains, are my friends, not yours, and they will join me to chase you down if you leave. You won't make it to New Mexico if you try to leave. Don't even think about it. Are there any questions?"

I smiled as I saw Geronimo slump back and glance at Perico. *Teniente* Scott was clever beyond his years as a Blue Coat. I liked him a lot. There were no questions about escaping, and so we began discussing when to plow and sow our winter cover crops.

# TWENTY-SIX

## FIRST GHOST FACE AT FORT SILL

BEFORE THE GHOST Face came roaring into Fort Sill, Geronimo had some-how learned that a big grove of mesquite was less than a day's run southwest of Fort Sill. Naiche spoke with *Teniente* Scott, who agreed to let us go on our rest days to collect mesquite bean pods, which, if we were in time, should still be good enough to make mesquite bread. We couldn't leave before the time of shortest shadows on the day the White Eyes called "Saturday," and we had to be back and ready to work the following Monday morning at seven by our watches. We hadn't had any mesquite bread in years, and we were anxious to get enough bean pods to make a few loaves for every family.

Those who had horses or mules brought them, and we carried provisions to eat, canvas to shelter us if it rained, and bags to hold the pods. My women didn't go because Helen had young ones to care for, and Nalthchedah and Banatsi had work on clothes and baskets they wanted to complete and helping Helen as she needed. Maud asked to go, and I let her come with me. It would be fun to test our endurance on two long forty-mile runs.

It was dark when we reached the mesquites, with Naiche following a map *Teniente* Scott had made for him. We made a camp near a slow creek, building good fires for coffee and trail food, and resting after a long day.

Dawn disappeared as the sun rose in a glow of pinks and oranges on high thin clouds over the horizon. We had a quick morning meal and went to check the quality of the bean pods dangling from mesquite branches. We were all wor-ried that they would show black spots and couldn't be eaten. But luck was with us. Few pods showed black spots. All that sun, we raced each other to fill our sacks with good bean pods.

We worked all day until dark and filled many sacks with the pods. As the sun was painting the clouds in the west with brilliant heart-filling orange, red, and purple colors, we ate, loaded our sacks on our ponies and mules, and began our run back to Fort Sill.

The moon had begun its descent toward the southwest horizon when we returned to our *wickiups* and unloaded our ponies, ready to rest from a long sun and a half and two nights of running and working. My women were happy to see us return with the many full bags of mesquite bean pods. I could already smell good mesquite bread baking.

LATER THE NEXT sun, *Teniente* Scott came to where we were cutting poles for lumber and firewood. He asked us to gather around him and said, "I much admire you for your strength and what you did in collecting the mesquite bean pods. In less than thirty-six hours, you ran nearly ninety miles and picked over three hundred bushels of bean pods. That is strength to be proud of."

I glanced at Geronimo. I knew he must be thinking of what we could have done if we hadn't become soft, living as prisoners of war. I thought, *Don't even think about it, Geronimo.*

NAICHE AND I spoke with the men who would have houses in our villages and showed them where we needed to plow to plant a cover crop to support cattle the *Teniente* wanted to buy. Most of our men had learned to manage a team and plow on their little farms at Fort Apache and soon had the ground turned, disked, and sowed in oats for the coming warm season.

A moon after we returned from the mesquite grove, wind from the north brought dark, almost-black clouds sailing over us with strong winds, and the air went from mildly cool to bitter cold and stayed that way, except for a few suns, until the Season of Little Eagles. Soldiers who had been at Fort Sill a long time said it was the coldest winter in their memory. Our *wickiups* down in the brush and timber bottoms along Medicine Bluff Creek had good wind breaks that kept the worst of the wind off us, but we still had to keep strong fires burning all day to stay warm. The men cutting fence posts, poles, and logs had to build big fires near their workplaces to warm themselves when they weren't swinging axes or pulling saws.

We used a sawmill driven by an old steam engine that Wratten had worked on at the request of *Teniente* Scott. Wratten understood how the steam engine worked and soon had it consistently running the big sawblades for cutting lumber we needed when we started building houses in the Season of Little Eagles. I worked at the sawmill, turning logs into lumber. It didn't take nearly as long to saw up a log as it did to cut down and haul the tree to the sawmill, but there were many more crews cutting logs than sawing them, and they kept the log and pole pile well supplied as the lumber stacks grew tall.

HELEN AND I decided to name the baby Blake. It was a soldier's name Helen had heard at Fort Marion and liked. I had been a scout and sergeant in the Blue Coats and had heard that name before. I thought it was a good name, too. She asked her father's second wife, Nahzitzohn, to make the *tsach* for the baby and conduct the cradleboard ceremony. Nahzitzohn was proud to be asked to make it and conduct the ceremony for the baby's introduction to its *tsach*. Helen gave her three of her best baskets for helping us.

The *tsach* Nahzitzohn made for Blake was a good one and kept him warm even as it got colder in the *wickiups*. The Blue Coats supplied the men with heavy coats to work in. As Ghost Face grew colder and the winds blew harder, we appreciated how those big, bulky coats kept the cold away even though it was awkward swinging an axe or pulling a saw wearing them. The women wrapped themselves in blankets as they worked in the *wickiups* and used another blanket when they went to the wood pile. Some days it was so cold and the wind so bad that *Teniente* Scott let us stay inside. The demand for firewood was quickly emptying the Blue Coat supply, which meant we had to cut more firewood and a lot of it before the fort supply was gone in the second or third moon of Ghost Face.

Cutting and splitting firewood in the bitter cold was hard, brutal work. A few of the men got what the White Eyes called "frostbite" on their faces and feet, but *di-yens* were able to make it go away without permanent damage. We all learned the value of the White Eye gloves for protecting our hands from the cold and to keep them from developing blisters from swinging an axe or a splitting mallet all day. Despite air so cold you could see steam from one's spoken words inside a *wickiup* and the cold we endured while working outside, we were still thankful we were no longer at Mount Vernon and never wished to return.

While we sat close around the fire eating, my women and I discussed what they wanted to plant when the Seasons of Little Eagles and Many Leaves came. After I listened to them sniping back and forth about what ought to be planted, I said, "I'll divide the space into four equal parts, and each of you plant what you want. Just remember, some of what you plant must get us through the seasons of Large Fruit, Earth Is Reddish Brown, and Ghost Face, and you have to take care of your plot in the growing season." That ended the arguments, and they agreed that they would plant what their sisters didn't. That way, we ought to have plenty of food across the seasons.

Although the cold and wind in the Ghost Face made life hard, not much snow or rain came. When the sun was warm enough to work the land for the coming season, the soil had become very dry, making it hard to plow or disk planting fields in the Season of Little Eagles. I saw as I plowed and disked our spot of land in the village field that unless we got some good rains by the Season of Large Leaves, we couldn't expect much harvest from anything planted. Nalthchedah and Banatsi decided they would plant sweet potatoes. Maud chose to plant cantaloupes, and Helen chose melons. They wanted to wait to plant as late as possible to increase the chances for rain to come and the plants to do well. I agreed to let them wait for the rain until the moon the White Eyes called "June" came, and then they must plant and carry the water to keep the plants alive until the rains came.

On the days it was too cold and snowy to work, I made Maurice a few playthings, including a toy bow with arrows. I taught him the correct way to shoot at a target from near the back of the *wickiup* and in the opposite direction from the fire. He learned the fundamentals of good bow shooting during that Ghost Face when he was not yet four harvests old. I was very proud of my fine young son. He might be a chief someday.

For reasons I was never able to learn, the old animosity Nalthchedah had for Helen when I took her for a wife at Fort Marion returned like a consuming fire. Although Helen had two young children to deal with and she was my choice for keeping my blankets warm, Nalthchedah went out of her way to show Helen no respect and, with flashing eyes and tender smiles, tried to get me to come to her even to the point of asking if I was coming to her blankets on that night in memory of our son Horace, who had died at Carlisle.

I glanced at Helen, whose face was an unreadable mask, and then stared at smirking Nalthchedah as her words settled around us, dark clouds ready to make lightning and thunder. I looked at her and said gently, "We were in the blankets many times before Helen and I were married. *Ussen* never gave us a child except for Horace, and he's already taken him to the Happy Place. *Ussen* favors Helen now. Already she has two children, and it has not taken us long in the blankets for us to have them. I don't think my coming to your blankets will give us another child."

I could see the fury in the squint of Nalthchedah's eyes as she raised her chin defiantly while the other women, including Maud, bowed their heads and with little smiles stared at the fire. Nalthchedah said in an even, menacing tone, "You surprise me, Chato. You speak like a chief, not the bloodthirsty war leader you once were under Geronimo. Now even he hates you. I'm surprised Chihuahua and Ulzana or Kaytennae haven't killed you yet, but mark my words, one day they will."

Deep in my gut, I wished I had a good solid stick at hand to make her wish she had shown me some respect. Another part of me knew everything she said was true. I also realized that she was trying to make me angry enough to beat her but knew that I wouldn't because the other women were around us. I decided she wanted to goad me into divorcing her, and although I badly wanted to do just that, I wouldn't then. If I had divorced her, then she wouldn't have to work and support my other women, and as bad as the Ghost Face was, she didn't think I'd force her out. My Blue Coat masters might not understand. I knew she'd divorce me when she had someone to take her.

I said, "Maybe what you speak will be so, maybe not. *Ussen* shows us the way. Has he spoken to you about this?"

Her mouth was a tight, straight line as she slowly shook her head.

# TWENTY-SEVEN

## FIRST SEASON OF BIG LEAVES AND LARGE FRUIT AT FORT SILL

AS THE LAST days of Ghost Face vanished and the winds died down, *Teniente* Scott shifted most of our work from logging to cutting fence posts we could use around our planted fields to keep out cattle he expected to buy for us soon. We were also plowing and disk harrowing the land near our future village sites to plant in Kaffir corn and gardens. The work was a gamble. We knew that if rain didn't come before the end of the Season of Little Leaves, we wouldn't get much for our labor. To get the gardens started, the women and children carried water to the new garden plants every other day. As the plants began to grow, they carried water to them as often as the plants seemed to need it. In the moons the White Eyes called "July" and "August," truly the Season of Big Leaves, the fiery sun dried up little creeks and reduced the big ones to trickles. We cut as much hay as we could with the mules pulling mowing machines and rakes *Teniente* Scott had found for us, but the hay we baled and had to sell to the Army was not nearly as much as it could have been in normal years. As *Teniente* Scott suspected, the Kaffir corn survived to make feed for the winter.

*Teniente* Scott also bought enough lumber and building supplies—which we hauled from the iron wagons stopping at Rush Springs—that even without the logs we had been cutting and sawing into housing lumber during the winter, we built the first twenty houses under the supervision of a master carpenter. I never met or saw the carpenter who made the door and window sashes. For all I know, he might have been the one who was supervising the building of the village houses. The carpenter, with Wratten's supervisory help, used men in groups of three or four to build the first twenty houses while the rest of us dug wells, put up fencing, or made and baled hay. *Teniente* Scott bought a mule-powered well-drilling machine that let us put the wells just about any place we needed them.

The first houses, on the east side of Cache Creek, were built in three villages on the eastern end of the string of twelve villages that were laid out west along Medicine Bluff Creek. All the villages were close to good springs for fresh water. The head men for the first three villages were Kayitah, Geronimo, and Perico.

The houses built in those villages were all the same design, called "picket houses," which were built on upright posts set in a frame. The outside boards were nailed vertically on the horizontal frame. The floor was supported by the outer frame and foundation piles of flat rocks midway under the joists. The houses had two rooms, each a square about five paces (fourteen feet) on a side, with a covered breezeway between them wide enough to drive a wagon through. Each room had a door, two windows, and a tile chimney. *Teniente* Scott had found cook stoves for one room in each house and a heating stove for the other room. Every man had learned to make tables and chairs and beds for their Mount Vernon houses, and so we rebuilt the ones lost in the New Orleans iron-wagon fires. Our houses at Fort Sill were larger and more comfortable than the houses we had at Mount Vernon but still hot in the Season of Large Leaves and cold in the Ghost Face.

SINCE THERE WAS then no fence around the reservation, we had to keep our cattle herded away from the boundary between Fort Sill and Comanche-Kiowa reservation land. Otherwise, if our cattle grazed on the Comanche reservation, it was theirs for a good meal, or if we went after them, we might be trespassing, and then they were free to attack us. For the good of us all, peace had to be maintained.

*Teniente* Scott began training men who wanted to herd cattle about a moon before they arrived. I thought this was something a leader ought to be doing and decided to participate in the training, as did most of the other men. When I learned *Teniente* wanted to teach us how to herd cattle, I thought, *It's foolish to teach us to herd cattle. In our raiding days, we herded cattle we took all the time.* I soon learned, there is a great difference between just running cattle along a trail, not caring if they lived or died, and herding them so they survived, grew fat, and had many calves. Tenientes Scott and Capron didn't know anything about herding cattle either, so they learned with us from soldiers who had once worked on cattle ranches. Many of us didn't yet have horses, so we just watched as those with horses were trained on how to approach cattle, what to do when one tried to change direction, how to rope and mark who owned the cattle, how to recognize when cattle were sick, what the sickness was, and the ceremony to cure the sickness along with myriad other small jobs and cattle herding tricks.

Our cattle were delivered early in the moon the White Eyes call "August." There were five hundred eighty mostly red cattle with short horns and white faces. Five hundred sixty were cows not yet bred—the White Eyes called them "heifers"—and twenty bulls. *Teniente* Scott assigned each family eight heifers, and the bulls were owned by all.

Soon after the cattle arrived, a few became sick and died. *Teniente* Scott was angry. We wondered if a witch was after us. He thought the man who sold them was trying to take advantage of us and sell us sick cattle. Di-yens who knew cattle sickness came and did their ceremony to learn what the sickness was and from where it came. They told *Teniente* Scott that the cattle had a sickness called "Texas fever" and that it came from them being held in the pens where the sickness had been among cattle used for our beef issue. The *di-yens* told us how to stop the disease spread, and we lost only a few cows.

When we let the cattle graze, they began to wander over the range looking for grass because the dry time left little grass on the prairie. Most of us who didn't yet have ponies to use for herding the cattle had to run on foot to keep up with them and use the same tricks herder horses used to guide the herd. Herding cattle on foot was dangerous. If they stampeded without the herders having enough time to get out of the way, we would be trampled. Herding on foot wasn't hard for us, but we had to have mule-drawn wagons to carry our blankets and rations. The cattle consistently wandered toward the grass on the Comanche-Kiowa reservation. We had to keep the cattle on our side of the line if we wanted our herd to survive. Twice, a few cattle slipped away from us and went over the reservation line, but we managed to cross the line and get them all back without being caught.

*Teniente* Scott placed as many men putting up fences around the Fort Sill line as he could but focused on getting us in houses before the Ghost Face, harvesting what hay and crops we could, and herders, many on foot, keeping the cattle together. There was so much to do that everyone—men, women, and children—worked all that burning-hot time in the Season of Big Leaves and into the Season of Earth Is Reddish Brown from the light of dawn until we could no longer see, into the night. The work was long and hard, but no one thought life at Fort Sill was harder than run, fight, raid, hide, and run again in the land the White Eyes and *Nakai-yes* had claimed.

WIND WAS GUSTING, growing stronger and colder as dark, heavy clouds tumbled across the sky. The cattle stirred, putting their tails to the wind, uneasy but not ready to run, as the sun peeked through the clouds just above the horizon. Naiche was one of the few Chiricahua who had a pony. It was given to him by one of the Comanche leaders as a gesture of respect and friendship. Naiche oversaw the herd at *Teniente* Scott's direction. His instructions were to make sure we didn't lose track of the herd if a storm came up.

Noche and I sat with Naiche by the cook's fire as we drank a hot cup of good coffee, deciding how best to handle the herd if the storm came.

Naiche said, "I don't like this wind. It's getting colder, and it's blowing directly toward the Comanche reservation line and pushing the cattle toward it. We need to do something soon or they'll be gone."

Noche nodded. "You speak wise words. What you think we should do?"

Naiche shook his head. "I have an idea but not sure it'll work. What do you think, Chato?"

I said, "We need to get the cattle out of this wind and hold them in place until the storm is gone. There's a deep, wooded canyon half a hand's run northwest of here. I don't remember its name. I saw it when we rode to look over Fort Sill in the time of Little Eagles. It had a good creek running along the bottom then, and good timber was there, but I don't know how well the grass or water held up during the moons of no rain."

Naiche crossed his arms and stared off into the growing darkness. "What you think, Noche?"

"Chato thinks good. Let's start the herd northwest. That'll keep their tails to the wind. We ought to hurry them to the creek out of that canyon and then point them up the canyon. Even if we have to drive them into the wind, it shouldn't take long before we're in the canyon and sheltered from most of the wind."

Naiche nodded and took a big swallow of coffee. "Hmmph. You're right, but if we run them too far to the northwest, they'll fall into the canyon and that'll be the end of the herd. Chato, you find the north end of the canyon and build a big fire for us to point on. Noche, you find the men and tell them as soon as they see Chato's fire to head for it and that we want the cattle to head southwest into the canyon. We need to hurry. It's getting colder, and the wind is coming up. Those cows could be on Comanche land before we know it. I'll get the cook loaded and find the men with horses to get them started."

Noche headed for the nearest herders. I took the cook's hatchet and a couple of sticks with pine knots from the cook's woodpile. I poured a little kerosene oil on the pine knots from a lamp, slid some big redhead matches in my vest pocket, and ran for where I thought the creek would be but stayed toward the north so I wouldn't run over the edge of the canyon like the cattle if we headed them too far to the west too soon.

I ran hard as the wind seemed to get colder, making my fingers cold and numb. I was glad I had the wind to my back and didn't have to face it. It pushed me along like I knew it would the cattle. There was just enough light in the gloom to still see pieces of the rolling hills near the horizon through breaks in the tumbling clouds. I could just make out a wide swath a little darker than the rest of the land. I thought, *There's the valley that leads into the canyon.* I turned a little to shorten my path toward it.

As I reached the edge of the wide, dark swath, the land began sloping down. I could barely see as I ran down the slope straight into brush, mostly saplings that slapped at my face and tore at my clothes. I stopped in the thicket I had run into. I wasn't hurt but could tell my face had a few scratches. I heard the weak gurgle of a flowing stream not far away. I found a match in my vest pocket and lit it with my thumbnail and held the flame against the kerosene-soaked pine knot that flared into a fine torch.

I was surrounded by a thick stand of saplings about the diameter of my thumb, tree leaves, and grass. Nearby was a dead pine tree blown over by the wind from a previous storm. I found another match and lit my second torch and fixed it in the pine tree limbs while I took the other torch, found the creek, and saw the area was filled with timber. The wind was shaking the tops of the trees, but here on the ground, there wasn't much. If we could get the herd down in these trees, we ought to be all right until the storm passed. I ran back to the pine and began chopping limbs that I dragged up the slope and out of the brush to make a big enough fire that would at least make a glow the herders could see.

I hurried to gather more wood to make the fire bigger until it was sending sparks into the wind and cracking and popping. In the distance, I heard, "Hey! Ho! Chato, is that you?"

"My fire! Come! Creek nearby!"

I heard cattle bawling and men yelling and decided to climb a tree nearby to get out of the way. I found a limb low enough that I could jump up and grab it, and I pulled myself up. The fire wasn't more than a hundred yards away from my tree when streams of jogging cows turned to one side or the other of the fire and headed into the timber along the creek. They must have been thirsty. Their bawling stopped, and I heard them drinking before they passed on into the timber.

The herders on foot stopped at the fire to warm themselves and catch their wind as the last of the cattle disappeared into the trees. I swung down out of the tree just as Naiche rode up grinning. "Chato, this worked out better than I expected. You're a good man."

I thought, *At least somebody in the chiefs and leaders thinks so,* but said, "Ussen was with us this time, Naiche."

# TWENTY-EIGHT

## DAKLUGIE COMES

TWO MOONS AFTER we had helped drive the cattle herd into deep timber to keep it off the Comanche-Kiowa reservation, Noche and I were watching the herd one bright sun in the Season of Earth Is Reddish Brown. We were sitting in tall, brown grass, enjoying the warmth of the sun glowing on our skin, when I saw a rider in a long duster and black hat jogging in our direction. He rode in among the grazing cattle and stopped to look them over. I pulled my soldier glasses from their case and watched him. He was a dark-skinned Apache, young, maybe in his early twenties, and when he pulled off his hat to wipe his face, I could see his hair was cut White Eye style like a scout. He seemed to look at every nearby cow, leaning down from his pony to study their legs and backs. Scowling and shaking his head, he plumped his hat back on and rode in the direction of the fort buildings three or four miles away.

Noche had been watching him too and said, "Who was that?"

"I don't know, but I thought he looked familiar. His dark skin, round face, and big body reminded me of someone I knew many harvests ago, but his face and name were foggy. The way he studied the cattle and scowled and shook his head, I thought, was strange."

"Uhmm-huh. I thought so, too. Maybe he's one of the Carlisle students coming back to us. You know Chihuahua's oldest daughter, Ramona, came back home about a moon ago. Didn't Chihuahua and Juh agree their children would marry when the time came? I think maybe it was Ramona and Juh's youngest son, the one who lived with Mangas at Fort Apache—what was his name?"

I remembered the boy Noche was talking about. Mangas's son and he were about the same age and lived in the *wickiup* of Mangas's wife, the expert *tizwin* maker, Huera. Kaytennae had been training the boy and Frank and two or three others when *Teniente* Britton Davis arrested him. One of Davis's spies told him Kaytennae had nearly murdered him while he was out turkey hunting. Most believed I was the spy, but I never spied on my People. The boy was very angry, and one day at the trading post, when I told Kaytennae's adopted son that Kaytennae would be chained to a rock in the big water for many harvests, the boy had practically shouted, "One day, you'll pay for that, you traitor spy. You're no better than a diseased dog that needs killing." I started to cuff him for being disrespectful but held my hand because I was a sergeant of scouts. He ran off before I could correct him. I saw little of him after that. I think he was avoiding me.

What was his name?

I said, "Daklugie. That was his name. Youngest son of Juh. He was very angry with me because he thought I was the spy who told *Teniente* Davis that Kaytennae had nearly killed him when he went turkey hunting. Said I'd pay for spying one day. Last time I saw him was from a distance in Florida, when he and the Mangas boy were brought to Fort Marion to wait for an iron wagon that was supposed to carry many of our children to the school at Carlisle. I think that fellow we saw was Daklugie. He looks a lot like the boy I knew at Fort Apache and Juh in his younger days."

Noche nodded and made a smile on one side of his face. "I think you're right. He was Daklugie. He must know something about cattle, the way he studied them. Maybe Naiche will use him to help with the cattle."

I grinned. "We'd be back to where we were at Fort Apache, except now he's grown. I hope he doesn't come after me. I'd hate to kill him."

I learned that night that I was right. The man Noche and I had seen looking over the cattle was Daklugie. My women were full of gossip about what happened when Daklugie went to ask Wratten for a job and Wratten had sent him to see *Teniente* Scott. The next thing anyone knew, *Teniente* Scott had run out of his workroom, jumped on his horse, and ridden away but showed up a little later at Wratten's store.

Nobody knew what had happened after that.

The women all knew that Ramona and Daklugie had been promised to each other by their fathers when they were young children and that Ramona had been living at Chihuahua's house for nearly a moon before Daklugie arrived. No one knew where Daklugie planned to live, but they decided it wouldn't be more than a moon or two before they married and lived in Chihuahua's village. Then the talk turned to Ramona being a Christian and whether they would marry the Apache way or the White Eye way. I wondered if Daklugie was a Christian or if he had kept to the old ways and prayed to *Ussen*.

I played with my sons while the women talked. They took much pleasure in all the talk about what Daklugie and Ramona might do, but I was thinking about what Daklugie and I might do. If he was not a Christian, then he might come after me or wait until I was off guard. Even threats made in childhood carried a burden of acceptance or formal rejection. My biggest allies were patience and the sharp knife in my boot sheath.

That night in the blankets, Helen whispered, "Blake grows fast, and we have plenty of room and sunshine now. We can see the mountains and eat mesquite bread. Please, husband, let us make another child soon. Think about us trying sometime in the next harvest. You should also know students now return to their parents from Carlisle, that Nalthchedah looks for one she can marry, like the young man Daklugie. Will you be sorry to divorce her?"

I snorted. "Nalthchedah is still a handsome woman, but I doubt a man the age of Daklugie will want a woman ten or fifteen harvests older than he is. It would be like having a mother for his wife. No. If she wants to leave us, I'm glad to be rid of her. She has been a pebble in my moccasin for too many harvests now. Tell me why you want another child so soon."

She paused a while before she sighed and answered. "Maybe you want another woman after Nalthchedah is gone? Would I become second wife and sleep without you nearby? I wouldn't want that."

I puffed my cheeks and blew into the cool black air. "You are a very good wife. *Ussen* smiled on us when I agreed to take you. I promise you I take no more wives. You are the first and the last wife for me."

She hugged me. "You are a good man, Chato."

I took her in my arms. "You are a good woman. *Ussen* blesses us. Yes, maybe we try to make a new child, soon."

"Please, husband. I would like that."

ONE NIGHT, LESS than half a moon after Noche and I watched Daklugie study our cattle, *Teniente* Scott called a council of all the men who worked with the cattle. We gathered around a big fire burning in the same place we had met when he told us the children were being sent to Anadarko. When we were seated, *Teniente* Scott and Wratten walked to the edge of the firelight, where we could all see them.

He looked over the faces in the flickering yellow light and, through Wratten, said, "It's been a long, hard summer and fall. You men have worked hard and accomplished much. We received our cattle the first of August, but it wasn't long before some died. We didn't know what was wrong. I had men come who knew cattle problems, and we learned it was a sickness they got from being penned where sick cattle for food rations from South Texas were kept. We were shown how to keep your cattle from getting that sickness.

"Now you have to keep the cattle away from the Comanche-Kiowa grass or those stray cattle might wind up roasting over their fires. I expect soon that all of you will have horses. You no longer will do this job on foot. We'll train you and your horse how to move and use your rope as you handle the cattle."

The fire popped and sizzled, sending sparks high into the night air. I wondered, Where is he going with this? We already know what he's telling us.

"I have asked Naiche to be chief of this work, and he has done a good job. I can always depend on Naiche when we need it done. But there is much about cattle, their care and breeding, that Naiche, like the rest of us, doesn't know. I think, in the future, cattle will be your primary source of income and the man or men with the most knowledge about them should be in the lead to take care of them.

"We are fortunate that a young man has returned to us from the Carlisle School who has spent the last seven or eight years learning about cattle and the best ways to take care of them." *Teniente* Scott paused and smiled. "We've had a talk, and he's told me what he sees as problems with our cattle. I've decided that his knowledge and experience with cattle will help you build up a fine herd under his leadership. He will now be cattle leader. What he says to do with the cattle, you do, and you will be better off for it. Naiche no longer has the burden of overseeing the cattle, and I personally thank him for his leadership."

I looked over at Naiche and saw him smile and nod. He was glad to be rid of looking after the cattle.

*Teniente* Scott said, "Now I want you all to meet the new cattle leader, just back with us from eight years of Carlisle School and working with cattlemen in Pennsylvania. Asa Daklugie, step up here and introduce yourself."

Daklugie stepped into the firelight wearing the same duster and hat Noche and I had seen him wearing when he stopped to look at the cattle. "Ho, brothers! I am the youngest son of the great Nednhi war chief, Juh. When you were in

Florida, I was running with Mangas, wild and free. Then Mangas surrendered, and I was sent to Carlisle to learn White Eye secrets. I didn't want to go while the rest of you were prisoners, but my uncle, Geronimo, insisted that I go."

I thought, *Geronimo made Chappo go to Carlisle, too. He outsmarted himself with Chappo, who got sick at Carlisle and died just before we came here. Daklugie, I wonder why you didn't get sick like Chappo? Maybe you make a bargain with witches?*

"I was at Carlisle for eight years and learned much. I speak the White Eye tongue. I read and write their tracks on paper. Most important, I spent much time with farmers who raised cattle and learned much about taking care of them and making money. I think raising cattle is work worthy of Apache warriors. When I first came to Fort Sill, I looked at your cattle. I expected better. It's a sorry herd."

I saw men frown and shake their heads. Maybe Daklugie had more in his mouth than he could chew.

"Ghost Face is coming. They should be fatter. When the heifers breed, they need that weight to make strong calves and give them the milk they need. I saw some with black leg, a sickness that medicine cures. Others had hide sores that looked like ringworm. That, too, needs to be looked after. We need to get the rest of the fencing up so the cattle won't wander onto Comanche-Kiowa land. You need horses to herd cattle. Those who didn't have horses when Blue Coats from ranches first taught you how to work, brand, and rope cattle will need to learn these lessons even as I do, too. *Teniente* Scott promises I will get the medicine for treating cattle diseases, wire for fencing, and horses for herding when I tell him how much and how many we need. This will be hard work. There is much to do. I tell you that if the herd is not bigger and better this time next year, then you should find someone else to be your cattle leader. This is all I have to say."

As the council ended, most of the men took a wait-and-see attitude, and others nodded their acceptance of Daklugie as the cattle leader, all, including me, were willing to give him a chance. I didn't like the boy, and I knew he didn't like me. I decided to keep the peace, but I wasn't going to step off any trail to make way for him or Geronimo.

# TWENTY-NINE

## MY WOMEN

GEORGE WRATTEN HAD opened a sutler's store at Fort Sill where the People bought supplies that supplemented those *Teniente* Scott provided us. We also sold garden produce from our wagons parked near or around the store. Wratten's store had become a community gathering place by the second-harvest Ghost Face. It was a place for us to gather, with its great stove pouring out heat, look over pots and pans hanging on the walls, and see and feel cloth of different colors on long rolls and many other things that women liked. The men came drawn by the sight of saddles and the familiar smells of new leather, *tobaho* and papers, and oiled hand tools, including a fine array of knives. On my days off from work, I was happy to take my women to Wratten's store, and while they looked at things they might want or need, I stood or sat near the stove and talked about work or the old days with the other men.

About a moon after the council when *Teniente* Scott told us Daklugie was the new cattle manager, I took my women to Wratten's store. It was again a very cold and dry time, and the wind seemed especially cold and sharp. I was talking with Noche about a run of fence we were putting up on the north edge of the Fort Sill reservation land when the door opened, bringing in a puff of cold air and a young man of average Apache height, wearing a soldier cavalry hat that he pulled off once he was inside. He waved at Wratten, who was behind the counter, and said in perfect White Eye tongue, "Hello, George. Sure is cold, ain't it?"

Wratten waved back. "Howdy, Dexter. Yes, sir. It's mighty frosty. Good to see you again. Get up against the stove with the other men and get yourself warm."

We made room for the young man to sit down with us. We spoke our Mexican names around the stove, with him nodding and repeating each one to remember it and then telling us his name was Dexter, Dexter Loco. We all knew he was the son of Chief Loco. He nodded toward me and, grinning, said, "I remember you, Chato. You stuck the business end of a rifle against my father's chest at San Carlos and said you'd kill him if he didn't lead our People to Juh's camp in Mexico. You seemed very angry. He didn't doubt you would kill him, so he led us as you told him."

I bowed my head and nodded. "Yes, I did that. I believed at the time it was the right thing to do—we were fighting the White Eyes for our rights and land and believed your father must fight too. After *Nant'an Lpah* came for us in the Sierra Madre, I learned better and helped the Blue Coats stop Geronimo's raids and killing that Loco was also against. I remember *Nant'an Lpah* chose you and other children to go to Carlisle School when we returned to San Carlos. Is that where you learned to speak the White Eye tongue?"

He grinned and hunched his shoulders. "I mean you no offense, Chato. What was done are only memories now. Yes, *Nant'an Lpah* sent me to Carlisle. I was there for eleven harvests, most of the time working for White Eye farmers and learning how to farm. I left there about a moon ago and went to Fort Apache to see about farming there, but after speaking with Alchesay, I decided I would stay with my father and the People here and help with the farming even if it meant living as a prisoner of war."

I nodded. *"Doo dat'éé da.* It is good you are here."

Out of the corner of my eye, I noticed Nalthchedah, who had been rubbing her fingers over and studying the pattern on a roll of cloth, standing as if frozen in a ceremonial trance as her eyes followed Dexter Loco's every move. I smiled to myself. Dexter has been to Carlisle and knows White Eye secrets. He can have any woman he wants. Why would he want a woman ten years older than him who was already married? Some women just don't have much sense.

Wratten kept a big pot of strong coffee on the stove and invited us to help ourselves while we talked. Some of the men wanted to know what Dexter had learned about farming around Carlisle. Others asked what he planned to grow next season. As the men were talking, Wratten, standing behind the counter, held up a clean cup during a pause in our talks and nodded toward him while pointing at the coffeepot. Dexter nodded and stood up to go get the cup. As he approached the counter, Nalthchedah tried to return a broom, handle first, into a small barrel holding brooms, but missed the barrel and the broom hit the floor with a loud thump. Nalthchedah's face turned red as she clapped her hand over her mouth in embarrassment and surprise. She reached to pick it up, but Dexter picked it up and handed it to her, nodded, and took the cup from Wratten. I thought, *Why would a man pick up a broom for a woman? White Eye custom he learned at Carlisle?* Nalthchedah had heard the children at Mount Vernon learning to say, "Thank you," and, "You're welcome." She said loudly enough for us to hear, "Thank you."

Dexter said, again for all to hear, "You're welcome."

Helen with Blake and Banatsi with Maurice stared with their mouths open. Maud, near twenty harvests, was then ready to do her own courting, although she hadn't spoken to me about a young man wanting to court her, and she watched the scene with a frown. She understood Nalthchedah's maneuvers better than her aunt and Helen. I saw Maud's frown at Nalthchedah dropping the broom and thought, *Maybe I lose an unhappy wife soon.*

AS THE SUNS of Ghost Face drifted into the Season of Little Eagles, Nalthchedah was in a much better mood than she usually showed. When the days were warm, she often took walks by herself between villages, looking, she said, for wild plants she might harvest in the Season of Many Leaves or later. One evening during the family meal, I asked her what plants she had looked for. She said she was trying to learn what we might eat that grew on Fort Sill land and was showing possible plants she'd found to old women, *di-yens* who knew plants, in Loco's and Naiche's village. A reasonable answer, but I didn't believe it. I didn't press her about who she talked to or if she had found any plants worth harvesting. She understood I knew the game she was playing.

In the Season of Little Eagles, as the prairie grass turned green and the larks called to each other from their ground nests and great white clouds sailed across the sky, I was harrowing ground I had plowed for our Kaffir corn and vegetables. Through the light haze of dust raised by the harrow, I saw Nalthchedah leave my village on one of her "plant-finding walks" that took her across Four Mile Crossing at Medicine Bluff Creek to follow the path toward Loco's village. But after she crossed the creek, she disappeared into the *bosque* west, following the creek. I rested the mules, spat out some dust grit, and, staring at the *bosque* where she'd disappeared, thought, *She's either going to meet a lover or finding a place to meet a lover. Maybe I'll find out tonight.*

In the middle of the night, before the moon reached the peak of its ride across the sky, I got up as I sometimes did to use the privy, went through the motions like I had made a personal-business visit, and returned to the open breezeway and opened and closed the door on the room where Helen and I slept, except that I stayed outside and quiet as steam floating in the cool air moved out into the brush shadows, where I could watch the house and not be seen. In about a hand on the horizon, a figure wrapped in a dark blanket, making it hard to see, left the house breezeway and headed for Four Mile Crossing. So, Nalthchedah, you're doing some night crawling.

Keeping in the shadows, I followed her across Four Mile Crossing and stayed outside the creek *bosque*, moving parallel to her, listening to her move through the brush on a path along the creek. I lost hearing the swish and clack of tree limbs knocking together and brush against her dress as she moved along the path through the *bosque*. I stopped to listen. I knew I couldn't be too far from her. Then I heard a low mumble of voices just ahead and crept down into the *bosque* toward them.

"I didn't know if you would come."

"Of course I came. I need you. I want you for my wife. The pleasures we share when we are together fill me up. How much longer will you stay with that dog Chato? Why haven't you left him?"

"Soon. I leave him soon, but not before I can take all I want and need to start a new life with you. First spread my blanket. Let us have our pleasures. Then we talk."

I was close enough to see the wisps of steam from their breaths in the moonlight as I heard the light swoosh of Nalthchedah's blanket being flipped open and the crackle and snap of grass and leaves as it settled down, clothes being moved or undone, bodies reclining on it, heavy breathing, and groans of pleasure. I moved silently toward them.

He was breathing hard like a fast runner, panting in the pleasure of the moment, when I laid the cold, sharp edge of my knife against his neck and whispered in his ear, "Freeze or you die now." He was instantly still.

Beneath him, Nalthchedah said, "Wha? What's the matter? Why have you stopped? I'm nearly to the top. When she opened her eyes and looked up to see my face, she nearly screamed, but I put my free hand edgewise to my lips for her to be silent. She made no sound, her mouth open in a circle, her eyes wide in fear.

I said, "Custom says it is my duty to kill this man who lays with my wife and calls me a dog. Custom says it is my duty to kill or cut off the end of my wife's nose so she's so ugly no man wants her." I heard Dexter swallow and felt his muscles quiver from not moving at all and cold fear filling all parts of his body.

"Relax. Lie on her, Dexter. Isn't she still warm and willing?" He sighed and relaxed against her. "I won't kill you. You have what you want. She's an unfaithful woman. I hope she honors you better than she did me." He sighed and nodded, his head next to hers, fear slowly leaving her face.

"Woman, it's time you left my house. Take only your clothes and a Blue Coat blanket. If I find you've taken more, I'll come for it and for you. The end of your nose will be mine unless Dexter wants to fight me for it, but you don't, do you, Dexter?" He shook his head.

"It's three hands before sunrise. Nalthchedah, I want you out of my house in four hands. If you're not, I'll make a big scene to let everyone know you're being thrown away like some dirty rag. Do you understand?"

She nodded, relief filling her face.

"I have said all I will say." I left them and disappeared across the creek on big, bare rocks glowing white in the moonlight to trot back to my house.

I stepped up to the breezeway, went to my room, opened and closed the door behind me, pulled off my moccasins, and slid into the blankets next to Helen's warm, soft body.

She said, "Husband, you are cold from the night air. All is well?"

"All is well, good wife. Your sister, Nalthchedah, leaves us within a hand of the sun's coming. Soon she is the wife of Dexter Loco."

She said through a big yawn, "I wondered how long that would take. You are better off without her."

I yawned and laid my arm over my eyes as she rolled next to me. "I think so, too."

"Husband."

"Hmmph."

"I think now is a good time for us to begin another child for our family."

I took her in my arms. I had hoped she would say that.

When Banatsi came to help Helen with the morning meal, she said, "What happened? Nalthchedah took her clothes and a Blue Coat blanket and left before dawn. She wouldn't tell me why she was leaving. Do you know?"

I took a swallow of coffee and played with Maurice and Blake as Helen smiled.

I said, "She is no longer my wife. She goes to live with Dexter Loco."

Banatsi giggled. "Good for you both."

Maud only smiled.

I SAT ON the edge of the breezeway, watching the sun fall into the far blue horizon painting high clouds in reds, oranges, and purples. The mouthwatering smell of roasting meat, frying onions, and baking acorn bread filled the air along with the shouts and squeals of our two boys playing hide-and-catch in the tall brown grass. I heard the door close in the growing darkness behind me and the shuffle of Maud's moccasins coming my way.

Her hand rested on my shoulder. "The end of the day and its colors fill us all with joy, Father. Do you want some company? It is a little while before our meal is ready."

"It's my pleasure, Daughter. Come, sit with me."

The weight on my shoulder increased as she eased herself down and fluffed out her skirt. As darkness fell, *googés* (whippoorwill) began their sharp, clear calls to each other and tree peepers took up their chorus.

"Father, have you heard any more about Mother and my brother and sister? Are they still *Nakai-yi* slaves?"

"After Chihuahua asked Wratten to write a letter to the Blue Coat chiefs, asking that Ramona be allowed to return home, and she came, I and others who had family in the hands of the *Nakai-yes* that *Nant'an Lpah* had tried to bring back asked Wratten to write a letter to the Blue Coat chiefs, asking that they return. The *Nakai-yes* say they have no slaves, and they don't know where our families are. They lie, of course, but *Ussen* told me a long time ago that your mother, brother, and sister weren't coming back but were taken care of."

Maud bowed her head while she listened to me and nodded when I finished. She looked up to the stars beginning to glow in the black-velvet darkness of the night and sighed. Staring out into the darkness, she said, "I've missed my mother, sister, and brother. I know your devotion and how hard you tried to get them back have made many on Geronimo's side say you are a traitor because you sided with the Blue Coats to keep the rules and bring those who left back to Fort Apache. You make me proud, Father. I know you're a good man. You try to do the right thing."

I had an idea where this talk was going. I pulled my *tobaho* and papers from my vest pocket and rolled a cigarette. I lighted it, smoked to the four directions, and handed it to Maud and nodded for her to smoke. She smoked as I did and coughed as she handed the cigarette back to me to finish. This was the first time we had smoked together for a serious talk. I don't think she had sneaked a try at smoking with the other children.

"I know you think much, and your heart is heavy. Speak, and I will listen."

Even in the low light of dusk, I saw the hurt in her eyes. "Father, I am not an ugly woman. I have many skills that make a woman a good wife. When we are in Wratten's store, I see young men watching me with warm eyes, but none have tried to speak to me. I know there are now many women, young and unmarried and widows, who want husbands but now live alone because most men no longer want more than one woman for a wife. I'm like that except I live with you."

Her voice cracked as she spoke. I clenched my teeth at the sorrow in my daughter's voice as she cleared her throat. "I've talked a long time with Banatsi about this. She thinks no men want me because they would have to live here in your village and be an outcast from their friends who follow Geronimo and think you are a traitor because he says so. I've asked other girls about this. They think Banatsi is right. They all think if the men didn't have to live in your village and support a traitorous father-in-law, I would get plenty of men wanting me for a wife. What can I do to make men want me, Father?"

To my mind, it was as clear as the rising sun what had to be done. I made myself relax so I didn't sound the rage I was feeling at the miserable man Geronimo was and what his ugly voice had done to my daughter. I wanted to kill him if I could, but I knew if we ever wanted to free ourselves, revenge wasn't in the future.

I said, barely above a whisper, "I know how to make the men see you, Daughter. You need to live in one of the villages to the east. Maybe in Kayitah's or Perico's but never with Geronimo. I'll make it so. Be ready to move in half a moon."

Her jaw dropped in surprise. "Father? You would do this for me?"

"Of course. You're a beautiful woman and deserve a good husband and family. I want you to come visit and help with the garden when you can, but you'll live in another village. That way, my reputation doesn't taint you."

Maurice ran out into the breezeway, yelling, "Father, Father! Mother say meal ready."

I saw water glistening in Maud's eyes as she hugged me and whispered, "I have the best of fathers."

A FEW SUNS later, Perico and I were on herd watch. It was a cloudy day. We were keeping watch for storms that could brew fast and stampede the cattle. I rode over to Perico sitting relaxed on his pony. He saw me approaching and scowled but kept his tongue civil, for which I was grateful.

I rode up beside him and said, "Perico, I want to speak with you."

He tilted his head back and looked down his beak-shaped nose at me. It seemed he waited a long time, but it wasn't more than two or three breaths before he said, "Speak. I will listen."

I rolled a cigarette, and we smoked. I told him how men who needed a wife seemed to be shunning Maud because they didn't want to serve a father-in-law Geronimo believed was a traitor. Perico's face didn't betray what he was thinking, although I could see a smile trying to form at the edges of his mouth.

I said, "Maud's aunt and her friends, married and unmarried, believe her chances of being taken by an eligible man are much better if she doesn't live in my village. I've always known you as a good, straight man, regardless of what you think of me. Now I ask that you help Maud and let her live in your village. She won't be your slave, but she's good with children and is willing to help your woman Biyaneta with the children you have. I ask this not for me but for a young woman whose mother, brother, and sister have been taken into *Nakai-yi* slavery. She deserves to have a good man."

Perico's black-obsidian eyes stared at me, nearing the point of insult. But he nodded. "I have a vacant house in my village. It needs cleaning and someone to live there. In four suns, send your daughter to my village. She will be welcome. If she helps with my children, Biyaneta will be glad for her to eat with us. Don't come with her. I have said all I have to say."

I waved my arm parallel to the ground in the all-is-well sign, nodded, and rode away.

MAUD WAS ACCEPTED and lived well with Biyaneta and Perico's family. She visited Helen, Banatsi, and me often. In the next two years, three or four young men came and asked me to court her knowing that if they married, they wouldn't have to live in my village. I knew their families and approved them seeing her, but Maud never felt a connection with any of them, and after a time, they went away. I noticed a couple of years after she left my village that she was showing signs of the same illness that had killed many of us. As her health carried her closer to the ghost pony, Banatsi went to stay with and help her. As she grew worse, Perico and Biyaneta helped Banatsi with her, too, and sent word that it was all right if I came to the village to visit. I thanked Perico for allowing me to come and bring *di-yens* who tried to help her. It was no use. She rode the ghost pony in the Season of Many Leaves in the harvest the White Eyes called

"1902." A great sadness filled the hole in my soul that Maud's leaving us had made. I think of her often, even now.

# THIRTY

## CATTLE THIEVES

DAKLUGIE MANAGED THE cattle herd very well. He knew how to stop losing cattle from black leg and anthrax and how to get rid of ringworm. He kept a careful count of the number of cattle we had and, after getting us horses, had men ride the fence lines between Apache land and that of the Comanche-Kiowa to ensure we didn't lose cattle through the fence. He often made these counts and occasional fence inspections with Perico. Daklugie's counts started showing one to three cows missing every count, and some of us occasionally found tracks that didn't belong to our herders mixed in with those of the cattle. He increased the number of night riders for the herd and was often riding among them in hopes of stopping the thieves.

One day in the Season of Little Eagles, the wind moaned across the grass in brilliant sunlight. Perico and Daklugie were riding across our range to look for holes in our fencing when they spotted a circle of pushed-down grass. The grass was around an old hand-dug well neither of them nor anyone else among us knew existed. They thought it might be used to help water the herd and looked it over. Looking in the well, they saw it was stuffed with rolls of something. Daklugie and Perico pulled sixty-seven hides, all with Apache brands, from the well and concluded they must have been taken by White Eye thieves, since no Comanche, Kiowa, or Apache would waste good leather like that. There were no signs of slaughter, offal, or blood-stained grass anywhere. After they returned to Fort Sill and told *Capitán* Scott and the rest of us in a leader council, we all knew the thieves had to be caught, and quick, or soon our herd would disappear.

Those of us who had been in Company I of the Twelfth Infantry were made a small cavalry troop, Troop L in the Seventh Cavalry, under the command of *Teniente* Capron, who had come from Mount Vernon to help *Capitán* Scott manage us. We had learned to drill as a cavalry unit, and the unit was kept at full strength by including Comanche and Kiowa men in with us who had also served in the infantry. When our time of service was complete, we were told we were free to go and were no longer prisoners of war, but our family members were still in Army custody. We couldn't leave our families. It was infuriating to think that the White Eyes were either such fools as to think we would leave or just cruel to use family to keep us in their prison reservation.

Daklugie and Perico had discovered the hides not long after we had been discharged from the Army. After Daklugie told *Capitán* Scott (who had been made a *capitán* during the second Ghost Face after we came to Fort Sill) what he and Perico had found and asked to catch the thieves, he told them that, without special permission from the big chief in the east, he couldn't give them authority or firearms with which to capture a White Eye, and even if we could track them, we couldn't leave Fort Sill without a pass.

*Capitán* Scott formed a troop of scouts who were under the command of *Teniente* Capron and whose primary mission was to help protect and manage our herd. The scouts in this new troop were for the most part men who had been in Troop L and scouts who were village chiefs who could easily be paid for their service.

Sixteen scouts, including volunteers like me, were in the troop *Capitán* Scott formed to track down the cattle thieves and help manage the herd. The extra men were a big help with Daklugie still up nearly every night to direct the cattle watchers. Even with all the close guarding, we were still losing cattle. Daklugie didn't look happy, but he didn't say anything when he learned that I had volunteered to join the scouts and help find the cattle thieves.

NOCHE, MY FRIEND who had also been a sergeant of scouts at Fort Apache and was now a village chief, had also volunteered to help with the herd. One rest day in the Season of Little Eagles, as the wind shook the trees and whirled through old brown grass, we warmed ourselves near Wratten's stove and smoked and talked, remembering old war days.

I said, though I don't to this day know why, "You were a good tracker in the long-ago days, Noche. You could find the trail better than me. I usually had to guess where the warriors went and use their bits of trail to make sure I had guessed right. Why don't we ride out and see if we can't track those thieves?"

Noche grinned, took a final draw on his cigarette, tossed it in the stove, and said, "I was just thinking the same thing."

It had been nearly a moon since Daklugie and Perico had found the hides. The sun after the hides were found, a few men had looked for tracks and found a faint trail they'd lost crossing a creek about a mile away. We didn't expect to find much in the way of tracks, but maybe the others had missed something. It couldn't hurt to look again.

We found the old well and the tracks of the wagon used to haul the hides Daklugie and Perico had pulled from the well and hauled them back to a bare place next to the horse corral, where we could lay them out and work on them to make them uncurl. We wanted to look the hides over and learn what we could. Those we could open without breaking showed that whoever had taken the hides was a man who knew what he was doing. We found no signs of bullet holes or of the hides being dragged, and their condition said they were all about the same age.

Riding in great circles around the well, Noche and I kept finding what we were certain was the trail the other trackers had found. It was hard to see, almost covered over by weeds. Daklugie told us in council that he had been noticing two or three cows gone every time he had checked the herd over the past two or three moons. I did some arithmetic in my mind like we had learned at Mount Vernon in I Company training. If the thieves took at most only three cows at a time and there were over sixty hides in the well, that meant they would have made over twenty trips to the well if they disposed of the hides as they took them, which would have made a much-clearer path that was easy to follow, or they brought only one or two loads from someplace where they were stored and ditched them here so they wouldn't be caught with hides having an Apache brand. I and Noche hoped maybe they were foolish enough to bring the hides here on a wagon.

We looked for wagon tracks, but there were none. That meant, by my guess, three or maybe four packhorses or mules would have been used to haul the hides to the well. I said, "Let's look around and see if we can determine whether they used horses or mules as pack animals."

Noche said, "I think it was mules. Look at that patch of bare dirt over by the well."

I slid off my pony and walked over to the dirt. Myriad faint horse tracks along with the track of one of the wagon wheels on the wagon we had used to collect the hides were slowly losing their form. I could pick out the tracks from our scout horses, and I even saw some that were so faint I knew they must have been from the thieves' horses. I studied them for a while and was able to pick out sets from three different horses.

I said, "I see tracks from three different horses that aren't ours, but I don't see anything that says any are mule tracks."

"Hmmph. See the pair just off center of the dirt patch? Then over toward this side is another pair beside those that are a little bigger and wider apart. See them?"

I stared at the spot until I followed what Noche was describing. "Yeah, yeah, I see them. One horse looks smaller than the other, judging by how wide apart their tracks are."

"Now look for the back tracks. See them?"

I studied the ground again until I found the back foot tracks for the smaller animal and the back foot tracks of the larger animal, but they were hard to find because the smaller animal tracks were not a good indicator toward the location of the bigger animal tracks.

"Yeah, I found them, too."

"Now, look at the difference in distance between the front and rear tracks of the large and small animals. That difference is what you would expect between a horse and a pack mule. They look like the kind the Army packers made in Mexico when we were with Crawford and Davis, chasing Geronimo and Chihuahua. I know. I looked at a lot of them."

I looked up at Noche and grinned. "You have a great tracking eye, Noche. I would have missed the back two sets of tracks. I bet you a sack of *tobaho* we find these tracks lead past that little creek where the other trackers lost them and on to the Anadarko Road."

Noche frowned. "Why you say that? How you know?"

"Daklugie says none of our fencing wire has been cut. They need a hole in the fence to drive the stock or lead the horses through if they're not cutting wire, and there's a long stretch of land off the Comanche-Kiowa reservation on the road to Anadarko where they could make meat like it was their own cattle.

"The horse next to the mule has iron shoes that look like they've been cut down from a bigger set." I pointed toward a track in good shape. "See how wide they spread more than usual toward the back? A man with your sharp eye can follow that easy." The sun was running fast to dive into the horizon. "It's getting late, and we're losing light. Let's go find *Teniente* Capron and see if we can't get a pass to go past the gate and look at ranches on the Anadarko Road. He ought to give us a pass. He gives them to women when they want to run to the school up there with blankets and something sweet to give their children."

"Hmmph. We go. Chato has a clear eye."

*TENIENTE* CAPRON, VERY interested in what we told him, gave us a three-day pass beginning the next day and told us to see what we could find. Not far from the Anadarko gate was a buffalo wallow that still held water. Noche found the tracks we were looking for. The man leading the mules had stopped to water his horse and mules.

We rode through the cattle gate and stayed on the road toward Anadarko. I noticed that today, unlike yesterday, there were cowboys with long, thin braids who rode on the hills above us and seemed to be studying us. I wasn't worried but thought we ought to keep up with them. We rode about half the distance to Anadarko. Our Comanche friends stopped at their reservation line, but they used soldier glasses to watch us as long as they could.

We began seeing White Eye ranch and farm buildings set a few hundred yards off the road, and we began looking for the iron horseshoe track with the distinctive spread across the back. We hadn't ridden far when Noche found the tracks on a wagon road that led from the Anadarko Road to a distant farmhouse.

Noche and I sat our horses in the shadow of the big gate in front of the wagon road like we were taking a break and used our soldier glasses to study the place. Near the barn, a windmill pumped water in a cattle tank and a small creek, probably dry by the Season of Large Leaves, edged on both banks with thick *bosque*, ran behind a big pole barn. The wind under the brilliant ice-blue sky was especially cold that day, and we had to keep blowing into our curled fingers to stay warm.

Something stirred the *bosque* brush. Out of the *bosque* walked three head of white-faced cows driven by a barefoot White Eye boy wearing ragged canvas pants and a shirt torn at by the wind. I knew he must have been freezing and felt bad for him. The doors to the barn swung open, and out walked a tall White Eye carrying a big sledgehammer and wearing a blood-smeared apron. A mule in harness stood tied to a post nearby. In a corral extension from the far side of the barn, three horses and three mules watched the boy driving the cows.

The man pointed to one of the cows, and the boy used a long stick he was carrying to separate the cow from the others and drive it toward the barn. When the cow turned toward the barn, I saw her brand. She was one of ours. I clenched my teeth, wishing I had a rifle so I could ride down there, kill them both, and burn the entire place down. But after the first blast of anger passed, I thought, *Calm yourself, Chato. You live in the White Eye world now. The White Eyes will settle this.* I glanced at Noche, who stared though his glasses, his mouth hanging open.

The cow's separation from the others was easy enough, and she appeared headed for the dark doorway, but when she saw the man with the sledgehammer, she took a quick turn. She nearly ran over the boy and headed back toward the creek *bosque* followed by the other two. The man was very angry, pointing and yelling at the boy in the ragged clothes. He carried the hammer back in the barn and then pulled the mule inside. The boy went in the barn, too. Soon he came driving the mule pulling a wagon with a load covered in white cloth that was showing splashes of red. The man followed the wagon out of the barn and tied a dark canvas cover over the white-cloth-covered load. He said something to the boy, who snapped the lines and drove across the barnyard toward the road from where we watched. The man closed the barn doors and walked toward his nice white house about three times the size of mine. I looked toward Anadarko and saw three cowboys coming in our direction. I didn't want any trouble with the White Eyes.

I said, "Noche, I think we've found our thief, or at least one of them, and those men yonder are coming our way. I think it's best we go."

Noche nodded. "We go. Tell *Teniente* Capron what we see."

*Teniente* Capron listened carefully to what we told him, made tracks on paper, and said, "It sure looks like you men have found at least one of the rustlers. The man is taking our cattle, making meat, and selling it in Anadarko." He grinned. "He may even be selling it to the Indian School people, which is kinda funny since it was Indian beef to begin with, but I think the joke is on him."

Noche and I looked at each other. We had no idea what he was talking about. I said, "When you take him?"

"I need to talk to Captain Scott first, but I expect he'll tell me to send a wire message to the tribal police in Anadarko and ask them to make the arrest. If the cows or their hides are still there, the man you saw will be tried and sent to the calaboose at Fort Leavenworth for a long time, and that will be the end of his rustling days. Men, you've done a great service for your People. They will be grateful."

Noche and I rode back to our villages and our families.

AT OUR NEXT council meeting, *Capitán* Scott told us the tribal police in Anadarko had caught one of the rustlers with proof he was selling our cattle for meat in Anadarko. The *capitán* said the man had been caught because of the diligent tracking by Noche and me. He asked us to tell the council how we did it. It was a good time like the old days, when we returned from raids and acted out what we had done on raids or in war to deserve recognition.

Noche said the tracks were hard to find, but he had found dimmer ones in Mexico and that I'd had the right idea about how the thieves had to be headed for the Anadarko Road. When I spoke, I gave Noche the credit for finding the tracks in the first place and then told how I had reasoned out where the thieves must have passed the fencing without cutting wire. There were many hums of approval, and some muttered, *"Enjuh,"* as I sat back down.

At *Capitán* Scott's invitation, Daklugie gave a summary of the status of the cattle herd, which was doing well and growing fast. Before he finished, he expressed thanks for the work Noche and I had done and said with a false smile filled with malice, "We all know Noche must have done the tracking and figuring out where the thieves went. Chato is famous for taking more credit and recognition than he deserves, but nonetheless, we're grateful for his work."

Geronimo and two or three others laughed out loud, but I noticed Naiche, *Capitán* Scott, and *Teniente* Capron, who had come to the council late, and a few others were frowning. I tasted the bile in my throat and thought, *In the long-ago days, little boy, your insult would not have gone unchallenged. Someday, maybe you and I have a talk alone and we'll settle this business.*

# THIRTY-ONE

## FINDING THE JESUS ROAD

AFTER THE COUNCIL where Daklugie made a point of insulting me, I rode back to my village, taking my time to let my hot blood cool. By the time I entered our house, I had decided these kinds of slights and taunts probably would haunt me for a long time. My knife was under White Eye rules. It must remain silent and not speak against insults if I wanted to avoid the calaboose or dancing on air at the end of a rope. The best thing I could do was ignore the insults until *Ussen* gave me an opportunity to take back my honor.

As I closed the door to our room, Helen said from the blankets, "Hi-yeh! My husband returns. The boys are with Banatsi. I have our blankets warm. Come to me."

With her inviting words, the door to my anger and irritation closed. I was thankful to *Ussen* for giving me this woman, already the mother of two fine sons. Perhaps this night another son would begin.

IN THE SEASON of Many Leaves the following harvest, our third son, healthy but a little small, was born. We named him Cyril. He was a pretty child but weak, and he fought sickness often. Helen and I spent much time finding *di-yens* who had ceremonies that might drive away the evil attacking him. But despite all they tried, their ceremonies did him little good. I decided Cyril must be fighting against a White Eye sickness and asked the Fort Sill White Eye *di-yen* to perform his ceremonies for him. This the White Eye *di-yen* did, but his medicine was not strong enough either. Cyril left us in the Season of Large

Fruit. We buried him where the Blue Coats told us, the place they called the Apache cemetery, where all our People from Nana to the youngest baby were buried. Our burials at Fort Sill were unlike those for our children at Mount Vernon, where we could pick the place we wanted for an unmarked grave deep in the woods.

Not long after Cyril went to the Happy Place, *Teniente* Beach, who had replaced *Teniente* Capron when he left in the Season of Many Leaves to fight the Spanish, called a council of the village chiefs and leaders. At the council, *Teniente* Beach had two men we didn't know sitting with him. One had the face and dark skin of an Indian. The other was a White Eye. They were introduced as Frank Hall Wright, a Choctaw *di-yen* who wanted to teach us about the Jesus Road and the White Eye God, and Walter C. Roe, a White Eye *di-yen* who had been teaching about the White Eye God in a Cheyenne mission school. With the approval of *Teniente* Beach, they asked how they could help us. They talked of plans they wanted to implement with our permission to establish a mission for worshipping their god, an orphanage, a meeting house, and a school near our villages for our younger children.

We were happy they wanted to build and start a school. That meant the younger children didn't have to go away to Anadarko, even if the older children had to go farther away to Chilocco. Geronimo spoke for us all.

He said, "I, Geronimo, and these others are now too old to travel your Jesus Road. But our children are young, and I and my brothers will be glad to have the children taught about the white man's god."

The faces of the Jesus Road *di-yens* broke into big smiles, and *Teniente* nodded and smiled, too.

THE BLUE COAT chiefs let the Jesus Road *di-yens* build the school buildings and their mission house where we could all learn about the Jesus Road in a hollow called "Punch Bowl" near Kaytennae's village. With the help of a skilled White Eye carpenter and our men working on putting up the building when they could, we built a one-room schoolhouse with an attached room where the teacher would live. The Jesus Road people called themselves the "Dutch Reformed Church." They found a White Eye woman named Maud Adkisson, a nurse and missionary worker they paid to come help with the school. A lady teacher, F. A. Mosely, came in the Season of Large Leaves. They shared the room attached to the school. The church also raised money for desks, lamps, and school supplies. When school started, it was discovered that twenty-three of the youngest school-age children had been overlooked, and the church hired another teacher, but she didn't stay long. Another came. Her White Eye name was Mary Ewing, and she stayed until the school closed when most of us went to Mescalero fourteen or fifteen harvests later.

The first school building we built was too small to hold all the students, and so a second was built to house mostly the youngest children, a large dining room, and a kitchen. The teachers had learned that many students didn't eat a morning meal before they came to school, so the teachers began serving a meal at the time of no shadows with rations provided by *Teniente* Beach.

The White Eyes called every seventh day "Sunday." On this day, before the time of shortest shadows, the students had lessons on the White Eye God and what it meant to walk the Jesus Road. The parents were welcome to listen to the lessons with the children and then to stay for something called "church meeting," where one of their *di-yens* taught their ceremonies by reading from the church's black book of papers with many tracks and explaining what it meant. Most of the leaders in the west villages went with their children to this Sunday school and became interested enough to stay and listen to the *di-yen* tell his story during the church meeting. Geronimo and others in the east-side villages were slow to value what the White Eyes had to teach us about their god.

In these Sunday teaching times for the parents, the *di-yen* spoke of many things about the White Eye God. This god was a great spirit with a son who appeared on the earth as a man. In this life, the man was named Jesus. He taught other men about what the White Eye God was like, what he expected from them, and how they should live to have a happy life. This son did many ceremonies to heal his sick people, and they were very thankful for them. He also made other powerful *di-yens* angry because he always spoke straight. These *di-yens* became so angry that they nailed the hands and feet of this Jesus to a post, stabbed him with a spear, and let him die. When I heard this story, I knew it couldn't be true. No god would allow his son nailed to a post to die. A true god would have destroyed all the men who did such torture. I was shaking my head in disbelief when the *di-yen* said that, after three days, the great God brought Jesus back to life. People who knew him saw him walking on the road, saw him when they fished, and saw him in rooms where they ate after they had seen him die, and he still had the places where his hands and feet had been nailed to a post.

I stopped shaking my head. This sounded like what the prophet, Noch-ay-del-kinne, had said. He claimed that *Ussen* would bring the great chiefs back from the dead when we did the Ghost Dance and all the White Eyes left the land. I thought, *Maybe the White Eye God is the same as* Ussen. *The White Eye* di-yen *said the White Eye God brought Jesus back from the dead to show that he has power over death and can forgive and make us forget all the bad things we do if we believe in Jesus and follow his rules for living so we can hear and understand when the White Eye God speaks to us.* This was the Jesus Road. I thought then, *This is much to think about. I need to learn what the other leaders think. We need to know more about this Jesus Road. It sounds like a good thing.*

*The* di-yen *said if we told Jesus all the bad things we had done, were truly sorry for them, and followed the Jesus Road, which meant we had to forget revenge against those for whom revenge is due like the White Eye God had forgotten his revenge against those who killed Jesus with hard torture, and lived by the rules for staying on the Jesus Road, so it was easy to pray to and listen to the White Eye God, then we would have peace and many blessings for our spirits. If all this means I can't avenge myself for all the slights and slurs and lies Geronimo and his crowd have given me, then I don't want the Jesus Road.*

ONE SUNDAY, AFTER we listened to the *di-yen* speak and were leaving church, Naiche said, "Let's send the families back to the villages ahead of us while you and I talk as we walk." I was glad to hear Naiche say he wanted us to talk. I had many questions about the Jesus Road and the White Eye God the *di-yen* was describing, and I knew Naiche must have them too.

It was a beautiful afternoon, warmer than usual but not uncomfortable. The sun, in the middle of its fall into the horizon, was a great golden ball in the sky, lighting up cottonwood trees growing in the Medicine Creek *bosque* where the leaves had changed color to orange and yellow. High above us, a red-tailed hawk slowly circled, looking for a rabbit or mouse to make a mistake and show itself for the blink of an eye—just long enough to become the hawk's meal. We told our women and children to go on ahead of us, that we wanted to talk privately as we walked back.

Meandering down the wagon roads back toward our villages, Naiche sighed and said, "Do you believe what the *di-yen* was telling us about the Jesus Road? He said if we told Jesus we were truly sorry for the bad things we had done, then he would forgive us, and our lives would be smooth again. Do you believe that's possible, Chato?"

"I'd like to believe it's possible. Sometimes I think of my wife and children in *Nakai-yi* slavery as my punishment for the bad things I've done, the enemies I've tortured, those I've killed. You have relatives who are in *Nakai-yi* slavery too. Is this what you think?"

He made a face and looked up into the trees down the wagon road. "Sometimes those thoughts cross my mind. I've done many bad things in my life that I wish I'd never done. I've drunk much whiskey and had women who were not my wife, but I never forced them. I've killed many White Eyes and *Nakai-yes*—men, women, and children. Killed them any way I could—shot them, hit them in the head with rocks, cut their throats, used them for knife-throwing targets, shot them full of arrows, some just to watch them die, or tortured them to hear their screams as they begged to die. I've burned some, dragged some across cactus, staked them in the sun over an anthill, and cut off their eyelids so they went blind while the ants feasted. The blood of those I've killed, I dream of flowing like a great river about to drown me, and I hear their dying screams. The dreams wake me up in the middle of the night, and I'm bathed in body water and my hands tremble. I know you've done some of the same things. Do you have dreams like that?"

I stared down the road at the orange cottonwood leaves in the *bosque*. "I think about these things more often than I should. It's been moons since I dreamed about them and woke up with the trembles. I just want to be rid of those memories. I want my family out of slavery. I want to be free to live as a good man. Do you think the White Eyes will ever set us free?

"Warriors do bad things in war and shouldn't think about them after they're done. *Ussen* doesn't care—it's just war, or so Geronimo used to say. I want to do the right thing. Is taking the Jesus Road the right thing? Will the screams and bad things I've done and I still see in my dreams go away if I take the Jesus Road?"

Naiche shook his head. "I don't know. Noche says he believes Jesus will help him do the right thing, and he's done bad things, too. He thinks Jesus will make his life smooth again. Maybe his dreams come no more. He'd walk the Jesus Road just to get rid of them. Noche is a wise man. And no, we won't ever be free until Geronimo goes to the Happy Place. The White Eyes fear him too much to let us go with him alive. I think it would be better for all of us if he walked the Jesus Road."

I said, "I've ridden many times with Noche, fought many battles, killed many White Eyes and *Nakai-yes*, and yes, even our own People. I killed Ulza-na's son—the boy was only sixteen harvests, and I think about him often. I trust Noche's thinking. He has a good eye for dim trails. Noche tries to do the right thing, but sometimes he takes a wrong trail. Let us see if Noche is taking the right trail. If he is on the right trail, then let us follow him to the Jesus Road. Maybe all the bad things we've done will be forgotten, and Jesus will help us be better men. Maybe even Geronimo will decide to walk the Jesus Road."

Naiche smiled. A cool breeze rippled through the grass as we climbed a low ridge, and the high clouds were beginning to catch the early colors of the dying sun. Ahead we could see lamplight in the windows of our village houses. It was a peaceful time.

"Chato speaks wise words. I will think on them even as we watch Noche follow the trail he sees."

# THIRTY-TWO

## WALKING THE JESUS ROAD

THE NUMBER OF people who listened to the White Eye *di-yen* talk at Sunday meetings about the Jesus Road fell to only a handful during the first Ghost Face after the school started. An old Chiricahua *di-yen* named Harold Dick, who wanted the People to keep their old ways, set up dances and ceremonies at the same time the White Eye *di-yen* talked to the People about the Jesus Road. Old Dick wanted to draw people away from the Jesus Road, and it looked for a while like he had. Noche, Naiche, Chihuahua, and I and returning students from Carlisle, like Jason Betzinez, Benedict Jozhe and his wife, James Kaywaykla and his wife—and of course, Ramona Chihuahua, Chihuahua's pride and joy, and her future husband, Daklugie—continued to listen to the White Eye *di-yen* with a few others.

The White Eye *di-yens* always followed the same pattern when they told their stories. They first sang a song praising their god and then prayed to their god before describing the background for what they read from the black book with many little tracks on paper. After the reading, they talked about what that story meant.

One cold Sunday, under a brilliant blue sky and with a wind whistling around the schoolhouse windows, the Choctaw *di-yen*, Frank Hall Wright, sang songs for us and was teaching us how to sing them. When he finished singing, he raised his arms and prayed to the White Eye God to open our ears and hearts and hear the message he would give us. Then he picked up the black book, opened it to a place where he had put a paper with his written tracks, looked around at us, and smiled.

He said, "Brothers and sisters, I'm glad to feel the warmth of your hearts on this cold and windy day."

As if in answer to him, the wind shook the windows and doors on the school and whistled even louder.

"Today I want to speak about one of the key questions you need to answer before you begin walking the Jesus Road. Jesus asked for an answer to this question from his followers in the long-ago times, and in your spirit today, he will also ask it of you."

I thought, *This Jesus has been in the Happy Place since the long-ago times. Is he back now to talk to us?*

"One day in the long-ago times, Jesus was sitting with his followers. He was already known as a great *di-yen*. He had done ceremonies to heal all kinds of diseases, from blindness to skin and flesh rotting even as a person lived, to being so crippled others had to carry them around. All his ceremonies had worked, and anyone who was sick or knew someone who was sick was after him to heal them. Sometimes after he talked in the open fields to great groups of people who followed him from place to place, awestruck and without provisions. he made the little food a few brought increase so there was always enough to eat. Everyone thought he was going to drive the enemies who controlled them out of their land and become a great chief. On this day, believing they were about to start a great kingdom, his closest followers were arguing among themselves about who would be the most important chief on the new range."

Wright lifted up his black book in his hands and said, "The story is told in the sixteenth chapter of the Gospel According to Matthew, beginning with the thirteenth verse. It reads:

*13. When Jesus came into the coast of Caesarea Philippi, he asked his disciples, saying, "Whom do men say that I, the Son of man, am?"*

*14. And they said, "Some say that thou art John the Baptist, some, Elias, and others, Jeremias, or one of the prophets."*

*15. He saith unto them, "But who say ye that I am?"*

*16. And Simon Peter answered and said, "Thou art Christ, the Son of the living God."*

*17. And Jesus answered and said unto him, "Blessed art thou, Simon Bar-Jonah: for flesh and blood hath not revealed it unto thee, but my Father which is in heaven.*

*18. And I say also unto thee, thou art Peter, and upon this rock I will build my church: and the gates of hell shall not prevail against it."*

Wright closed the black book. "May God bless the reading of his word.

"Jesus' question, 'Who do you say I am?' bears as much meaning for us here now as it did in the long-ago times for his followers. Who was Jesus? Some say he was a good man killed for his beliefs. Others say a man of great moral courage who eventually lost the big battle with the big chiefs of his day. Others say he was a prophet and great teacher and *di-yen*. Still others say he had a great mind and was carried away with his own popularity."

I studied and listened carefully to the *di-yen*. He had my full attention. He's right. This is a question we all needed to answer before we start on the Jesus Road.

"To those who answer that Jesus was just a good man who died for what he thought was right, I want to tell you a story from the long-ago times about a man who was a chief in the Roman tribe far away across the big water. The Romans were at war with the Carthaginian tribe, who had a war chief winning many battles with the Romans. Most Romans believed it was only a matter of time before they were wiped out or became Carthaginian slaves.

"The fighting went on for more than twenty harvests, with the Romans getting the worst of the battles nearly every time. Valuable prisoners were taken on both sides. One captured Roman chief was named Marcus Regulus. He was a great warrior with a spotless reputation. He was known on both sides for his courage and honesty. The Carthaginian council of chiefs decided that a valuable trade could be made with the Romans by swapping Marcus Regulus for a large group of less-well-known Carthaginian prisoners. Marcus Regulus was brought before the Carthaginian council of chiefs and asked to go to the big Roman town called Rome, present the offer, and give his word that if it was not accepted, then he would voluntarily return to the council in their great village, a place called Carthage. He gave his word that he would come back."

This Marcus Regulus had honor, but he was a fool. What if the Roman chiefs say no? He can't go back to Carthage and be a prisoner again. He's a chief.

"When Marcus Regulus got to Rome, he told the council of chiefs the Carthaginian offer. Then he begged the council not to accept it, saying that the Roman tribe would lose an advantage it couldn't afford to lose with the Carthaginians so close to winning. The council thought and argued a long time but finally accepted his recommendation and refused the offer.

"Marcus Regulus returned to Carthage as he'd promised he would. When the Carthaginian council learned what he had done, they were so angry they had a box built, which he could easily stand in. Then they filled the sides with sharp, thin spikes. If he stood perfectly straight, the spikes didn't touch him, but if he slumped just a little, then the spikes would start to stab him. The Carthaginians locked him in that box and left him to die."

*He should never have gone back to Carthage. The Carthage tribe could have taught us a thing or two about torture in our war days. I'm glad those days are done. We won't see them again.*

"By anyone's standard, Marcus Regulus was totally dedicated to his tribe, a man of high principles. He was so trustworthy he kept his word knowing that it would get him killed. Since the long-ago times, there are many stories of good men who always kept their word regardless of what it might mean for them. Not one of them claimed to be the Son of God. Not one claimed to do exactly what God wanted. None of their lives, or the fact that they lived, fills my spirit with joy, peace, love, or feeling closer to God. The long-ago times shows the lie that Jesus was just a good man who always kept his word."

*Hmmph. He's right. All our great chiefs in the long-ago days never claimed to be a son of Ussen. I don't feel any kind of presence from them.*

"Others say Jesus was just a prophet and great teacher. No one denies Jesus was a great teacher. I think he was the greatest teacher. He gave us the clearest description of what God is like and what he wants from us more clearly than any man who ever lived. Other teachers may have sensed God and tried to tell their ideas to others, but they never reached the standard Jesus set. For example, we know Jesus taught the Golden Rule we learned a few Sundays ago, 'Do unto others as you would have them do unto you.' Another great teacher from the long-ago times and from far away tried to teach the silver rule, which was something like, 'Don't do to others that which you don't want done to you.' It sounds like the Golden Rule, but when applying these rules, you get two different results in real-life situations. Both rules say you shouldn't burn a man's house down. But if it catches on fire, the silver rule says you shouldn't feel obligated to put it out. The Golden Rule says you are obligated to put it out. These rules sound very much alike, yet their demands on the hearer are much different."

*There is much to learn and study here. No wonder the Jesus Road people meet every seven days.*

"The belief that Jesus was just a prophet seems hard to deal with. Most people who saw Jesus when he was a man thought he was a prophet. Why would we think different from the people who saw him in the flesh? First, no prophet in this book ever claimed that if you saw him, you saw God. Second, Jesus spoke with an authority that none of the other prophets had. Any prophet in this book will begin a statement with something like, 'The Lord says,' or they will end a prophesy with, 'thus says the Lord.' Jesus, on the other hand, amazed and made the *di-yen* chiefs of his day angry with statements that began, 'You have heard it said… but I say…' Jesus believed he had the authority of God. There was no 'thus says the Lord' from Jesus.

"This leads us to two alternatives—either Jesus was the true Son of God, or he was totally crazy. My faith, what I've seen in my lifetime, and my understanding of the long-ago days leads me to the belief that he was the Son of God, the Christ, the Spirit of God fully in man, the Spirit of God that is with and within us even today."

*From all I've learned about Jesus, I wouldn't believe he was ever lost in his mind— what the White Eyes call "crazy." But why would he think he's the Son of God in the first place? Where did he get that idea? Maybe from God?*

"In our study, we always come face-to-face with the question, 'Who do you say is the man called Jesus?' Time and again, we find people asking Jesus who he was. Peter's answer always comes ringing back, 'You're the Christ, the Son of the living God.' Think about that for a moment. The Son of the living God. The all-powerful creating God. The God of all the great men in this book. The same God of these men is our God, too, or he can be. This God chose to commit a part of himself, a beloved Son, to a world populated with people like you and me. To a world populated with races of men who, since time began, lied, cheated, murdered, stole, warred, and denied God on one hand while on the other attempted to draw near him and to seek fellowship with him. It seems incredible that God would risk on us that which he loved. To our great good fortune, he did take the chance, knowing, I think, full well what would happen. That's how much God loves us. Can we try to love God any less than with all our heart and mind and being, and our neighbor, as the Christ has loved us. Dare we be any less than all that we can be? And not what we are?

"How do you answer, 'Who is this man called Jesus?' If you've learned the answer and truly believe Jesus was God in man, then you are ready to walk the Jesus Road. You have much to learn, and sometimes you'll stumble and fall. That doesn't matter if you get back up and keep walking. You may feel there are many who have done you wrong and deserve your vengeance, but none as badly as those men in the long-ago time who nailed God's Son to a tree. If you feel God speaking to you, telling you to follow the Jesus Road, then I invite you to come up here as we sing the invitation song and accept my hand of fellowship and become a member of this fellowship walking the Jesus Road. Come while we sing."

The Carlisle students who had returned to us as Christians sang the song with Wright because they could sing in the White Eye tongue. The rest of us hummed the melody. Before the song ended, Noche went up and took Wright's hand, and then Chihuahua followed him. I felt the pull of the invitation to walk the Jesus Road, but I wanted to think more on what I was hearing. I glanced over and saw Naiche with a set jaw, staring at Noche and Chihuahua standing there by Frank Wright, and could tell Naiche felt a strong pull too, but I knew he also wanted to think more about it and learn how the Jesus Road affected the lives of Noche and Chihuahua. I knew he would probably talk to Geronimo to learn what he thought before he made his decision. It was a hard choice to make. I hoped Naiche wouldn't listen to Geronimo, who I knew was bitter at the White Eye *di-yen* whose group was reducing Harold Dick's Power and his own over the People.

# THIRTY-THREE

## THE TENT MEETING

NAICHE AND I could tell Noche and Chihuahua were changed men within a moon after they took the hand of the Jesus Road *di-yen*. They were slower to anger and seemed happy and relaxed. One evening late in the Season of Many Leaves, Naiche and I sat with Noche and Chihuahua by a small fire we'd built under the cottonwood trees in the *bosque* along Medicine Creek near the mission school. After smoking to the four directions, we talked about how their lives had changed and what they thought about the Jesus Road. They were glad we had asked to hear them and willingly came to talk with us.

It was a warm evening. Googés called, and frogs on the creek, tree peepers, and insects were singing in full voice. We sat bathed in the fire's warm yellow and orange light and were quiet for a time.

Naiche said, "Brothers, tell us what your lives are like now that you walk the Jesus Road. Chato and I think we will join you on this road if we believe it's the right thing to do to leave *Ussen* and walk with Jesus."

Noche looked at Chihuahua, who smiled and nodded. Noche said, "We've prayed with the *di-yen* Wright, and we pray every day for strength to do what Jesus wants. My life is fast becoming smooth again. I hated Geronimo for what he did. We were innocent of any raids he made. We quietly worked our farms and minded our own business. Yet because of Geronimo's war, we became prisoners of the White Eyes. Two moons ago, I wanted to kill him but knew, while we were under the control of the Blue Coats, that could not be. Many would suffer for anything I did to him. I had bad dreams of things we had done before *Nant'an Lpah* came. But after much prayer, I now sleep in peace. I no longer want to kill Geronimo. I pray for him to find the Jesus Road. Then we will be like brothers."

The chorus from the insects, tree peepers, and frogs all seemed to pause as Noche stopped speaking while he collected his thoughts and then continued.

"Keeping yourself always ready to hear God is hard. The Jesus *di-yens* say, to hear God, we mustn't drink whiskey, play cards, beat our women, fight, or gamble racing our horses. We should encourage all people we know and even strangers to walk the Jesus Road to a better life. We hope you hear our words and watch our lives so you want to join us. That is all I have to say."

Chihuahua leaned into the firelight so his face was easy to see and looked at me. "Chato, after you killed my nephew, my brother's son, just a boy, I vowed that one day I would get my satisfaction and kill you if Ulzana had not done so already. But now that I'm on the Jesus Road, that is no longer a thing I can or will do. For my part, I don't hate you any longer. Jesus has forgiven me for all the bad things I did in the wars, and now I tell you, I forgive you for what you did to my family. You have nothing to fear from me, and if Ulzana walks the Jesus Road, you will have nothing to fear from him for the killing of his son. God forgives you of the bad things you have done in the past, even for killing my nephew, and you and Naiche for not fighting at Aliso Creek when so many of our People died. We've all done many bad things. Jesus wipes our record clean and remembers no more all the bad things we've done. I sleep in peace now. My family is together again even if we are prisoners. My life is smooth like it's never been before. This Jesus Road helps us all even if we can't have whiskey, play cards, or race our horses for money. This is all I have to say."

I was glad to learn Chihuahua no longer planned to take revenge against me for killing his nephew or thought bad of us for hanging back at Aliso Creek when the *Nakai-yi* soldiers attacked Loco's People and killed many women and children. I saw Naiche nod that he was happy to hear this too.

Naiche said, "I talked privately with Geronimo three suns ago. I asked if he could give me any advice if I decided to walk the Jesus Road. He said there were still plenty of revenge accounts against others that he must settle, that he didn't have bad dreams in the night visions, and what was done in war was normal and the Blue Coats were supposed to wipe them clean from the record. I know now, Geronimo doesn't understand what the Jesus Road means. I don't claim to know that yet, but I tell you now, I intend to."

I said, "My brothers speak with straight tongues, and so will I. I know I have many faults and much to regret. I'm very sorry that Chihuahua's nephew and Ulzana's son was killed in the land of the *Nakai-yes*, but he was fighting like a man, and yes, I killed him and was sorry when I did, but the way he was trying to kill us, I believed I had no choice. I'm sorry for many things that happened before *Nant'an Lpah* came to us in the Sierra Madre camps and brought us back to San Carlos. I've wanted to do the right thing since then.

"I've avoided Geronimo because I wanted to kill him for all the bad things he's done, and I know he wants to and has tried to kill me or have me killed. Now I think that because there is a better way with the Jesus Road, I no longer want to kill anyone. I know there are people who dislike me for trying to do the right thing and for things I've said and done in the past that were not the right thing."

I stared at the fire a moment as I made up my mind. Off in the distance coyotes yipped and then grew quiet as the little fire snapped and popped as my friends watched me.

"Next Sunday, I join the mission fellowship. I hope that you'll accept me. I'll try hard to walk the Jesus Road to a smooth life. But as the *di-yen* Wright said, if I fall, I need only to get back up and keep on walking to stay on the Jesus Road."

Noche, Chihuahua, and Naiche were smiling and nodding and almost with one voice said, *"Enjuh!"*

Naiche said, "I'll be with you, Chato. We will join these good men together."

We talked together a long time by the little fire that night and looked deep into each other's soul. I thought then we were all changing for the better.

THE NEXT SUNDAY, Naiche and I took the hand of the *di-yen* Wright and began walking the Jesus Road. A few suns later, we went to a deep pool in Medicine Bluff Creek and did the baptism ceremony. We learned to pray as the *di-yen* said Jesus wanted us to pray and learned all the things we shouldn't do if we wanted Jesus to hear us when we prayed. I felt better and happier with my life and had peace in my mind I had not known before. I had decided to drink no whiskey after Ishchos and the children were taken, but I admit I took a swallow occasionally for medicine to make me feel better. I decided to keep that path. I gave up occasional card games and betting on horse races. I never missed losing those times. Naiche dreamed no more bad dreams and felt such peace that he decided to take the name Christian Naiche and later named a son Christian. I admired Naiche and was glad we were friends. He had grown much from when he first became a chief and was a true leader of the People.

As the number of our People walking the Jesus Road increased, their use of Chiricahua *di-yens*, including Geronimo, decreased. Geronimo withdrew into his village and stayed there except to go to his fields or take his wife, Zi-yeh, and daughter, Eva, to Wratten's store. I rarely saw him except at the store. When we did cross paths, he gave me a hard, menacing stare, but I was on the Jesus Road and gave him a smile and nodded, which seemed to make him even more angry.

As the People made less and less use of Geronimo's *di-yen* Power, he somehow became of greater interest to the White Eyes. The harvest before the Jesus Road *di-yens* came, Geronimo, Naiche, and a few others went to a big White Eye gathering called "exposition" in a place northeast of us called "Omaha." Naiche told me that, there, Geronimo sold his souvenirs and his signatures and photographs to more White Eyes than he could count, made much money, and faced *Nant'an* Miles to argue that he'd lied to get Geronimo and Naiche's band to surrender, and Miles laughed and admitted it was true. The desire of the White Eyes to see Geronimo, who had killed many of them, brought him invitations to other White Eye gatherings, and the Army let him go to many of them.

During the Season of Big Leaves after the other leaders and I started on the Jesus Road, the *di-yens* who spoke to us on Sundays decided we should have a "tent meeting," where they taught two or three times a day and Comanche and Kiowa also attended. We set up a big tent where the People sat in its shade on benches and chairs and stayed out of the rain if it fell while the *di-yens* did their talks, prayers, singing, and other ceremonies.

There was much singing under the big tent. Most of the People didn't know the White Eye words to the songs, but with George Wratten's help, they learned to sing them in our tongue. The *di-yens* always extended the hand of fellowship to those who wanted to walk the Jesus Road, and many accepted the hands of the *di-yens* during the seven days and later the baptism ceremony in the nearby creek where I had the ceremony.

IN WHAT THE White Eyes called "the year 1902," we had our third tent meeting. Geronimo's wife and daughter, as at the first two tent meetings, came and set up a little tent to live in nearby, visited with the other women, and listened to the *di-yens* and their talks and ceremonies. The first two harvests when we had tent meetings, Geronimo never came with them, but on the last day of the third tent meeting, he rode his pony to the meeting and sat outside Zi-yeh's tent. Many who were camped there watched him with questioning eyes and wondered what he planned to do. When the *di-yens* who were conducting the tent meeting ceremonies learned he was camped nearby, they went and talked to him. I saw them speak with Geronimo but heard none of what they said except what others who were nearby heard and repeated. Their talks were relaxed and easy. They told Geronimo to come to the meeting that night and learn about the Jesus Road. Geronimo thanked them for the invitation and said he would think about it after his nap. They shook hands, and the *di-yens* left.

That evening, Geronimo came and sat on the first row with his hands in his lap. He seemed to enjoy the singing, and after the *di-yen* made a call for people to come forward and take his hand in fellowship, Geronimo stood and raised his hands, gave his own talk about how good the Jesus Road was, encouraged people to follow it even though he had not yet, and closed his speech with, "Now we begin to think that the Christian white people love us." There were many who came and shook hands with Geronimo, said kind words to him, and patted him on the back. I heard the *di-yens* talking to him, and he was saying things like, "This singing is a good thing. I want to include it in my *di-yen* ceremonies. There is much to Jesus Road that I like."

The Jesus Road *di-yens* decided not to offer the baptism ceremony to Geronimo until he learned more about Jesus and encouraged him to come there to the mission church every Sunday and hear the *di-yens* talk. Geronimo said that he would come with Zi-yeh even though she was part of the Catholic tribe of Christians. That seemed to please them all.

# THIRTY-FOUR

## WITCH

DURING THE HARVEST that followed Geronimo's first tent meeting, he came to the mission almost every Sunday to hear the *di-yens*. Those of us who knew him believed that, on the Sundays he didn't come and wasn't off traveling somewhere, he was sleeping off a drunk in the Cache Creek *bosque*, the Blue Coat calaboose, or his bed. On the Sundays when he came to the mission, he even nodded to me without hate in his eyes and spoke kindly to all.

Geronimo wasn't present at the first tent meeting the next harvest, even though he had come often to the mission on Sundays, and Naiche's face filled with sadness near to eye water. Chihuahua had ridden the ghost pony two harvests earlier, a few suns after the tent meeting. He had been a good man, a strong warrior, and had walked a straight path on the Jesus Road. We were all sorry that he had left us. His son Eugene, who worked with Wratten at his store, became the village chief. Chihuahua's village was southwest of Geronimo's and the next village west. Naiche found Eugene after the morning meeting and asked him if he knew why Geronimo had not come to the first meeting.

Eugene nodded and sighed. "Geronimo was trying to show Zi-yeh, his grandson Thomas, who lives with them now, and Eva what a fine horseman he was, riding Zi-yeh's mare. He did something with her that made her do an unexpected crow hop. She threw him off. He sailed high and landed hard on his lower back. Thomas says he's hurt bad and been lying in bed for the past three or four days, barely able to even get up for his private business. He's lucky he didn't break his back. He keeps calling himself an 'old fool.'"

Naiche puffed his cheeks and blew. "Whew, I hope he gets better soon. We'll pray for him. That's about all we can do."

Eugene squinted, looking out across the hot, dry fields, and nodded. "Yes, sir. I suspect it is. It sure is getting hot, ain't it?"

Naiche wiped the sweat from his face with his pocket handkerchief. "Hmmph. Very hot."

BY THE TIME we ate our midday meal, the sun was at the time of no shadows and cast fiery, blinding light on all of us. A strange quiet settled over the camp. No birds sang. Even the insects were quiet. Most men found a shady spot after they ate and tried to take a little *siesta*. Several of us found shelter in the shade of a big cottonwood next to the meeting tent. We sat and talked with the *di-yens* about what we had heard and understood from them that morning.

As we were talking, I saw a lone rider in the shimmering heat waves hunched forward on his pony, slowly walking it down the hill toward the tent. I squeezed Naiche's arm to get his attention and nose pointed toward the rider. Naiche's attention locked on the rider. I heard him whisper what I was thinking, Geronimo.

Geronimo rode the pony up to the tent and slowly, in obvious pain, slid off holding on to the saddle horn to steady himself for a few moments before, leaning forward and bent over, he shuffled into the tent. We didn't waste any time following him inside. He was slumped in a chair near the front, and Naiche sat down beside him.

Geronimo, in his dry, wispy voice of an old man, spoke in Apache, and Benedict Jozhe interpreted what he said for the *di-yens*. "Geronimo says he's in the dark. He knows that he's not on the right road and wants to find Jesus."

The *di-yens* had big smiles, but Naiche's face was aflame with happiness as he gently hugged Geronimo's shoulders. "You are very close to the Jesus Road, Grandfather. Come to my tent and let my woman Ha-o-zinne serve you a meal, and then you get some rest before tonight's message, and in the days to come, the brothers and I will tell you what we have come to believe is true about Jesus and why it is so."

"Come on, lean on me and, we get you some food in your belly and rest for your bones."

As he was standing, his bloodshot eyes locked with mine for a moment before he reached for the back of a bench to steady himself. He was a proud man brought low, and I had never felt such sorrow for a warrior before. I prayed then that Jesus would make Geronimo strong and useful again. Naiche had one of his boys take care of Geronimo's pony and sent another with a wagon to get his family. But before he could leave, Zi-yeh, Eva, and Thomas rode into the camp with their tent and a week's worth of supplies.

Naiche told Zi-yeh that Geronimo was resting and to put their tent next to his and use Ha-o-zinne's cooking fire. Zi-yeh had been sick for a long time and was getting worse, but the last thing she was about to do was let her man be uncomfortable at a tent meeting.

When the night meeting began, Zi-yeh and the children had helped him move up to a front-row bench so he could hear the *di-yens* and their ceremonies, and he sat with bowed head listening to every word. For the next six days, many of the men who had joined the mission assembly came and sat around Geronimo, telling their conversion stories, their challenges, and how God had blessed them despite the troubles they had as prisoners of war.

At the last meeting of that tent meeting, Geronimo accepted the Jesus Road as he took the speaker's hand at the invitation to join the assembly, saying, "I'm old and broken by this fall I've had. I'm without friends, for my People have turned from me. I'm full of sins, and I walk alone in the dark. I see that you missionaries have got a way to get sin out of the heart, and I want to take the better way and hold it until I die."

This time, the Jesus Road *di-yens* decided that Geronimo understood what a commitment to Jesus meant and that he was ready for the baptism ceremony. Three days later, Geronimo joined the assembly of baptized Christians during much singing and many prayers. The brothers helped him with his farm work while his body healed, and he thanked God for us. In a few moons, just before harvest time, he was strong enough to do his own farm work.

FOR MORE THAN two harvests, Geronimo stayed straight on the Jesus Road, this despite Zi-yeh riding the ghost pony in the next harvest. He spoke often with Naiche about Jesus, even with me listening and occasionally adding what I knew to their conversation. In the harvest year the White Eyes named "1905," Geronimo went to another exposition at a great village named Saint Louis. There, he found his nineteen-year-old daughter, Lenna, whom he hadn't seen since she was a little child. Lenna was the daughter of Ih-tedda, the Mescalero woman Geronimo had divorced to get her and Lenna out of Mount Vernon and sent back to her father at Mescalero. Geronimo learned from Lenna that Ih-tedda had been married off to an old, retired scout a few days after she returned to Mescalero and, seven or eight moons later, had given birth to a son she named Robert. Geronimo knew the boy could easily be his even if Ih-tedda claimed he was not. After seeing Robert at the Chilocco Indian School, he was certain the boy was his son.

During those harvests when Geronimo traveled the Jesus Road, he also rode in the Great Father Roosevelt's parade in the big village of many stone buildings where I and my group from Fort Apache had gone to beg another Great Father to let the scouts continue living on their farms. On this trip, Geronimo sold many of his photographs, hats, and toy bows and arrows, and made much money. I think all the recognition by the White Eyes, all the money he made, and Zi-yeh riding the ghost pony made him stumble off the Jesus Road. He started to drink whiskey more often and to gamble again. A time or two, the police found him passed out in the weeds with an empty whiskey bottle nearby. They put him in the calaboose to sober up. When he was let out of the calaboose, a few in the mission assembly saw him leave. Word spread fast that Geronimo was going wobbly on the Jesus Road. When I heard the story, I didn't doubt it.

A new *di-yen*, Leonard Legters, came to speak on Sundays. Within a moon after he began to speak and teach, or so Naiche told me, Legters spoke with Geronimo privately about asking Jesus to forgive his fall and help him back to the Jesus Road. Geronimo told him no. He had decided that the *di-yen* rules for being on the Jesus Road were too hard and that he was turning back to *Ussen* as his god. Naiche was near eye water when he told me this. He had so wanted Geronimo to know the peace Jesus had given him.

GERONIMO HAD A White Eye friend named Barrett who was a chief of schools in the area where a new village was built and growing not far from the Fort Sill gate. The village was named after *Capitán* Henry Lawton, who had chased Geronimo in the land of the *Nakai-yes*. Barrett wanted to write the true story of Geronimo's life, and after the Great Father gave him permission to do it, the Army agreed to let him make the tracks for a book if they had final approval of what was written. Geronimo told Barrett he would speak about his life at times they both agreed to and only he, Barrett, could write down what he heard from the interpreter, who was Daklugie.

One early sun, during the moons Geronimo was telling his stories to Barrett, Noche and I sat on Wratten's store porch drinking a cup of coffee before we rode out to inspect the boundary fence. It was in the Season of Little Eagles. The sun, still low, looking like a red egg on the eastern horizon, was growing brighter and gave a little warmth to our skin, but there was still a chill in the air. Larks called from their ground nests, and our horses stood peacefully at the hitching rail, unbothered by flies and other insects.

Lot Eyelash and a couple of other young men I knew had ridden with Geronimo in his reservation escapes rode up the hitching rail, tied their ponies off, and, acknowledging us with head nods, went in the store. Soon Eyelash led the others out with cups of coffee in their hands and walked over to Noche and me. Eyelash, with a slight frown of curiosity wrinkled on his brow, said, "Brothers, we want to ask your wisdom about something that we worry about."

I looked at the other two and saw the same little frown that Eyelash carried. Noche gave me a little head nod, and I said, "There are chairs. Come, sit with us." They brought the chairs and sat close together in front of us. After they sat down and had a slurp or two of the steaming hot coffee, I gave a little head nod. "Speak. We listen."

Lot Eyelash said, "You know Geronimo tells the story of his life to the White Eye, Barrett, and that Daklugie is their interpreter. We hear that the Blue Coats will read and approve the story tracks made by Barrett before it is sold to the White Eyes. We all rode with Geronimo and did many things to the White Eyes and *Nakai-yes* for which we're sorry. Do you think Geronimo tells of these things? Will their telling get us in trouble? What can we do so the Blue Coats don't come after us?"

I looked at Noche and then Eyelash. "I don't know. If Geronimo puts stories of what we did in that book of many tracks, the Whites Eyes might want revenge, but I doubt it. Just because Geronimo says something doesn't make it so, and the White Eyes learned that many harvests ago. He knows if he gets you in trouble, he'll be in trouble, too, so I'd guess he'll be very careful about what he says. You should keep your ears open in case he does make a mistake, and be ready to run if you have to. But I think it'll be all right, especially if you stay out of trouble and no one thinks to use the book to tie you to something bad."

Noche's thoughts were about the same as mine, and when he finished speaking, Eyelash and the others looked a little more relaxed than before. We talked a while longer about what Geronimo might say that we should all watch for, rinsed our cups from the rain barrel, and rode off to take care of our work for the day.

NOT LONG AFTER Noche and I spoke with Lot Eyelash and his friends, Eyelash claimed *Ussen* had given him Power and special ceremonies to identify witches. I wondered if this was true or if Eyelash claimed it so that he might hear the latest gossip on what tales Geronimo might be telling the White Eyes.

Geronimo's daughter Eva seemed to be getting ill. As he thought about all his children and family he had lost and why, he began to think that a witch was taking his family members and, to save Eva, he had to find the witch. He decided to pay for a big ceremony for a *di-yen* to identify the witch. There were several *di-yens* among us who knew the ceremonies for identifying a witch. But Geronimo had ridden in war with Lot Eyelash following him. Eyelash seemed the perfect choice to help him identify the witch.

In the harvest the White Eyes named "1908," Geronimo invited all the villages to come to the big witch-finding feast and ceremony. Most of the old Apache came but not those who were Christians. They didn't believe in witches and thought Geronimo should just pray to Jesus to save his children. My curiosity about the outcome of this ceremony, knowing what I did about Eyelash, led me to sit in brush on a nearby hill where I could see and hear what was going on.

The ceremony was held in a field next to Cache Creek. There was a big roaring fire, where Eyelash led the People in dancing around it, feasting, and singing until the moon rose to the top of the arc, and then Eyelash disappeared for a time. The People found places to sit down and quietly wait for Eyelash to reappear.

Eyelash came out of the shadows like smoke from the fire and began a dance that would involve the four directions. Depending on his Power, his songs and dances might continue until sunrise to make known the witch taking Geronimo's children. His dances and songs were strange. I had never seen anything like them. He went through two songs and dances as the fire slowly burned down to blue flames among the orange embers. The drummers paused and then shifted to a new rhythm. Eyelash began to dance and sing his third song.

Eyelash suddenly raised his hands toward the sky and yelled, "Ho!" The dancing and drummers stopped, and all eyes turned to him. His left arm lowered, but his hand on the raised right arm made a fist with his index finger raised. Slowly the hand came trembling down and stopped, the quivering finger pointing directly at Geronimo.

Eyelash yelled, "You did it! You did it so you could live on."

There was a kind of collective gasp from those who sat around the fire as Geronimo, with crossed arms, stared at Eyelash, his black eyes glittering with outrage, and walked to within four paces of the singer. He said, "I don't know where you got your Power, Eyelash, but it wasn't from the same *Ussen* who has given me my Power to help the People since before you were even born. I would never take the lives of my children for mine, which I risked many more times than you ever did when you were my novitiate. I know, after all these years, none of the Powers *Ussen* gave me demand my children's lives that I might live."

Eyelash raised his chin and looked down his nose at Geronimo and said through clenched teeth, "I have said all I'm going to say."

Geronimo smiled. *"Doo dat'éé da!* Then the dance and ceremony are done. Go and say no more."

The People were fast to leave the fire, Lot Eyelash with them. Geronimo stood with his arms crossed, staring at the dying fire a long time before he turned and walked toward his house across Cache Creek.

I didn't move until he was gone. I thought, *Only Jesus can save your children from evil, Geronimo. It's sad you didn't and haven't prayed for that and stayed on the Jesus Road. You are a good lesson for us all.*

# THIRTY-FIVE

## GERONIMO RIDES
## THE GHOST PONY

NAICHE AND I checked the reservation fence a few suns after Lot Eyelash
had accused Geronimo of being a witch and trading his death for those of his
children so his Power would not take him. The accusation and Geronimo's re-
sponse to it had swept across the villages like a prairie fire in a strong wind, and
Naiche knew the story like everyone else. As we rode along the fence under the
shining, blue, cloudless sky, Naiche said, "What do you think of this story about
Lot Eyelash accusing Geronimo of witching the deaths of his children so he can
live longer?"

I pulled the brim of my hat forward for more shade on my face and said, "I
know for a fact what happened at the ceremony. I saw and heard it all."

Naiche turned to me with a frown. "You, a Christian, went to a *di-yen* ceremony when you promised to stay on the Jesus Road?"

"I didn't attend the ceremony. I watched it from brush that was close enough
for me to see and hear what was going on. Not long into the ceremony, Eyelash,
with a sneering frown, pointed at Geronimo and said he had done the witching.
Geronimo, his teeth clenched and creases of anger covering his face, said *Ussen*
never told Eyelash that and the ceremony was over. People left in a hurry, but
he stayed there a long time, watching the ceremony fire burn to coals, and then
prayed to *Ussen* before he went home. I felt bad for him. I know he's done everything he knows to do to save his children. You might remember that he even
divorced Ih-tedda to save her and little Lenna from dying at Mount Vernon."

Naiche pulled up and looked at me with a squint against the bright sunlight.
"You saw and heard it all?"

"I did."

"Why do you think Eyelash would do something evil like that?"

"Survival."

"What do you mean?"

"Early one morning back in the Season of Little Leaves, Noche and I spoke to Eyelash and two of his friends at Wratten's store. Eyelash was afraid that Geronimo might tell bad tales about his old warriors to the man writing down his life's story. He thought these tales might get him and his friends in trouble when White Eye chiefs saw it. That was about the time Eyelash claimed to have his witch-identification ceremony revealed to him by *Ussen*. I think he believed that if he could make Geronimo look bad, to his own People, then the Blue Coats wouldn't think about coming after him because Geronimo told a White Eye some story.

"When Geronimo asked for Eyelash to do the witch-identification ceremony, Eyelash probably thought he could run Geronimo back into the shadows and make the People stay away from him. I don't think anyone believed it except for maybe a handful of old Apache who were there."

Naiche looked out over the rolling green prairie, shrugged his shoulders, sighed, and said, "You're probably right. It's just too bad that Geronimo left the Jesus Road. Jesus could have helped him and healed his children, too, without resorting to things we shouldn't believe in anymore.

"Come on, we've got several more miles of fence to check before it gets dark."

We trotted down the fence line until dark but found the fence was untouched and in good shape.

THE ASSEMBLY *DI-YENS* held another tent meeting a moon after I talked with Naiche. Geronimo came to speak with Legters, the chief *di-yen* leading the meeting. Legters asked Naiche and other church leaders, including Noche and me, to attend the meeting with him. Geronimo rode in after the morning service, took his fine roan pony to the corral, and unsaddled her before coming to sit with us in the shade of the tent. After we prayed for guidance, Legters told us Geronimo wanted to return to the Jesus Road and asked him to tell us why he wanted to seek Jesus again.

Geronimo explained why he had asked Eyelash for his ceremony and what happened. He knew the ceremony was a lie and decided he had to follow the god with the most Power. Heads around me nodded. Legters started to speak, but Naiche raised his chin and said, "Tell us, Geronimo, do you still drink whiskey?"

"Yes. Sometimes an old man needs his medicine."

"Do you still believe in *Ussen,* or have you returned to Jesus?"

"I believe in both. If the White Eye God is in three parts, then why can't *Ussen* be a fourth part?"

"Do you still play card games like monte, games of chance?"

"All of life depends on chance. Why not understand chance with games?"

"Will you marry Azul as the White God directs?"

"Azul and I are happily married in the Apache way. There's no need to do the White God marriage ceremony. He knows our hearts are good for each other."

"Do you still wish to die fighting?"

"Yes. That is how I want to die. I want to die fighting like a warrior, but *Ussen* has told me that won't happen."

Naiche, frowning, stared at Geronimo and slowly shook his head. "Return to *Ussen,* Geronimo. You're not ready for the Jesus Road."

Geronimo looked at each of us in the group. When his eyes found mine, I saw that little squint that hate brings as I slowly nodded as the others had. Naiche was right. Geronimo was not ready for the Jesus Road.

He stood, looked at each of us once more, and then walked to the corral. Legters stood up holding his big Bible with many black water tracks in both hands and called after him, "Geronimo, wait! Stay with us! Jesus will save you!" Geronimo never looked back. He went to his pony, saddled him, and rode away.

GERONIMO LIVED WITH his new wife, Azul, in Guydelkon's house in Chihuahua's village. He enjoyed life making his souvenirs, for which visitors always paid much money, and playing card games with the boys who visited him. I only saw him a few times the rest of that harvest. Each time, he looked more and more frail, losing weight and a little height, and he never acknowledged seeing me.

One morning in the Ghost Face near to the Season of Little Eagles, I went to Wratten's store for supplies. It had rained the night before, making the ground too wet to do anything outside and giving me a good excuse to sit by Wratten's stove and swap stories and plans for planting with the other men there.

When I walked in the store, there seemed to be more people than usual sitting around the stove. Wratten was busy, so I told one of his helpers, a young boy, what I needed and walked over to the stove to get some coffee amid a low buzz of talk from the people sitting around the stove. As I was pouring my coffee, one of the old men said, "Ho, Chato, what you think about Geronimo?"

I stuck out my lower lip and frowned. "What you mean? I haven't seen him in half a moon. What's he done now?"

The old man made a face. "We hear he got drunk and slept out all night in the rain. Sounds like he has what the White Eye *di-yens* call the 'pneumonia sickness.' He's over to the Apache hospital now. You go in that place and you don't come out alive. Daklugie, Eugene Chihuahua, and Azul are all over there with him, but the *di-yens* won't let anybody else visit with him. The Blue Coat *di-yen* says he'll be lucky to live more than two or three days."

I finished pouring the coffee and looked at the men around me. They all had sad eyes, and I guess I did, too.

As the men talked about the raids and fights in which Geronimo led them in the days before surrender and the Power he had as a *di-yen*, my mind flooded with images from all the years I had spent with and against him. I remembered the fury in his face when Clum arrested us and took us back to San Carlos. For reasons I never knew, Clum set me and other warriors free but put Geronimo and his leaders in the guardhouse, there to wait for the Tucson sheriff to claim him for hanging. But the sheriff never came, and Clum left as reservation agent, angry at his big chiefs. The new agent freed Geronimo and his leaders. Geronimo claimed it all happened because *Ussen* answered his prayers. I remembered the surprise in his eyes after we found *Nant'an Lpah*'s scouts had attacked my village in the Sierra Madre and how deferential he became to the *nant'an*. After *Teniente* Davis arrested Kaytennae and then made me his first sergeant, Geronimo looked at me with angry eyes turned red and called me a traitor and a liar, but I didn't think keeping your word and not telling lies made you a traitor and a liar. I remembered how he laughed and enjoyed killing *Nakai-yes*. I remembered his despair and desperation when the *Nakai-yes* took Chee-hash-kish prisoner and how he tried to free her. The memories of Geronimo in my past were a never-ending stream as I sat and slurped my coffee with the low rumble of voices in the background surrounding the stove.

I was staring into space, watching those memories, when the boy helping Wratten finished gathering my supplies, put them in a burlap bag, and called to me stopping my drift down the river of memories. I took the sack, left the store, and rode to the Apache hospital. Despite it being cold and wet, many of the People were gathered all the way around the building, waiting on any news whether the old man had died or lived on.

I stopped and asked an old, gray-haired man I didn't recognize standing at the edge of the crowd what had happened. "We all came to see Geronimo, but the only ones they let in the place are his wife Azul, the nephew Daklugie, and his grandson Eugene Chihuahua. My nephew, who's an orderly in there, told me Geronimo probably won't live more than two or three days. Daklugie and Eugene are takin' turns staying up with him. The rest of us are waiting to learn if he'll live or ride the ghost pony."

I waved him good luck with my hand parallel to the ground and left. Returning to my house, I gathered my women and son, who were sorting seeds and making ready to plow and harrow our crop ground, and told them what I had learned and that I expected we would attend his funeral in two or three days. Helen's and Banatsi's eyes looked on the edge of water, but they only nodded and said they would be ready.

My son Maurice said, "I guess he wouldn't be sick if he had kept on the Jesus Road. Do you think Jesus will save him now, Father?"

I shook my head. "I don't know. I know he could if Geronimo asked him, but Geronimo has chosen his path and doesn't pray to Jesus but to *Ussen*. I think his time has come."

"Father, Geronimo hated you for all you did to track him down during his last breakout. Are you glad he's about to ride the ghost pony?"

I puffed my cheeks and sighed. "I'm never glad when a man, regardless of who he is, rides the ghost pony. I've never known Geronimo to be anything but mean, full of deceit, and only caring for himself, and I was just as bad when I rode with him. After I talked with *Nant'an Lpah*, I decided he might get my wife and children out of Mexican slavery, and that there was a better way to live. I tried to be a better man and live peaceably with the White Eyes. I found the Jesus Road the best way to live. Sometimes I fall off that road, but I always pick myself back up and get back on it. I hope you will do that, too."

All my family members said they were trying to stay on the Jesus Road, and that warmed my heart.

GERONIMO DIED IN the early morning of the sun the White Eyes named February 17, 1909. He was laid out in his favorite clothes in a little stone building at the fort. Old women grieving, wiping water from their eyes, and praying walked through to tell him goodbye. The men, their shoulders hunched as if standing against a cold wind, sad beyond description with words, stayed outside and watched in silence.

The funeral was the next day. We waited in a long line for Geronimo's children, Eva and Robert, to arrive on the iron wagon from Chilocco School before beginning the ride to the Apache cemetery. The Blue Coat in charge of us, *Teniente* Purington, didn't notify Geronimo's children how sick he was until it was too late for them to come and see him a last time before he rode the ghost pony. As it was, we had to wait half a hand before they arrived filled with grief, water spilling from their eyes, their faces twisted in pain, before we could start for the Apache cemetery.

Geronimo's grave was dug next to Zi-yeh's—she had ridden the ghost pony about four harvests before. The ceremony for last-remembrance words was held by the side of the grave. I was with the leaders in the first row of the people surrounding the grave. Naiche, tall and straight, standing at the very edge of the grave, spoke first in the strong, clear voice of a true chief. He remembered times Geronimo was on the warpath, spoke of his bravery, how fine he was as a war leader, and how he kept the peace without failure after he surrendered. He said that Geronimo in his old age had found the Jesus Road, life's greatest blessing, but had lost his way on it, and thus was an utter failure in the chief thing in life. Naiche urged us to profit by Geronimo's example. I thought, *Naiche, you've never spoken truer words.* The *di-yen* Leonard Legters from the church assembly then gave the Jesus Road ceremony for burying the dead, with Eugene Chihuahua interpreting his words into Apache.

Daklugie wanted to be sure no one would dig up Geronimo's grave to take his favorite things buried with him or chop off his head for a traveling sideshow to show off his skull. He organized crews of two men each night to guard the grave and make certain such an outrage didn't happen. The guards were there every night for moons all through that harvest and then, after a while, every other night, before finally stopping after we were sure no one would desecrate the grave.

# THIRTY-SIX

## BLAKE RIDES
## THE GHOST PONY

GERONIMO RIDING THE ghost pony unlocked the doors that kept us prisoners of war. The Blue Coats would never let Geronimo, and consequently our People, loose again for him to take vengeance once more against the White Eyes or them against him. After he left for the Happy Place, it took four years for them to let us go—this after the Army had decided it wanted the land we had worked for nearly twenty years. They wanted to use our land for teaching soldiers how to shoot big guns that could kill many in one shot.

The harvest Geronimo rode the ghost pony, Daklugie and Eugene Chihuahua began asking the big chiefs to free us and let us have our own land. Daklugie had listened to stories from Mescalero about their reservation in the Sacramento Mountains of New Mexico. He believed that if we had a place to go when we were released from captivity, then the Blue Coat big chiefs in the village of the Great Father would be more likely to release us. A moon or two after Geronimo went to the Happy Place, Daklugie got permission to buy his own ticket and visit Mescalero. Snow was still in patches on the ground, but he rode all over the reservation, hunted with a couple of Mescalero, and talked to the Mescalero agent and leaders. He thought the Mescalero reservation land could easily support a large cattle herd and that there was plenty of game to hunt and forests to supply firewood and timber for lumber. He asked the Mescalero if they wanted the Chiricahua on their reservation. Their answer was solid. "Come to us."

Daklugie also visited the Blue Coat big chiefs in the place of the Great Father. Daklugie made the argument for why we should be freed as prisoners of war. After he returned, we held a council, and he told us he thought the Mescalero Reservation would be a fine place for us. It had enough range for a large herd of cattle, good hunting, plenty of timber, and the possibility of good wells anywhere on the reservation. After hearing this, most of the men wanted to go to Mescalero. Others, who had lived at Ojo Caliente before Clum came, wanted to live there, and a few others liked the Fort Sill land, remembered all the labor we put into it, and wanted to stay.

A few moons after Daklugie returned, *Teniente* Purington called a council of the men in a shady oak grove next to Cache Creek, not far from the main post. He made black water tracks in a book of paper as a record of all the questions and answers, conflicts of opinion, and who wanted to go where. He asked Daklugie to describe again what he'd found at Mescalero. Before he could speak, Daklugie and Naiche argued over whether the Chiricahua had agreed to share their cattle herd with the Mescalero. Daklugie wanted all the cattle and farming tools sent to Mescalero and half the herd to go to the Mescalero. Naiche said the council had never agreed to such a deal. *Teniente* Purington said that issue could be resolved later. He let Daklugie tell again what he had seen, about his meeting with the Mescalero and their agent, and what they had discussed.

*Teniente* Purington noted that the Chiricahua had eighty men, sixty-four women, twenty boys over twelve, forty boys under twelve, fourteen girls over twelve, and forty-one girls under twelve years of age. Sixteen scouts on duty were all Chiricahua.

The council talks determined that thirty-eight men wanted to go to Mescalero, eighteen wanted to go to Ojo Caliente, and fourteen wanted to stay at Fort Sill. There were about seven thousand head of cattle, which *Teniente* Purington said would probably have to be sold to avoid the risk of spreading Texas fever into New Mexico, but that was talk for another time.

After Purington's council, those who wanted to stay at Fort Sill were involved in much haggling with the Army as it built new buildings for becoming a place to shoot big guns. If they were to have land at Fort Sill, they asked, why didn't the Army ask them what they thought about the new buildings?

Two harvests passed into the harvest the White Eyes called "1911" as the big chiefs argued back and forth and the Chiricahua who wanted to stay demanded to make their wishes heard. The Army sent our old friend and commander when we first came, now a colonel, Hugh Scott to convince us of the need to move. Another council of leaders meeting with Colonel Scott decided to send a small group with him to independently check what Daklugie had reported and then see what land was available at Ojo Caliente. Eugene Chihuahua and Goody were sent to represent the Chiricahua who wanted to move to Mescalero and

Toclanny and James Kaywaykla to represent the Chihenne who wanted to return to Ojo Caliente.

When they returned, Eugene Chihuahua and Goody reported that the Mescalero Reservation looked better than what Daklugie had described in glowing terms when he returned. (Daklugie had seen the land in the Season of Little Eagles, when patches of snow were still on the ground. Eugene had seen it in the Season of Large Fruit, when it was at its most fruitful). Toclanny and Kaywaykla learned there was little useful land left at Ojo Caliente, not enough to support the number of families who wanted to return there. Those people would have to decide if they wanted to stay around Fort Sill or move to Mescalero.

DESPITE GERONIMO RIDING the ghost pony and fanning sparks of hope for a release from captivity to a blaze in the long, dry grass of our dreams, shadows of sadness still filled my house. Four moons before Geronimo went to the Happy Place, my youngest son, Blake, rode the ghost pony. He was a good son with a sweet soul, smooth and easy in temperament. He had attended the mission school. He could speak the White Eye tongue as well as most White Eyes, and his mind worked fast with numbers. I tried to teach him and his brother, Maurice, how to use weapons and to bring home game from the hunt. Maurice was a natural hunter, good with every weapon from a sling to a bow to a rifle or *pistola*. Blake, on the other hand, preferred to spend his time studying how White Eye black water tracks on paper spoke the maker's words and to follow and learn from them.

I had learned to speak the White Eye tongue, could read some of their black water tracks on paper, and work with their numbering system when I was in the Army. I didn't learn enough to easily read the water tracks on paper. Blake thought it funny that I wouldn't call writing anything but "tracks on paper." The terms had been in my head too long to change for new shorter words.

The harvest Blake rode the ghost pony, he was showing all the signs of the sickness I had seen at Mount Vernon that took many good people. They grew weak and listless and went through uncontrolled coughing spells, eventually showing spots of blood in the rags they held to their faces when they coughed. Apache *di-yens* believed the sickness was caused by worms, but all the Apache *di-yens* I knew, from Geronimo down, had no ceremony to cure what the White Eyes called "tuberculosis" or "TB," and neither did the White Eye *di-yens*.

When Blake first showed signs of tuberculosis, I took him to the White Eye *di-yen* who served the Blue Coats and asked for medicine. The *di-yen* went through his ceremony to identify the sickness by feeling the boy in different places on his body, using ropes in his ears to listen to Blake's breathing, and holding Blake's wrist while he looked at the watch he carried in his pocket. When the *di-yen* finished his ceremony, he motioned for me to follow him out of the room while Blake put back on his shirt and pants.

We stood next to a window, one side of our faces in the sun's golden glow, our arms crossed, the *di-yen* with his head bowed thinking of words to say, me staring at him and wanting desperately to protect my son. The *di-yen* sighed, looked me in the eyes, and said, "Mister Chato, I'm very sorry to tell you that your son has tuberculosis. It looks like a fast-moving, very deadly variety. There is little I can do except give you medicine to ease any pain he has and perhaps ease his breathing."

My head felt like it had been hit with a war club. Blake was still a child. He knew little of what life meant to a grown man. I thought we had left this sickness at Mount Vernon, but it was still with us. *Ussen* must be punishing my family because I became a Christian.

I knew the answer before I asked the question. "There is nothing but this medicine you give us that you can do for the boy? You cannot do ceremonies to heal him?"

The *di-yen* looked at the floor and sighed. "No, I can't heal him. We don't know enough about the disease to cure it. We just know enough to ease his suffering. It'll be worse, before he leaves us."

I couldn't stop my stutter. "How... how much... long... longer will... will he... will he live?"

The *di-yen* crossed his arms and shook his head. "I don't know, but in cases this advanced, I'd guess no more than six or seven months. There's just nothing we can do except pray that somehow God heals him and keeps him with us."

Riding back to our house under a blazing blue sky, with birds darting after insects in the grass, Blake reined up close to me and said little above a whisper, "What did the doctor say to you out in the hall, Father?"

I was tempted to say nothing, just shake my head and ride on, but I said, "To-night, I will do my own ceremony, make my own medicine, and then we talk."

I saw the sadness in the boy's eyes, but he just nodded, knowing what the *di-yen* said was not good.

We rode on home in silence.

WHEN BLAKE AND I returned to our house, I told him to rest on his bed and then, in the house breezeway, told Helen and Banatsi what the *di-yen* had said. Their eyes filled with water, and they covered their mouths with their hands to keep the wails under their tongues, hidden from the boy. When Maurice came in from working in our crops of squash and beans, we had the evening meal Helen had made us.

As we ate, the boys bantered back and forth as they usually did about who was the best shot or who could plow the straightest furrow or who had the fastest pony, but it seemed Blake's pokes and thrusts at his brother's digs didn't have the fire they usually did. Helen and Banatsi told me they wanted to go to Wratten's store soon to sell baskets they had finished. They said Wratten had told them there were many White Eye women coming in the store and asking for them. Few women made baskets as good as Helen's, and Wratten's customers who asked for them said they were willing to wait until more came in. I promised to take them in the wagon in a day or two.

After Helen poured us the last of the coffee, I said, "My sons and I will make a ceremony at the circle of stones under the big oak behind the house tonight."

Helen nodded and, looking at Banatsi, said, "Can Banatsi and I watch your ceremony from the breezeway?"

I said, "Come sit with us when you are ready. You are always welcome at my ceremonies."

The boys looked at each other, and then Blake looked at the floor and gave a hard, barking cough.

I SAT WITH CROSSED legs, the boys on either side of me, near the little crackling fire under the big oak tree behind my house. The women sat nearby but back a respectful distance. The sky was a soft black cloth showing uncountable brilliant points of white light, and the insects were making much noise. We could even hear the frogs in the distant *bosque,* and the tree limbs above us were filled with a loud chorus of tree peepers.

I waited for the fire to die down to blue with occasional orange flames and then said, "My sons, we hold this ceremony because of what I learned from the White Eye *di-yen* who did his ceremony for Blake today."

Maurice frowned and looked at Blake, who raised his eyebrows in curiosity. Blake said, "Speak, Father. We will listen."

I knew no other way than to speak directly. "Hmmph. The *di-yen* told me he's certain that Blake has the disease the White Eyes call tuberculosis. He says there is nothing he can do to treat it, and Blake will probably ride the ghost pony in six or seven moons. I believe him. I saw many with this disease leave us on the ghost pony when we were at Mount Vernon. Blake shows all the signs of being attacked by this sickness."

Maurice hung his head, and I could see his eyes were bathed in water. Blake sat straight and erect with his chin tilted up. "I'm not afraid to die, Father. I've learned in the mission school there is a better place where Jesus takes our spirits after we die. I am ready to leave this place when he's ready to take me."

I heard a snuffle from one of the women at the edge of the circle of light.

"I know, my son. I wanted to have this little ceremony so our family knows where Jesus leads us in this, and so we can know our own hearts in this."

I reached in the leather pouch Helen had given me many harvests past and handed each boy a large pinch of sage and then kept one for myself. "I have given you sage to put on the fire, that you might bathe in its smoke and be purified. Blake will bathe first, then Maurice, and then me."

I nodded to Blake to go ahead. He tossed the sage on the fire, yielding a little cloud of smoke that washed over him, making him cough. Then I motioned to Maurice to bathe in his smoke. His sage made a brighter flame and produced less smoke than Blake's had made, but Maurice bathed in it and sat back. I tossed my sage on the flames and a good cloud of smoke bathed us all.

When the smoke cleared, I stood and raised my arms to sing a prayer for Jesus to help my son and to give us all the courage, like he had when the evil ones nailed him to a post, to still believe God was with him in a time of trial. I asked for strength in the days to come and for him to guide us in his will even if we did not understand it as we traveled the Jesus Road.

It was not a long prayer, but when I finished, Blake said in a clear, strong voice, "May God bless you, Father," and Maurice said, "Amen and Amen."

AS THE MOONS passed, Blake grew weaker and coughed more. We all knew he wouldn't beat the sickness, and he had accepted that soon he would ride the ghost pony to meet Jesus. I kept Maurice away from his brother. I didn't know if nearness was how the sickness was given to another but knew, if it was, it wouldn't take both my boys.

In the Season of Earth Is Reddish Brown, I sat by my son's bed, ready to give him the medicine the White Eye *di-yen* had given me for his pain. Blake had a deep wheeze for each breath, and he had water leaking from his body like he was working in the fields at the time of no shadows in the Season of Big Leaves.

His sleep was short naps without much rest. He opened his eyes after his last little nap, took my hand, and said, "Now I ride the ghost pony, Father, to whoever is on the other side, *Ussen* or Jesus. It makes no difference to me. I'm proud to be your son. I know you have always done the right thing." He was puffing like he had just run many miles up across the hills.

I heard the door creak and saw Helen sweep into the room with the coffeepot followed by Banatsi with a jug of water. I said, "Helen, come tell your son goodbye. He mounts the ghost pony."

She put the coffeepot on the table and swept to him, saying as she took his other hand, "Jesus waits for you, my son. We will find you on the other side."

He managed to wheeze, "I see you then, Mother," relaxed his hold on both our hands, and was gone.

Banatsi reached to touch his face and then held Helen as she shook with grief but made no sound. Water filled my eyes, and I walked to the window to stare at the life around us that was no more for my youngest son.

# THIRTY-SEVEN

## MAURICE MARRIES
## LENA KAYDAHZINNE

MY *AMIGO* TIM Kaydahzinne, his wife Dashdenzhoos, and four children lived in Naiche's village just across our jointly cultivated fields from my village. He had been a scout who had left the Army but reenlisted when Geronimo and others left for the land of the *Nakai-yes* in the harvest the White Eyes called "1885." Tim was with me, tracking those who had left with Geronimo, Chihuahua, and Naiche, who had all run far into the land of the *Nakai-yes*. Tim helped track and attack camps of the escaped Chiricahua when we could find them. Now, like most of the other Chiricahua men and me, he farmed, worked the cattle herd, and did many of the community tasks we all had to do for everyone's benefit.

One sun in the Season of Large Fruit during the harvest when Geronimo rode the ghost pony, the time the White Eyes called "1909," both our families were picking their cotton crops on a cool, easy day, the sun glowing behind thin clouds, Kaydahzinne and I stopped to smoke and talk a little while at the end of a row of waist-high cotton in a field where the brilliant white bolls made it look like it had snowed. I saw his four surviving children at work in the field. (I think he and Dashdenzhoos had had seven children—she was very fertile.) His oldest child looked to be a young woman of maybe sixteen or seventeen harvests, but I thought the child they'd brought with them from Mount Vernon had ridden the ghost pony the next harvest after we came to Fort Sill.

I said, "Old man, I thought Hannah, who you brought with you from Mount Vernon, had ridden the ghost pony. Now she's a fine-looking young woman."

He grinned and shook his head. "That's not Hannah over there talking to Maurice—she has her eye on him, you know. That's Lena. She's had her *Haheh*, about this time last year. She's really bloomed into a full-grown woman since then, but she's only eleven harvests."

My jaw dropped. "That young woman is little Lena? How can that be?"

Tim shrugged. "I don't know, but *Ussen*—or as the White Eyes say, God or Jesus—formed us all. I guess some just grow up faster than others. I've even had young men come around and ask permission to court her, but she didn't want to court them, and I didn't want her to be a source of fun by a young man I didn't know, even if his family was trustworthy."

I glanced over at the children as they bent over talking and laughing while dragging their sacks of picked cotton bolls down parallel rows. "Hmmph. I'll tell my son to stay away from your daughter."

"Leave them alone, Chato. Maurice is a good boy, and I know his father well. Despite her age, I think Lena wants him to court her. If he comes and asks to court her, I won't say no, and Dashdenzhoos likes him, too. Let us watch and see and not interfere with the natural course of things. Maybe he courts her, maybe he doesn't. Maybe he takes her to wife, maybe he doesn't."

I stared through the dust at our children's fast hands picking cotton bolls as they dragged their sacks behind them while they advanced down their row aisles.

"Hmmph. My friend speaks wise words. Yes. Let us watch if something blooms between them. I won't interfere, but she is very young."

Tim nodded, smiling. *"Ch'ik'eh doleel,* Chato. You make a wise choice."

LATER THAT HARVEST, early in the Season of Earth Is Reddish Brown after the cotton was picked, I took my family in our wagon to Wratten's store. Helen and Banatsi had baskets they wanted to sell, and they wanted to pick up some supplies. As we walked in the store, I heard a woman at the counter laugh and saw Maurice's eyes light up. Tim Kaydahzinne was there with his family. He was standing by the stove and held up a cup of coffee and motioned us over while Helen and Banatsi carried their baskets over to the counter where Wratten stood. Maurice and I filled our cups and turned our backs to the black and shiny-metal-trimmed stove whose heat pulled men to it like moths to a flame.

We had our usual conversation about the progress being made to free us and how the cattle herd was holding up. The *di-yens* predicted a cold winter. We all expected a few cattle would be lost. A much larger number of heifers than usual had been dropping calves before the weather was supposed to turn bad, and we hoped they would enrich us all next harvest.

The conversation reached a quiet time, and I noticed Maurice with a squint of concentration watching every move of the young woman, Lena, at the counter. She would occasionally look over her shoulder with a smile toward us standing around stove.

I thought, *That child acts more like she's twenty than twelve harvests.*

Tim smiled and put his finger by his nose, where I could see it but others couldn't, a signal we used for a coming joke.

He looked hard at Maurice and said, "Hey, young man. You're about to stare a hole through my daughter. You got something on your mind?"

"Oh? No, no, sir. Nothing on my mind. I was just admiring her. I wasn't thinking about anything I shouldn't have. She's a pretty woman. Good for the eyes."

Tim frowned and practically growled (I could tell he was choking back a laugh), "Well if you think she's that nice, why ain't you come to ask me about courting her?"

Maurice's jaw dropped. "Well, uh... I knew you'd run off several of my friends who wanted to court her. I just thought I'd get turned down, too."

Tim nodded. "You just don't charge ahead like your father. Why don't you come see me about sundown this evening? We'll have a meal she'll cook, and afterward, we'll talk about you courting her. That sound reasonable to you?"

Maurice had the biggest smile on his face I had seen since before his brother rode the ghost pony. "That would make me very happy. Your willingness to talk to me is a very good thing. I just hope Lena is interested in me coming to court her."

He looked at me, and I nodded. "You have to make your interests known or you can't dance, my son."

IN THE SEASON of Little Eagles, during the next harvest, the one the White Eyes named "1910," Maurice and Lena planned to marry at the mission. The *di-yen* at the mission was Leonard Legters, who, when he learned how old Lena was, didn't want to do a Jesus marriage ceremony for them but said he would when she was sixteen harvests. They told him that if he didn't do the ceremony for them then, they would marry in the Apache way and then do it again for Jesus when she reached sixteen harvests. Legters changed his mind, and they married at the mission in the Jesus way. Maurice was nineteen. Lena was twelve or thirteen. Legters asked that the ceremony be small, with no big feast to celebrate their marriage. He didn't want it spread about that he was letting young girls marry or he might have to do more. We had a small celebration at my house but only invited people in my village and Naiche's who knew what was going on.

Naiche had an empty house in his village and let them use it to start their married life. They worked together in the fields, helping Tim with his crops. I thought I had lost my son's help. It was his duty to support his father-in-law, but after doing a day's work, he'd slip over to my part of the fields and use the mules and whatever tool he had hitched up to help me. I thought I was a lucky man to have such a thoughtful son. He and Lena often came with Tim and Dash-denzhoos to visit Helen, Banatsi, and me during that harvest. We sat out under the big oak tree and told stories of the old days. Our children leaned forward, listening and soaking up every word we had to tell. By the time of the Season of the Earth Is Reddish Brown, they could tell many of our stories word for word like we had told them.

In the Season of the Ghost Face, it was too cold to sit outside. Then we did most of our visiting during trips to Wratten's store. As the suns drew near to the Season of Little Eagles, Lena looked like she was gaining weight, but then she and Maurice told us they expected their first child in the Season of Large Fruit. It suddenly dawned on me that this would be my first grandchild unless my children in Mexican slavery had children I knew nothing about. It was stunning to think that I had enough harvests to be a grandfather. I didn't feel old like a grandfather. I wasn't even sure how "old" was supposed to feel. Old people moved move slow. I didn't feel I moved slower, yet I knew I moved slower but only in the eyes of those around me.

As the child grew in the belly of Lena, I noticed that Maurice didn't seem to have the fire of life he'd had last harvest. He coughed much more than he used to and always seemed to be tired. Lena told Helen sometimes Maurice awoke in the middle of the night coughing and choking on stuff he needed to spit out. When Helen told me this, a feeling of bad times crept into my bones. I saw Banatsi bow her head and give it a little shake.

The next sun, I saw Maurice using a hoe in the vegetable part of Tim's fields. He saw me coming and stopped to watch me approach. Although the sun was only three or four hands above the horizon, Maurice looked weary like he had been running all day. He cleared his throat, spat, and coughed in his hand as I came near.

"Your melons, squash, and potatoes do well racing the weeds for the sunlight. You should have more than enough to sell after you take what you want for your growing family."

Maurice smiled. "It is good to see you, Father. Your patch of melons and beans looks like it, too, will produce much this harvest. I know using a hoe is woman's work, but my woman has the rest of our family that we have to help support."

We bantered back and forth a little about whose crops were better before I asked, "The sun is not yet halfway to the time of no shadows, but you look like you've been working sunrise to sunset. Are you sick? I have bad memories of the sickness of your brother. Do you have the same thing as him? Let me help you."

"I feel weak sometimes and strong in others. I don't think I have the same sickness as my brother. It's just something I need to shake off. Maybe you have a ceremony for me or can pray to Jesus to make me better?"

"Yes, we're Christians now. I'll follow the Jesus Road and pray for you. I want you to see the White Eye *di-yen* and let him tell you the best medicine if he can find out why you tire so quickly."

"I intend to do that, Father, if what I have gets worse."

I shook my head. "I go to get my pony now. You go get your pony and tell your wife you'll be back before sundown. We'll meet where the roads from our villages join."

He frowned and started to shake his head but thought better of it, shrugged, and started for his house. I went for the barn where our horses were kept.

A YOUNG WHITE Eye *di-yen* did the same ceremonies with Maurice that were done with Blake. I could tell from his frowns as he did his ceremonies that he would not have good things to say. When he finished his ceremonies, he sat on a stool and talked to us.

"Maurice, I think you are in the early stages of tuberculosis. The best thing we know to do now is to send you someplace where dry air and rest can help your body fight it off. I think I could get you into a place farther west, maybe up in Colorado. I can talk with your commander and see what we can work out if you like."

Before the *di-yen* even finished speaking, Maurice was shaking his head. "My wife carries our first baby. I won't leave her alone. How long before I have to go to avoid riding the ghost pony?"

The *di-yen* frowned. "I don't know. I just know, the longer you have TB, the harder it is to get rid of it. I think if you go maybe within a year to rest in a dry place with medical attention, it could do you a lot of good. Much longer than that and you won't live to see your child reach two or three harvests. I can check to see where we might send you, but you need to tell me what you want to do."

Maurice said he would think about it and tell the *di-yen* what he wanted to do. I knew his moons were numbered, and so did he. We talked on the ride back home and decided that he and his family ought to go to a place where he might get better after Lena had their baby. That night, I told Helen and Banatsi that the White Eye *di-yen* had told Maurice he had TB. There was water in their eyes, but they didn't moan and weep. I knew they were thinking, just as I was, that maybe the little family might make it. Every day, I prayed to Jesus that it might be so, but my spirit heard nothing in reply.

# THIRTY-EIGHT

## THE ROAD TO MESCALERO

MAURICE AND LENA'S child was born in the moon the White Eyes called "September" in the Season of Large Fruit—a little girl, and they named her Esther. She was born strong and healthy, and for that, we all gave thanks to Jesus. Maurice's sickness didn't seem to be getting any worse, and he often told us he was feeling better, and for that also, we all gave thanks to Jesus. About the time Esther was born, Colonel Scott had come to learn who wanted to move to Mescalero or Ojo Caliente or stay at Fort Sill. After the men went with him to visit Mescalero and Ojo Caliente, it was clear no one could go to Ojo Caliente. There was not enough land left to support even a few of our People. How to settle our People on land in or around Fort Sill was a question the councils of the big chiefs in the place of the Great Father still had to answer.

During the Ghost Face of the harvest the White Eyes called "1912," Esther cried more than she should and wouldn't nurse on any kind of schedule. The White Eyes *di-yen* checked her often but couldn't identify what was making her sick. The faces of Maurice and Lena were masks of worry. They got little sleep, taking turns rocking the child or walking while holding her in one of the house rooms. Maurice's illness returned. Despite having little energy, he stayed up long hours helping Lena with the baby.

Late in the Season of Little Eagles, Tim appeared at our door early one morning before our meal. His face was painted in long, sad lines of grief as he told us that Esther had ridden the ghost pony the night before. My women wailed, and I wanted to, but only water leaked from my eyes. The mission *di-yen* made a good ceremony over Esther's little brown burial box, but I noticed while standing in the cold wind during the ceremony that Maurice's cough had returned.

The next sun, Maurice came to visit and said that he and Lena were ready to go to a place where he might be cured of his disease. I told him I thought that was wise. The White Eye *di-yen* who had seen him before told us that he would recommend sending them to Fort Apache and make arrangements for them to go. In less than a moon, Maurice and Lena left for Fort Apache. The mission assembly prayed to Jesus that Maurice be healed, and so did I, every day.

ONE SUN IN the Season of Large Fruit, we learned that the big chiefs' council named Congress had passed a law that said the Chiricahua were no longer prisoners of war, that we could choose whether to move to Mescalero or stay on land around Fort Sill, and that money would be provided for us to move.

Colonel Scott returned to Fort Sill and met in council with all the Chiricahua on the first day of the moon the White Eyes called "December." He told us what a fine place Mescalero was but that we should feel free to do what we thought was best for our families in choosing whether to go to Mescalero or stay near Fort Sill. I decided after Helen and I talked, and Banatsi had her say, that since our leaders were going to Mescalero, then that's where we ought to go. The next sun, 176 Chiricahua decided for Mescalero and 88 for Fort Sill, and it was so recorded in the tracks on paper. At the close of the council, Naiche said to Colonel Scott, "I'm glad that the War Department and Interior Department have given us a chance to get a home and set us free."

Eugene Chihuahua said, "We feel happy today because we think you are going to free us."

Preparations for the move began both at Fort Sill and at Mescalero. We who were going to Mescalero gathered our farming tools and household items we wanted to take with us. We were told that, at Mescalero, the agents were gathering a stockpile of additional clothes and blankets (it would be colder in the mountains than we were used to or dressed for), tents (we would have to live in tents until we could build our houses), heating stoves (we could bring our cooking stoves), and lumber for flooring and tent frames. We had over seven thousand head of cattle at Fort Sill that had to be sold (to avoid bringing Texas fever to New Mexico), with some money going to those who had individual herds and some for the tribe.

WE DROVE OUR possessions to Lawton, broke down our wagons, and loaded them on iron wagons along with our household goods, our harnesses, and our farming tools. On the morning of the sun we left Fort Sill, our horses and mules were loaded in an iron wagon that would travel with us. We were told to leave our dogs because they might be carrying ticks that carried Texas fever. We said we understood the need to prevent Texas fever and the need to leave our dog friends behind, but few wanted to do that. After we loaded our horses and mules onto freight cars waiting at the Lawton iron-wagon house on the day the White Eyes named April 2, 1913, all the Chiricahua and Chihenne who had chosen to live on the Mescalero Reservation had a midday meal with our families and then climbed into the iron wagons that would carry us and our things to our new home. I wore my big silver medal the Great Father had given me to show that I was a leader despite being ignored by other leaders, especially Daklugie and Eugene Chihuahua. I sat next to the window so I could see the stars and judge our direction as we traveled in the dark. Helen and Banatsi sat on the seat opposite, facing me with a blanket over their laps. It was the middle of the Season of Many Leaves, and the evenings were still too cool for comfort without a fire.

I looked around at those with us in the iron wagon. I saw Naiche and Daklugie with their families at the other end. It was the first time some of the children had been on an iron wagon, and they shivered with the excitement and nervously giggled. At last, all the iron-wagon seats were claimed, the end doors closed, and through an open window I heard the man the White Eyes called "conductor" lean out and wave from one of the iron wagons in front of us. He yelled, "Boarrrrd!" to the man in the front iron wagon controlling the demon used to pull the iron wagons behind it. The White Eyes called that man "engineer," and I told myself to remember that word. The engineer made the lead wagon give two short, lonely moans acknowledging the conductor's call. There were jerks and clanks as the iron wagons hooked together began to move in the direction of the big golden ball floating three hands above the western horizon. In a gentle rocking motion, the line of iron wagons loaded with the People and their things gained speed, making the brush near the iron road go by in a blur.

Helen and Banatsi pulled out a sack of warrior trail food from under their blanket. It was for us to eat that night, and they put it within easy access for when we grew hungry as we watched the low rolling prairie hills with a few trees scattered near pools of water and bent in one direction by the unending wind from the west flash by. I thought of the iron-wagon rides I had taken, first to the city of the Great Father, then to the school place the White Eyes called

Carlisle, and then home toward Fort Apache, only to stop at Fort Leavenworth before the ride to Fort Marion in Saint Augustine. Then there was the ride across Florida to Mount Vernon Barracks, and seven years later from Mount Vernon to Fort Sill, where we had stayed for nearly eighteen years before hav-ing to give up our farms and herds because the Army chiefs wanted our land to train soldiers to shoot their big guns.

For most of the old Apache returning to the deserts and mountains, this was a much easier ride than they had endured on the way to the Florida forts. Then, the windows had been nailed shut and it was the Season of Large Fruit, when the desert heat trapped inside the iron wagons made them all suffer. Their only facilities for personal business were buckets at either end of the wagon that, aside from depriving them of privacy, made a stench so bad it burned their noses just to take a breath.

The shadows from the falling sun stretched into darkness, and yellow lights making stars scattered lying across the land—no doubt from ranch *casas*—could be seen far across the *llano*. We napped through the night, jerked awake two or three times by the stops to reload the supply wagons carrying black rocks to burn and water for the demons that pulled the iron wagons.

The day passed crossing a *llano* that seemed to never end. We napped and watched the land go by or paced up and down the walkway where we rode in our iron wagon. The Army fed us with the rising and the setting of the sun from an iron wagon set up with stoves, and soldiers who were cooks made the meals. Naiche told me the way we were fed from big pots was the same way the Army fed the Naiche-Geronimo People when they were held for nearly two moons at Fort Sam Houston while the Great Father decided how to deal with the lies from General Miles.

As the sun began falling into distant mountains, the land became desert-like with cholla cactus and prickly pear appearing more and more frequently in the tall grass. Distant mountains began to appear in the gray horizon haze, and mesquite and big bushes began to line the tracks.

We stopped for water and coal several times either in the mountains or with mountains nearby. Even though my watch and the moon said it was close to the middle of the night, I could feel the excitement begin to fill our iron wagon as some of the older Apache stared out the windows, trying to recognize the mountain shapes against the stars of some places they might know. I thought we were probably no more than three hands from the Tularosa iron-wagon place the White Eyes called "station," where we would stop and unload our wagons and other things and then follow the wagon road up the Río Tularosa to the Mescalero agent's house. I wondered if the Mescalero agent would be there if we arrived deep in the night.

THE DEMON IRON wagon following the iron road through creosote bushes and mesquites near what must be the Sacramento Mountains made three short moans. I had learned that was a signal the demon wagon gave to warn it was approaching an iron-wagon house. The iron wagon began to slow with the clanking and squeal of iron rubbing on iron. Soon we were rolling no faster than a man might walk and then stopped with our wagon directly in front of the station porch where, in the yellow light of lanterns held high by a group of Apache in blue coats, their hair trimmed like that of White Eyes, surrounded a white-haired old man wearing a conductor's hat and two younger men, one older than the other who looked not much older than a boy.

As soon as the iron wagon stopped, Daklugie was out the iron-wagon door and down the steps to the ground, where Eugene Chihuahua, Goody, and Major Goode, the Army commander in charge of us until we were formally accepted by the Mescalero agent, joined him to meet the two White Eye men with the Apache. I soon learned the older man was named C. R. Jefferis, the Mescalero agent, and the young man was Ted Sutherland. Jefferis introduced him to our men as the reservation livestock superintendent. They shook hands as White Eyes always do, talked a bit with much nodding of heads, and then our men returned to us while Sutherland and the Apache with them walked holding lanterns high down the tracks toward the wagons, carrying the horses and mules and our belongings.

Daklugie came through the door and held up his hands, and the talking stopped, and all eyes quickly turned to him. He said, "The Mescalero agent and Major Goode have agreed that we take the horses and mules off the train first and get them to water and then leave them in the station corral until we're ready to leave. We'll unload and assemble the wagons, then hitch the horses and unload our belongings and equipment directly into the wagons. We'll form a line of wagons and follow the road up the Río Tularosa to the reservation, where tents and lumber for floors await our use and a big feast is being prepared for us while we visit with friends and relatives. Any questions?" There was nothing but silence. "Good. If the men will come with me, we'll take care of the horses and mules and then get started putting the wagons together and unloading our belongings."

We followed Daklugie out of the car and down the side of the iron road to the wagons holding our animals. Ted Sutherland was waiting for us and frowning. He said, "The noise from that car sure don't sound like horses."

Daklugie frowned and shook his head.

A railroad man pulled the door open and a flood of dogs of every size, breed, and color tumbled through the horse's legs and out the opened door, barking, yipping, twisting, and turning with excitement. They were overjoyed to see their friends. The solemn faces of the men turned to laughs and grins as some dogs barking and wagging their tails ran up to lick their masters' hands before running up the iron road, where the women and children were climbing down from the iron wagons.

Daklugie puffed his cheeks and, shrugging, turned to Sutherland. "We didn't know the dogs were on the train. We hated to leave them. Maybe the train crew put them in with the horses. Can we keep them, or must we kill them?"

Sutherland smiled and said, "There're no cattle here now. Get any ticks off them. You have medicine for that and know how to use it. We ought to be all right. Just understand that if Texas fever shows up in any of your livestock, they'll all have to be put down, sick or not. It'll be your loss."

Daklugie crossed his arms and nodded. "We'll live by the rules you require. We've lived with the White Eyes for twenty-seven years now and know we must do this."

I thought Daklugie very wise in the way he spoke to Sutherland, who grinned and said, *"Ch'ik'eh doleel.* Now let's get you folks unloaded, fitted up, and on the road to Mescalero."

In addition to nearly forty men from Fort Bliss who Jefferis had requested for help unloading and reassembling our wagons, the Mescalero policemen, and women and children who were able, helped with unloading the animals, getting them water, and unloading the farm equipment and personal possessions. Teams of the men from Fort Bliss working together on getting all the wagons rolling made fast work of positioning the wheels and tongue back on the wagons. Teams also helped load each wagon with family farm tools and personal possessions, which also made that work go quickly. It was a good time for the People, and after eating our last meal from the iron wagons, we had our wagons rolling up the road to Mescalero before the time of shortest shadows.

# THIRTY-NINE

## APACHE SUMMIT

OUR LINE OF wagons followed the rough, gullied road in the distance looking like two pieces of brown reata lying side by side, winding up Tularosa Canyon beside the Río Tularosa toward Mescalero. The horses strained against their harness. The pull wasn't too steep, but the incline was long and the loads heavy. It was surprisingly quiet. Children and adults had little to say above the creak and groan of our wagons and the gurgling of the Río Tularosa as they took in the stark beauty of the desert in the bright sunlight. A couple of hands past the time of no shadows, we passed a soul-expanding view of the White Sands lying like early-morning mist low against the base of the gray San Andres Mountains. In all the suns I've lived at Mescalero, I had to travel this road often and passed by that view, but I always stopped for a short time to enjoy its beauty and serenity.

Near dark, the pleasant air was becoming bitingly cool in the long shadows stretching off the ridges. As we approached the agent's white house among a scattering of other buildings at the reservation's headquarters, we saw many small fires and *tipis* scattered around the agent's house. Smiling Mescalero were there to greet us, the women working over great pots of food steaming over their fires, to welcome us to our new home. From the Mescalero *tipis*, dogs barked and children laughed as they waved and watched us pass by while the agent led our wagons to places where we could set up the big walled tents the Army had provided for us.

Agent Jefferis spoke with the village leaders from Fort Sill and told us it might be a good idea if we gathered our tents in the same groups the villages had used, but there was no rule that said we must. He also told us the Mescalero would help us put up the tents and we could leave our horses and mules in the big stone corral near the agent's house. We thought organizing by Fort Sill villages was wise, and the Mescalero helped us in any way they could. Since nearly all the men from Fort Sill had been in the Army and had lots of experience putting up tents, we were done in less than a hand. We waited to put up any floors under the tents until we knew where we would stay.

It was dark as we gathered around the Mescalero fires to share their good company and food. Many Mescalero knew distant Chiricahua family members and greeted them as long-lost brothers and sisters. My family had no Mescalero family connections, but I recognized one of their tribal policemen with his Yellow Boy Henry rifle. In fact, he was named Yellow Boy for his Power with his rifle. He was a Mescalero legend who could hit anything with his rifle he could see. As my women and I sat together by ourselves, many of the other Chiricahua ignoring us, we ate our share of this fine feast. Yellow Boy stopped by to visit with us.

He nodded and smiled at the women. "We are glad you come to us. You and your People are welcome here. Ho, Chato? You remember me?"

"Yes, I am Chato. You are Yellow Boy, scout with *Nant'an Lpah* when our village was raided and burned nearly thirty harvests ago when Tzoe led him into the Blue Mountains to bring the Chiricahua back to San Carlos in a 'good way.'"

"Hmmph. Chato, you have a very good memory. I'm curious to learn what happened to you and your People during your captivity and where you got that fine silver medal you wear. I don't understand how the White Eyes and Army took scouts who worked for them and made them prisoners of war after giving them medals and paying them for their work. It makes no sense. Maybe we can talk about those times one evening over a cup of coffee?"

"Yes, we can talk together. There is much to tell. Our story will take many cups of coffee."

"*Doo dat'éé da*, I look forward to enjoying your story. I know it will teach me wise lessons at the same time."

We made the all-is-well hand-wave symbol before he moved on to another fire.

We visited and feasted five or six suns with many Mescalero families who became our friends for many years. During those suns of rest, we learned many things about the reservation and how a knowledge of them would help us. We saw Blazer's sawmill and watched it turn out lumber from logs much easier than the rig we had at Fort Sill. We visited Blazer's trading post and met the clerks who would sell us our supplies and buy things like Helen's baskets, and we saw the schools for Indian children. The tribal police showed us maps that had the best trails marked for traveling the reservation and told us the best times to hunt in the high places.

On the fourth day, after many of our questions were answered, the Chiricahua had a council meeting. As chief of the Chokonen, Naiche spoke first. "The Mescalero have welcomed us to their reservation with great kindness and generosity. Truly, they are our brothers. The suns slip away while we visit and feast. We must do all we can to prepare for the coming Ghost Face while the suns are warm and peaceful. Agent Jefferis has a supply of blankets and warm clothes for the cold suns, but he may not have enough. We must have shelter to protect our children and let our women do their work. There is not enough time or materials to build houses for us all. Many will have to live in the tents where they sleep now. Many men have asked me where our camp will be and when we will go there. I answer, 'I don't know.' I've heard Daklugie and Eugene Chihuahua, who looked over the reservation earlier, speak of several places where we might want to camp. I ask them to tell us what they think."

Daklugie stood and crossed his arms and looked at us. "Yes, I spent a little time looking over the reservation in hope that it could support a large cattle herd, which I think we all want to start after our money comes from the sale of our cattle at Fort Sill. I believe Mescalero Reservation can easily support large Chiricahua and Mescalero herds. I think the Chiricahua need to stay out of the way of the Mescalero people. I believe we need to stay in a place we can call our own and not bother anyone else with our farms and cattle. From what I've seen of the reservation, that place is called 'Whitetail.' It's about twenty miles from here, up on a high butte with valleys filled with good grama grass and water. It will be cold there in Ghost Face, and there is not much land for crops, but I think it is a good place for us to live as Chiricahua in good houses. I think Eugene agrees with me on this. It's where we ought to ask Agent Jefferis for our camp."

Chihuahua nodded his head and said in a voice loud enough for us all to hear, "Yes, I agree."

I stood waiting to speak. Daklugie wrinkled his face when he saw me stand but said with a sneer, "Sergeant Chato? You want to speak?"

I said, "I do." I lifted my medal off my shirt and turned so all could see it. "The Great Father gave this to me because he respected my words when you were little more than a boy and had not yet gone to the White Eye school where you say you learned all about cattle. That is a good thing to learn all about cattle, and your work at Fort Sill shows you learned your lessons well while Eugene was catching baseballs and helping George Wratten sell women cloth in his store.

As an old warrior who worked hard at Fort Sill, I have also learned many White Eye lessons, one of which is not to trust White Eyes. We trusted the White Eyes, expecting to have Fort Sill for our reservation. Now we must share a reservation with the Mescalero."

Daklugie scowled and looked at Eugene, who didn't look happy either. He said, "We can't listen to you ramble all day, traitor. What's your point?"

I grinned and crossed my arms, already knowing the answers to my questions. "I'm not the traitor your uncle Geronimo was. My point is, are you sure Whitetail is the best place for us? Have you looked at all the possible places for our camp this reservation has to offer? Or is Whitetail what Agent Jefferis wants us to take?"

The scowls on the faces of Daklugie and Chihuahua deepened. Daklugie said, "I looked at many places while I was here, and Eugene saw many when he was here to confirm my opinion of the place, but no, we haven't looked at every camp site we might use. Agent Jefferis has said he thinks Whitetail is probably the best place for us. So what? I'd take the word of a White Eye agent over a traitor any day."

My knowing smile seemed to infuriate Daklugie, but before he could add more insults, Naiche stood with his arms up and palms forward. "Enough! Let us quickly find the place we want and then get started establishing our camp. Ghost Face comes soon for all we must do. We must finish or suffer in a cold, snow-filled time."

All the men nodded and said, *"Ch'ik'eh doleel."*

As the council broke up, most of the men wouldn't look at or acknowledge me. I realized then that if I lived in the Chiricahua village, wherever it was, I would be an outcast.

That night, I dreamed I was an eagle sailing on the mountain winds with a nest high in the mountain crags above crows in trees far below me. The crows feared me but sometimes attacked me from above when I was flying. I always defeated the crows by flying so high they had to drop away because the high, thin air exhausted them. I always won these battles until one day, under attack, I flew into a cloud and never came back.

I awoke and sat up shivering in the cold mountain air. Helen said, "My husband stirs. You are well?"

"I am well, woman. *Ussen* speaks to me. I have not heard him since I started walking the Jesus Road. I think *Ussen* tells me much this night. Much I must think on. I'm all right. I need nothing. Stay in your blankets."

Daklugie and Eugene Chihuahua asked the agent where we were to live. They told him we wanted to get on with the work of establishing our village. Jefferis told them to ride the reservation and pick any spot that was not claimed already, and he would give it to them. Nearly all the men wanted to go with them. We planned to ride our horses to look at several places on the reservation where we could raise another herd of cattle, have gardens, and live comfortably.

We left the agency to look for a Chiricahua village site on the sixth day after we arrived from Fort Sill. A couple of Mescalero policemen acted as our guides. We rode up the wagon road toward Apache Summit. At the summit was a spectacular view of the great sacred mountain of the Mescalero, Sierra Blanca. Daklugie and Eugene Chihuahua stopped for a short time to parley with the policemen and then announced we would go first to Whitetail.

I looked around at where we were. It had tall pines, and I could see grassy meadows through the trees. I raised up in my stirrups and called to one of the policemen, "Does anyone claim the summit?"

He said, "No one claims the summit. There is no reliable water here."

I grinned. "Then I will ask for it and make a well or haul my water here if I have to. I won't live in Whitetail with Daklugie and Eugene Chihuahua."

The policeman shrugged his shoulders. "Maybe Agent Jefferis lets you have it. I don't know. You ask him. We go on to Whitetail."

I saw Daklugie and Eugene Chihuahua with big smiles, happy that I wouldn't be with them when they went to Whitetail. I laughed out loud and shook my fist in the air. My dream vision must be coming true, an eagle above the crows.

I RODE BACK DOWN to the agency on the wagon road to the summit and found Agent Jefferis at his worktable in the agency headquarters. He looked up from his work, saw me standing at his door, raised his brows in surprise that I had returned from the other group, and motioned for me to sit down. We had a long talk after I told him where I wanted to put up my house. He said no one else wanted that space because water wasn't reliable. He was curious why I wanted to live away from the rest of the Chiricahua. I told him of my service to the Army and that, because of that service, Geronimo had called me a traitor. It was a name other Chiricahua had picked up because Geronimo said so, but it was a lie. I was no traitor. I believed, and so did other scouts who helped me, that our service had saved many Chiricahua lives and prevented much suffering.

I was proud of my service, even if the Army had treated me badly by making me and my family prisoners of war. Many of my family had died in the prisoner-of-war camps in Florida, Alabama, and Oklahoma, but those who survived had the strength and courage to endure.

Jefferis studied me for a long moment and then nodded. He pulled out a map from several rolled up on his desk and made some measurements with a stick with many black marks and then looked in a book with many black tracks. He turned to me and said, "Apache Summit is yours. I hate that you'll be outcast from your People, but you've earned my gratitude for your Army work, and I know you'll be a solid citizen. I may be able to help you with a well in the future. In the meantime, you'll have to haul your drinking water and catch rain and snow in ponds for your livestock. Since it's just you and your wife, I'll give you the lumber so you can start your house pronto. You need to finish your house before snow flies. It gets very cold up there in the Ghost Face. If you must use a tent, as many of your People will, you'll suffer worse than those at Whitetail." He pulled a list of lumber cuts and lengths I should collect from Blazer's Mill to build a house like we had at Fort Sill, ran his eye across the pages, and then handed it to me. "Here's a list of materials for you to pick up with your wagon at Blazer's Mill. You can get a keg of nails from the trading post. Just show the clerk this list. After you have your materials hauled to the summit, I'll get one of the Mescalero policemen to help you get started with the heavy lifting for your house."

I nodded, shook hands with two solid pumps, and thanked him.

It was a time of long shadows at Mescalero. I put up my horses and found Helen to tell her what I had done. Her face was a mask. I couldn't tell if she was happy or angry. When I asked her what she thought, she said, "It will be hard to live at the summit, but I understand why you do this. It is the right thing to do. We'll do well."

"Hmmph. I'll start hauling the lumber next sun. Maybe so I can finish the house before the snow comes."

The men who went to Whitetail returned in a few suns, and as I expected, they asked Jefferis that we be allowed to build the Chiricahua village at Whitetail. Jefferis agreed to the village at Whitetail but warned them that there were only enough materials and money to build about thirty houses that year and that the rest of the families would have to live in tents made ready for winter snow until more money or supplies came.

The men moved their tents and set them up where they wanted at Whitetail but with the entrances always facing east for morning prayers. Even though it was still the Season of Many Leaves, they began to make the tents ready for winter by cutting much more firewood than they needed then, for their women to cook during the warm moons, and stacked it high on the north side of the tents, which would protect the tent entrances from blowing snow when the cold moons came. To help hold the heat in the tents, they packed dirt up the tent walls. I thought, in some ways, those in tents were better off than those in the poorly built houses that had many cracks and holes where the wind could blow through. I was glad I had learned to build a good solid house when I was in the Army at Mount Vernon Barracks, had worked for master carpenters building houses even before that, and had kept my carpenter tools when we went to Mescalero.

# FORTY

## LIFE ON APACHE SUMMIT

I PICKED OUT a spot for the house near the intersection of the wagon road from Apache Summit to Whitetail and the wagon road past Apache Summit from the village Ruidoso to the Mescalero agency headquarters. The house I planned was on the south side of the road and faced the mountains east up the road to Whitetail. Across the road on the north side was a high ridge that helped block cold wind sweeping off Sierra Blanca. It took me twelve days to haul all the house's building materials up to the spot from Blazer's Mill and the trading post. Yellow Boy, the Mescalero policeman, tied his pony to the back of the wagonloads and rode with me to the summit, where he helped me unload and stack the lumber in nice stacks that let air circulate around the cut boards.

Yellow Boy was there helping me when I first began building the floor on the stacks of foundation rocks I'd prepared in the string layout. When we took a break, he said, "Why do you work so hard to live in a house when a *tipi* lets you sleep on Mother Earth and it's easier for your women to cook?"

Yellow Boy had been a great help to me, and he was asking the same things I had asked at Mount Vernon when the master carpenters were teaching us to build a good house.

I nodded. "I can answer your question from my living both ways. After living with the White Eyes for twenty-seven years, we Chiricahua have learned a few things. One is that houses are much more comfortable than *tipis*—cooler in warm moons, warmer in the cold moons. Once our women learned how to cook on the iron stoves, they thought it was easier than cooking over an open fire... although we can still build houses that will let them cook over an open fire."

"Hmmph. Maybe one day I try a house. All my women and I want and need now is a *tipi*."

After I hauled the last load of building materials, Helen and Banatsi insisted on my moving our farm tools, stove, and other possessions to the summit and as my family living with me while I built the house. We put up our tent at the summit site, and it didn't take me long to build a floor for it. With the women being there, I had more time to work. I warned them that if they lived with me, then they would have no company from their Chiricahua and Mescalero friends. They said they weren't leaving me.

Agent Jefferis gave me the plan for the Chiricahua houses. The house was much like what we had on the ridge at Mount Vernon. Every day, a nearly constant stream of wagons carrying material or men to work on the thirty houses at Whitetail passed by. I knew most of the drivers, but few ever looked in the direction of me or my women. Most drivers stared straight ahead, ignoring us as if they were horses with blinders on their harness. They were fools listening to tales told about me by my enemies.

Blazer gave me a couple of barrels to use for hauling water. Three or four times a moon, I took the team and the wagon with a barrel in the bed down the long decline to agency headquarters to fill up with water from the Río Tularosa. I planned to dig a tank to catch and hold rainwater as soon as I finished the house for my horses and for bathing. The barrel water, we used for drinking and cooking. There were two or three low places near our tent that had caught rainwater my animals used.

AFTER I FINISHED the house, I put in the stove and built beds, a table, and chairs for my women much like we had at Fort Sill. Next, I built a shed for my animals to stay out of the weather and to protect my farm equipment. Then I took my plow and shovel and dug a water tank in a little bowl-shaped hollow that would hold enough water for my animals once it rained. I also put a barrel under a drain spout off the house roof to catch rainwater we could use. By the end of Season of Large Fruit, Helen, Banatsi, and I were settled in our new house as cold winds blew off the mountains. I also spent time in the Season of Large Fruit finding and cutting grass for my horses and cutting enough firewood to get us through Ghost Face and into the next Season of Little Eagles. The Chiricahua who planned to live at Whitetail the first Ghost Face were cutting firewood, finishing their houses, or making their tents ready for the Ghost Face while their families stayed in their tents next to the agency. As high as Apache Summit and Whitetail were, Ghost Face came sooner and was fiercer than for the lower land around the agency. Many, including Naiche and his last wife Haozinne, who planned to winter at Whitetail, changed their minds and decided to wait until the Season of Many Leaves to move to Whitetail.

The Dutch Reformed Church, which had started the Jesus Road assembly of Chiricahua at the Fort Sill mission, also had a Mescalero assembly. Their *di-yen* was a White Eye named Richard Harper. He had a young, educated Mescalero interpreter, Solon Sombrero, who had much light behind his eyes, to speak his White Eye words in Apache during his talks. Solon also helped with other interpretation needs, such as singing Jesus Road songs in Apache and translating church documents so the People could understand them. The second day after we arrived, Harper with Solon Sombrero and two White Eye women—Hendrina Hospers and Martha Prince, who had worked at the mission at Fort Sill and had come to Mescalero with us—came to our tents to introduce themselves. After telling us who he was, Harper said the Mescalero church would be very happy to have us worship with them and to come when we could. He said that if we wanted to transfer from the Fort Sill mission to the Mescalero assembly, then Miss Hospers had all the transfer papers she needed to make it so. I liked Richard Harper and the two women with him. I promised we would visit the Mescalero mission soon. A moon after I had picked the place for our house at Apache Summit, Helen, Banatsi, and I decided to attend the Mescalero assembly.

I knew it would be especially good for Helen and Banatsi to get out and visit with their friends they hadn't seen since we moved to Apache Summit. The assembly building was a big white house near the bigger schoolhouses.

We arrived with a bell high in the mission tower on the white house slowly clanging to announce it was time for the People to come hear the Jesus Road words Harper had that day. Many Chiricahua came from their tents close to the agency, and Mescalero were riding their ponies and walking from nearby camps to join them. I met Naiche at the door, and he welcomed me with a big smile. He said it was a fine assembly, and he expected it to reorganize in a couple of months so everyone would be a new member, and he encouraged me to transfer my membership to this church. I told him I would probably do that.

The women and I went in to where the People sat to hear Harper, and since few seats had yet been taken, my women and I sat near the middle of the center row of the chairs. As women came in to take a seat, they waved at my women, but their men looked away from me and made it a point not to sit near us.

The bell stopped calling. I looked around. Most of the seated people were from Fort Sill. About half as many were from Mescalero. The chairs in a row in front and behind, and to our sides, were empty. No one, not even Mescalero who did not know me, sat near us.

In the stillness of the gathering, I grew bitter, and anger burned in my guts. All the years the Chiricahua had attended the mission at Fort Sill had taught them nothing about the forgiveness the *di-yens* often said Jesus spoke of. I stared at my hands as we listened to Naiche speak about what the assembly was planning. I had done the right thing for my People, helping the Blue Coats hunt down Geronimo, but Geronimo, who tried and couldn't walk the Jesus Road, had called me a traitor. I had done the right thing going after him when he left Fort Apache, and I believed I had saved many lives. I didn't believe Daklugie or Eugene were deliberately spreading tales about me, but now that the Chiricahua were free, there was no longer any need to put on a unified face for the White Eyes. Now I was shunned by my People, who sided with Geronimo, and by the Mescalero who had heard their stories about why I should be an outcast. If I could get my hands around how those stories were spread, I might be able to stop the evil that was being told about me. But I knew those things came out of hearts that were a trackless desert.

I leaned over to Helen and whispered, "I'm leaving. You and Banatsi stay. I'll be at our wagon when you leave."

Helen looked at me with sad eyes and nodded she understood. When the song leader had us all stand for the singing of "Come Thou Fount of Every Blessing," I turned my back to the song leader and walked with my head held high down the aisle, toward the entryway, and out the door.

I didn't return to the mission the rest of Ghost Face. In the Season of Little Eagles, Naiche, who was one of the men to be an elder in the new church organization, came to visit and tried to talk me into returning to the assemblies. He said that he was sorry the People had acted the way they did and that he had asked Harper to talk about forgiveness, but it did little good. He tried to convince me that going back to the assembly would make me a better man than the others, but I told him there was nothing I could do to change their minds. Geronimo had spoken, and they believed him. How the Mescalero learned the evil things the Chiricahua believed about me, I didn't know, and if the truth be told, I didn't care. They were fools, but it didn't make me feel any better or feel less an exile to understand that.

IN THE SEASON of Many Leaves, many Chiricahua who had stayed camped at the agency headquarters through the Ghost Face were ready to move to Whitetail. The sun before they were to move, I had taken my wagon and water barrel down to agency headquarters, where I filled the barrel with a bucket from a little waterfall that fell from a bench up on a butte. While I was working, Naiche's wife, Haozinne, wandered by, smiling, and waved. She said she was taking a last look around the headquarters area before they left the next sun for Whitetail. I told her, now that Ghost Face was gone, she and Naiche would enjoy Whitetail. It was a beautiful spot. She nodded and passed on to climb the butte to the bench where the water for the fall began.

I finished filling my barrel and left for Apache Summit. I never saw Haozinne again. She seemed to disappear. People looking for her found her body on the bench where she was going after she spoke to me. The climb to the top had been too much for her heart, and she left us, riding the ghost pony. I was sad to learn the news and thought I was probably the last one to see her alive.

The Chiricahua put off their move to Whitetail until after the burial ceremony was held for Haozinne. Out of respect for my friend Naiche, whose spirit was badly wounded, my women and I attended the burial ceremony. When I spoke with him privately after the ceremony, I told him I thought I was probably the last person she had talked to and why. Naiche's sad eyes spoke much as he nodded and said, "Thank you, Chato. You're a good friend. Come to Whitetail for visits when you can."

"This I will do, *amigo*. Stay strong. Your People need you."

# FORTY-ONE

## MAURICE COMES TO MESCALERO

ONE SUN IN the same moon that Haozinne rode the ghost pony, I and my women were sawing and splitting logs I had cut for firewood. Yellow Boy came riding up the road from Mescalero and stopped, I thought to visit, but he was playing messenger for Agent Jefferis.

"Ho, Chato. I see you gather much firewood with your women for your fine house."

I smiled and gave him the all-is-good sign. "Ho, Yellow Boy, climb down from your pony. I think Helen has coffee still hot on her stove."

He dismounted from his fine paint pony and said, "I drink your good coffee. Then I return to Mescalero. Agent Jefferis sends me to ask that you come to speak with him."

I frowned. I couldn't imagine why Jefferis wanted to see me. "Why does he want to speak with me?"

Yellow Boy shrugged his shoulders. "I don't know the agent's business, but he wants to see you in the next day or two. Maybe you want to keep me company on the way back to Mescalero?"

I nodded. "That I will do. I tell my women I go after we have a little coffee."

THE RIDE TO Mescalero with Yellow Boy was a good time as we shared stories and gossip about what was going on at Whitetail and the rest of the reservation. When we came to Mescalero, I tied my pony to the hitching rail in front of the agent's office and waved at Yellow Boy as he rode off on other police business.

Yellow Boy told me that his son, Hígh*á*h, had returned from school in the east. He was helping Jefferis with his work and sometimes taught at the school, and if I needed help, to ask for him. Reservation headquarters was a big white building. The entrance door opened into a dark hall with doors along its back wall. I knew the agent's office was three doors down the hall. Jefferis's door was open, but I waited there until he saw me and motioned me in and toward a chair next to his worktable covered with papers having many tracks.

"Thank you for coming so quick, Chato." He held up a piece of paper with the talking-wire symbol. "You have a son, Maurice, with a wife and little boy who moved to Fort Apache from Fort Sill about two harvests ago? I understand the Army doctor suggested he go there for his health?"

I crossed my arms and leaned back in my chair as I stared at Jefferis. My heart was racing. A frown was lining my face with dread and worry. He had news of Maurice. I hoped it wasn't bad. I nodded. "Yes, Maurice, his wife Lena Kaydahzinne, and little son Alexander, sent there by Fort Sill *di-yen*. He say air in our homeland help cure him."

Jefferis smiled. "There's nothing to be alarmed about, Chato. This telegram here says the health of your son has improved, and since your People have moved to Mescalero, where the air is as good for treating tuberculosis as it is in Arizona, Maurice is moving here to Mescalero to be with his family as he tries to get better."

I sagged back against the chair weak with relief. "My heart sings, Agent Jefferis. When they come?"

Jefferis grinned, looked again at the tracks on the paper in his hand, and said, "This telegram says they will be on the train from El Paso arriving in Tularosa three suns from now at nine in the morning. I was wondering if you wanted to pick them up and bring them here to the office where I can register them, give them papers for a tent and rations, and determine where they'll stay."

He laughed out loud at the grin on my face as I said, "Hmmph. This I do!"

I SAT ON the porch of the iron-wagon station and stared down the iron road as it disappeared into the creosote bushes and mesquite sweeping away southeast toward the brilliant blue sky behind the Sacramento Mountains. I was happy Maurice and his family were returning, but I worried the sickness he had still lingered on him and there was nothing any *di-yen*, White Eye or Apache, could do to stop it from killing him. Baby Esther had already been killed by a White Eye sickness before she was off her *tsach*. His son, Alexander, was more than a harvest old and hadn't shown any signs of being sick, nor did his wife, Kaydahzinne, when the family went to Fort Apache. I could only pray to Jesus or ask that *Ussen* save them all.

The old white-haired man in charge of the iron-wagon station came out on the porch and stood staring with me at the tracks disappearing in the brush south. He pulled a big yellow watch out of his vest pocket, snapped it open, checked its reading, and nodded. He turned to me, saying, "Yep. She's right on time." He pointed toward the tracks disappearing in the brush where a thin black cloud floated in the distance. Soon we heard the low, moaning whistle of the iron wagon with its demons pulling the other iron wagons behind it, and we saw the long black plume strung out behind it. I glanced over my shoulder and saw the water tower and black rock supply for the demon-filled iron wagon. Then, like a great black bird swooping out of the sky, it came rolling, huffing, and puffing out of the brush, down the iron road, straight for the water tower and the bin of black rocks next to it. There was a squeal of iron on iron as the wagons slowed to a stop where water and black rocks could be given to the thirsty lead wagon. Three of the wagons carried passengers, but most stayed in their seats. I scanned all the wagons but saw no one through the shining windows reflecting the sunlight who might be Maurice with his family.

A man in an iron-wagon uniform stepped out of the last wagon with people and put down an extra set of steps that reached from the iron-wagon steps all the way to the ground. After he had them in place, he motioned the passengers waiting in the wagon door to come down the steps. I clenched my teeth, expecting to be disappointed. It was rare that what the White Eyes promised and what happened were the same. Several men in suits and two women in fancy dresses and hats came down the steps and then a long pause. Disappointment was coming—I could taste it like a bad meal filling my stomach. But then a young man in a big flat-brimmed hat pulling a trunk came through the door to the steps. It was Maurice. I was running for the steps even as the man who put them there helped him get the trunk down the steps.

Maurice was followed by a child whose mother behind him held his hands high over his head as he tried to run after his father. With the trunk on the ground, Maurice stood up straight and saw me coming. He grinned and then coughed hard a couple of times while waving at me as Lena and little Alexander came down the steps. She picked him up and held him on her hip as they joined

Maurice and waved as I ran for them. It wasn't polite, but I didn't care. I hugged them all and, in my mind, gave thanks to Jesus and to *Ussen* for their return.

WE SPOKE OF many things on the wagon ride back to Mescalero. I told them why I had decided to live at Apache Summit with only my sister and my wife and not at Whitetail with the rest of the Chiricahua. They told me of life at Fort Apache and how calm it was without the constant tension between the White Mountains and Chiricahua, and they were friends with the White Mountain chief, Alchesay, who visited with them and sent his hopes for them and my family to do well in this land when they left Fort Apache. Maurice told me he still had the sickness that sent them to Fort Apache, but he was getting better, and the *di-yen* at Fort Apache said if they wanted to live in Mescalero, then the air was as good there as it was at Fort Apache, and they should go to Mescalero to be with family and friends. When they learned this, they immediately asked to go to Mescalero. I was happy that they had returned, but I knew after seeing Maurice cough when getting the trunk to the ground that he was weak and would take a long time to get better if the sickness didn't kill him first.

I took them to Agent Jefferis in his office and waited as Jefferis played with Alexander and then asked questions before making black water tracks on papers and in big books of their answers. Jefferis's last question asked where they wanted to live. They could stay near the agency and be close to a *di-yen*, live near me at Apache Summit, live at Whitetail, or, for that matter, live any place they wanted that wasn't already taken.

Maurice looked at Lena, who nodded before he said they should live at Whitetail, near her parents, as was the custom among the Apache. I sighed in my spirit that they would live somewhere besides my place, but I understood and had expected that they would live at Whitetail. Jefferis told them the White Eye *di-yen* would come to Whitetail twice a moon and they would have to live in a tent until their house could be built. Maurice and Kaydahzinne nodded they understood that was the case, and it didn't seem to matter. He entered their names in a big book of tracks that showed where everyone on the reservation lived. Then he made tracks on paper for rations and a tent, which we picked up before I headed for Apache Summit and the good meal that I knew Helen and Banatsi must be preparing.

MAURICE AND HIS family settled into their place near her family, and his tuberculosis seemed stable. I helped build a floor for their tent and put dirt against the walls to keep it warm. My women and I visited them often until the Ghost Face came. Then our visits depended more on the weather and how deep the snow was rather than customary times.

The Dutch Reformed Church *di-yen*, Harper, put up a tent in Whitetail for the regular assembly of those who lived in Whitetail. Maurice and Lena, who attended the assembly in the tent, decided they would have Alexander baptized into the church in the Season of Little Eagles, but on the day this was supposed to happen, the child was very sick with something the White Eye *di-yen* called "whooping cough." The church *di-yen* performed a ceremony that did the same thing for the child as if he were there. I didn't understand how this was possible, but Maurice and Lena accepted it for Alexander.

As the Season of Little Eagles warmed into the Season of Many Leaves, my women and I went to visit Maurice and Lena two or three times every moon. Maurice was weaker every time we visited.

One morning in the Season of Large Leaves, I sat with my women, drinking our morning coffee on the house porch, when Nelson Kaydahzinne, Lena's brother of about twelve harvests in age, came galloping up to our porch. He slid off his pony and ran up to us, breathing as though he had run ten miles instead of riding his pony.

He said, "Chato! Lena sends me. You and your women need to come quick. Maurice soon goes to Jesus."

Without a word, Helen and Banatsi were out of their chairs and inside to put on their traveling clothes. I said to Nelson, "I'm grateful you bring us this hard news. Water your pony at the tank behind the house. There is a bag of oats in the shed you can use. I'll saddle the horses for my women and me, and we'll ride."

The boy gave me a salute and headed for the tank.

I SAT BY the side of my son's bed, listening to the gurgle in his chest, and knew that soon he would go to Jesus. He was gray as cooking-fire ashes, and there was blood on the cloth he coughed into. My spirit mourned for him. There was nothing anyone could do—even the White Eye *di-yen* said so. His eyes fluttered open, and he made a crooked little grin as he spoke quietly. "*Nish'ii'*, Father. I'm glad you're here. Soon I go to Jesus in the Happy Land. Is there anything you want me to tell him?"

"Tell Jesus I said you are a good man, my son. I know he'll be glad to see you there with him. I promise to see that your family is cared for."

He struggled like a man climbing a steep mountain to speak. "You're a good man, Father. Please ask my wife and mother to come to me."

I was quick out of the chair and motioned for Helen and Lena to come speak to their son and husband.

They came with red, teary eyes. I stayed in the other room to give them time alone with Maurice. In a little while, I heard their low wails and knew that he had left us. I looked out the window and through the tall pines to the wide valley below and asked Jesus why he had taken my children and not me. I listened a long time, but there was no answer except for the beat of my heart.

# FORTY-TWO

## ALL I HAVE TO SAY

### MESCALARO HOSPITAL, MESCALARO, NEW MEXICO
### AUGUST 5, 1934

THE WHEEZING AND gurgling in my chest, the medicine the White Eye *di-yen* was giving me for the pain from broken ribs and collarbone, and the sad eyes of Helen and my friend Yellow Boy, who were sitting with me, said soon I would ride the ghost pony to *Ussen* or Jesus at their Happy Place. Helen had her chair in the corner, weaving a new basket while keeping a close eye on me. Yellow Boy sat by my bed, waiting to hear the rest of my life's story I'd told him over many visits to my home fire. Helen listened, too, for there were things I'd never told her after we married to save her from death and separation from her family at the White Eye school.

I wheezed, "I asked you to come so I can finish the stories I have told you so at least one man knows the truth and can tell it if he is asked after I'm gone. Now I tell you more of my time here at the reservation?"

Yellow Boy nodded and smiled. "You need to sleep, Chato, but if you speak, I listen."

I coughed to clear my voice, but I couldn't breathe deep enough to speak much louder than a whisper. "Yellow Boy, you are a good *amigo*. Now you learn the end of my life as I lived it. If you hear lies about me, you will know the truth and can speak it. The harvests I've lived at Mescalero pass like arrows shot from the bow of time, every shot taking its own measure of life from my body and leaving my hair whiter. Many friends and enemies have ridden the ghost pony—now it is my turn to ride. For many seasons, there were few moons that passed when I didn't attend a funeral ceremony of a friend or enemy riding the ghost pony. The funeral that cut my spirit like a sharp knife through living flesh was that of my son, Maurice, who went to Jesus as a good young man and left behind his young wife, Lena Kaydahzinne, and my grandson Alexander to carry on my family line. After a respectful time, Lena married Morgan, a Mescalero. They have lived well, and for that I am grateful. Now I tell you about the rest of my life and the puzzles I see here at Mescalero.

"Once we Chiricahua were free from our prisoner-of-war chains and came here to Mescalero, we who never quarreled openly among ourselves in captivity divided into two groups—those who had followed Geronimo into war and wanted, like him, to return to Arizona and those like Kayitah and me, who had wanted to keep peace with the White Eyes even if it meant never returning to Arizona.

"It was hard to keep the peace because many White Eyes could not open their mouths without lies flying out. We learned to carefully sort their words and then to make sure they were used as we understood them. This we learned from true White Eye friends who knew if what was spoken was true or false, real, or just a stumble in a blind man's dream. We all did this and stayed straight without White Eye trouble.

"Daklugie always assumed that what his uncle Geronimo told him was true, and because I was a leader for peace with the White Eyes and acted to end our fighting with the White Eyes by finding Geronimo's, Naiche's, Chihuahua's, and others' camps for the Army in Mexico, Geronimo told all who would listen that I was a traitor. I tell you, I was never a traitor to our People, and I'm proud of what I did to help the Army hunt down Geronimo. My work saved many lives even if Army leaders told lies and betrayed the peaceful People who stayed at Fort Apache by sending them to the great water in the east. They believed this would help stop Geronimo's raids and killings. These men stole our lives. They are thieves."

I coughed hard for a while and had to spit in the night pot. Yellow Boy waited, calm and unmoving like a deer hunter. My breath returned, and I began again to give him the rest of my story.

"We Chiricahua had good luck when we started our new cattle herd at Whitetail. It began in the Season of Large Fruit in the same harvest when we rode the iron wagons here. All but about twenty of the two thousand heifers and the eighty bulls that Ted Sutherland bought in the Season of Large Leaves for us with the money from the sale of our cattle at Fort Sill produced good strong calves in the Season of Little Eagles. Sutherland said he had never seen anything like it. I tolerated Daklugie telling the Mescalero that I was a traitor to the Chiricahua, and his pride and arrogance, because he worked hard with Ted Sutherland and helped us grow our herd into one of the best in New Mexico."

I puffed my cheeks and blew. I had to rest for a little while. Yellow Boy said, "Speak when you are ready, Chato. I wait and listen. I want to know how this pneumonia and broken bones happened to you."

After a while, the pain in my lungs and wheezing lessened. I tried slow, deep breathing to calm my wheezing and gurgling. I coughed again to clear my throat and said, "One of my old friends—I won't tell you his name, as a former tribal policeman, you might slip and tell your friends we had been drinking whiskey and we'd go to the calaboose—got his hands on a bottle of good White Eye whiskey."

Yellow Boy crossed his arms and nodded. "There are many White Eyes who have whiskey to sell to the Apache. We'll never catch them all."

"Hmmph. You have a clear eye, Yellow Boy." I wheezed and coughed again before I said, "I drove my old T-Model to Whitetail, planning to see how the cattle looked there on the grass. Before looking at the cattle, I stopped to visit an old friend who had his house in the Whitetail village. He grinned like Coyote while we talked. I asked him what was so funny. He reached under his chair and held up a flour sack showing lumps and bulges. He pulled out the long neck of a brown bottle far enough to show me he had a bottle of whiskey. I couldn't help raising my brows when I saw it. He says, "You want some? We can't drink here in the village. If others living here see us, they'll tell the tribal police." I hadn't drunk any whiskey in a long time. The memory of the fire it made in my belly made me nod yes. My friend was old like me and slow to get out much, so with a wink, I told him to come on with me if he wanted to see the cattle. He nodded and put the sack with the bottle under his coat, and we left.

"I drove slow down the rutted road out of the village and stayed in the ruts as they ran in the middle of the Whitetail valley. Near the road, we saw a few cows with big calves and some branded yearlings, but none carried our cattle brands, but we believed our cattle were like the rest of the herd. After a while, I saw a truck in the dust behind us with two or three men in the seats. They looked like they were looking at cattle, too, and waved to horsemen out in the trees, who kept the herd moving slowly south toward a big corral used for separating cattle when medicine, branding, and castration were done.

"My friend pointed for me to turn into a nearby canyon that would keep us out of sight while we drank his whiskey. It was hard to get out of the ruts, bumping and grinding across the road's dirt ridges, and into the canyon. We drove to the end of the canyon, where I parked the T-Model so the front faced back down the canyon and it sat in the shade of some big pines. That way, we were hard to see from the road and could leave quick if we needed to. About the time I stopped the engine, I thought I saw the truck behind us pass the mouth of our canyon.

"You know my second wife, Ishchos, and two of our children were taken by Mexican soldiers when I had been drinking in Juh's camp. I had tried never to taste whiskey again, and it was rare that I did. I didn't plan to drink much that day, just a little between friends.

"I remember that day seeing many orange-and-black butterflies flitting from tree to tree and then to any flowers left standing. I heard men keeping the cattle moving slowly down the valley, saw pools of bright afternoon sunlight falling across the grass and wildflowers, and smelled the tart pine sap tickling my nose. It was a good day to be alive. My friend and I sat down in the grass and leaned against the T-Model wheels, letting the day comfort us like a warm blanket on a cold night.

"He pulled the bottle from the sack, uncorked it, took a couple of long swallows, and then handed it to me, and I, too, drank some. The whiskey started fires in our bellies and loosened our tongues. We talked about the great changes we had seen in our lives and the many betrayals we had endured at the hands of the White Eyes and from our own People. We stopped talking for a while, and I thought of my first wife, Nalthchedah, whom I had divorced when I found her on her back under Dexter Loco. I wondered what had happened to them after I put a knife to Dexter's throat and told them to get out of my sight before I killed him and cut off the end of her nose.

"My mind filled with images from many people I had known. I was becoming drowsy from the whiskey when I thought I heard a horse snort on the little ridge behind the trees where we parked. My friend was already dozing in the warm heat and holding the whiskey bottle cradled in his arms like it was a baby. I slipped around the car and crawled up into the trees and brush where I could see everything on the little ridge, but I saw no sign of people or animals and crawled back into the T-Model. Like a fool, I eased the bottle away from my friend and took a couple more swallows and decided that was enough whiskey and time to leave while I could still stay in the road ruts. I shook my friend awake and cranked the motor, and we drove back down the canyon to the ruts of the main road. My T-Model jumped back into the ruts toward Whitetail to take my friend and his tasty whiskey back to his house. I was sorry I drank it. It made me want more to warm my belly.

"It was early evening. The light was soft in the sky, making the clouds off to the west blood red. The ruts in the road made it seem like we were riding an iron road. We were nearing the village when the truck that had followed us down the road appeared in a cloud of red, hazy dust, headed straight for us in the same ruts we were in. It was like the driver wanted to smash into us head-on. There were men whooping and yelling and holding to the frame of the truck bed. They made me angry. I wasn't going to move out of their way. If I died, then they would, too.

"My friend pleaded for me to get out of their way. I kept moving, expecting them to move over, but they stayed headed straight for us and seemed to go faster. At the last moment, I gunned the motor and jerked the wheel to turn out of the ruts to go up on the top bank of a field watering ditch. I turned the steering wheel hard to the right to avoid driving into the ditch, but the T-Model flipped on its side and slid down the bank into the shallow stream of water. My friend landed on top of me. I could still hear the whooping and yelling in the distance as the truck went racing away down the ruts.

"It was a good thing there was little water in that ditch or I would have drowned. My friend had taken a hit on the head. He was conscious but dazed and confused. I tried to push him up, but my arm wouldn't work.

"I said, 'Are you all right? Can you move?' He groaned and moved his legs to pull himself to a sitting position before struggling to sit on the edge of the seat where he had been before we flipped on the T-Model's side.

"He groaned again and said, 'I took a good knock on the head, but it's not bleeding. I'll be all right. Can you sit up?'

"I tried but felt great pain in my ribs, and I could do nothing with my shoulder on that side. 'No. I don't think I can move without help. My left side hurts bad and gets worse when I try to move it, and I can't find anything to push against and use my right arm to pull myself up.'

"He said, 'Hmmph. It's a good thing we don't run water down this ditch on this day of the week. You'd be in trouble, and I'd have to pull you out, bad side or no. Can you hold on where you are while I go for help?'

"I said, "You go. I ain't going anywhere."

"He told me, "I'll be back."

"My friend was still dazed and confused when he left. It was dark, and he turned down the road the wrong way and walked back toward the canyon. It was well into the night before he realized he was going in the wrong direction and turned around to head for the village. In the meantime, I was lying in a few inches of water, half drunk, and probably with something broken in my chest or arm. When my friend got back to where I was lying, he called to me and told me to hang on, that he had gone in the wrong direction for help and would be back as soon as he could, but he was walking slow."

"I WAS SHIVERING in the cold air and my wet clothes. The sky was turning gray when I heard a motor stop on the road above me. My friend had finally come with three or four friends. They worked quick and got me to their truck, where they helped me take off my wet clothes and dry off before wrapping me in a blanket and giving me hot coffee from a thermos. They pulled my T-Model out of the ditch so it wouldn't back up the next water release and carried me down here to headquarters and the Mescalero hospital.

"Somewhere along the way, I developed what the White Eye *di-yen* calls 'lobar pneumonia.' I had two broken ribs and a broken collarbone. When my friend told the doctor we'd been run off the road, the doctor told the tribal police. They came and talked to my friend and me, but I played dumb and told them I didn't remember any of the faces of the men in the truck that ran us off the road. I lied, and they knew it but didn't push for an answer. I'd take care of my blood right of revenge myself when I healed up. Those young good-for-nothings are going to learn there's a price to pay when they cross an old Apache."

Yellow Boy shook his head. "At your age, you need to let the tribal police collect your debt for you. It's their job. At least tell me. I'll help you."

I shook my head. "My honor says no, I will take care of my own debts. This is all I have to say."

# EPILOGUE

I AM YELLOW Boy, Chato's Mescalero friend to whom he told many stories about his life. I visited with him every sun that he lived at the Apache hospital in Mescalero. He was strong for his age, and the White Eye *di-yen* thought for a handful of suns that he might be strong enough to survive the pneumonia. But as the suns passed, I could tell that his time had come and that he would soon ride the ghost pony. For thirteen suns, Chato fought. Then three hands after the time of no shadows, with Helen and me by his side, he mounted the ghost pony and rode away to the Happy Place.

The Dutch Reformed Church claimed him as a member, and its *di-yen* did his burial ceremony even though some in that assembly shunned him. Chato was buried at the Mescalero cemetery. The Chiricahua didn't want to bury him in their Whitetail cemetery. I thought this was a sad thing. I sang and prayed to *Ussen* that Chato's journey to the Happy Place might be a fast one.

THE MOONS PASSED, and the Season of the Ghost Face came to cover our houses and *tipis* with ice and snow. One sun during this season, I took my women to the store in Mescalero for supplies. The store was a fine, warm place filled with good smells from *tobaho*, cloth, spices, and leather and was heated by the big potbellied stove that sat in the middle of the room, surrounded by chairs where the men could sit and talk while their women shopped.

I left my women to do their shopping and went to the stove to feel its fine heat. Two Mescalero, men I knew well, were talking as I sat down beside them and pulled out my *tobaho* and paper to make a cigarette.

Old Juan, who had been in the tribal police about the same time I was, was speaking to our friend Stands Straight. "My best pony got out of the barn last night. Had to track him down this morning. Wasn't hard to do with snow on the ground and no wind. But you know that fool horse wandered over to the cemetery. You'll never guess where he had found a little grass—right there on top of old Chato's grave. I sure hope that grass ain't contaminated with his betrayals and lies. They might make that old pony downright ornery like old Chato was."

Stands Straight raised a brow as if he didn't believe what Old Juan was saying. "I knew old Chato. Never had no trouble with him. He helped me out with my cattle a time or two. I think he was a good man. What lies and betrayals are you thinking about?"

Old Juan used his thumb and forefinger to stroke the edge of his jaw as he thought to answer Stands Straight. After a long pause, he said, "Well, I don't remember any stories about lies he told except that Daklugie and Eugene Chihuahua claim Chato didn't lead the raid that killed the father and mother of the McComas boy they took in 1883. Daklugie calls him a traitor because he was a scout who led the Army to Apache camps down in Mexico during Geronimo's last breakout from Fort Apache."

I heard my women asking the clerk about some heavy cloth as Stands Straight said, "Why, I heard most of the Chihenne People and quite a few Chokonen wanted Geronimo caught. Daklugie was Geronimo's nephew and listened to everything Geronimo told him about Chato. Geronimo hated Chato because he helped the Army in a good way and that eventually made Geronimo surrender. He worked harder than the other scouts at finding Geronimo, but I don't know why."

I finally joined their conversation. "I drank many a cup of coffee sitting by Chato's fire, listening to his life stories. I think I know why Chato worked hard for the Blue Coats. It was love."

Old Juan and Stands Straight frowned and looked at each other before Old Juan said, "Love? What's love got to do with it?"

"The Ghost Face before Crook led scouts into the Sierra Madre, Chato with his second wife was camped with Juh in the Sierra Madre about twenty-five miles south of Nácori Chico when the Mexicans, using Rarámuri as soldiers, attacked the camp early one morning and took many, including two of his three children and their mother, Ishchos, as slaves, and they also took a wife of Geronimo's.

Chato dearly loved that woman and those children. In the Season of Many Leaves a few moons later, the Chiricahua planned to raid over in Chihuahua and take hostages of their own to trade back for their women and children, but Crook came along to take them back to San Carlos, and it didn't happen.

"Chato begged Crook to use his influence to get his wife and children back, and Crook promised he would do all he could to get them out of Mexico. When Geronimo and the others broke out of Fort Apache Reservation, the Chiricahua with relatives who were slaves in Mexico thought Crook wouldn't do any more for them, but they were wrong, and Chato, believing Crook was the only chance of getting his family back, did the best he could scouting for Crook. Crook tried hard to get Chato's family out of Mexico, but the Mexicans claimed they didn't have any slaves and wouldn't send them back. Chato was heartbroken, but he did all he could for *Teniente* Davis and General Crook to end the Geronimo wars."

Stands Straight and Old Juan nodded as they stared at the stove. Old Juan said, "A man has to do everything he can to protect his family. I wouldn't blame Chato for that. But what about all the lies Daklugie says Chato told?"

I stood and poured a cup of coffee out of the pot on the stove and sat down again. I shrugged my shoulders. "I don't know. Guess it depends on the story. I know Chato wanted to be a great chief, and that was another reason he worked so hard as a scout for the Army. He expected he could do a lot more for the People working with the Army than fighting against it. I guess that's another reason Daklugie and Eugene Chihuahua hated him so and believed he told lies."

Old Juan said, "Well I expect they were right. Chato wasn't a great chief."

"Maybe you need to think about that some more. You remember that big silver medal that Chato had pinned to his coat or vest every time a big chief White Eye or a photo taker was around?"

Stands Straight and Old Juan nodded.

"You know where he got that medal?"

They lifted their hands and shrugged their shoulders to show they didn't know.

"The Great Father in the east pinned that big silver medal on his vest when Chato led representatives from Fort Apache to ask him that they stay there. The Great Father believed Chato was a great chief to give him that medal. I think he was, too. What do you think?"

I heard my women laughing with the clerk. Stands Straight and Old Juan crossed their arms, slumped in their chairs, and stared at the stove.

After a while, Stands Straight said, "Maybe so. I don't know."

Old Juan looked at me, made a little crooked smile, and shook his head but said nothing.

I thought, *It's time I found out who tried to murder you Chato and give them some payback for the way you were treated. Maybe they were witches. I know how to take care of witches.*

# ADDITIONAL READING

Ball, Eve, *In the Days of Victorio: Recollections of a Warm Springs Apache,* University of Arizona Press, Tucson, AZ, 1970.

Ball, Eve, Lynda A. Sánchez, and Nora Henn, *Indeh: An Apache Odyssey,* University of Oklahoma Press, Norman, OK, 1988.

Barrett, S. M., *Geronimo, His Own Story: The Autobiography of a Great Patriot Warrior,* Meridian, Penguin Books USA, New York, 1996.

Bourke, John G., *An Apache Campaign in the Sierra Madre,* University of Nebraska Press, Lincoln, NE, 1987. Reprinted from the 1886 edition published by Charles Scribner and Sons.

Bourke, John G., *On the Border With Crook,* Charles Scribner's Sons, New York, 1891.

Cozzens, Peter, *The Earth Is Weeping,* Alfred A. Knopf, New York, 2016.

Cremony, John C., *Life Among the Apaches,* University of Nebraska Press, Lincoln, NE, 1983.

de la Garza, Phyllis, *The Apache Kid,* Westernlore Press, Tucson, AZ, 1995.

Debo, Angie, *Geronimo: The Man, His Time, His Place,* University of Oklahoma Press, Norman, OK, 1976.

Delgadillo, Alicia with Miriam A. Perrett, *From Fort Marion to Fort Sill,* University of Nebraska Press, Lincoln, NE, 2013.

Farmer, W. Michael, *Apacheria: True Stories of Apache Culture 1860–1920,* Two Dot, Guilford, CT, 2017.

Farmer, W. Michael, *Geronimo, Prisoner of Lies: Twenty-Three Years as a Prisoner of War, 1886–1909,* Two Dot, Guilford, CT, 2019.

Goodwin, Grenville, *The Social Organization of the Western Apache,* Original Edition Copyright 1942 by the Department of Anthropology, University of Chicago, Century Collection edition by the University of Arizona Press, Tucson, AZ, 2016.

Haley, James L., *Apaches: A History and Culture Portrait*, University of Oklahoma Press, Norman, OK, 1981.

Hutton, Paul Andrew, *The Apache Wars*, Crown Publishing Group, New York, 2016.

Mails, Thomas E., *The People Called Apache*, BDD Illustrated Books, New York, 1993.

Opler, Morris Edward, *An Apache Life-Way, The Economic, Social, and Religious Institutions of the Chiricahua Indians*, University of Nebraska Press, Lincoln, NE, 1996.

Opler, Morris, *Apache Odyssey, A Journey Between Two Worlds*, University of Nebraska Press, Lincoln, NE, 2002.

Robinson, Sherry, *Apache Voices: Their Stories of Survival as Told to Eve Ball*, University of New Mexico Press, Albuquerque, NM, 2003.

Sánchez, Lynda A., *Apache Legends and Lore of Southern New Mexico, From the Sacred Mountain*, The History Press, Charleston, SC, 2014.

Sweeney, Edwin, *From Cochise to Geronimo: The Chiricahua Apaches, 1874–1886*, University of Oklahoma Press, Norman, OK, 2010.

Thrapp, Dan L., *Al Sieber: Chief of Scouts*, University of Oklahoma Press, Norman, OK, 1964.

Thrapp, Dan L., *The Conquest of Apacheria*, University of Oklahoma Press, Norman, OK, 1967.

Utley, Robert M., *Geronimo*, Yale University Press, New Haven, CT, 2012.

Worchester, Donald E., *The Apaches: Eagles of the Southwest*, University of Oklahoma Press, Norman, OK, 1992.

W. MICHAEL FARMER combines fifteen-plus years of research into nineteenth-century Apache history and culture with Southwest-living experience to fill his stories with a genuine sense of time and place. A retired PhD physicist, his scientific research has included measurement of atmospheric aerosols with laser-based instruments. He has published a two-volume reference book on atmospheric effects on remote sensing as well as fiction in anthologies and award-winning essays. His novels have won numerous awards, including three Will Rogers Gold and five Silver Medallions, New Mexico-Arizona Book Awards for Literary, Adventure, Historical Fiction, a Non-Fiction New Mexico Book of the Year, and a Spur Finalist Award for Best First Novel. His book series includes The Life and Times of Yellow Boy, Mescalero Apache, and Legends of the Desert. His nonfiction books include *Apacheria, True Stories of Apache Culture 1860-1920,* and *Geronimo, Prisoner of Lies.* His most recent novels are the award-winning *The Odyssey of Geronimo, Twenty-Three years a Prisoner of War, The Iliad of Geronimo, A Song of Blood and Fire,* and *Trini! Come! Geronimo's Captivity of Trinidad Verdin.* The first book in the Chato Saga, *Desperate Warrior: Days of War, Days of Peace, Chato's Chiricahua Apache Legacy Volume One,* is also a finalist for this year's Will Rogers Medallion Award for Traditional Western Fiction.

Printed in the USA
CPSIA information can be obtained
at www.ICGtesting.com
LVHW020043250824
788918LV00006B/13